Blood of the Albatross

**Center Point
Large Print**

ॐ श्री गणेशाय नमः

Blood
of the
Albatross

Ridley Pearson

Center Point Publishing
Thorndike, Maine

To Franklin Heller,
my literary agent and dear friend
who made this possible.

This Center Point Large Print edition
is published in the year 2001 by arrangement with
St. Martin's Press, LLC.

The text of this Large Print edition is unabridged.
In other aspects, this book may vary from the original
edition. Printed in Thailand. Set in 16-point
Times New Roman type by Bill Coskrey.

ISBN 1-58547-127-5

Library of Congress Cataloging-in-Publication Data

Pearson, Ridley.
    Blood of the albatross / Ridley Pearson.
      p. cm.
    ISBN 1-58547-127-5 (lg. print : lib. bdg. : alk. paper)
      1. Large type books. I. Title.

PS3566.E234 B56 2001
813'.54--dc21

                                                    2001028170

ACKNOWLEDGMENTS

Although a work of fiction, this story was plotted with the help of information gained through interviews with Dr. Donald Reay, The King's County Medical Examiner; Joseph Smith, of the Seattle Federal Bureau of Investigation; and Gary Flynn, Public Information Office of the Seattle Police Department.

Information on radio phones and navigational equipment was provided in part by Raytheon Corporation.

A two-week sail researching the islands of the Northwest was made possible by the time and efforts of Fletcher Brock and Aileen Denton and the fine forty-two-footer of the McCorkles. Julie Scott and Paul Bates added to the team.

The Greenlake Grill exists, has nothing to do with spies, and offers one of the nicest atmospheres and some of the best food in Seattle.

Shilshole Marina is one of the finest marinas in the state of Washington, and also has nothing to do with spies or illegal activities.

Brian DeFiore was the book's editor at St. Martin's Press. He worked long and hard on this novel and contributed much.

Thanks, Brian.

My wife, Colleen, helped from start to finish, as always. She did most of the research for this novel, and along with my father, Bob Pearson, copyedited the various drafts. For both of them a smile and hug will have to do.

My special thanks to the many musicians I have played original music with in the hundreds of halls and bars that string a trail through the last fourteen years. We played our hearts out for small change and applause. And the dreams. It's been worth every minute:

Robert Otis Reed, Jacques Pierre Bailhe, Tony Asa Morse, Robin Pfoutz, Adam Berenson, Charles Read, James Corwin, Hank Stahler, Chris Turner, Jocko Whimfiemer, John LaMoia, Peter Wetzler, Chan Lyell, Ronald Martinez, Todd Holland, Tom Iglehart, Brad Pearson, Gregg Mazel, Larry Forbes, Chief Kubichek, Jeff Rew, Mia Carroll, Lorainne Duisit, Aileen Denton, Fletcher Brock, Amos Galpin, Johnny Shoes, Luther Child, Jay Drange, Mike Boylston, Bruce Laven, Rod Cashin, Linda Terry, Lynette Hart, Chris Mercer, Nat Weiss, Chris Daniels, Eddy Dolbear.

Larry the Lizard is the house pet of the children of Tim and Laurie Haft.

"God save thee, ancient Mariner
From the fiends, that plague thee thus!
Why look'st thou so?"

"With my cross-bow
I shot the Albatross."
     —from *The Rime of the Ancient Mariner*

1

The man, dark and handsome in a rented tuxedo, spoke quietly to the demure woman across from him. He had last worn a tux at a State Department dinner so long ago that in the interval he had forgotten how to tie a bow tie. His attempt hung crooked at his Adam's apple, a propeller ready for take-off.

The young woman's sleepy eyes contained a shade of her cocoa-colored hair, which she wore curled under at her shoulders. Her chin was hard and jutting, her nose small and out of place on her face, but her neck was long and elegant. Her pearl-white gown shone in the candlelight, clinging tightly to her modest curves, which were made more imposing by her impeccable posture.

Around the couple, the Hotel Regensburg dining room hummed with conversation, wine glasses glinting, winking with the sudden movement of an arm. White-gloved waiters weaved silently through the close tables bearing trays of *gänseklien*, *hechtenkraut*, and *kugel*. The Regensburg's patrons had just attended a recital and so feet tapped beneath the tables, keeping time to memorable melodies.

Outside the hotel windows the approaching darkness of early evening enveloped the city, enhanced by storm clouds blown in from Czechoslovakia to the east. The low rumble of distant thunder and bolts of lightning on the horizon warned of summer rain. Sporadic gusts of wind swayed red geraniums rooted in brightly painted window boxes—the only color on the drab façades of the buildings that lined the narrow, cobblestoned streets. The wind teased the tree-tops, bending branches and flashing the silvery undersides of leaves as pedestrians hurried below.

Inside the dining room the man turned to his companion and asked, "Do you know your way to the train station, Sharon?"

Her lips pursed. "I'll have no problem getting out, Brian. Please, don't worry so much."

"I wish I shared your optimism."

Sharon wasn't concerned. Brian had staged it well: they were both hotel guests, both Americans; he had made an obvious pass at her in the lounge following the recital. He had led her to a table in the hotel's crowded dining room. In his tuxedo, he blended in to the surroundings. She looked radiant. During the first course he had given her some important information. All that remained was to give her the photo. No reason to be concerned. Tomorrow she would board a train for Paris.

He sipped his tea, glancing over the cup's delicate rim. "You look fit. You must exercise regularly."

"Yes, I do," she said, and added, "Thank you."

"Are you as healthy as you look?"

"I suppose so," she conceded.

"That's nice. I haven't felt well for weeks. It's this food. Too much meat and potatoes. It's all you can get. You'd think the Germans would be smarter than that, wouldn't you?" He didn't wait for her response. "Too much meat. Not enough grains and vegetables." He looked at her again. "I bet you eat a lot of fruit and vegetables."

She nodded. He suddenly seemed more nervous to her, his attention fleeting. Distracted. She found it disconcerting.

"The two in the doorway. I can't make them out.

Describe them to me."

This caught her by surprise. He had obviously been studying the reflection in the window behind her. She glanced casually over his shoulder in the direction of the lobby. Normally two men in business suits wouldn't have attracted anyone's attention; but with everyone else dressed in formal attire, these two stood out like weeds in a well-tended garden. The taller of the two scanned the crowd. His closely set eyes met her curious expression and steadied. She did not break the eye contact. She smiled at him and then lowered her eyes shyly to the table. She lifted her napkin and patted her lips.

Still looking into the window, Brian stated, "He saw you."

"Yes." Her mouth was hidden behind the napkin.

"The smaller of the two I don't recognize. Describe the taller one. Black hair? Big lips?"

"Thick lips, yes. Hard eyes and a pronounced brow."

Brian shifted in his chair restlessly. The wood squealed.

She returned her napkin to her lap, head held rigid, shoulders square, and looked into Brian's eyes. "Anything in particular you would like me to do?"

"Just keep talking. Enjoy yourself."

She smiled.

He continued, "That proves it: my cover's blown. It's up to you now."

"I have no problems with that," she said confidently.

"I screwed up somewhere," he said to himself, ignoring her. Then, "I hope I haven't blown you as well."

"Calm down," she instructed.

"Calm down?" he whispered. "What if I've blown

you as well?"

Sharon laughed theatrically. Very convincing. It would appear that they were a couple enjoying each other's company.

Brian was not hysterical—agents learned to block hysteria—but he was anxious. "I may not have all the proof just yet. But I tell you, I *know* when I'm right."

"Brian," she chided, hoping to shut him up, laughing to cover, again. Sharon Johnson had been re-routed here, unexpectedly, from her embassy post in Bonn. Now she was a mule with "vital information" for Washington. Just like that. Few knew of her assignment; no local authorities were to be involved. With each gust of wind, triangular pennants snapped outside the window behind her, sounding like hands clapping. Or gunshots.

She knew Brian had been here, in Regensburg, West Germany, just over six months, working out of the CIA's Special Operations. His cover as a lawyer had evidently worked well enough, but the going had been rough: no real progress for the first five months. Then he had stumbled onto a disgruntled employee and, after a so-called "courtship," had managed to buy a few pieces of hard information. And now Sharon was to deliver this information to the directors of both the CIA and the FBI. No one else.

She had reviewed case histories of deeply buried agents in her first year at Langley. Brian fit the description of a *blowout:* an agent whose cover unravels, whose mind frays. The problem with becoming someone else was that in order to be convincing you could never—*never*—fall back, never break your cover identity, not even to yourself. *Especially* to yourself. You had to live every moment of your life as that other person; in doing so, you crossed a thin line where make-believe was real, and real no longer existed. You ate, slept, thought like that other person. However, this other person was only a shell—a cardboard character of names, numbers, and places—fifteen pages of double-spaced, twenty-weight bond—a memorized past, a creative present. There was no solid ground beneath you, just a manila folder, some photographs, and all those "facts." Never allowing your real self to be present, it quietly hid behind a door never opened.

Yes, Brian certainly fit the description of a *blowout:* a nervous twitch to his left eye; his index finger tapping throughout the dinner; odd facial expressions; dull, penetrating eyes. Small beads of perspiration clung to a few unshaven stubs of whiskers below his lower lip. "What are they doing now?" he asked, the skin beneath his left eye still jumping. A *blowout.* Brian was falling apart right before her eyes. Of course she would have to report it; she would have to tell *them.* She knew his condition might negate the importance of his information in the eyes of her superiors.

She smiled at him—a patronizing smile—and reached out in an attempt to quiet his tapping finger. Rule number one: settle him down.

He jerked his hand away and placed it in his lap. He looked frightened.

"Perhaps we should go," she recommended, becoming nervous herself now. She envied a woman two tables away who seemed to be trouble-free and enjoying the meal. The low light of the room made the woman seem far away.

"Perhaps we should go?" Sharon repeated.

"No, not yet," he snapped at her.

She withdrew her hand from where it rested on the linen tablecloth and dabbed the edges of her lips with her napkin, saying, "Brian, it's nothing to worry about."

"It's him! The tall one is the henchman. He's come for me."

"Henchman? Brian, is there more I should know?" Spoken like a mother to a guilty son.

He sputtered, "Companies, within companies, within companies." The beads of perspiration had grown to small droplets. One trickled down his chin. "Boxes within boxes, within boxes. Free samples. Just free samples."

She had read that when the mind finally broke through the imposed wall that separated the real person from the contrived identity, it would take hold of any familiar image. Brian had chosen free samples.

He told her, "You walk to the end of the lane. The trees are turning and Sam Kane is burning leaves. You go to the mailbox and open it up. There's a box inside the mailbox, and a box inside of that. A box of dishwashing soap, or fabric softener . . ." He was scaring her now. How to take him out of here? ". . . or cereal. Kid's cereal. Captain Crunch. Frosted Flakes." He cocked his head, now Tony the Tiger, "They're grrr*eat!*"

They've drugged him, she thought, as he continued on mindlessly. He's under stress, certainly, but they've drugged him. Her eyes danced between his fixed gaze and the food on the table. *She* felt fine. So how had they drugged him? Salt? Pepper? No.

He raised his voice and then his arms, illustrating his sudden enthusiasm for bicycles, which was now his topic.

He and his sister, he explained, had once rented a tandem bicycle while on vacation with their parents in Bermuda.

His *entrée?* Unlikely.

Some of the guests at nearby tables were noticeably upset, shifting restlessly in their seats and casting glances toward their table. Whatever the drug, he was approaching light-speed. She guessed it might be a combination of amphetamines and mild hallucinogens.

"Jesus!" he shouted. "I'm fucked up."

An older woman sitting at the table next to them gasped.

"Brian," Sharon said calmly. But it was the wrong thing to say, and she realized it too late. He was too high, and he wasn't Brian. Brian didn't exist except in some folder. His real name was Robert Saks. She reached for his tea, held it under her nose, and sniffed: no way to tell.

His face reddened. He was having trouble breathing. She grabbed his hand. "Let's go."

He drew back violently, accidentally tipping his chair. He reached for support but took hold of the linen tablecloth. His chair went over backward; the tablecloth followed, and the tableware with it.

Sharon stood up abruptly; her chair also tipped over. She hurried to Brian's side, her tight evening gown restricting her movements. Spilled food covered him grotesquely. She saw in his face a young boy, in his eyes, an old man. She had never seen anyone die before, but she knew this was death. He reached for her and pulled her down by her hair. A matronly woman at the next table screamed as if her own hair had been pulled.

He withdrew a black-and-white photograph from his inside coat pocket. Then the pain hit and his hand clamped

14

down on the photo. Sharon tried to pull it loose; he wouldn't let her. She tugged, but he held on. She rocked his wrist and looked at the photo: a group of men, a single face circled in black. She studied the face, pulling again on the photo. Brian held it tightly.

"I'm scared," he gasped. His final words.

Two waiters hurried over quickly. The tall thick-lipped man by the lobby began to walk toward Sharon.

She stared down at Brian. Unthinkable. A man who had spoken to her only moments before now lay staring at the chandelier, a twisted grin pasted on his face, beads of sweat still clinging to his lower lip. She glanced up and saw the waiters standing over her.

The tall man edged closer, his attention trained on Sharon. Again their eyes met, but this time she did not smile. She stood.

The frantic waiter called loudly, *"Doktor! Doktor, bitte."* He knelt down and pounded on Brian's chest, pinched the dead man's nose, and bent down to apply mouth-to-mouth.

The tall thick-lipped man reached over and grabbed Sharon by the forearm. His hand was cold. She broke his grip and squeezed between two chairs. Her gown hooked a loose tack on the back of a chair and ripped. She pushed through, frantic now herself. Her pursuer followed but, being bulkier, had to force his way between the tables. A man at one objected. The tall man shoved the protester back into his seat. Sharon slipped between two chairs at the next table. *"Hilfe!"* she pleaded. A large man with pink cheeks and bushy eyebrows rose to confront Sharon's pursuer. He, too, was pushed into his seat.

Sharon made her way into the kitchen and was suddenly

surrounded by overpowering aromas and a handful of overweight men, all eyeing her torn dress and grinning. She took hold of a large knife and stabbed through the fabric between her legs, dragging the knife from thigh to ankle before dropping it on the floor. One of the fat cooks whistled at the sight of her thighs.

Her pursuer came charging in behind her, his face flushed and angry. She pressed past two of the cooks, kicked off her high-heeled shoes, and sprinted for the outside door. "Help!" she shouted as she yanked open the door. In the kitchen, one of the cooks blocked the aisle, stopping her pursuer. The other cooks ganged up on the man. As she rounded a corner, she slipped and tumbled to the cobblestones, bruising her elbow badly. She looked back: there he was, running toward her. She pulled herself up and fled down a narrow lane past wooden, numberless doors to ancient rowhouses. Thirty yards farther up the lane she spotted the spire and ornate façade of a church. She could hear him—a half block back perhaps, and gaining quickly. She reached the stone steps and again looked back at him. He ran with single-minded determination. She pulled on the giant door and opened it a crack, slipped inside, and pulled it shut. She walked briskly past row after row of dark wooden pews. Her wet feet slapped the stone floor and echoed around her. Only the altar was lit: Jesus nailed on the cross, bleeding from wrists and ankles. "Hello?" she pleaded, her voice reverberating aimlessly.

As she heard the large door groan open she dove between two pews and folded herself under one of them, quickly trying to slow and quiet her breathing.

Echoing footsteps. She bit down nervously on her index

finger. What to do? *Think of something!* Nowhere to go. Hiding in the House of God. A shredded piece of her dress lay where it might be seen. The squishing of his wet soles drew closer. She tugged the fabric out of sight.

He walked slowly, looking down each pew, searching for her. She held her breath. She could hear him breathing, like a man snoring.

"You are looking for something?" the soft High German of a man some distance away inquired calmly.

The black shoes stopped right next to her. She felt dizzy. Blood pulsed loudly in her ears.

"No, Father."

She wanted to cry out for joy. A priest! Thank God.

"You appear to be searching for something. Did you lose something?"

"No, Father. I . . . I came to pray."

"Then we shall pray together. Come, my son. Approach the altar. Pray with me."

The shoes squished past. She heard knees creak as the two men knelt. The priest began a monotone prayer that lasted several minutes. Then the black shoes came back down the aisle and past her. She heard the large door open and thump shut. She sighed, on the verge of tears.

"You may come out now. Let me see you. He is gone," the priest's voice echoed.

Surprised, she inched her way out and cautiously poked her head above the pews, looking first toward the rear doors, then turning to face the priest. He was an older man with hair the color of Christmas tinsel and the sapient face of a man of God. She was a mess: wet stringy hair, her white dress soaked through and clinging to her. She crossed her arms, covering her breasts. He walked slowly toward her, unhurried, serene.

"What is it?" he asked.

She shook her head, frightened. "I seek refuge."

2

A single moment, either way, can dictate the course of an entire lifetime. Jay Becker slapped the string mop against the white fiberglass decking of the thirty-foot sloop, wishing he had light hair instead of dark, convinced that dark hair in the sunshine made a person feel hotter. The single moment he was thinking about had occurred two weeks ago: the brakes had failed—it was that simple—and he had totaled Linda's car. He kept thinking about the if's: What if he had stopped for a 2:00 A.M. breakfast after work? What if he had serviced the car the week before as Linda had asked him to? What if? He wouldn't be a few thousand bucks in the hole; he wouldn't be swabbing the decks of someone's thirty-footer. Summers were the most lucrative months for his band, The RockIts—three months when the abundance of engagements ("gigs") provided enough income so that band members didn't *need* day jobs. But here was Becker, looking over at the top of Seattle's Space Needle and wondering what the other band members were doing while he swabbed decks. They were probably still asleep, or wandering down to a laid-back, mid-morning breakfast. They were probably enjoying the same heat and humidity that he was finding distasteful. He knew that if he hadn't been working, he would have been out riding his chrome racer, *The Streak*, putting in the first leg of a thirty-mile loop. He would have been pumping hard, sweating, enjoying the fact that as a musician he had his days free. Instead he was overly tired, hungry, and bored—a bad combination for Jay Becker. He loved racing—sailboats, bicycles, it didn't matter—but swabbing other people's decks was another thing entirely.

Jocko Kunst ambled down Pier L with his permanent comical grin pasted above his thin goatee and a pink paper bag in hand. His gait signaled his confidence, his smile belied a peculiar insecurity. One couldn't tell if Jocko was happy or afraid. But as he approached his friend of ten years—eleven next month—Jocko Kunst appeared carefree, a man unaware of schedules and calendars, even though one could set a watch by his arrivals at Shilshole Marina. Jocko was a people person. That's why Becker knew what was in the paper bag: one of the coffees would have cream, one of the doughnuts would be whole-wheat, glazed.

"What's zis?" Jay insisted every day on appearing surprised by his friend's visits. Never take anyone for granted: that was Jay Becker's rule.

"Emergency relief," Jocko said with his distinct lisp, a lisp that was not in the least bit effeminate, but more like that of a cartoon character. "What else have I got to do?" He shrugged. "Moral support can do wonders for a blown bank account." His voice jumped from high to low, high to low, and often cracked mid-word. Jocko *was* a cartoon character, a human Wiley Coyote who had given up on ever catching the Road Runner. The breeze ruffled Jocko's kinky hair; Jay's lifted off his head and settled back down.

Becker had piercing blue eyes, a round face with pink

cheeks, and a crisp jaw line. Friends teased that he looked like Clark Gable. He pumped the mop into the pail and rinsed it, watching the water change color like steeping tea. "I thought you weren't coming."

"Me? I never pass up the chance to watch a friend do hard labor. It does wonders for the trust-fund side of my personality."

"You should feel guilty."

"You should accept a loan when it's offered."

"Money now; money then: its all money. We've been over that." Jay jumped down onto the cement pier.

Jocko handed him the coffee with the cream. Jay spotted Shilshole's dockmaster and waved to indicate he was taking his ten-thirty coffee break. The dockmaster waved back and tapped his wrist. Jay and Jocko had a way of stretching the breaks.

"You should be riding."

"Tell me about it."

"How are we going to get you ready for the race if you keep this workaholic thing up?"

"We?"

"I'm your trainer."

"My *trainer?*"

"You're past your prime. You *need* a trainer."

"I turned thirty-one last week and now I'm past my prime?"

"Now you're catching on." Jocko sat down on the edge of the cement pier, as did Jay. A film of rainbowed colors, caused by floating gasoline, moved below their feet. Jocko admired its beauty.

"Aren't *we* forgetting something?" inquired Jay.

"What's that?"

"We're the same age."

Jocko shrugged. "Trainers only get better with age. Experience, you know."

Jay laughed. "I bet you've never ridden a bicycle in your life."

Jocko flashed his friend a disappointed look. He handed Becker the glazed-wheat. They both bit into their doughnuts at the same time. Jelly spilled from Jocko's and fell into the water, disturbing the surface and disrupting the colors. A glob of jelly clung to the whiskers below his lip. He lapped it away with his tongue.

Jay was tempted to tell Jocko that he ate like a slob, but he'd told him many times before, so what was the point? "So what's my routine, Coach?"

Jocko reviewed his plan. It was rigorous. He finished by saying, "If I didn't think you wanted this badly, I wouldn't bother. But knowing you, you'll win the damn race, and I like being associated with winners." He paused for a sip of coffee. "I do this for you for free," he said, imitating his Jewish father.

Jay laughed. He always laughed when Jocko imitated his father. Doughnut crumbs bombarded the water and disintegrated.

"You eat like a slob," Jocko scolded.

Jay sipped his coffee and then asked, "Any luck on Labor Day?"

"No. Everyone's booked. I even called the Met Café. Booked."

"Sully should have honored our agreement. We were booked first. It's his fault. We shouldn't be the ones screwed. He should at least pay us a percentage."

"No contract."

"We *never* sign contracts with Sully."

"Exactly." Jocko finished his jelly-filled and licked his chops. "So we get our first Labor Day weekend free in ten years. Who's complaining?"

"I am. It's the *principle* of the thing. Besides, I need the money."

"You need a rich uncle to die."

"Look who's talking."

"Don't fight a successful formula. It worked for me, didn't it? You never know what lies ahead. That's what makes life so damned exciting. So I got lucky. It could happen to you, too."

"Speaking of what lies ahead."

Jocko followed Jay's gaze. A woman with blond hair, nice legs, and an intoxicating rhythm to her hips was headed toward them, down the pier. "Meaning?"

"She's taking sailing lessons, starting tomorrow." Becker lifted his eyebrows. "This job has its benefits, you know." She drew closer to them. Jay said, "Hi."

"Hello," she said in passing, her accent German.

Jocko was ogling her. He whispered, "Introduce me."

They both watched her from behind as she headed down the pier. She didn't have a contrived, hip-heaving prance. She didn't need it. Everything on her was well connected and working in unison, like a finely tuned engine. From the back she had long legs and firm buttocks; she appeared to be strong, her shoulder blades clearly visible beneath tanned skin as her arms rocked at her side. Her bathing suit was light blue and gossamer.

"What about Linda?"

"What about *Linda?* I'm going to give the woman sailing lessons, Jocko. I'm not marrying her." Becker shook his head.

"Try telling that to Linda," Jocko said, adding, "If she ever sees that one, you're in deep trouble."

"Linda's history."

"Meaning?"

"Is there something unclear about that?"

"Is there something I don't know? You've said that about a hundred times over the past few years."

"Yeah. Well, this time I mean it."

"You've said that, too."

"What's your point?"

"My point is: you have yet to *do* anything about it."

"So I should tell Linda to get lost?" Jay shook his head, pained. "I've tried that."

" 'Under my thumb . . .'," Jocko sang out of key.

"Lay off."

"Just making a point."

Jay jumped to his feet. "I gotta get back to work."

"Sorry," Jocko said.

Jay turned and paused before saying, "It's complicated, Rocks. I feel one way but I act another. I *hate* the idea of hurting her."

"Hurting *her?* You've taken it on the chin so many times you're numb. I like Linda. You *know* I do. But she treats you like shit. Sorry." He rose. "None of my business."

Jay looked stunned. "Guilty," he said quietly.

"Be back around five. Wind sprints at five-fifteen at Golden Garden." He started to walk away.

Becker called out, "Thanks for the coffee."

Jocko raised a hand to acknowledge, paused, and then continued on as if reconsidering.

Jay reached the pail, bent down, and picked up the handle to the mop. He slapped the deck forcefully. Then he looked up. The woman was reading a paperback on the bow of a boat several slips down the pier. The horseshoe-shaped flotation device attached to the boat's railing read *The Lady Fine*.

Jay studied her without her knowing and thought, No kidding.

3

The Seatbelt and No Smoking signs glowed yellow, the aisles clear for the descent into Washington, D.C.'s Dulles airport. Roy Kepella watched the tiny overhead spotlights blink on and off randomly, according to use, a private art form. Below the jet, suburban lights shone like holiday ornaments, their twinkling mirroring the stars. He missed seeing the stars—stars were a rare sight in Seattle. He chuckled once to himself, thinking, The *sun* is a rare sight in Seattle.

Memories of Washington, D.C., still occupied a corner of Kepella's mind. He could recall the exact day when he had first stepped off a train in the nation's capital. August 25, 1950: two months behind the North Korean invasion and capture of Seoul. The heat and humidity had almost gagged him that day. His native Oklahoma had its share of hot days, but that boilerplate humidity belonged to D.C. alone.

Stepping off the plane, he realized things didn't change, gasping as the oppressive heat closed in around him. Once inside the terminal Kepella did not have to wait for his luggage. He carried all he would need in a soft-shell flight bag: a change of clothes and a dog-eared address book.

The taxi ride took him past new sights. Even in the dark he could discern that what once had been farm-and-horse country was now condominium-and-Mustang-convertible country. Six- and eight-lane highways carried him to his destination, a Holiday Inn in Arlington. The driver, a black man named John, never stopped talking—shouting actually—above the grating sounds of gospel rock from the radio.

Kepella knocked twice on the door to room 210, and it opened. The man had a Marine brush haircut, a trimmed mustache, and a clear, deeply tanned complexion. He signaled Kepella to take a chair across an oval formica table bearing orderly stacks of papers and file folders.

"Good to see you, Walter. Thank you for coming." The uppers always called him Walter. His personnel folder had him as Walter. "Kevin Brandenburg," his host stated, as if Kepella didn't know who had summoned him three thousand miles to a secret meeting. "It seemed a waste of time to meet at the Agency, what with your traveling so far. This matter is rated highly enough that I prefer not to draw attention to it, and you know how the Agency is, as regards outsiders. . . ." No, Kepella didn't know. He was accustomed to the Seattle regional office, not Washington. Brandenburg continued, "The room is secure. We may talk freely."

Kepella nodded. The room was standard Holiday Inn: king-size bed, lamps, endtables, telephone, television, an oval table lit by a green-shaded hanging lamp. The curtains were drawn, hiding a sliding glass door leading to a balcony. Kepella shifted uneasily in his chair. Brandenburg studied a folder, his brow furrowed. It was a typical gesture of the uppers, an intimidating pause meant to reestablish the pecking order. Kepella wondered how often one had to get a haircut like Brandenburg's in order to keep it so perfectly uniform.

"You're a hard worker," Brandenburg said, as if reading from Kepella's file, but Kepella knew better; his file was much thicker than that. He grunted, shifting again in his chair. Brandenburg would get to the point when he saw fit.

"I'm sure you're familiar with all the technology we've been losing lately."

Kepella nodded.

Brandenburg saw the nod and looked back at his folder. "The CIA was running an agent outside of Regensburg, West Germany. He may have penetrated Wilhelm's network. Due to the security rating of the operation the data are slim at the moment. But, a few days ago he requested a mule—something he was not supposed to do unless standard courier lines could not be trusted. So, we have to assume he had something of value. He's dead, Walter. No word from the woman at all."

"Woman?" Kepella interjected.

"The mule."

Kepella nodded again.

Brandenburg looked up. His forehead was creased, eyebrows cinched toward the bridge of his nose. "We know that your area is next, Walter. Seattle is next. We have reason to believe that they will follow the same pattern as

26

Los Angeles—"

"Go after an agent."

"Exactly." Brandenburg shut the file, stacked it, and opened another. His fingers were thin, with manicured nails. "Tell me about your family life."

"Nonexistent," Kepella replied quickly, uncomfortable with the question.

Brandenburg waited.

"What can I tell you that you don't already know?" He pointed to the file folders. "I live alone, I work, I eat, I shit, I sleep."

"There's no need for cynicism." Brandenburg studied Kepella. "Your son paid you a visit, did he not?"

How the hell did he know that? Kepella remembered mentioning it to Mark Galpin, the Seattle Director of Operations and a close personal friend, but he had a hard time believing Mark would have routed the information to Personnel. "Last year," Kepella admitted.

"And?"

"I don't see how it pertains to Agency business," reluctantly adding, "sir."

"I don't know you, Walter. I *need* to know you. I have little time to get to know you. What good does this crap do me," he asked, tapping the file, "if I can't get word one out of you?" Brandenburg knew people. If informal was what Kepella wanted, then informal he would have. "Tell me about your son's visit."

Kepella sighed. "I don't know what you have in that file. I threw the kid out when I lived in Oklahoma City. He was a drunk at eighteen—"

"But you used to drink rather heavily yourself, Walter.

27

Did you not?" Intimidating.

"Do you want me to tell you or would you rather tell me?"

"Continue."

"I threw him out." Kepella ran his hand through his thick black hair, his pain apparent. "Didn't see him for years—"

"How many?"

Kepella closed his eyes. When he opened them he said, "Ten. A little over ten years." He hooked his fingers on the edge of the table, as if the table might hold him up. "He showed up sometime last year. February, I think. We went out together. He married some Irish woman, knocked her up. He didn't want the baby coming into nothing. He wanted cash. Ten years, and all he really wanted was some money. I gave him five grand. I didn't have much more than that saved. I'm not particularly good with money." A weak smile. "The next day he was gone. Haven't heard from him since."

"Tell me about your early days."

Kepella gave in. "I was raised on football, beer, and the back seat of a Chrysler New Yorker. Oklahoma was okay, I guess. I never liked it much. My dad drove trucks. Mom cleaned houses. I suppose I wanted more than eighteen wheels and dust mops. I enlisted, signed up for a tour of duty in Korea. Did okay.

"After the war they moved me to Washington. The Bureau recruited me, ran me through college, and stationed me back in good old Oklahoma. I married a gal who was too young for me. Stupid move. We had Tommy. Things went to shit, it all fell apart on me. Tommy grew up real quick. He was drinking heavily by the time he was eighteen. I threw him out. The wife never forgave me. She fooled around. I found out about it and raised hell. Next thing I knew her lawyers had won my house—*my* house, can you believe that?—and had left me nothing. I transferred to Seattle.

"I don't really like Seattle." He pointed to the folder. "But if you know anything, you know that much. One cloudy day after another. I got into the booze pretty heavily myself. Nights first. Then lunch. You know how it goes. No, maybe you don't. I did my job okay. I got wise about a year ago. I told Mark . . . Galpin, the director . . . about the drinking problem. I dried out. Here I am." He looked up. Sadness creased his face.

"What about your love life there?"

Kepella's life had moved like the moon over water, its reflection more beautiful than the real thing. Sure, he had learned how to avoid the booze; but besides work, what else was there? Love was not a word in his vocabulary anymore. "Nothing going."

It was Brandenburg's turn to nod. "We think they may come after you, Walter. You fit what they're looking for."

Kepella knew that was no compliment. He didn't like Brandenburg. "Why do you say that?"

"You had a problem a few months back with a co-worker."

"What if I did?"

"You were suspended for two weeks."

"That was political. Ask anybody. I went right back to the job. Full responsibility."

"I know. You're right, of course. But it wouldn't look that way to someone outside the Agency. You were suspended. You are a man in a position of extreme national security, Walter. Many of the latest domestic military technologies pass across your desk. And you have access to others. You have no family to speak of—a loner. They seem to like that. As you said, you're not great with money. You see, Walter, I think you're perfect for them."

"You don't have to worry." He could see twenty years going down the tube to some young assistant deputy director, some baby-boomer who, having nothing better to do, had decided to do a little Agency weeding. Culling. "It's not my style. If I was going over to the other side, Brandenburg, I would have done it long ago. I've held this post for some time, you know."

"Yes. Nearly eight years. That's good, Walter. That's very good." Brandenburg slid the folder to one side, leaving the table in front of him clear. "How's the drinking now, Walter?"

"Don't you have that in one of your files somewhere?"

"I might. Why don't you tell me?" He smiled patronizingly. "Your words." He reached down and pulled a bottle of Popov out of his briefcase. He stood, and when he came out of the bathroom he had two glasses in hand, each filled with ice. "Care to join me?"

A pretty clumsy test, Kepella thought to himself. "No thanks," he said.

Brandenburg poured himself a drink like a scientist might mix chemicals. He was no drinker, Kepella thought. He poured vodka on the rocks: Kepella's drink. Brandenburg pushed the drink toward Kepella.

Kepella looked at it. "No, thank you."

"Don't you want some, Roy?"

Brandenburg had switched to calling him Roy. So this was the friendly part? Business was either over, or just starting. Brandenburg was well informed. Kepella said, "The agent was CIA. Why are we involved?"

"So was the woman."

"Was? I thought you said she hasn't made contact." The statement rattled Brandenburg somewhat, Kepella thought.

"Is, was, you know what I mean. It's either us or the Secret Service on U.S. soil, you know that, Roy."

"I thought the Secret Service generally handles Special Investigations."

"Who said anything about Special Investigations?"

"Why else would you fly me all the way out here? And you even made me call in sick rather than tell the Bureau where I was going. You need a spy. You want me to watch for any shit going down. Right? I've got news for you, Brandenburg. I do that anyway."

Brandenburg finished the drink and immediately poured himself another. Kepella felt the saliva running in his mouth. The urge never stops.

"This has nothing to do with SI. There are only four people involved in this operation, *the* director, myself, my secretary, and you."

"What operation? Which *the* director?"

"Washington. Your man Galpin in Seattle knows nothing about this. As for the operation . . . we're coming to that. You were going to tell me about your drinking."

"No I wasn't."

"You said you're off the stuff."

"I am."

Brandenburg took a deep breath. "Roy, these folders,

31

reports, personnel statistics don't do shit for telling me about you, the person. Christ, I know about your marriage, your ex, your son, even your bank accounts. I know you dried out and that you seem to be okay now. I need stability, Roy. I don't have a lot of time. Not much at all. And I need to know who the hell you are."

"So you offer me a glass of booze and expect me to spill my life story?" He knew if he had been drinking, the warmth would already have reached the top of his spine. "I'm not like that, Brandenburg. Read your files more carefully. They should tell you somewhere that I don't like being led around the bush. I like to get straight to the point. I like to get work done. I'm good. I came to Washington on your orders—orders I wasn't thrilled about. Here I am. If you know anything from that pile of . . . crap . . . then you know I'm not particularly happy in Seattle. I've been there close to ten years, hoping to earn my passport to Washington. I like this town. This is where I was recruited. Where I spent some of the best years of my life. I've been leaning on Mark Galpin to drop a few hints out here. He said he would. I got your call and figured maybe my time had come. Come to find out, I get drilled by a man twenty years my junior, who just happens to be my superior, who calls me Walter for the first forty minutes and then pours himself a drink and switches to Roy.

"By the way," Kepella continued, "how do I get reimbursed for this?" He reached into a breast pocket and withdrew his airline ticket. He had big hands with thick fingers and flat nails. He still wore his wedding ring.

Deftly, Brandenburg removed his billfold and counted out seven hundred and fifty dollars. He handed

Kepella the cash.

"Cash?"

"I told you," Brandenburg said, returning the wallet, "this isn't even listed as an operation. Just the four of us. Can't very well route expenditures through accounting, now can I? The whole damn department would know. Probably a senator or two, as well. We're having hell keeping information locked up lately. Too many people willing to sing to the press. The director has sent out a white-paper memo."

"I read it."

"Then you know."

"Yes. We're more fortunate. A small, tight group, that's Seattle. It has its advantages, I suppose."

"That brings me to my point, Roy. We know you want Washington. You've passed your twenty, so we assume you're sticking with us. The director likes to see men stay past twenty. I suppose that may have had something to do with you being selected for this run." He went back to the folders. "I'm in a position to offer you a trade of sorts, Roy. You do this job for us, and we'll see you here in Washington."

Kepella placed the crisp bills in his wallet and stared at Brandenburg. "What run?"

"I told you that we—the CIA actually—have reason to believe the next target may be Seattle. Maybe you."

Kepella didn't say anything, though he wondered how anyone could possibly have determined this. But then, the CIA was another world entirely.

Brandenburg said, "We'd like to sting them."

"A video sting?"

"No. More involved than that. It's an old technique, I'm told, dating back to the war." When he wiggled his nose, Brandenburg looked like a ferret. "I've consulted with a man named Stone. Ever heard of him?"

"No."

"He's retired now. He used to run counter-intelligence agents."

"Doubles?"

"Actually, agents who sought out doubles."

"You're talking about the SIA?"

"Then you *have* heard about it?"

"Only recently. A man named Lyell runs it, doesn't he?"

"Stone used to run things over there," Brandenburg said, avoiding a proper answer. "At any rate, Stone was very helpful. He knows a great deal about this sort of thing. Years of experience. We discussed the possibility of stinging the other side. Really letting them have it. It's an involved operation. Not at all our normal sort. Details will be forthcoming once I've made my decision. The director likes the plan. We'd like to have a go at it. We're seriously considering you for the run, Roy. But, as I said before, I would like to know you a bit better, and I'm afraid I haven't the time. You see, we need somebody we can trust. Absolutely trust."

"You studied overseas, didn't you."

"Yes, England, why?"

"Cambridge?"

"Oxford, actually." He blushed. "Rhodes scholar."

"You speak like a Brit. I knew a fellow who spoke the way you do. It's not very common."

"I'm afraid I've never quite given it up entirely. Three

years was all, but it's stayed with me. My wife is a 'Brit,' as you say. I suppose that doesn't help matters any."

"Children?"

"No. None," Brandenburg said, disappointment written all over his tanned face. He sipped the vodka.

Kepella said, "So what does this entail?"

"It entails nothing less than breaking this network. We want another shot at Wilhelm. That's what we have in mind. It's a good, solid plan, Roy. Most unusual. But . . . well, the point is . . . you haven't really ever been an operative. That's partly why we chose you, and partly why we are uncertain about you."

"An operative?"

"Yes. How does that strike you?"

"It would have to be clarified." He patted his stomach. "I have a bit of a gut. Not the most fit person in the department. Too many years behind a desk is what it is. My training was years ago. Oh, I can still pass target range, that sort of thing. But hand-to-hand? Not for a minute. It would depend on what you have in mind."

"It wouldn't require any extra training. Nothing of that sort. I'm going to level with you, Roy. My concern is whether you can take the pressure or not. It's a difficult assignment; would be for anybody. With your life-style, your drinking record, your suspension, you both qualify and worry us. It's a delicate line I have to tread. Unfortunately, it's all been put onto my shoulders. I have to make the decision. There's no one else we have in mind, you understand. It's you, or no one. It has to be you." He finished his drink.

"And?" Kepella asked.

"I'm sorry?"

"What is your decision?"

"You wouldn't ask if you didn't already know, Roy." He tapped a file folder. "That's just not like you."

4

A color picture of the president hung on the wall behind Mark Galpin's desk. The president was smiling; Galpin was not. His office reeked of the acrid smell of perspiration. The view from the seventh floor of the New Federal Building looked out across Puget Sound. One could usually see Mount Rainier, but not today. Too hazy. Galpin wore a navy blue blazer, white ever-press shirt, and a rust-brown necktie. His sun-bleached blond hair helped him look younger than his fifty years. His large, dark oak desk seemed more an intended barrier than a work place. Free of even a single sheet of paper, it held a green blotter pad bordered in dark leather, a name plate, and a black-plastic telephone called a Merlin. Next to the phone was a paperweight that doubled as an ashtray—a brass housing for an anti-aircraft shell from a World War II destroyer—MARK GALPIN peppered neatly into its side. Galpin struggled to compose himself, a teacher at wit's end. His jugular veins pulsed on either side of his flushed neck, pumping along in time with his rapid heart rate. His mandible muscles flexed in unison as if he was chewing.

Sit, his hand instructed silently.

Kepella chose a chair facing away from the large window, not wanting the distraction of a beautiful summer day, and sat down, breathing heavily.

"What gives, Roy?"

"It won't happen aga—"

"Why? Why start drinking again, Roy?" Galpin stared out the window, avoiding his friend's eyes. "You take a sick day. The next day you don't show for work. That night— last night—you run three red lights, you smash into a car, you end up piled into the side of a delivery truck." He hesitated. "You smell like booze, so they haul you downtown. Close so far?"

Kepella studied the telephone.

Galpin continued, "Then you have the nerve, the gall, to bring the Bureau into it. What were you thinking? What could you have possibly been thinking?"

"I wasn't. That's just the point."

"You don't need to tell me that." He looked back at Kepella, who had crossed his hands in his lap. "You've put me in a bind, Roy." He paused and added, "One heck of a bind."

"Mark, it's just that things have been awful lately."

"I don't want to hear it, Roy," he snapped, waving his arms. "I told you: no sale. I can't get into this. You made a mistake. You should have never brought the Bureau into it, you know better than that."

"I thought—"

"I know what you thought. Everyone knows. Page four, for Christ's sake."

Kepella remained silent. He wondered what Galpin saw when he looked out the window. The boats probably. Galpin loved to sail. Some of the agents and stenography pool even called him 'Skipper.' Tempted to turn around and look for himself, Kepella concentrated on the photo of

37

the president. The president smiled like an actor.

"What follows next, Mark?"

"Next?" he asked, unable to look Kepella in the eye. "Darn good question, Roy. What is next? What am I supposed to do with you? You're a good agent, Roy. But you're pissing up a rope, my friend, and it's coming right back at you. What choice do you leave me? I hate the thought of breaking someone else in at your desk. You've run a darn good show, Roy. You're one hell of an archivist, and a good friend. Shit." Galpin knotted his hands and lowered his voice. "It's the sauce, my friend. You had a problem, Roy. You never let it interfere with your job. Before any of us even knew about it you had it under control. But it's different now, isn't it? It makes it even harder that we're friends. The committee won't let a former alcoholic who's drinking again run our archives. You know that. That's how they're going to see this, Roy: too risky. Let's be honest."

"You know me better than that."

"I thought I did, Roy. I thought I did." His face showed the pain of betrayal. "We put a lot of faith in you . . . after the recovery."

"The drunk farm."

"I thought you were off it."

"I was, Mark. I really was."

"As a friend, Roy. As a friend I'm here when you need me."

"Is that it?"

"It won't be long now. A day at best. There's nothing more to be said."

"Yes there is."

"What's that?"

38

Kepella stood and offered his hand. "Sorry, Mark."

In order to be opened, Kepella's office door required him to slip his magnetic-coded ID card into a plastic slot to the right of the door. A buzzer sounded and Kepella turned the doorknob. The room had no windows. All but one wall held columns of government-gray, five-drawer steel filing cabinets, stacked side by side. Kepella's small desk was also government-gray and occupied the remaining wall. A picture had once hung on the wall, as was obvious by a rectangular ghost several shades lighter than the wall paint. Kepella had titled the space "Alaska in a Blizzard." He studied the office now as a stranger might, noting the blandness, the harsh fluorescent light, the gray, gray, gray. The filing cabinets were grouped according to security rating:

(C) CONFIDENTIAL

(S) SECRET

(TS) TOP SECRET
(SCI) SENSITIVE COMPARTMENTAL INFORMATION

(WNINTEL) WARNING NOTICE: SENSITIVE INTELLIGENCE SOURCES AND METHODS INVOLVED

(NFD) NO FOREIGN DISSEMINATION

(RD) RESTRICTED DATA

Each cabinet had its own numeric pad, its own special

master combination code. Each drawer of the filing cabinets was labeled with an alpha-numeric sequence. Three of the cabinets required the agent's magnetic coded card to be inserted before the combination could be entered. The files. Year after year: the files. A custom copier and shredder occupied the far corner, behind Kepella's small desk. A blue enamel box sat alongside the shredder—the only color in the office—a high-voltage incinerator the size of a trash compactor, used to further negate security risk by reducing the shreddings to ash.

Kepella kept an IBM PC on his desk, independent of all the other Bureau computers. He used it for filing purposes: a database management system. He switched it on. The hard copy files in the cabinets were libraried into the PC by a number of different subject headings, allowing for multiple-tag searches. Only Kepella, Galpin, and some deputy-something-or-other in Washington knew the password: ZOWEHOTE. He entered the password and then worked his way through a variety of menus. A few minutes later Kepella began scribbling down a series of file codes. He didn't bother to exit the search mode because the computer automatically cleared if no key entry was made within fifteen seconds. His heart pounded. This was the beginning.

He photocopied the files in a matter of minutes, returned them to the proper cabinets, and locked them away. He carefully folded each photocopy so that it would fit inside his shoes. He stepped into his shoes and re-tied them, the knot of the bow terribly symbolic for him. That done, he sat back in his chair and tried to relax. What he really wanted was a drink.

5

Jay Becker walked with determination down the cement pier toward *The Lady Fine*. It wasn't that he felt determined. Quite the contrary—if anything he felt apprehension: today he would *meet* her, not just toss out a casual hello as she passed by. No, today he would spend *time* with her. For nearly two weeks he had eyed her: the woman who appeared both shy and lonely; the woman who spoke softly; the woman who seemed afraid of something. He could sense this fear in her, and he knew his interest was due as much to curiosity as hormones. Still, he was sweating, his heart beating quickly. He dragged his hands across his cut-off blue jeans, attempting to dry them off. Curiosity was a driving force in Jay Becker's life: the need to observe, a passion for the unknown. The two-hundred-plus songs he had written were full of his observations, from industrial smokestacks to whaling ships.

He had once written a song about a moth. He and the band had watched the moth during an electrical storm when the lights had been switched off in favor of candles. Soon the featured attraction was not the spikes of lightning but, instead, the moth. Time and again the moth flew through the flame of one of the candles, and with each pass burned a little more of its wings. But it wouldn't quit. Finally, in one last heaving effort, it flew up off the table, flapping its singed wings hysterically, and plummeted into a pool of hot wax just below the wick. Jay had named the moth Marvin, and had written the lyrics as an allegory. That had been nine years ago, and Jay still felt like that moth at times. Despite the repeated setbacks, he continued to play music for a living, refusing to give up his dream. Marvin. Marvin knew, of course, but Jay Becker was still learning.

The mystery in her compelled him. She held a secret of some sort, something stowed way down inside her, hidden away. Find the key and she'll open up.

He knew his track record with her kind of beauty. For him there was a fine line between pretty and attractive; once this line was crossed, Jay turned into a bumbling idiot with a postage-stamp I. Q. He was much too aware of his own shortcomings to get a big head about himself. He was human. "Very human," was how he put it to close friends. And he figured that in a world where people tried to be anything *but* human, he stuck out like Sissy Hankshaw's famous thumb. He spent his energies on observation and expression, not acting, and beautiful women were notoriously professional actresses. He was no match for them. Oh, he could act on stage without any problem. He could have a fever and still pull off an energetic night of music. But once offstage Jay Becker was a different person altogether, he knew that, though many women had never fully understood this about him. He finger-combed his hair and continued down Pier L.

"A series of lessons," is how the dockmaster had put it. A series of lessons. "She wants to race in the Labor Day Regatta off of Whidby. I told her you were the finest skipper we had. Finest *available* skipper," he had added, excluding himself from consideration. "I warned her that between your damn bicycle races and your combo"—the dockmaster always called the band a combo—"she would have to check with you about Labor Day."

42

"One day at a time," Jay had replied, to the obvious disgust of the dockmaster, who in turn had said, "That's the attitude I can't stand. It's got no darned future in it. You young people gotta think about the *future*. It's always me, me, me—now, now, now." And with that he had huffed away.

Jay had checked with Jocko. Labor Day weekend was still free. He had felt like clicking his heels.

He made the mistake of glancing to his left, across to Pier K where *The Lazy Daze* was tied up. He had been varnishing on that boat last night when Linda had arrived. He wondered how a person could end up living with another person for so long, knowing the whole time it was wrong, and never do a thing about it. It had taken him until last night to do anything about it and strangely enough he did not feel guilt now, just relief. For four years he and Linda had struggled to hold something together. Month by month their love had diminished. Month by month the problems had mounted. And Jay had never had the strength to do anything about it. That was it, he had realized last night after it was all over: until that moment he had never found the *strength*. He felt so strong in so many ways. He had the legs of a champion, and could out-ride anyone in his age class. He had the strength to endure the hardships of playing original music in clubs for ten years, a strength of the mind. But strength of the heart? A weakling. He could give his love. No problem. But take his love away? Heaven forbid. He had stayed with Linda longer than he should have, and all because he had no strength of the heart. Or perhaps it was too much strength. He wondered: Is the strength in staying with somebody, holding on to the bitter end, or in being able to cut loose?

She had cried. Linda knew Jay Becker's vulnerabilities. She wouldn't go down without a battle—not Linda. Jay had always felt more like Linda's trophy than anything else, and last night, when push came to shove, Linda had not been about to hand over the trophy without a final scene. So she had cried, and Jay Becker had found strength of heart, at last. He had waited for her to stop. Though he felt relief now, he also felt a distinct hollowness, a sense of loneliness, that he had not felt in years. Perhaps it had been this loneliness that had kept him awake last night. Perhaps it had been his continual re-playing of the ugly scene with Linda. Perhaps it had been anticipation of what today might bring.

One day at a time, he thought. One minute at a time. He stopped by the bowsprit of the forty-two-foot ketch and studied *The Lady Fine*. She wasn't the best ever made, nor the worst. He was hungry to have her out under sail, to test her and put her through the moves. Sailing, like bicycle racing or music, demanded one live a moment at a time. He gritted his teeth and knocked on the hull. He knew somehow that after this moment, things would never be the same.

"Hello," spoke a voice with a German accent. She was backlit by the morning sun, and all he could make out was the sweeping line of her shoulders and the nervous tapping of her right foot. She moved toward him and suddenly the sun pierced his eyes, blinding him, but not before he caught a glimpse of her. She was wearing white pants and a pink-and-white collared blouse; her hair was brushed out and held back by a single barrette. "You must

44

be Mr. Becker," she said.

Jay felt himself standing there in cut-off blue jeans, a rugby shirt with a hole in the shoulder, and two-year-old Topsiders, and felt like dying. What had he been thinking? What kind of a damned fool impression had he planned on making dressed like a kid out of junior high on summer break? Here was a woman of the Riviera, of the Greek Islands, of Marina del Rey, West Palm Beach, and Cancun. Who was he? A hired hand here to win her a trophy for some oak-burl mantel in some goddamned castle in Bavaria.

"You are Mr. Becker, are you not?"

He was staring. "Yeah, yes. Jay Becker." He climbed aboard and stuck out his hand. "Nice to meet you."

She took the hand gently and they shook hands quickly. He noted that she had none of the calluses of a sailor. She was new to this. His hands, in contrast, were tough from fingertip to wrist. Between the music and the boats and the occasional bicycle spill, Jay's hands were anything but tender.

She said softly, "I do not know whether the superintendent informed you, but I am hoping to learn how to sail. I would like to race *The Lady* in the Labor Day Regatta. It is not my boat, so the final decision will not be mine . . ."

"The decision?"

"Whether or not you skipper the boat . . ."

"I see . . ."

"The decision is not mine, but my . . . employer's."

And there it was, plain as day, Jay realized. The mystery. Her mystery. Whatever was bothering this woman had something to do with her "employer." She had nearly choked on that word.

"So what do I do?" she asked innocently. She had the most vivid green eyes Jay had ever seen.

Only you,
You've got the eyes . . .

Lyrics. Always lyrics. He thought her eyes looked sad. Not a permanent sadness, but the presence of sadness, as if she had just finished a long, hard cry. He felt like taking her into his arms to comfort her. He wanted to say, "Tell me what's bothering you. Tell me. I'll listen." Instead, he said, "Let's have a look around."

She followed him. She studied him. He stopped at every cleat, every winch. He tugged on this, pulled on that, pushed against the rail. He ran his fingers along the sail-cloth, checking the stitching, banged on the teak, and ducked his head through the companionway and went below.

The Lady Fine was equipped as a pleasure craft, not a racer. He noticed an open briefcase on the counter that contained a telephone. He had seen them in catalogues. Fancy stuff. A portable phone. "Cellular phone?" he asked.

"Yes."

"Quite a luxury. It's no good once you're out to sea, is it?"

"No. I do not think so. The owner—my employer—does not like using the ship-to-shore radio."

"I don't blame him."

"This is his."

"All the comforts of home," Jay said, noting the television, stereo, and video recorder. He could have added a comment about expensive taste: the TV was a Sony, the stereo looked like something from *Star Wars*; but everyone who owned a boat had to have bucks. The expression was: a boat is a hole in the water you pour your money into. It was not a new expression, and it did not surprise Jay to see all these luxuries. It was fancier than some, less than others. All relative. He pulled on the tiny closet door and noted that the latch needed repair. The door was loose, even when closed. It would clatter endlessly under sail. Jay had sensitive ears—he hated it when things clattered. He went forward to examine the sails. They were stored below the two forward bench/beds. There was a blue-and-white spinnaker, a genoa jib, and an extra mainsail in the bench to port. Stored to starboard he found the jib and some skin diving equipment: masks, snorkels, and spear guns. All the luxuries. "Do you dive?" he asked. When she didn't answer he turned around. She was standing back in the galley watching him. "Do you dive?" he asked again. She seemed so frightened of him.

"No. I do not dive."

"What does your employer do?"

She hesitated again. This time longer. "He is a businessman," she replied finally. Then, changing the subject, she asked, "What do you think? How is the boat?"

"She's a beauty." Jay offered one of his patented smiles, to which he got no response. "Can't tell much until we put her through the moves," he said, thinking, Just like you. He stuffed the jib bag back into the hold and closed up the storage area.

Once they were topside Jay asked her, "What do you

know about sailing?"

"I have windsurfed before."

"Great sport," Jay said, lifting a seat-hatch in the cockpit and leafing through the contents somewhat carelessly. "Have you ever crewed before?"

"When I was younger," she told him.

He turned to look at her, and again the sun was behind her, giving her an ethereal quality. Twice in a matter of minutes, he thought—twice in a matter of minutes you've looked more like a ghost than a person. "Your name," he said, squinting in her direction. "What's your name?" And despite the lighting he could sense her smile. When she spoke he knew she was smiling. He could hear it.

"Marlene," she informed him. "Marlene Johanning-meir."

"That's a mouthful."

She nodded, still smiling, and then put on her stone-sober face and looked away. He let the hatch fall shut, banging as it did. He noted that the sudden sound did not jolt her. She remained calm, her arms crossed. Her eyes caught the sun and seemed to glow. Perhaps that was all there was to her mystery: those eyes. Perhaps it was nothing more than appearance and his own runaway hormones. Perhaps.

"Should we take her out?"

She shrugged. "You will teach me?"

"Yes." He paused. "I will teach you. Let's take her out."

"Tell me what to do."

So he did.

A few minutes later Marlene tossed the bowline onto Pier

L, and Jay backed the craft out of the slip, the diesel humming. A sea gull spooked and lifted off the top of a piling, its wings carrying it effortlessly into an indigo sky. The breeze caught Jay Becker full face and a smile curled his lips. He was aboard a fine boat with a beautiful woman, being paid to sail. There were others in glass towers not far from Shilshole Marina probably looking out right now and spotting the tiny vessel as it motored out past the long breakwater. Had his life taken a different turn it might have been him looking down from just such a skyscraper. It might have been him in the suit with a large desk, two phones, and a secretary. And he thought about that now, thankful for where he was. Despite his debt to Linda for the wrecked car, despite his eight hours at Shilshole and five with the band—every day—he felt gratitude overwhelm him. Who else was this lucky? Who else was being paid to sail today? Who else could win demanding bike races at thirty-one years of age? No, Jay Becker knew his fortune: he was a rich man, and he counted his blessings as he hollered forward and had Marlene pull in the inflatable bumpers and store them in the cockpit seats. He had his health, his friends. He had his dream, his optimism. He believed. What else was there?

They studied each other for the first hour out. Jay had no intention of forcing himself on her. The dockmaster had said *a series* of lessons; there was no sense in coming on strong and jeopardizing a week or more of this kind of work. So he held *The Lady Fine* pointing upwind and studied her sails.

He knew in the first fifteen minutes that *The Lady* would never win a race. He had entered plenty of regattas where a boat like this would be lost at the gun, a good five lengths out by the first buoy, out of sight by the end of the course. But that wasn't his problem. He had been hired to make the boat move as fast as it could and give the woman aboard the chance to feel like she was part of the race. That much he could do.

Marlene had smiled once, a few minutes earlier, though it had seemed more a mistake than anything else. She had looked back at him, the green of her eyes mixing with the green of Puget Sound, her lips curled at the edges, her teeth peeking through briefly only to retreat back behind pursed lips. It had happened during a nice gust from the port side, and *The Lady* had lurched to starboard, causing spray to splash across their faces. That's why she smiled, he figured, so he cinched in the mainsheet, cranked the jib's self-tailing winch two clicks, and pointed her up a bit farther. Again *The Lady* heeled heavily to starboard, again spray tossed up over the gunwales and smacked them both in the face. But she didn't smile at him, white-knuckling a teak rail instead. So Jay let the wheel slip to starboard and righted the boat, slowing it down and eliminating the spray. "What do you think?" he asked.

She looked back at him and he felt her holding back the smile, keeping it to herself. "It is fun, yes. But I am not learning. I want to learn."

A woman of purpose, he thought. "Okay, deal. Come back here."

Now the smile was genuine and her enthusiasm evident, and Jay suddenly realized that she had allowed herself to believe she might never get a chance at it. Perhaps, he thought, she had had to fight like hell just to get these lessons. Perhaps this was her only chance at "fun." If that was the case then Jay would give her all the fun she could handle, for a pleased customer keeps coming back for more—and who could beat this for work? "Did you see the way I've been trimming the sails?"

She nodded.

"Here, I'm going to let her fall off some," he said, quickly loosening both the mainsheet and the jib sheet and moving the bow of *The Lady* downwind a few degrees. The boat hesitated a moment. Then the mainsail snapped loudly and *The Lady* began moving smoothly again. "As I point her back upwind, trim the mainsail . . . just like wind-surfing . . . you let me know when you think you've got it." He spun the boat's wheel to port and watched Marlene as she studied the luff in the mainsail and went about trimming it. He noted her concentration, and realized immediately that Germans and Americans were two different beasts. Her attention to detail, her determination, impressed him. This was *important* to her. Then he noticed that her pink blouse was spotted from the spray. Her hair whipped behind her, and he thought she looked quite at home on a boat. "Perfect!" he announced. "You're a natural. Now the jib." *The Lady* leaned back into a steep heel and Marlene squealed and smiled quickly. She saw him notice her smile and turned away from him.

Puzzled, Jay told her, "Nothing in the *Boatsman's Guide to Better Sailing* that says you can't enjoy it, you know."

"Is this a book?" she asked, dead serious.

He shook his head, disappointed.

And then she laughed: one quick bark into the stiff breeze, eyes sparkling, teeth white. Jay felt his heart pound and then race away from him, like *The Lady Fine* jumping into a good heel. One smile. Look out for her, he warned himself, she's a powerful one.

"Are *you* having fun?" she asked.

He wanted to answer her, but found himself staring into those green eyes—and no words would come out. He nodded.

The spray hit them both at the same time. They laughed together, Marlene's blouse wet and sexy, salt water running from Jay's chin. He reached out and took her hand and placed it on the wheel.

Boom, boom, boom.

"It's all yours," he told her. And he slid out of the way and let her take control.

6

It had begun to rain and, even though a commonplace occurrence in Seattle, it seemed terribly symbolic to Kepella. Nature's tears, wasn't that what rain was? In the past few days he had photocopied and removed too many FBI files to count. Hidden in groups of three, he had scattered them around town in safe deposit boxes, lockers, and storage areas. It had begun. The "eyes only" material, printed in light blue ink so it could not be photocopied, he had read into a cassette recorder. He had enough information spread around this city to set the military complex back years. Decades perhaps. One man. He switched on his blinker, the green indicator light pulsing across his face. The thrill overwhelmed Kepella: action, real action!

There was no turning back now. Just over twenty-five minutes ago he had been suspended indefinitely, pending further investigation of his car wreck. As expected, the committee was making a scapegoat out of him. His story had moved from page four to page two for the last three days. He was an unwilling celebrity, a target for the anger and animosity of thousands of total strangers. A Richard Nixon of Seattle. He had screwed up, and was not about to be forgiven. Just as Brandenburg had hoped.

Kepella turned right off of South Washington and onto 6th Street. When he reached South King he turned left and parked. The section of Seattle he was in is known as the International District, though many prefer to call it China-town, in spite of the variety of people who live there. The streets are not particularly clean, there are no fancy high-rises, but there is a unique energy—like the energy in a hive of bees or a nest of red ants.

Kepella walked past a grocery store, the sign in Chinese characters. Through the rain-stained glass he noticed several women rummaging through the bins of roots and beans, scooping and weighing, marking and wrapping. A small, wide-eyed child held against a hip watched her grandmother shop. Kepella grinned spontaneously and winked at the child. Children had a way of making Roy Kepella smile.

Fu Won's, a ratty bar on the north corner of South King and 8th Street, hadn't been remodeled since the early six-ties. But Kepella liked it. It was one of those places no other FBI agent would be caught dead in, the kind of place where you had to get to know people before they gave you the time of day. Everyone called the bartender Georgie. His real name was Lon Wong, but that name had been the cause of so many jokes and bar fights that Fu had ordered him to change his name to Georgie, and the name had stuck. What Fu said, went: he had the aura of a Buddhist monk, the toughness of a drill sergeant, the face and teeth of a man somewhat deformed. It was rumored that at the age of seventeen, in Bangkok, Thailand, Fu had slipped while running to place a bet at the Bangkok Sports Club. The Sports Club's golf course was partly contained within a horse track. Golfers inclined to place a few *baht* on a thoroughbred would send a "boy" in with the cash. Fu and the other "runners" had long since abandoned the route to the betting cages sanctioned by the club. They chose the short-cut instead: straight across the track. Fu had been knocked down by Galloping Dream. He had been stepped on by Darling Dancer. Dancer had gone down with a broken leg. Miraculously, Fu, in need of two dozen stitches, had stood up and run. He knew that one didn't drop a race horse and live to tell about it. He had not stopped running until he had reached Seattle. That had been forty-one years ago.

Kepella's right fist was clenched. "The usual, Georgie."

"Yes, sir, Mr. Roy." Georgie's hands worked beneath the bar and produced a drink for Kepella.

Kepella smelled the man before he felt him lean across his shoulder. Fu always smelled bitter, like lemon juice. Old lemon juice. Kepella said, "How's it going, Fu?"

"Just fine, Mr. Roy." He moved closer and whispered, though no other patron was within earshot, "You will join us today?" Fu tended toward the dramatic. Kepella could never tell what the old goat was thinking.

"Could be."

"You win real big last night," Fu stated.

"If I didn't win now and then, Fu, I wouldn't keep coming back."

Georgie was leaning against the bar, sharing in all of this, his acceptance of Kepella obvious. All three men laughed.

Iben Holst sat in a rented luxury car with white walls and nice comfortable seats. Kepella's old beater was parked nearby. Holst knew all about Roy Kepella. He had been tailing him, off and on, for several weeks. These latest news stories were what he had been waiting for. Kepella was going down, and Holst, like a circling vulture, was waiting to pick the meat off the carcass. He felt like he had all the time in the world. In truth he had but a few more weeks.

Holst sat, quietly, wondering if the old Chinaman was doing his bit. Holst had paid handsomely for results; now it was simply a question of whether or not the Chinaman could deliver.

An agonizing ninety minutes later, Holst entered Fu Won's. Kepella wasn't at the bar. That meant they had to be in the back room, for Holst knew Kepella had not left. A fireplug of an Oriental guarded the door to the back room. He was short and had a ruddy complexion and dull black eyes tightly hidden inside folds of tawny skin. He wore an ill-fitting T-shirt advertising the Summer Olympic Games. On his right forearm, a tattoo of a mushroom cloud erupted into his elbow. Beneath it, a set of Chinese characters spelled out what roughly translated as "Peace Brother." It was what everyone at Fu's called him, though he appeared anything but peaceful. In the past few weeks, Holst had come to know him well. Peace Brother opened the door as Holst approached. Like Fu Won, he was on Iben Holst's payroll.

"Ah, welcome, Mr. Holst." Fu's scar, in the shape of a horse hoof, stretched from just below his nose to his right ear. His teeth, yellowed from constant smoking, clamped a nonfilter cigarette, a permanent fixture in his lips. The Camel bobbed up and down, continually dropping ashes on his lap.

The room was small, filled with smoke, and dark except for the strong glare from the light above the green felt poker table. Kepella was there. A respectable-looking Chinaman in a business suit, whom Holst had never met, sat next to Fu, his brow knitted, his concentration fixed on the hand he was holding. Patsy sat next to this man, drinking her dark drink, testing her horsehair wig to make sure it hadn't slipped. Patsy and Holst knew each other. A young man named Kim sat to Fu's left. He wore a black leather jacket, as did Holst. Holst sat next to the boy. The chair creaked. Smoke swirled beneath the lamp.

Fu said, "I think you know everyone but Mr. Lu and Mr. Kepella," pointing to each. "Mr. Holst."

Lu nodded without taking his eyes off his cards. Kepella looked over and offered his hand. "Roy Kepella."

"Please call me Iben." Holst spoke with a strong German accent. He had bright turquoise eyes, short flaxen hair, and hard, imposing features. His light eyebrows, like brushstrokes, pointed sharply in the direction of his lobeless ears. His lips were nearly purple. His teeth were as white as polished porcelain. The leather jacket fitted his muscular body snugly. "The name Kepella sounds familiar to me."

Fu interrupted, as planned. "An unfortunate coincidence, Mr. Holst. You are thinking perhaps of the recent news, the FBI agent by the name of Kepella?"

This drew businessman Lu's attention. He looked at everyone at the table.

Kepella said, "No relation."

Holst nodded. "What a coincidence. I've never heard that name before."

"It's fairly common in this area," Kepella said, looking Fu in the eye, thankful the man had some degree of character. He appreciated a businessman who knew how to protect his clients.

Fu dealt.

7

Sharon Johnson found sanctuary. The priest offered her a small room in a stone building behind the church. A number of canvas cots had been stored in the catacombs years before as part of a civil defense plan. The priest set one up for her, supplied her with bedding, and even bought her a toothbrush. She spent two days and nights there, frightened, wondering how to get her passport. Hidden in the passport, in code, was a phone number: the conduit. The priest brought her picnic meals of hot soups, cheese, bread, apples, red wine. Late the second evening, over a game of cards, they talked. Death had touched her, and no pious solicitude could tame its horrible impression. The fear on Brian's face haunted her with the same persistence as the dank odors haunted the halls of the stone building.

The tall, thick-lipped man returned the first morning, looking for his "cousin." He questioned a deacon but learned nothing.

On the second morning she ventured into the streets, a scarf about her head. She wore an olive green skirt and white cotton blouse that the priest had given her, claiming to have borrowed them from a friend. She knew, in fact, he had purchased them, because he had neglected to remove the price tags.

She wanted her own clothing badly but, more importantly, *had* to have the passport and money. But her luggage and passport remained in her hotel room. Knowing that someone—if not many people—might be watching for her, she knew she couldn't just waltz inside and go upstairs to her room.

A café across from the Hotel Regensburg seemed a good place to collect her thoughts and form a plan. The waitress, a bosomy blonde with large hips and hands, brought her a cup of strong coffee, which Sharon paid for using one of the five deutsche marks that the priest had loaned her. She stirred two heaping teaspoons of sugar into the espresso and drank it. The café's five tables were crammed together, each no larger than a large tray. The leaded windows' colorful curtains were tied back and framed the glass like festive bunting. A few customers came and went; most came and stayed. Within an hour, all the chairs were filled and the noise level had increased considerably.

Sharon finally spotted three of the hotel's chambermaids, still in uniform, walking down the sidewalk across the street. One of them, an attractive red-haired girl, crossed the cobbled street and stood near the café, apparently waiting for a ride. Sharon stepped outside and approached her. She spoke in English. "Hello?"

"Yes?" The girl answered nervously, shying away. She had lovely gray eyes, a flat chest, and tiny wrists.

"I'm sorry to bother you, but aren't you a chambermaid from the hotel?"

"The Hotel Regensburg, yes." Spoken beautifully.

"I wonder . . ." Sharon hesitated. "I have a favor to ask you. I can pay you, actually."

"Yes?" Curiosity.

"I am a guest at the Hotel Regensburg—*was* a guest. Room Three-twenty-one. I've had a terrible falling-out with my husband, you see." She performed well, knitting her brow painfully. "Another woman."

The chambermaid's face expressed sympathy.

Sharon went on. "I ran away, you see. However, I left all my belongings in my room. My husband has left town . . . on to Bonn. With *her.*" She frowned. "But I'm quite sure he's having the lobby watched. Possibly even the room, though I doubt that."

"And you need your belongings?"

"I'd like them very much. Would you?"

"I shouldn't. It is not allowed."

"I can pay you thirty U.S. dollars, or the equivalent in deutsche marks. You'll have to pack for me. My wallet is in my purse, in the room." She glanced at the hotel and then back to the young woman. "There's plenty of cash. I'll have to trust you. Please pay the hotel bill. Tell the desk you found the payment in my room. I owe for three nights. No other charges. A bellboy can take the bags and bring them to the front door. I'll wait in a taxi. I don't know what else to do."

"Here is my ride."

A small car pulled alongside. It had tiny wheels and room for two. The chambermaid opened the door, stooped down, and talked briskly in German. The driver, another young woman, listened and then nodded. The car drove away. The chambermaid stood and said, "I will do this for you."

Nearly an hour later, with a dull sky the color of dirty snow covering the city, Sharon made a phone call. A woman on the other end gave her another number and hung up. She dialed this number a dozen times. No one answered. She decided to take a train.

The train station, beneath a giant translucent green canopy, was mostly empty. She walked briskly to the ticket counter and, using an Agency credit card, bought a one-way to Bonn, departure in seventy minutes.

She noticed the two when she turned around. They were staring at her. Neither looked familiar, but even so, she evidently looked familiar to them. She wondered what to do, her training evaporating, replaced by sudden panic. What did they intend to do? What *could* they do?

Kill you, her mind answered immediately. Just like Brian.

They approached slowly, casually. Professional killers, she thought. She picked up the two bags, her purse slung over her shoulder, ticket in hand. She moved quickly toward the door marked DAMEN. Her heels clicked against the stone floor. The two walked silently behind her, closing the distance.

She pushed through the door, into a small room with wash bowls and a mirror on the right-hand wall. An inner door took her on into the toilet room. She realized suddenly that it was empty. Even the toilet-maid was gone, probably on a break. But she had left behind a pair of shoes and a smock. Would they dare? She quickly put down her bags and hurried over to the small wooden cabinet below where the smock hung. In the second drawer down she found a wicker basket containing sewing materials, including a small pair of scissors, which she seized.

She heard the outer door open noisily on its hinges. She rushed toward the inner door, slipped, and fell to her hands and knees as she reached it. The inner door swung open. She saw a long, thin blade jutting from the man's right hand. He stopped, sensing her behind him. Before he could turn she drew the scissors over her head and brought them down hard, sinking them into his back. The two of them screamed simultaneously, the volume magnified by the tiled walls. The stiletto fell from his hand. She kicked it and then stepped back, biting the knuckles of her right hand, wondering what to do.

The man was not dead. He wasn't even unconscious, though he appeared to be in shock. He had fallen onto his back—onto the scissors—puncturing a lung, and now lay on the floor, his arms and legs flailing like he was a turtle flipped onto its shell. He tried to speak, but no sound came out.

She edged around him and reached for her most important bag, her purse still slung over her shoulder. She heard the groan of the outer door opening again. Could it be . . . ? She found the stiletto, grabbed it, and scooted to the right of the door, where she squatted. The door swung open. A man's trouser leg. She plunged the knife into the man's thigh. He yelled, doubled over in pain, and fell forward onto the other man.

She fled through the doors and ran from the station. It had begun to rain.

8

Jay spotted her across the room, alone at a small table, a tall glass of iced tea in front of her. She was resting with her chin on her palm, staring out the window, her green eyes unfocused it seemed, gazing nowhere, seeing nothing. He believed in serendipity, and although he had stumbled in here to buy an ice cream cone, it did not shock him to see her here. She didn't see him at first: she continued to stare, her sad, green eyes frozen in her head like the eyes of a marble statue. She wore white shorts, a madras blouse, and flip-flops on her large feet. Her toenails were painted red, her fingernails not at all. She had her hair pulled back and held with a terry cloth headband, which made her look like a professional tennis player with the wrong shoes on. He ordered two chocolate cones and approached her table. He stood there until the chocolate was running down his hand. Finally, he cleared his throat and she turned to look at him. He pushed the cone toward her. "Chocolate," he said, grinning.

She appeared confused. "The lesson is not for another hour. You said one o'clock."

"I know that."

"I don't understand."

"Chocolate. I said, 'chocolate.' I bought you a cone."

"No, thank you," she replied.

"It's dripping all over my hand." He paused. "Please?"

She took it from him, carefully avoiding contact with him. "Thank you," she said lifelessly.

"May I?" He hooked a leg of an empty chair across from her.

She shrugged and licked at the scoop of chocolate.

"Ah, you're a licker," he said.

She looked curiously at him, her tongue halfway out of her mouth.

He explained, "Some people nibble at their cones, others lick. You're a licker."

She drew her tongue back into her mouth and nibbled.

"Nothing wrong with lickers." He winked.

She smiled, covering her open mouth with her hand. "It is good," she acknowledged.

He nodded. "They make a bunch of the flavors right here. Homemade. Best in the city."

She nodded and returned to licking.

"Did you enjoy yesterday?"

"Yes. I particularly liked to steer it. It is a good boat, is it not?"

"Yes and no," he replied truthfully. "It's not a racer, Marlene. We won't stand a chance in the regatta. Not in *The Lady Fine*. She's too broad in the beam and low in the water. We'll have fun, but we won't win."

"Who is to say? Maybe *The Lady Fine* will be lucky." She purposely avoided using "we" and Jay didn't miss it. No one had asked him to race the boat with her. Only the dockmaster had mentioned it and who could trust him?

She licked, he nibbled. Their ice cream cones shrank. She said nothing and he began to feel in the way. "Am I interrupting?"

The question clearly broke her train of thought. She shook her head. She had chocolate stains on both sides of her lips, making her twenty-some-odd years seem more like twelve. She licked away the stains. "No," she told him, "I am just missing my home, I think."

"Germany?"

She nodded. When she bit into the sugar cone it crunched; some crumbs fell to the table, along with a drop of chocolate.

Jay felt foolish; she obviously didn't feel like talking. "Well," he said, rising from his chair, "see you in a little while."

"You are leaving?"

"I interrupted. I didn't mean to."

"Stay." She looked directly into his eyes. "Please."

Boom, boom, boom. He sat back down. They both started talking at the same time. The result was gibberish. Jay stopped and smiled. She crunched into her cone. "Go ahead," he said.

"I was going to say to you that you are very nice to buy this ice cream for me. Thank you."

"You're welcome."

"How do you think we can make *The Lady Fine* faster? Is there a way, or is this not possible?"

Jay thought a minute. "Anything's possible—" She laughed before he could continue. He asked, "Why do you laugh?"

"I am sorry. It was funny . . . 'anything is possible.' This is very American, I think. Yes, very American. We think differently, you and I."

Jay didn't like the idea. He wanted to think the same. "You don't believe it?"

"That anything is possible?"

"Yes."

"No. I do not. It is foolish. Some things are possible, yes. Anything? Of course not. Some things simply are as they are. They can not be changed. I am a scientist. Scientists know there are limits. You are a sailor." She smiled. "Sailors think there is paradise just over the horizon."

"Scientists once thought the world was flat."

"I am not defending science."

"Sailors proved them wrong." He let her think about this while he finished his cone. "What kind of scientist?" he asked after a moment, and not without a tinge of humor in his voice.

"An electrical engineer," she replied formally.

"Computers?"

"Not exactly computers, but I understand them. Why?"

"What then? What kind of electronics?"

She noticed an American flag flapping on one of the moored boats. "My work is boring. I would rather not discuss it." Changing subjects, she asked, "Will we use the spinnaker today?"

He glanced out at the flag, noting the direction of the wind. "We could on our way in, if this wind holds. You didn't answer my question."

She studied his face. A long, intriguing silence passed as the two locked eyes. Marlene finally said, "I feel as if you are reading my mind."

Still staring, he said, "No," and paused before adding, "I wish I could."

"Do you?" she asked skeptically.

"Yes, I do." His eyes were blurring, beginning to burn, but he would not flinch, would not look away from her. "You're hiding something."

She blanched. "Why do you say that?"

"I can tell when a person is hiding something."

"Then you *do* read minds." She looked back out at the flag, breaking their eye contact, and pushed the remainder of the sugar cone into her mouth. "You're a musician," she said after a moment.

"Yes. Yes, but my work is boring. I'd rather not discuss it."

She grinned. "I thought musicians always like to talk about themselves."

"Is that so?"

"Musicians, painters, poets, people of the arts love to talk about themselves."

"Musicians have two personalities. There's the stageman and the normal Joe. Most people never see the normal Joe."

"Is that what I am seeing: the normal Joe?"

"No," he admitted. "This is the Jay Becker that wants to impress a pretty woman." He blushed; he couldn't believe he had said that. Was he nuts? She seemed stunned. "Where did that come from?" he asked, trying to recover.

She said quietly, "And this is the Marlene afraid of the handsome man."

Boom, boom, boom. Had she really said that? He felt as if he were melting from the feet up. She was reaching into

66

her purse to leave money for the iced tea. He didn't know if he should offer to cover it or not. In fact, he couldn't think of anything to say, and he wasn't sure anything would come out if he tried. She placed two dollars on the table and stood. Her face was red. Think of something to say, dummy! He couldn't think.

"It is time I go," she said, in almost a whisper. Embarrassed.

Think of something! But he couldn't. He watched as she walked toward the door. "Wait!" he finally managed. The couple at the next table looked over at him. He hurried to Marlene, who had reached the door. He held it for her. "Someday you'll tell me," he said flatly.

With far-away eyes, Marlene nodded sadly. Her words were barely audible. "I know."

It was all she said. She seemed on the edge of tears. Then she turned and walked away.

He watched her. When she was some distance from him she glanced over her shoulder quickly, obviously not expecting him to still be staring. When she saw him looking, she snapped her head back around and raised a hand in the air to wave.

He waved back. But she didn't see.

9

There had been power failures for the last two evenings. The late news blamed them on air conditioners—a lame excuse in a place like Seattle, where no one owned air conditioners. Both nights Kepella had been at Fu's in the middle of losing more money. Both nights the game had continued right on through the blackouts. So on this, the third night, when the lights browned and dimmed, Kepella slammed his cards down on the worn-felt table and said, "I fold. My eyes can't take another night of emergency lights and candles." He went into the bar and ordered "the usual."

She wasn't much over five feet tall. She wore a fire-engine-red rayon blouse with Chinese buttons and black pants that fit her so tightly the seam disappeared into her crotch. She was bent over the darkened jukebox. She hit it once angrily. Kepella wanted to go up and . . . She turned around and looked him right in the eye, as if she had read his mind. Cutest little Chinese face he'd ever seen. Not a day over twenty-five, with black pupils the size of snow peas. She smiled and then giggled like a school girl. "Took my quarter," she complained. She walked straight toward him, moving like an ambling mountain lioness, the slick shirt shifting across small, pert breasts and hard nipples. As she passed him she said, "You fly's open," and giggled. She walked on down to a bar stool, leaving four empties between them.

Kepella checked his fly. It was a gag. He watched her toss her leg up over the stool and ease up onto it. She wiggled, adjusting herself on the stool and it damn near made him stiff. It was then he realized she wasn't *trying* to be sexy. She just couldn't help it.

"That was a cheap shot," he said.

She didn't seem to hear him.

He raised his voice. "I said, that was a cheap shot."

"You stare at me," she told him. "Jukebox has a

mirror on it."

Kepella looked at the jukebox. Then he looked at Georgie, who shrugged and smiled and said, "Looks like she caught you, Mr. Roy."

10

The Streak was aptly named. It was an Olmo racing bike with a chrome finish: in the sun, it shined with the same intensity as the bumper of a '59 Caddy. It sported Campagnolo hardware and Cenneli handlebars. Jay stood alongside of it nervously. "So what do you think?" Jocko's lisp made him sound like Sylvester the Cat.

"I think the race starts in a couple of minutes."

"I mean about your chances, birdlegs."

Jay looked down at his legs. They were tanned, muscular, and hairy—anything but birdlegs. "My chances would have been better without Rossi showing up."

"Who cares about Rossi? You should be thinking about the course."

"He's the best in the state. Olympic starter in Los Angeles in '84."

"Technicalities. You're on home turf. You're on the goddamned slickest-looking bicycle this side of Rome. If anyone gets behind you they'll be blinded."

"He grew up here. He's on a Masi."

"If the rain would stop I'd feel better about this. A bike race isn't worth a broken wrist or something."

"It adds to the challenge."

"You're a sick puppy."

They were interrupted by the voice shouting into the bullhorn. "Two minutes to the start of the race. Bikers only please. Two minutes."

Jocko slapped Jay on his numbers. "Remember those two gear changes you told me about."

Jay snapped on his chin strap and worked his jaw, nodding at the same time. He started hyperventilating, gradually increasing the pace. "Shitty position," he gasped.

Jocko nodded. "Luck o' the Irish. You'll have to make your move early."

"On the first hill," Jay replied, huffing like a steam engine.

Jocko said, "Break a leg," and moved through the crowded bicycles toward the sidewalk.

"One minute," the starter announced from a perch high atop a ladder, starting pistol in his hand.

Jay glanced over at the sidewalk, hoping to catch a reassuring nod from Jocko, but he didn't see him. He didn't see anyone but her. He felt like he was in one of those corny shampoo commercials in which the macho man sees only one face in a sea of hundreds. And what a face. She was smiling because she knew he saw her. She didn't wave, didn't nod, didn't blow him a kiss. She just smiled.

"Thirty seconds," the starter barked. An odd clatter, like the sound of crickets in summer, as a hundred and sixteen people mounted their racing machines. Jay hooked his foot into the metal loop on the pedal. Sometimes he tied himself into the pedals, but not today. With the rain and a street full of amateurs he had decided against it. Rossi would be strapped in. A few of the others. "Fifteen seconds . . ." He couldn't remember telling her about the race. When had he told her? It was strange to see her standing there. Strangely wonderful. It bridged a gap—this made them friends, not just professional acquaintances. She had obviously made an effort to be here.

"Ten, nine, eight . . ." called the voice. Tension rose. Muscles flexed. Jay could see the back of Rossi's helmet: the Italian was up on his pedals, perfectly balanced, his handbrakes keeping him behind the start line. He was ready to release the brake and tromp down on the pedals. Rossi wanted this race.

"Seven, six . . ."

Jay had only raced against Rossi once before, and had blown a tire with a quarter mile to go. Rossi had won that one. But at the time of the tire failure Jay had already passed twelve bikes and was within three of Rossi. He might have beaten him.

"Five, four . . ."

Something distracted Jay. He snatched a quick glance to his left, over toward Jocko. Linda was standing with Jocko. Linda! And she had fixed her concentration on the face Jay had been staring at. Marlene's face. "Shit," Jay said.

"Three, two . . ." *Bam!*

Rossi shot out into the lead. Where Jay had been positioned he had to wait a beat for the bikes in front of him to start moving. Someone went down off to his right and two or three bikes crashed into the downed rider. He paid no attention to it—his first coach had taught him that—except that he prepared himself for the quick surge of riders avoiding the pile-up.

Rossi took the first corner comfortably. He had a

length's lead already. Jay swerved left and passed two bikes, pulling in front of a thin guy with curly hair. He heard the familiar Jocko war cry echo off the buildings—his coach approved.

Two more bikes lost it on the corner, their skinny wheels slipping on the slickened pavement. The resulting crash was noisy. Jay figured at least another six bikes had gone down. He shifted gears and passed another guy. Rossi was eight bikes up. The riders began to string out. Jay took a gamble and left himself in low gear. He leaned on it and passed two more riders. This was not a good place in the course, or in the strategy of the race, to put a move on. Jay caught the two unsuspecting. He snapped *The Streak* into fifth gear. Rossi still held the lead, six bikes up.

It had been Jocko's idea to fix a fiberglass fender to both wheels. They were tiny fenders, made in Spain, and they added perhaps a pound to the overall weight of the bike. None of the riders in front of Jay had elected to use the fenders, but Jay had liked Jocko's reasoning: water sprayed onto your front and back and absorbed into clothing weighed more than one pound worth of fenders, which prevented ninety percent of the water from hitting you. It was the kind of good, clean, streetwise sense typical of Jocko. He knew absolutely nothing about bike racing, but his logic was impeccable. Jay was moving a lighter load. He looked ahead. All the riders had brown lines down their backs, across their numbers, their T-shirts getting soaked by the spray from their tires. Jay peered into the rearview mirror mounted to his helmet: everyone was behaving. Not one of the top twenty bikes was making a move. Riders were settling in.

It was fun to have the city close streets for you, to have cops guarding all the intersections. A mobile TV van parked at the next corner had a crew of vid-heads trying to get footage for the six o'clock news. Jay smiled as he flew by them.

Rossi shifted gears and pulled out ahead of the pack—wicked move considering the upcoming hill. The strategy frustrated Jay—this was where he had intended to make his first push, but Rossi's move kicked everyone, and Jay had to lean on it just to hold seventh. He felt the tingling in his hair: he was beginning to sweat.

Jay's training as a sailor warned him of the gust: he saw the ripples on a puddle on the road up ahead. The wind swept across the intersection, carrying rain with it. Jay watched as it hit Rossi and caused him to swerve left. It had to be powerful to rattle a rider of Rossi's abilities.

Mr. Second Place evidently didn't sail, because he didn't see it coming. When the wind hit, it blew the bike out from under him. He yelled and went down, one foot holding in the pedal. He was dragged along behind his bike and slid into a cop car with enough force to cause a hell of a racket. Jay didn't see the rest of it. He tucked low over the handle bars and edged his front wheel to the right, preparing for the gust. As it hit he pedaled harder and held the handlebars tightly. He swayed but didn't lose an inch to the wind. He quickly closed the gap left by the downed rider. Rossi was five bikes up.

Now was his shot. He had planned this, and once Jay Becker planned something, he followed through. No going back. And nothing like competition to spur him on. It wasn't just a race; it was Rossi—and Rossi had beaten him before. Jay had an appreciation for the unexpected. This came in part from calling set lists at the band's gigs. If the crowd looked like they wanted a slow song, you gave them one more fast song first—then the slow dance. If it was a quiet crowd you wanted to excite, you didn't jump right into a rocker; no, you handed them a real mellow number—match their mood—and then, song by song, brought them up to a frenzy. He reasoned that this same theory might work against a person like Rossi: if no one ever passed on a hill, then pass on the hill. Why not?

The most common racing strategy is to shift to your lower gear at the bottom of a hill and work like hell just to hold your position. Jay downshifted twenty yards before the rider in front of him did. His theory was simple: get the momentum required to hit the base of the hill at top speed. In order to keep pace he had to pedal harder than the man in front of him, and in doing so, *The Streak*'s gears complained. The rider in front of him heard the change of gears. Jay could *feel* the man check his rearview mirror, but by the time number four had figured it out, Jay was taking him to the left, rising off the seat and pumping like hell. Number three dropped behind next. Jay pumped hard. It wasn't so much that the other riders couldn't have defended their positions—it was Jay's timing. Their positions had been challenged and won before they knew it.

Jay had no strength left to take on number two. He calmed down and regained his strength, ready for the men behind him to fight for the positions they had lost. To expend energy on number two would be an exercise in futility. He might win the position, but for how long? With weakened legs he would be an easy target for the angry two behind him. He watched as Rossi crested the hill. Jay hunkered down low as a strong gust caught him from the right. Rossi shifted and shot out ahead. Number two followed suit. Jay saw the former Mr. Three making a challenge off to his left. The two were even within seconds, wheel to wheel. It was all a matter of who went for the gear change first. Jay didn't hesitate. In the split second before the gears caught his opponent surged a half-wheel in front, then reached down to shift. Jay bolted past and leaned hard into the sharp left turn. The man had miscalculated Jay's "kick," and when Jay made the turn, was forced to rescind. Jay regained third, shifted, and settled into a series of quick turns too tight for any of those behind him to make a legitimate bid for the position. He still had two men in front of him. And one of them was Rossi.

He battled with the rider behind Rossi. The man was good. Each attempt to pass was met with equal determination. Turn to turn, they rode along the wet streets, sweating, huffing, changing gears. The gears and chains whined; the narrow tires cried in the water. Handlebar to handlebar, wheel to wheel, they struggled with each other. And then the man looked over.

Jay estimated they had been fighting for the position for close to fifteen minutes. Both were tiring. Rossi pedaled effortlessly ahead of them. Jay had resisted the temptation to look over at his opponent, thinking it odd that the more he tried not to look, the more he wanted to. But he didn't. In these close battles for position, even the slightest turn of the helmet could cost you the race.

Out of the corner of his eye Jay saw the flash of white

as the man's helmet moved. In that fraction of time, Jay cut in on him. It was a ruse more than anything else. He knew what it felt like to see that jerk of the arms. This rider overreacted as all riders do. He, too, jerked his wheel, but harder than Jay. Jay's wheel nudged in front of his opponent's. To avoid the crash the man had to stop pedaling. Jay rose onto the pedals and his bike jumped ahead. The spray from Rossi's wheel hit him. Rossi, who had probably been watching their contest in his mirror. Rossi, who seemed to be out for a Sunday ride, not leading a pack of bike enthusiasts in the summer's biggest race. God, he wanted Rossi.

They came around the final turn and were headed toward the finish line, the crowd much larger than Jay had expected. A roar went up. Some kids barked encouragement. Others applauded.

Applause. People rarely realized what applause meant to a musician. The truth of the matter was that at fifty to sixty dollars a night, by the time a musician had arrived at a gig, set up all the equipment, tuned the instruments, changed into show clothes and ate dinner, he had earned all but fifteen dollars of his pay, and that fifteen *might* cover the hour and a half to break down and reload the equipment back into the van at the end of the night. This meant that the musician played for free. People didn't understand that. The real "pay" was the crowd's enthusiasm, applause. It was the only fuel to a performer's fire.

The cheers increased, and so did Jay's energy. His legs hummed in perfect unison with Rossi's. Gears whined. The crowd roared louder.

Suddenly, Rossi shifted.

Jay reached for his gear lever too late. Rossi broke the tape.

Jay coasted past the finish, the flagman's fingers held in the V that indicated second place. He glanced to his left looking for Marlene and saw her wave. He coasted ahead and pulled alongside Rossi. "Nice race," he shouted above the roar of an overhead jet. Rossi nodded. Still moving, the two reached out and touched hands. A light cheer went up from the crowd.

Two blocks later Jay followed the route back around a block to the starting point. Jocko greeted him with the same casual smile that had become his trademark. They said nothing to one another. They locked *The Streak* into Jocko's van and then Jay asked, "Where is she?"

"Linda?"

"No, Marlene."

"Who?"

"The woman from Shilshole."

"She was here?"

"Oh, shit." Jay hurried back to where he had spotted her. Some kids approached him and stopped his advance, asking for autographs. He rose to his toes. He and Marlene saw each other, her eyes as green and sparkling as ever. Then she disappeared. He briefly saw the back of her blond head round a corner. Gone.

Jocko had caught up to him. "Nice race," he lisped. "I knew you'd place in this sucker."

Jay turned and said, "I should have had him."

"He's one of the best in the country. Take what you're given, you fool."

Jay's face tightened, sweat rolling off his chin, shoulders still heaving from the race. "You *accept* what you're *given,* Rocks. You *take* what is rightfully yours." Jocko handed him a towel and Jay patted himself dry. Then he said, "That's the difference."

"You look beautiful." He wondered what made him say such things. Perhaps a hidden desire to fail. Is she too much for you, boy, is that the problem? Do you plan on scaring her off with clichés and little-boy smiles?

"Thank you," she replied sincerely. She wore a fashionable but scant two-piece: a few strings securing three well-placed patches of sky-blue Lycra. Her breasts were small enough to require little support. This suit had been made with her in mind. A bustier woman would have looked cheap. Marlene looked tantalizing.

She offered him a hand and pulled him aboard confidently, smiling broadly. As he came aboard, she kissed him on the cheek.

"What's that for?" He was grinning like a schoolboy, wondering again why he said such things, why he made his stupid faces. He walked past her trying to let her out of an answer.

She shrugged. He didn't see it. "For coming in second."

"I'm sick of almost," he mumbled. He turned to her and added briskly, "Let the bowline go as soon as I have the engine running."

She obeyed and moved forward. Jay moved aft, started the diesel, and unfastened the stern line.

The Lady Fine moved slowly past the breakwater, Marlene on the bow watching Jay, who stared out to sea.

The sky to the east was azure, to the west dotted with soft gray clouds. A fifteen-knot wind blew out of the west, causing occasional whitecaps on Puget Sound. The summer sun beat down on them. Her bathing suit, indeed, her whole being, was provocative. Jay couldn't keep his eyes off her. Every time she moved, the thin blue fabric shifted teasingly. She would lean over here, bend over there, pull on a strap or reach down and tug the tiny bikini bottom. Maybe he felt this way because she had shown up to see the race. Maybe it was the kiss on the cheek as he had come aboard. Maybe it was her smooth, oiled skin, or her tiny suit. Europeans are different, he thought. Sophisticated, strong, and mature. Linda didn't hold a candle to this woman.

"What are you thinking about?" she asked.

"Why do you ask?"

"The sails . . ."

Jay looked up: both sails were luffing. He didn't even remember having put the sails up. He fell off some; the sails snapped back to life.

"How long will you be in Seattle?"

"Why?"

"I'm curious."

She grinned. Jay felt himself blush. She said, "I do not know." In certain light her hair glowed red. "I am to begin working soon. Hopefully, you and I will sail the regatta—"

"Labor Day . . ."

"Yes." She paused. "I imagine sometime after that I will be leaving. Your brow is furrowed."

Marlene had told him about her boss, a man named Iben

Holst, who ran an overseas sporting goods chain. She had left out most of the details. "Trim the Genny," he instructed. "A little more. Good. See the difference?"

She studied the genoa jib; Jay studied her. "Yes. And I can feel it, too." The boat had heeled noticeably.

Jay was thinking, And I can feel you. I'd like to tell you that I'm infatuated, but I'm scared of you. He said, "That's right. Now you take the wheel. Point her upwind and trim the mains'il. I'll take the Genny." They switched places. Jay brushed a hand across her back as they did. She didn't seem to notice. A moment later *The Lady Fine* heeled even farther into the water. She cheered and her chest swelled. The bottom of the stanchion caught the sea. Foam slapped the white fiberglass.

"Fall off a bit . . . yes, great," he said.

She cheered enthusiastically; the wind whipped her hair.

"Let go of the wheel," he commanded.

She did so. *The Lady Fine* headed immediately upwind. The sails flapped noisily. The sheets banged against the boom and mast frantically. He took two steps toward her, raising his voice to be heard. "Marlene," he said loudly. She looked up at him. The green eyes. The tiny suit. Her chest heaved in and out, in and out.

He wanted to kiss her. He wanted to wrap his arms around her and pull her close. He wanted to feel her heart beat against his. He wanted to smell her hair and feel her cheek press against him. He took her face in his hands. The sails continued to flap, the sheets continued to raffle. It sounded as if the boat was shaking itself apart. They stared into each other's eyes, their hearts pounding, their breathing shallow and uneven.

80

It seemed to him an eternity. He didn't need to kiss her—not that he could get up the nerve. A warm and vibrant energy passed between them, through his hands, through her soft cheeks. They were making love, sharing each other, eyes locked, the boat trembling in the wind. Had he been holding her a minute, an hour, a lifetime?

"Never mind," he said.

She sighed.

He lowered his hands; he noticed they were shaking.

And so were hers.

Jay had left an hour earlier. Running the engines on the way into Shilshole had warmed enough water for a quick shower. She was still thinking about him as the ship's clock rang seven times. She wore white cotton pants, white sandals, and a pink blouse. A thin gold chain encircled her neck. With her feet kicked up on a sofa/bench midship, Marlene watched the news on a small Sony, a rum sunrise in hand. A paperback lay beside her.

She never watched the lead stories, only tuning in to catch the weather forecast. Tonight's called for a chance of rain. What else was new? She sipped her sunrise. As she switched off the set, Holst came aboard. Always the same time of night.

He ducked to keep from bumping his head on the companionway and said, "It's me."

"Who else?"

"It might have been your sailor friend."

"Leave him out of this!"

"Do not be sharp with me, Marlene." Holst unzipped his black leather jacket. His turquoise eyes, always oddly distant, held her. Evil. "Let us not forget who is in charge."

"Do not try and make it sound like I *wanted* this job."

"You are here. You are a smart girl to cooperate. You would have been foolish to do otherwise."

Marlene hated being called a *girl*—she pictured braids and knee socks. She was a woman. "Just do not involve Jay any further. Leave him out of this."

"He likes you. He will not suspect anything." Holst mixed himself a drink.

She hated him. She despised his arrogance, his self-control, his self-assurance. He used people. Was there anything lower than a person who used others?

"You use people. You used my father to get to me, now me to get the data. Where does it stop?"

"It does not." He stirred his cocktail. "Why should it stop?"

"And this man Kepella. You use him, too."

"Of course."

"And none of this bothers you?"

"Listen to me. You make it sound like I have a remote control device on everyone I work with. Not so. I have power over them, yes. But it is only power they willingly allow me to have. Your father made an illegal contribution—that was his mistake. Because of this, you agreed to help us here. That was your choice. This Kepella is all confused. He gambles too much. That is his problem. I simply take advantage of what is already there. You make me sound like the devil himself."

"To me you are," she mumbled.

"What did you say?" he asked angrily, as if he had not heard her.

"Nothing."

Holst pushed her feet off the pad and sat down. Marlene straightened up—she didn't like sitting this close to him. He placed his hand on her thigh, touching her ear with his other hand.

She squirmed and pushed his hand away. "Keep your hands to yourself."

He put down his drink and kneeled in front of her. "You still do not understand this, do you, Marlene?" He looked into her eyes, then reached over and touched her breast.

She slapped his hand away. "You are disgusting! Get away!"

He shook his head. She had struck him. His face flushed. He felt tempted to beat her, right there and then. A good beating. He liked to beat girls. No girl had ever slapped Iben Holst. "Marlene, you will never strike me again. Never! And I will do whatever I like. Is that clear?"

She looked away from him.

"Your father's reputation, his *future,* rests in your hands. It would be foolish not to cooperate with us. We all know how much you love your father." Again, he touched her breast.

She slid away from him.

He grabbed her by her hair and wrestled her into submission. He tried to kiss her unmoving lips, slobbering her face with his attempts. Then he grinned lasciviously. "Of course, you can always change your mind." He laughed pathetically. "But you will not. Your father means too much to you, does he not?"

She didn't answer.

He yanked harder on her hair. She squealed in pain. He

asked, "Does he not?"

"Yes," she conceded.

He released her. "That's a good girl." He smiled. "Be thankful I do not ask for *more*." The smile widened into a grin. "I came to tell you that we are getting close now. It will be soon. I will be back tomorrow."

And with that said, he left her.

11

Trapped in a collapsing spiral, Roy Kepella began to worry. Maybe he wasn't cut out for this operation after all. Oh, he'd had his share of thrills in earlier years, though few and insignificant for the most part. His real service had begun when he'd been moved to Archives. Christ, he'd taken to it like a duck to water, reorganizing, restructuring, making himself an expert, so that he had to be noticed, had to be involved. He had seen others his age be quietly moved out of the inner circles. Not Roy Kepella, no sir. *Make yourself important and they need you.* That was why he had eagerly accepted the job from Brandenburg: they would notice him this time, probably hang a goddamned medal around his neck.

Fritz Wilhelm. The Bureau had been after Wilhelm for a couple years now. Wilhelm trafficked stolen technologies—everything from computer parts to heat-seeking missiles. They had the proof. But they didn't have Wilhelm. Not yet. The only one real chance at the man had been in Montreal, and somehow the network news had found out about the whole thing going down, and no FBI operation could be pulled off smoothly with the press lurking around, so they had been forced to let Wilhelm walk. The anchorman tore the Bureau apart on the evening news, and the heat followed from Capitol Hill. But policy was policy, and, like it or not, the director . . . *the* director was not about to have his boys attempt a major operation in front of network news cameras.

Kepella kept trying to convince himself he was doing the right thing for his career. What would become of him if Wilhelm never showed? What if, for some reason, the operation fell apart on him? What then?

Kepella left his apartment at 5:45. He drove carelessly, his mind on Wilhelm and Brandenburg rather than driving. He didn't see the state trooper in time. The cop turned on the overhead lights just past the floating bridge. Kepella had been clocked at seventy-two mph.

Fu Won's provided small chunks of roast duck along with cocktails. Kepella wolfed down a few bites.

Holst waited in his rental for twenty minutes, wanting to time his arrival to seem coincidental. Peace Brother let him pass.

Kepella had lost one hundred and eighty-three dollars by the time Holst joined the game. They sat across from each other. Kepella looked terrible. He had obviously been sleeping poorly, if at all. Bags hung beneath his eyes. His hair was oily and unkempt. His face showed worry and neglect. He had leather lips and a nose like a yellow squash. He looked sad.

Cocaine was passed around the table. Kepella didn't touch it.

Holst drew a pair of tens and bet ten dollars on the hand for good luck. Next to Kepella and Holst, an old white-haired Chinese everyone called Nim sat picking his teeth free of duck. The alcoholic woman named Patsy was there, as always. Fu dealt. He smiled often and sucked air through his teeth whenever shuffling.

"How you, Iben?" asked Nim, showing off his pitted teeth.

"Just right," responded Holst. "And yourself?"

Nim nodded and blinked. "How's tricks, Roy?" he asked Kepella.

"Shitty! Things have been going shitty, lately." Kepella shrugged. "What the fuck do I care?"

"What the fuck do any of us care?" questioned Patsy in her whiskey-cigarette baritone. "Let's play poker, eh, boys?" Patsy was originally from the Bronx and had not a trace of Chinese to her accent, despite her Oriental appearance. She was missing her right incisor and her wig was awry on her head: she appeared to be leaning to her left, and top-heavy. She took a belt of a dark drink and threw two cards at Fu. "Hit me."

A few minutes later Kepella counted his chips—now two hundred and fifty down. After a fold, Fu asked to speak with him privately.

The tables in the restaurant area were empty—no one eating. One of the waitresses was programming the jukebox, the other, cleaning ashtrays. Kepella and Fu sat down at a booth.

Fu said, "Mr. Roy, I like very much to have you play. But business is business. I been extending you credit too long. I think it time you think about how you gonna pay me back. You see?"

Kepella looked over at the man. What a scar. "I thought we had a deal?"

"We do, Mr. Roy. I loan you plenty. But business is business. Cash only from now on. We talk about loan tomorrow, yes? We make it straight. Okay, Mr. Roy? How that sound?"

"I don't have any cash on me, Fu. I'd like to keep playing."

Fu shrugged. "I no make trouble, Mr. Roy. Cash. Business is business. Maybe ask Mr. Holst. He win plenty last couple days. Maybe he help you."

"But I hardly know the guy." Kepella tossed it out there, like Georgie the bartender tossed duck scraps to the alley cats.

"He nice man. Maybe he help you out." Fu shrugged.

Kepella's pulse quickened. Perhaps this was the contact he'd been waiting for. His stomach grumbled.

When they returned to the back room, passing the unmoving Peace Brother, Kepella said, "Iben"—he had never called him by his first name—"think I could bend your ear for a minute at the bar?"

"Sure," replied Holst, without asking any questions.

Kepella's excitement built.

Holst was forty-one dollars ahead. He rose from his chair and left the room. Patsy passed some brutal wind and Fu said something to her in Chinese. She snarled at him and finished her drink.

Georgie the bartender, an extremely short man, wore a ridiculously loud shirt. Kepella ordered, "The usual," which meant he would be served a glass of water with a squeeze of lime that everyone else would think was vodka. Kepella paid Georgie well to pour water instead of Popov—and to buy the man's silence. Georgie had not said a thing to anybody. Mr. Roy got what he paid for.

Kepella asked Holst, "Know how much I'm down?"

"No, Roy. No idea. Why?"

"Nine grand."

Holst nearly smiled. "Sounds like a lot of money."

"Sounds like? It's a fortune! Fu just handed me the riot act."

"I do not understand."

"I'm out of the game unless I play with cash. I have this feeling that tomorrow the shit hits the fan. He wants to meet with me." Kepella studied Holst, wondering what the man was thinking. "I could win it all back in one good night, you know I could. And seeing how you've taken a good bit from me, well, Christ, I'm flat out, Iben, and I wondered if maybe you could go me a couple hundred, you know, stake me. One good night, Iben, one good night is all. I can feel it, my friend. Tonight. I'm going to do it tonight!" He smiled and finished the drink, grimacing as if it was vodka.

"Sure."

Kepella jerked. "What? No fooling?"

Holst shook his head.

"Hey! Great! Tonight's the night, Iben, I'm telling ya."

"I'll need something to back it up."

"Yeah, sure. Name it. What's mine is yours."

"What do you have, Roy?"

"How much are we talking?"

"You tell me. How much are we talking, Roy?"

"Five hundred?"

"Sounds like a car to me."

"Hey! The car is worth five thousand easy."

Holst let some time lapse. "Sounds to me like in a few days Fu may own your car anyway. What else?" He wanted Kepella nervous.

Kepella, feeling like the fisherman who, having waited all day for the bobber to move, suddenly feels the rod bend, said, "One good night, Iben. Tonight I buy Fu's whole joint. I'm telling ya. I can feel it!"

Holst glanced at his watch. "I must go." He removed his checkbook and scribbled out a check for five hundred dollars. He handed it to Georgie. "Cash this for Roy." Then he said in Chinese, "Tell Fu this guy plans on buying the place by sunset." Behind, him, Peace Brother, who had overheard the comment, laughed loudly. Holst patted Kepella on the back, nice and intimidating. "You are all set, Roy."

"Christ, Iben. I didn't know you spoke Chinese."

Holst winked. "Only a few phrases, Roy. Be lucky." He dropped a quarter on the bar and left without saying another word.

Peace Brother grinned from his position against the far wall.

Kepella lost the full five hundred within the hour. All according to plan. When he reentered the bar, the young Chinese woman, Rosie, was waiting for him, as she had for the past several evenings.

He bought her a drink. "What brings you by this place?"

"You," she said bluntly. "I been thinking about you, Roy Kepella."

This was unfamiliar ground to Kepella. He assumed that

89

Holst had hired the girl, so he tried to play along—but playing along was difficult for him. He moved awkwardly on the stool. "Good things, I hope," he said cautiously.

"You lonely. I lonely. We like each other." She went back to the drink, taking small, uninterested sips.

That's a simple way to put it, Kepella thought. "Can't argue with that."

"We the same, this way."

"Yeah, but you're pretty and young. I'm old and—what's the right word?—weathered."

"I don't think so. I think you cute." She blushed.

Seeing her blush surprised him. The line seemed practiced. But how does one practice a blush? "We're friends, Rosie. I like that."

"We talk. You and I talk. I like that very much." She looked down at the bar. "You take me for a drive, Roy?"

Kepella squelched a grin. "Where to?"

She glared at him. "Just a drive. I don't know."

"Why not?"

"I don't know why not."

"Just an expression. Sure, Rosie. What say we drive up to a view somewhere? Take in the city lights."

"We leave now?"

"You haven't finished your drink."

"Who cares. We leave now." She reached out and took his hand.

Once in the old beat up car she asked, "Know why I like you?"

"It is curious."

"Know why?"

"Because we talk. Isn't that what you said?"

"No, never said that. It's because you different."

"Amen."

"You not like the men my age. They all try and be someone they never be. They think they all movie stars, big men, like that. You just Roy. Cute Roy. I like you, Roy."

"I'm glad, Rosie. I like you too." He thought, And this is one of the strangest conversations I've had in my life. "Now, where should it be? Golden Garden has a nice view of the Sound. Gasworks has a good view of the lake—"

"Take me to your home, Roy. I want to see your home."

He swallowed. So you *are* part of it, Rosie. Disappointment caused his face to sag. "Sure thing, Rosie."

"You mad at me for saying this?"

"No, Rosie, I'm not mad. My place is a great idea. From the roof of my building you can see at least a block."

"You make fun of Rosie."

He turned a corner and stopped at a light. "Yes, I suppose I did, Rosie. I'm sorry for that."

She cheered up immediately and laughed. "At least a block . . . that funny, Roy. That funny."

Rosie sat on the couch, moving a dirty shirt out of the way. Kepella went into the kitchen, took down the bottle of Popov—Papa, as, he called it, his old drink—broke the seal, and asked her if she wanted one. She said yes. Hidden from her view, he poured a shot of vodka and swished it around in his mouth, spitting it out without drinking any of it. It was a trick he had been pulling for a while now. His breath smelled like vodka, just like it had in the traffic accident. Very convincing. He poured a short glass of water for himself, vodka for her. The charade had worked so far, but each time he swished the booze around in his mouth he thought about just gulping it down. Why not? He hadn't been to a meeting in a few weeks, and it was beginning to take its toll. But he hadn't taken a drink yet. He couldn't. He returned with the drinks and downed his water in the first toast to bury the evidence. He glanced over at Rosie, wondering if Holst had hired her.

Of course he had hired her, he told himself. Why else would a young broad with her looks come on strong to an old fart like him? He didn't want to believe it. He liked Rosie.

She reached over and placed her hand on his chest. She smelled good, like moist flowers. She pressed against him.

He didn't want this. He liked her too much. They were *friends*. She fumbled with his buttons. Not like a whore to fumble with buttons, he thought. Kepella had taken an occasional weekend to Reno, once, twice a year. Two hundred dollars would buy him a grind. The whore would moan and squirm and make him last a long time, make him feel young. She knew her business. A few times. But he had quickly learned that sex didn't come close to love. It was one of those things Roy Kepella had learned too late in life.

Rosie ran her fingers over his pale, hairy chest. Her hands were warm. She bent over and kissed a nipple. It felt good, too good. He was utterly confused. He *liked* her. Was she part of this or not? If not, then he should turn her away now. Keep her away from it all.

He kissed her black hair, reached out and drew her close to him. She was a wisp of a woman; he could almost connect his hands around her waist. She giggled and kissed

him on the mouth, tasting like sweet cinnamon. She giggled again, pulled back, and reached behind herself. The
zipper sang. She pulled the dress off her arms. Her chest
was bare. Beautiful. She had the firm, pert breasts of a
young woman. She pulled his head down between them
and slowly lay back on the couch.

"Can I stay with you tonight?" she asked.

He didn't answer. He didn't need to.

Iben Holst was staying at the Washington Plaza, adjacent to
the majestic Four Seasons Olympic. The Plaza had small,
comfortable rooms, a rickety elevator system, steam radia-
tors that kicked on in the cool Seattle evenings, and a great
breakfast spot next door. It cost thirty-three dollars a night.
He had intended to stay aboard *The Lady Fine* with Marlene. But following the long ride to Seattle on an oil tanker
out of Panama, he couldn't conceive of even another five
minutes on a boat. He had been sick to his stomach for the
entire ten-day voyage. That was why he needed a skipper.
Someone had to get *The Lady Fine* into Canadian waters,
and it wasn't going to be him.

He plugged the phone line into his Hewlett-Packard
portable computer and selected the configuration that automatically dialed and logged-on to CompuServe. A few seconds later he was hooked up to Electronic Mail. He left a
message on the service for user number 52-765-00012-9:
The Mariner.

The beauty of the EMAIL service was that it was
entirely private, inaccessible to anyone without his password. No need to write in code, no worry the information
might fall into the wrong hands. Even so, he used a stylized

notation, so that a computer hack stumbling into this user-area would not go running to the authorities.

He typed in a message that read:

MARINER: MARK FIXED. POSITION SECURED. REQUEST INFORMATION BIOGRAPHY ON A JESSE CLYDE BECKER. AGE APPROXIMATELY 30 YEARS. ALL ACCORDING TO PLAN AND SCHEDULE. MARK DOWNHILL. PHASE TWO BEGINS TOMORROW. LOOKS GOOD. PLEASE ADVISE ON BECKER SOONEST.—ALBATROSS

He felt uncomfortable with his code name. He had read *The Rime of the Ancient Mariner* as a youth. The arrival of the albatross brought good fortune; but the blood of the albatross had brought bad luck. Iben Holst had no use for bad luck.

He left the message area, typed "BYE," and CompuServe disconnected him. Connect time: 7 mins. 54 secs.

He put the computer away.

The sign at Beji's read ALL NUDE GIRLS. He had seen the sign a few days ago. Last night he had parked across the street, slipped a man ten bucks, and now he had a name.

First Avenue, teeming with winos and whores, pimps, loners, and perverts, was cooking. Beji's rocked, with tassel-swinging dancers on the stage behind the bar, oiled and shining, grinding and thrusting, dipping and writhing, doing their best to earn another buck or two from the toothless strangers staring goggle-eyed from the stools they had owned for the past five hours and would own until closing. One of the girls got daring and flashed some beaver at a customer in a cowboy hat who had already laid three twenties on her. She yanked her G-string down, dropped down onto her back, and parted fur practically in the big spender's face. Sweat broke out across his forehead and before he knew it the glimpse was gone; he wasn't even sure the flash of pink had been real, or just a fantasy image floating on the sea of booze in his mind.

Louis Mendez, half Hispanic, half black, sat arrogantly in the corner, a girl on each arm, a chinchilla draped around his neck. He wore earrings in both ears—two in the left— a little lipstick, and his shirt open exposing a rug of black body hair down to his navel, in which he had miraculously affixed a paste sapphire. Louis Mendez's street name was King Rat, given to him by a street bum, a former Berkeley professor who had hit the skids.

Holst walked over to Rat and stood facing him. He wore his usual black leather jacket, blue jeans, and leather running shoes. A toothpick bobbed in his lips, below his dark glasses.

"You catch that beaver, Short?" Rat called every white man Short. The two black girls smiled. Holst liked black girls. The one to Rat's right stared at Holst's crotch and licked her lips. She wore a surprisingly simple red dress with a thick black belt. Her breasts bulged from the dress. Her face was hard, her hair straight; she wore lipstick the color of the dress and blue eye shadow. The whore to Rat's left had coffee skin and Oriental eyes. Her left breast poked out of her wallpaper-print shirt, its olive-skinned nipple looking like a third eye. She appeared far too high to see clearly. She stared past Holst. Her third eye bobbed up and down when Rat adjusted his posture.

Holst said, "I understand you provide certain escort services."

Rat smiled. His teeth were flawless—three thousand dollars' worth of flawless. "The bitches provide the services, Short. The man do the business." The girls giggled. The one on the right still stared, making Holst warm. "You got some business?"

"I would like to speak with you."

"Vell, vell. I would like to shhpeak vith you, too. Yah! Sit down, Short. We do business."

"Not in front of the girls."

"Sit down, my man, or take it elsewhere. I don't like it when people stand. You dig?" One look from Rat drew a bouncer's interest, who moved toward the table, inspiring Holst to sit. "That's better. You want a babe, no problem. Rat's your man."

Holst acted like a man afraid to touch the furniture for fear of germs. He folded his hand in his laps. Behind the dark glasses he was blinking repeatedly. Nerves.

"Speak," Rat demanded.

The girl who had been staring now rubbed Holst's leg under the table with a bare foot. She licked her lips again. Sweat broke out on Holst's forehead. "I need a *special* girl. I would rather talk alone."

"What kinda *special*, my man? Believe me, you couldn't a dreamed up what these two 'escorts' have been through. You ain't gonna surprise no one."

"S and M," Holst practically whispered.

Rat smiled again. "No sweat, Short. No big deal. Relax. I'm sure you understand—as one businessman to another—that certain services of my escorts come for a higher fee."

"How much?"

"Depends how rough, dude. Three bills for an hour with one escort. Two girls for five bills. If it's too rough, they walk. That's how it works. Let's say they walk and you decide you don't like the deal? Then Harry over there tears your cock off." The three-thousand-dollar smile lit up again.

Holst smiled privately, barely a twist on his lips. He nearly said, "What cock?"

"I do it," said the black girl on the right. "How 'bout me, daddy?" she asked Holst, still sliding her foot up and down his leg.

Rat continued, "Now mind you, my girls can take it. They can give it out. Whatever you like, you dig? Sadie here will make you shoot before she's got her clothes off. You want Sadie, it's an extra fifty bills. You dig? She's like what they call 'private reserve.' I got others you can check out, if you'd rather. I do business, my man. I don't fuck around. You call it, or you move on. I got other customers."

"She's fine." Sadie rose. Holst said, "Not now. Tomorrow evening. I'll leave the stairway entrance to the Washington Plaza open. You know where that is?"

She nodded. Rat asked, "The stairway?"

"She doesn't use the lobby. *You* dig? The stairs or nothing."

"It's cool, Short. Be easy. It's cool."

Holst gave him the room number and the time. He was about to leave when Rat reminded him, "Cash up front, Short. No cash, no gash." He grinned. Sadie licked her lips and lowered her eyes.

12

Sharon Johnson had stabbed a policeman, not one of her pursuers. The incident had made the front page, with all kinds of speculation about who "the woman" was. Now the police wanted her as badly as the others. And Brian had *demanded* that the local police not be involved. She had taken a hotel room not far from the train station, and from there had tried again to reach the conduit by phone. She waited and waited, her impatience mounting, afraid to venture outside the room. Finally, two days later, a deep voice answered.

"Thank God," she said, hearing him speak the code. He repeated the phrase and Sharon quickly answered with the proper response.

"Where are you?" he asked.

She supplied him with the name of the hotel, hung up the phone, and murmured a short prayer. Sharon Johnson believed God helped steer one through life, and finally getting through to the conduit had reinforced this belief. She had allowed herself fear, an agent's most formidable foe, but now the conduit was on his way and she knew there was a chance. Hope had driven off fear for the moment.

She was washing her face in the small bathroom when the phone rang. The phone! She counted the rings. Except for the hotel desk clerk, whom she had paid handsomely to alert her of visitors, no one knew she was staying here. Perhaps the conduit was calling back, taking precautions. But after two rings the phone went silent. The signal: a single person had inquired at the desk and was headed up. She tried to collect her thoughts. What to do? How long had it taken the clerk to phone? How long did she have?

She was tempted to head for the stairway, but whoever was after her might have sent the elevator to the top floor empty, rendering it useless, while he, or she, used the stairs. The fire escape was another alternative, but again, her visitor might not be alone, and by now, only seconds from the confrontation, a backup might be in place. She was trapped. She studied the room, wondering what to do. No use hiding behind the door. Under the bed? Ridiculous. That left only the small bathroom, and it made no sense to trap herself in a room the size of a prison cell that had but one exit. She could feel the sweep hand of the clock counting down the seconds. What to do?

The idea struck her in a flash. She could clearly see the progression of events of the next few minutes. She quickly shed most of her clothes and piled them on the bathroom floor, leaving on only her pantyhose and shoes. She reached into the shower stall and opened the hot water. Steam wafted from behind the drawn shower curtain that enclosed the porcelain tub. She moved the pile of clothing so that it could be seen from the room's door. Then she pulled the medicine cabinet door open to change the angle of the mirror. Steam crowded against the ceiling of the small room and worked its way down the walls like an ominous cloud. She studied the scene she had created: bra and clothes piled on the bathroom floor, steam, the sound of water running—it looked convincing. Her time was up. She slipped under the bed, at the same time trying to slow her breathing. Her bare chest heaved against the carpet.

She had to wait only seconds. A knock on the door was followed by silence. Then she heard what sounded like cat claws scratching the door: the lock was being picked. She tried to turn her head, angry that she had positioned herself facing the wall with no view of the door. The scratching stopped; the door brushed the carpet, opening a crack. Her heartbeat sounded like a drum to her, and she was afraid he might hear it. The door clicked shut quietly. The intruder waited patiently by the door. A professional.

Her ruse worked well. The intruder walked past her, slowly moving toward the bathroom, obviously taken in by the sight of the clothing and steam. The shoes told her it was a man. He exaggerated his walk, heel to toe, heel to toe, to avoid being heard. He had obviously done this before. She restrained herself from making her move too quickly. With the medicine cabinet opened slightly and the mirror partially fogged, there would be no way he would see her as she came up behind him. Still, if she moved too soon, he might hear her—too late, and her angle of attack would be all wrong. In such a small space a strong man would have the advantage. He inched closer to the bathroom door. In his right hand he carried a black nine-millimeter Beretta with a bulky silencer. One more step; Now!

She slipped out from under the bed. He had stopped and was looking down at the clothes, the steam swirling around him. She rose to her knees, suddenly, unsure of herself. The year of study, the months of training, and now this.

He lifted the gun.

She took three large steps toward him, swung back her foot, and kicked straight up between his legs and into his crotch. As he yelled and crumpled over, she pushed him forward, smashing his head into the edge of the sink. She kicked again, this time at his hand. The Beretta fell onto the pile of clothes. The blow to his head did not knock him out, but stunned him momentarily. She had a split second to decide: the head again, or the gun? She reached forward, took him by the hair, and pounded his forehead into the edge of the sink. He reached behind himself quickly and hooked the waistband of her pantyhose, gaining leverage. She screamed. She had lost her advantage. He twisted his fingers into the fabric and muscled her slowly to his right. She pounded a fist into his back. He hooked a leg around hers and leaned against her. She felt herself falling. She spotted a red stain on the edge of the sink. His forehead was bleeding. If it was bleeding enough, his vision would be impaired. In what felt like slow motion, she fell to the bathroom floor beneath his weight. His instinct was to drive for the position of advantage and dominate her quickly. She fell onto the clothes, trapping the Beretta beneath the small of her back where she couldn't reach it. He came crashing down heavily on her, dazed by the blows to his forehead. The sight of his bleeding forehead was so revolting that she found a reserve of strength she didn't know she had. She rolled strongly to her right, dumping him under the sink, and searched blindly for the gun behind her. He wedged his palm beneath her chin, pushing her head back.

She touched metal. The Beretta. Her fingers searched for the butt of the gun, down the silencer, down the barrel, then she had it. His fingers had tightened on her throat. He banged her head into the door frame and rose to his knees. She swung the gun around, but before she could aim—long before she fired—he batted it out of her hand. The gun bounced on the tile and slid into the corner. She drove her shoe into his chest, driving him back and off balance. He struggled to his feet. She knew there was no time to try for the Beretta—that would be his move.

She ducked her head and charged him, forcing him against the sink. His head snapped back against the open mirror with enough power to crack the glass. Someone, she thought, someone hear us, someone call the manager, someone stop him. Please . . . someone stop him! Despite her training, she knew a man this size would overpower her given enough time. Training was training—this was now, and she was frightened. They could teach you how to defend yourself, even how to kill, but overcoming fear could not be taught, only learned through experience, and Sharon had had little field experience.

The knee! she remembered suddenly. She could hear her instructor say, "The knee is one of the most vulnerable joints on the human body." She knew the rest of the lesson.

She pulled back her right leg and kicked his kneecap. He cried out and collapsed into the shower stall, tipping the curtain from the rod and scalding his face and upper body. He flailed his arms, attempting to shield himself from the near-boiling water.

Instinctively, she dove for the Beretta. She found it, aimed, and pulled the trigger rapidly, three times, the muffled report sounding like hands clapping. Blood spurted from three small holes. Then the bleeding ceased.

Stunned, she sat staring at him. Finally, she inched closer and, reaching quickly, turned off the water. Silence. Absolute silence, punctuated only by the pounding of her slowing heartbeat. Water dripped from his hair. He was dead.

She gathered her clothes up, unable to take her eyes from

him, and backed up step by step into the bedroom. With her mind caught up in planning the next few minutes, she dressed quickly.

What now? Was another person waiting somewhere for a signal? Would a backup enter any minute, having not heard from his accomplice, or, having heard the commotion inside this room? And what of the agent—the conduit? She had summoned him here. Would he now be led into a hotel teeming with police, or worse? Think! she demanded of herself. She weighed her options. The police? No. The fiasco at the train station had made her a fugitive. What then?

Escape.

She moved to the door, pulling her skirt to fall correctly, tugging the sleeve of her wrinkled blouse. She opened the door a crack, the Beretta in her right hand. The hallway was empty.

How had he known she was here? Had someone followed her from the train station? Had they traced her one phone call back to this hotel? She pushed the thoughts aside and opened the door farther. The hallway was empty, the exit at the far end dimly lit. She crept down the hall, her shoulders pressed against the wall. After what seemed like an eternity, she entered the poorly lit stairway. She told herself that the conduit—all else—came second to her own escape. No one was going to show up and rescue her; she had to do this alone. Landing by landing, she worked her way down the stairs, the weapon aimed at the ceiling, arm bent at the elbow. She rounded each landing carefully, arms extended, aiming the heavy gun. No one. Floor by floor she descended, anticipating opposition. Ready.

She had killed.

The stairs seemed endless. Finally, she reached ground level and stopped by a door that opened onto the street. What now? Step out onto the street with a gun and silencer? She untucked the blouse from her skirt and stuck the Beretta between skirt and skin, forced to keep a hand on it due to its weight. She pushed against the door. It was locked. Frustrated, she threw a shoulder against the door. It did not budge.

Behind her, another door led into the lobby. She cracked it open and peered down a short corridor that led past the hotel kitchen. She edged into the narrow hallway, moving cautiously toward the lobby. Looking around the corner of a wall, she spotted the desk clerk, the man she had paid to warn her. Beyond him, a young woman sat in an over-stuffed chair flipping through a magazine. The woman's apparent lack of concentration alarmed Sharon. Was she an accomplice playing the part of a bored tourist? Or *was* she a bored tourist? How long had she been there? Was she a guest of the hotel?

Sharon pressed herself against the wall. One option was to try and locate an alternative exit; her other option was to simply walk out the front door. She clamped the gun against her body, holding it firmly in place. If she left through the kitchen she would attract attention. The lobby was better. She prepared herself for trouble, rounded the corner, and walked straight toward the front door.

The bored woman turned a page, looked up from her magazine, offered a pained and contrived smile, and crossed her legs. Sharon Johnson stepped outside.

Dusk had softened the street. A solitary car was parked

halfway down the block. As she glanced toward it, a small, thin man stepped from the passenger door and hurried after her. She walked steadily in the opposite direction, careful not to run, keeping track of him with quick glances over her shoulder. He was walking briskly. Again she looked back. The car pulled out from the curb and headed toward her.

She opened a door and stepped into a restaurant, worming her way through the tables, reminded of the night of Brian's death. A doorway to her left led to a portico covered with hanging flowers. Checking over her shoulder, she hurried onto the portico. Well-dressed people sipped cocktails and wine. In her wrinkled clothing she stood out. She had not waited for the maitre d', and the squat, balding man now caught up to her. He rattled on in German, waving his arms. The Beretta slipped out of her hold and clunked onto the stone patio. The portico became hushed. The maitre d' stared at it. She heard a gasp behind her. A few people stared, frightened. All eyes. It felt like she had stood there for several minutes, when, in fact, it was only a matter of seconds before she grabbed the Beretta and broke into a run, making for a wooden gate at the end of the patio.

The thin man was close behind. She moved through the gate and turned right, breaking into a run down a narrow, cobbled lane. Slowing to prevent a turned ankle, she glanced over her shoulder and saw the man come through the gate. She ran left through an open doorway and hurried down a dark hallway, seeing a lighted door at the other end of the building. As she reached the door, a police car, siren wailing, zoomed past, another behind it.

She heard footsteps behind her and jumped into the darkened corner by the doorway, the stairs to her right. The thin man's shadow stretched against the far wall, moving toward her. He came into view, holding a weapon in his left hand. She raised the Beretta, not wanting to fire. He stopped, his breathing loud in the narrow hallway.

"I see you," he said in German, turning his weapon on her.

But he did not see her. He saw a shadow.

She fired first, wounding him. His gun discharged, sending a bullet into the wall. Her next shot hit him too. He slumped to the floor. A cloud of bitter gray smoke hung in the air.

She fled out the doorway, stuffing the Beretta into her skirt and burning her skin. She buckled with the pain but forced herself to keep moving. An alley to her immediate left took her north. She walked quickly. He was back there dying; she had left him to die. She had killed. Again. Her head was spinning. She turned right, then left, and threaded her way through the narrow, back streets of Regensburg.

13

Holst, trading in a nine of diamonds and three of spades for a fresh pair, glanced up and caught Kepella's eye as he entered. The back room held less smoke than usual because Patsy had not showed up. Fu had arrived a few minutes earlier, the ever-present cigarette glued to his lip. Dull-colored poker chips, the texture of smooth bone, lay stacked in piles by the five men around the table. Four were Chinese. They rattled to each other in their staccato tongue, casting suspicious looks across the green felt table. Poker is as

106

much a game of what you don't have as what you do have, and these men were very good at poker.

The defeat written on Kepella's face made Holst feel good. Fu grunted, signaled Kepella, and rose from his chair. They left the room together; the arguing began immediately.

Holst had been waiting for this all afternoon. Fu was following orders to the letter, doing everything he was being paid to do, and doing it well. Holst folded and left the table. Peace Brother stood guard by the door to Fu's rarely used office, scraping dirt from beneath his nails with a toothpick.

"Are they in there?" Holst asked his other hired hand rhetorically. Peace Brother nodded, not looking up from his nails. Holst knocked once and opened the door before Fu answered. He stepped inside.

Kepella, his face flushed and sweat-covered, stood glowering down at Fu, who was seated behind a battered desk. "What do you want?" the small Chinaman asked angrily. Perfect.

"Lemme in the game," whined Kepella, ignoring Holst's entrance. "I have the cash."

"Cash you owe me," insisted Fu.

"I thought maybe I could help," interrupted Holst, answering Fu's initial question.

"I have agreement with Mr. Roy, Mr. Holst. It none of your concern. Please return and enjoy game. We can settle this."

"Is that why Peace Brother is outside the door?" Holst asked.

Kepella blanched.

"John Chu helps me when I need help," explained Fu calmly.

"And who helps Roy?" asked Holst.

"There's no need for rough stuff," Kepella interjected anxiously. "I just want to play poker."

"You owe two percent for game. Minimum. That two hundred sixty dollar. Then you no play here—or anywhere until daily interest paid. I explain yesterday."

"And how much is that?" inquired Holst, already knowing the answer.

"None of your business, Mr. Holst," Fu told him.

"Go ahead and tell him." Kepella slumped into a chair, defeated—the consummate actor.

Fu rattled the numbers off. "Nine thousand one hundred seventeen dollar in principal on gambling debt. Two thousand seven hundred forty-three dollar interest. This total eleven thousand eight hundred sixty."

"Is that right, Roy?" Properly astonished.

Kepella shrugged and rubbed his eyes.

"Have you got it?" asked Holst.

"Tapped out, Iben. I'm tapped out."

"There must be something you can sell," Holst suggested, watching Kepella rub his eyes and nose. "How about your wife's jewelry or something?"

"I'm single. I've sold everything I own. The banks own the rest. I'm tapped out, I'm telling you. Tapped out."

"Gentlemen, gentlemen. This no concern to Fu. I want interest this minute. And if I hear you play other games around town, Mr. Roy, before I repaid, I send John after you. You understand me?"

"Now listen here, you Chinese son-of-a-whore—"

Fu leaned across his cluttered desk.

Kepella appeared to back down. Holst asked, "Fu, would you leave us alone for a minute?"

Fu rose with the difficulty of an old man, sighing. He coughed loudly and took a drag off his cigarette, then left.

Kepella sounded desperate. "Iben, do you think you could go me the interest . . . I mean just today's interest? If this asshole puts Peace Brother on me, I'm history."

Holst thought, You're history already, Kepella. He said, "I do not know, Roy. Without something to back it up . . . I just do not know. I loaned you five hundred yesterday. Sounds like you need some *big* money."

Kepella shrugged. "You know of someone? Shit, I didn't even think of that. A street loan?"

"The interest is high of course. A point a week at least. Without collateral maybe a point-and-a-half. You must pay the interest every week. You do not pay, they cripple you." He waited. He wanted to say, Come on, Kepella.

Kepella repeated, "You know somebody?"

"I might. But remember, if you default, it is on my reputation, my credit. If I arrange the deal . . . I am taking a risk as well."

"Yeah, yeah. No worries, Iben. I can pull a couple hundred a week no problem."

"You will have to stop the gambling. Absolutely stop."

Kepella had a good sweat going. He dragged his hand across his mouth and chin. "I know, I know."

"I will stake you to today's interest now," Holst said, withdrawing several hundred from his right-hand pocket. "You give Fu what he needs, and we will go see the man, right away."

Holst played it well. He drove Kepella to a seedy apartment house on Holgate and left him sitting in the car. The sky was the gray of the filing cabinets in Kepella's old office. The sun hid behind the cloud cover like a night light behind a faded towel. After a few minutes, Holst reappeared and climbed in.

"Where can I drop you?"

"What's up?"

"He won't deal with you. He doesn't know you."

"God damn it."

"It is okay, Roy. I told him I would act as middleman. I do not know why I should be doing this for you . . ." He tried to sound reluctant.

"You won't regret it, Iben," Kepella assured him.

"I must leave you while I make the arrangements. Have you a pen?" Kepella shook his head. Holst searched the glove compartment and found one. He scribbled the address of the Washington Plaza on a gas receipt and wrote his room number on the bottom. "I am sticking my neck out for you, Roy."

"I understand."

"Are you sure?" Holst's glare was like the warning rattle of a poisonous snake about to strike.

"I won't screw it up, Iben. I promise." Kepella grabbed Holst's hand and shook it eagerly.

An hour later Kepella knocked on the door to Holst's room. Holst opened the door and let him in. The room smelled of hotel disinfectant and stale air. Holst offered a chair, but Kepella elected to remain standing. He kept his trench coat on.

"I borrowed five thousand to start with, Roy. I thought it

110

best to start slowly, make sure you can handle this kind of load."

"That's great, Iben. How many points?"

"It is worse than I thought, Roy. Three points a week. That is steep, I know. If you want out, say so. I can still return the cash."

"Three points, huh? What's that work out to?"

"One hundred and fifty a week, interest." Very German now. "Ten percent of the principal every twenty-eight days. Those payments will be six hundred and fifty. But listen carefully, Roy: if you miss even one interest payment, they tack on a point a week, and that point stays there. You follow that? You screw up some week and your interest is up to four points; two weeks, five, just like that. And that stays fixed. You better think about this, Roy."

Kepella appeared to be considering the deal. He paced the small room for a moment, wondering why Holst didn't open the window occasionally. Through the window Holst had a view of a cement parking facility. Down on the street pedestrians hurried about, a few limos cruised by, headed, no doubt, to the Four Seasons, nearby. Kepella didn't want to jump at the deal. It would seem out of character. It was funny, he thought, that in order to assume a deeply buried cover you had to *become* the person you were establishing. You could not, even for a moment, be the true Roy Kepella. You had to stay fixed in an identity, fixed like the interest rates. You acted and acted, and pretty soon you lost touch with the real Roy Kepella. You laid in bed at night, tempted to try and remember, but Rosie would reach over and take hold of your crank and get you all worked up, and you realized *they* were everywhere. They hovered around you like vultures waiting to feed off your mistakes. And you laid in wait yourself, awaiting the sound of your trap closing on *them*—a sound you had given the last month of your life to. If the job was to trap a loan shark, the job would have been done—but it was not. Each and every day it was as if the operation was just beginning.

"I'll do it, Iben. No problem."

Holst grinned. It occurred to Kepella that until now he had never seen the man smile. "That is fine, Roy."

"Take what I owe you . . ."

"You sure?"

"Damn straight. I want to get things settled. You take your dough, then I'll go pay Fu."

Holst counted out eight hundred, which he pocketed, and handed Kepella the rest of the money. Kepella counted it quickly and asked, "How much trouble would it be to get another five thousand?"

"No trouble, Roy. But I think we had better see how this goes first."

"Yeah, sure. Right." Kepella appeared both nervous and elated. "Do I pay you?"

"Yes, you pay me every Thursday afternoon. The first two or three payments are critical, Roy. You miss those and that makes you look bad. When these people give their customers reminders, they are the kind of reminders that one does not quickly forget. You follow me?"

"Yeah, I follow. They break your knees with baseball bats. Don't worry, Iben. No sweat. I've got this covered. No sweat."

"I just thought you should see the full picture, Roy. I would not want to surprise you. You understand."

"Clear as a bell, Iben. Thanks again." They shook hands. Holst's hands were cool, Kepella's warm and sweaty.

14

The gig had started promptly at nine.

The bar, less crowded than the dining area, contained the usual crowd: tanned bodies dressed in the vivid colors of L. L. Bean, Eddie Bauer; and Land's End. The long wooden bar patrolled by two bartenders stretched the length of the room, ferns separating rows of bottles, their numbers doubled by the mirrored wall behind them. A hand-lettered poster taped to the mirror advertised Seattle Slews, a mixture of rum, orange juice, coconut, and grenadine, for three bucks even. Voices were shouting rather than conversing. The waitresses wore Danskin tops, cut low, and all well-filled. Apparently they were allowed to choose their own skirts.

On stage, at the far end of the low-ceilinged room, under the lights, Jay turned to Jocko and counted softly: ". . . two . . . three . . . four . . ." The drummer tapped his sticks together to the same tempo and the band started into a smooth rendition of "High Wire." Several people turned, some smiling as they remembered the song, while others shifted in their chairs restlessly, and still others, apparently deaf, took no notice at all. Conversation grew louder. The waitresses weaved through the throng, drawing male glances, delivering weak drinks with pink umbrellas, chunks of pineapple, and an abundance of ice. The thirty-dollar hair cuts, the perfect teeth, the arch smiles, all marked a typical summer night at the Blue Sands.

Jay sang strongly and moved well on stage. He had moved well on stage damn near every night for ten years. Eleven next month. For the last three nights The RockIts had been drawing capacity crowds at the Sands and had enjoyed the scene. Most everyone knew each other, often slept with each other, and ate dinner for something to do. Money was no object. Many owned boats, either on Lake Union, Lake Washington, or the Sound. The Sound was the hip scene this summer. Last year it had been Mercer Island. The women were all just a little too pretty, and the guys a little too cool. Jocko called it a herpes convention—but he liked to watch the waitresses walk by; the elevated drum platform afforded nice glimpses of cleavage.

The band was into a smooth rendition of Buddy Holly's "Well All Right" when Marlene entered with Holst. Jay noticed her immediately and tried to catch her eye. After a few moments she turned to look at him and returned his smile. Seeing her paired with Holst hurt Jay. He was the sensitive type, and he had already come to think of her as his. Seeing her with the strong, confident, blue-eyed Holst made him realize just how tentative his position was. How would it look to Jocko for Christ's sake? Hey, that's my girl—my woman—on the arm of that boot-camp type over there. Damn.

Holst noticed her interest in Jay and placed his hand on the small of her back as they were led to a table. The gesture signaled ownership, like a dog pissing at the edge of his territory. Jay and Holst exchanged stares and both knew what the other was thinking. Male games.

Holst tried to seat her, but she switched seats on him so

that he sat with his back to the bandstand, Marlene smiling over his shoulder. His face flushed with anger. Although he had not slept with her, had not even kissed her, he nevertheless considered her his property. She was part of this job, under his supervision, and therefore his.

He studied her across the table. She used restraint and taste with makeup. Never too much. Her lips were red, her eyes faintly shadowed; two gold studs in her ears matched the thin gold chain around her neck. Her hair was wavy and blond, except when the light caught it just so, and then beautiful reddish highlights showed. Her body was athletic and firm. He wondered what the rest of her looked like.

She ordered a rum sunrise and he a vodka gimlet. To her, dining with Holst was tedious. Like dining with your prison guard. She wondered if this was like a marriage that had gone stale. Tedious. She hated Holst. If only her father had not tried so hard. If only Holst didn't have it on tape. The thought stole her appetite. She hated Iben Holst.

She ordered the Dungeness crab with broccoli and a salad with house dressing. Holst ordered another drink.

Marlene looked at his empty gimlet. "That was fast."

He shrugged. "Lost my appetite."

"But not your thirst."

He shrugged again.

She fiddled with her silverware and patted her hair absent-mindedly, looking away.

Holst looked up from the table slowly. "You think of me as a monster. I can feel it."

She toyed with the spoon, not answering. On stage Jay counted off the next song.

"Soon, it is over," Holst tried.

A short waitress with a cranberry top delivered the vodka. Holst grunted at her. The music stopped. Marlene and others applauded.

Jay Becker's voice boomed through the speakers. "Thank you, dancers. We'll be back after a short intermission. Don't forget tonight is Seattle Slew night at the Blue Sands. See ya in twenty—after a short pause for the cause." Jay made it seem fresh every night. That was his job: do the same thing every night and make it seem fresh.

Marlene said to Holst, "Are you going to ask him over?"

Holst nodded. "Yes, of course. You know I am." He turned to signal Jay, who was already looking at Marlene. Holst raised his index finger like a person signaling a cab. Jay noticed the gesture and raised his own index finger, indicating he would be a minute. Holst was annoyed. Male games. When Jay arrived at the table, Holst remained seated.

"Sit down, please," Marlene offered, angered by Holst's rudeness.

Jay dragged a chair up, still catching his breath. Holst and Marlene had fresh drinks. Jay drank from a glass of beer with a lemon floating in it.

"Jay Becker." He and Holst shook hands.

"Iben Holst. You have met Marlene," he said, reasserting his ownership.

Jay nodded.

"We would like to hire you, Mr. Becker, full-time. Marlene is enjoying her sailing lessons and there is much to do to ready *The Lady Fine* for passage at the end of the month. I will pay you three dollars an hour more than the marina is currently paying you, and one hundred dollars a day when you travel north with Marlene. Are you interested?" Holst made it sound demeaning but attractive.

Jay looked at the smooth German features; no hard lines creased his face or eyes. Even so, the man exuded evil—what some called "bad vibes." There was no mistaking it. His nose had a thin little scar most people would have missed. A knife wound perhaps, Jay told himself, an extremely sharp knife to leave so thin a scar. Maybe not a knife, but a razor blade. Yes. He noticed a similar scar just inside the man's shirt collar. A neck scar curved like a frown. "I'll have to clear it with John. He's the dockmaster. I don't want to jeopardize my job at Shilshole."

"And if John agrees?" Holst asked.

"It's very tempting," Jay said, glancing at Marlene over the rim of the beer glass.

She smiled rather formally. Jay understood: this was business. Holst was obviously a jealous type. Like Jay.

"When will you have a definite decision?"

"Tomorrow noon."

"Fine. Marlene, you'll let me know?"

She nodded at Holst.

"Excellent. Now perhaps we can continue with dinner. Thank you, Mr. Becker. That will be all for now."

You didn't have to say that, Jay thought. He rose, pushed the chair in, and walked away, refusing to look back at Marlene.

When he reached the stage, Jocko said, "She is a fox."

"Shut up, Jocko. Just shut up." Jay slammed his hip into the panic bar on the exit door and stepped out into the chilly Seattle night.

117

It was eight-forty-five, just past sunset and at the edge of darkness, when clear images gradually lose their sharp edges. Seattle residents are accustomed to such light, for the city is often overcast with low, ominous clouds—with or without rain—dark, charcoal clouds that blow in relentlessly off the Pacific, blow in from Siberia, from the Aleutians, or from the vast swelling ocean. A few brave seagulls still swept through the twilight gloom, sounding their hollow, eerie cries, their white bodies like kites in the wind.

Pedestrians jammed Alaska Way near Pike's Market, mostly tourists after that one small item that was easy to carry, that one simple reminder of a vacation that could be tucked beneath the socks for little Ben, Dodge, Ted, or Blair. Not aware of exactly what they were after, they were lured into this, that, or the other store.

Roy Kepella steered his way through the crowded sidewalks. He had decided on a three-stage shake. The first phase was to wander the market until dusk. He poked his way through stores he had not visited for years and found himself enjoying them. He could feel the energy in the market, and it reminded him of the stockyard on the outskirts of Oklahoma City he had visited with his father as a kid. All those cows—as Roy called any four-legged beef animal—and all the people wandering around talking about heifers and milkers and calves and culling and bids and veal and flanks and rounds. He remained alert for anyone following him. It had been years since he had done anything like this. He had read enough files, had been involved in enough cases, to know that this was where many agents screwed up. Kepella had no intention of screwing up.

He entered a men's store by one of the market's three entrances, going first to a glass display case, where he inspected an assortment of cuff links. A large mirror behind the display allowed him a view of most of the store behind him. He paid special attention to the doorway he had entered, keeping an eye out for anyone keeping an eye out, although he didn't think he had been followed. But just in case Holst or some stranger was keeping him under surveillance, he continued to check the large mirror. Then he quickly left the store through a different exit. He walked briskly, but not so fast as to attract attention. He made his way out of the complex, crossed the street, and climbed into his old beater of a Dodge. He drove away.

He spent as much time looking in the rearview mirror as he did watching the road in front of him. He drove due west, one, two, three blocks, and parked near the Nordstrom department store, near 5th and Pine. Phase two. He bought a ticket for the monorail and boarded at the last possible second, pleased with himself because no one had had time to enter behind him.

Phase three. The cab, requested an hour earlier, was waiting for him with its engine running. The advantage of a cab was that it left Kepella free to fix his attention on the traffic behind them. He instructed the driver to take a certain route, running down one-way streets and making a series of four right-hand turns onto other one-way streets. It was a technique designed to expose any surveillance, even the most professional.

No one was following. He told the driver the address, a

residential area just over the hill.

The house, a blue two-story Cape, overlooked Lake Washington. The variety of plant life out here still amazed Kepella. It wasn't as apparent in the heart of the city—where Kepella had spent over eight years—but here, five, ten minutes out of town, every variety of shrub, tree, flower, fern, and bulb thrived, all neatly tended, property after property, like one might expect to find in Japan.

He unlatched the white picket gate and closed it quietly. A flagstone path led past tall, trimmed hedges. He followed the path around back as he had been instructed. He knocked on the back door twice, rang the doorbell, and knocked once more, all according to instructions. He let himself in, as he had been told.

The kitchen smelled of turkey and mashed potatoes. Water boiled on the stove. A Thai maid appeared through the inside door and nodded to Kepella. She swept an arm toward the door and nodded again. Kepella smiled graciously and pushed through the door. Brandenburg was sitting at the head of a long table. He stood. His haircut looked the same, as did his boyish face, his smooth skin, and penetrating look. "Good of you to come, Roy," he said, sounding somewhat British. The two shook hands. Kepella removed his trench coat, brushed off his sport jacket, and sat down. Silence. Kepella sipped his water and waited for Brandenburg to say something. The furnishings were Colonial, antiques and a simple flowered wallpaper. The polished dining table reflected the plain white ceiling. The candles were lit and the overhead light was dimmed. A not unpleasant room, Kepella thought.

"I thought you might be hungry." Brandenburg hesitated.

"Pahn has cooked a bit of bird, turnips and the like. I do hope you like bird."

"Fine"

"Oh good." Brandenburg buttered a roll and, stabbing the air with his knife, said, "Help yourself."

Kepella withdrew a steaming roll from the basket and had to place it down quickly.

"How's it going?" Brandenburg looked up and waited for Kepella to answer, his butter knife resting on the hot bun.

"They've made contact. I'm certain. I'm into them for five thousand. Got the loan today."

"Who?"

"The man's name is Iben Holst."

Brandenburg smiled. "Holst is it?" He buttered the bun carefully. "He's the right-hand man, you know?"

"Of course I don't know. I don't know a thing about this."

"You needn't be cross." Brandenburg took a bite of the bun and chewed vigorously. "I know this is difficult for you, Roy. But it sounds like you've hit pay dirt. It shouldn't be long now. Did you get the files clear?" He looked over again, jaw muscles flexing.

"Yes."

"SOSUS?"

"Yes. Everything you asked for."

"Wonderful job, Roy."

Kepella wanted to hit the man. There sat Kevin Brandenburg, a couple of years older than his son, chewing on a steaming roll and telling him that everything was wonderful. Bullshit. Everything was not wonderful. He had

121

been acting out a role. His nerves were frayed, the seams were ripping, the foundation rattling.

"The drinking?"

"I have an arrangement with the bartender. He pours water for me."

"Excellent." Brandenburg blinked, chewing on the edge of his lip, and examined Kepella more closely. "Are you up to this, Roy? It shouldn't be much longer."

Kepella wiped his mouth. Pahn entered, burdened by the platter of turkey. She made several trips back and forth: mashed potatoes, peas, turnips, gravy, cranberry, oysters, a tall glass of whole milk for Kepella, and white wine for Brandenburg. "Looks like Thanksgiving."

Brandenburg said, "It's your favorite, isn't it, Roy?"

They ate for a few minutes without discussion. When Brandenburg was finished with his glass of wine he asked, "What's your plan?"

Kepella felt better. The food *had* helped. "I'll default on the note. I'll get in nice and deep. I'll ask Holst to arrange refinancing. I already checked with him. He said he wanted to see how this went first. He'll bear down and I'll become desperate, just like you said."

"Nothing important at first, you understand. You can't pass along bullshit, but you want to watch how sensitive it is. You must make it look like you're trying to get away with something. They sucker in better that way."

Kepella nodded. He had studied similar routines.

"We'll try and meet once more. Same signal: three rings, I ask for Eddie, we hang up. A day later, here again."

Pahn cleared the table. She brought dessert. Cherry pie.

Kepella asked, "What about Washington?"

Brandenburg seemed confused. "I beg your pardon?"

"My job."

"Oh, yes. All cleared, I should think, by now."

"But what sort of post?"

"What did you have in mind?"

"I hadn't thought about it."

"Sure you have. What's your preference, Roy? I'll see what's available."

"After all this . . . well, I have kind of changed priorities. I think I might like something in Operations."

"You know there's not much there anymore. We're after a few federal judges at the moment, there's a few things down in Florida, though most of the money laundering is handled by the Secret Service and you know how tightly knit they are. There's some political stuff going on out in California, but that's not passing through Washington. It's being handled regionally. I'm not sure Operations is worth the effort; might be something more exciting at another desk. I'll make some phone calls."

"Will you?"

"Yes, of course."

"But Washington *is* on?"

"You bet. For you, Roy? Jeez, you're top dog at the moment." Brandenburg tasted the pie and smiled. "Good pie, isn't it?"

Kepella asked, "What if *I* need to contact *you?* How can I do that?"

"I'm afraid that's out. Security, you know. If anything should go wrong—if you were to be interrogated—we couldn't very well have you lead them back to me, could we?"

"But I've already got your name."

Brandenburg shook his head. "No, Roy. You have *a* name. Isn't that what you meant? A name." Brandenburg smiled. "Precautions, Roy. In this day and age, one just can't take too many precautions."

Kepella had never heard of an upper using a cover to run an operation. "That's a little unusual isn't it?"

"This whole operation is unusual, Roy. We're taking a huge risk here, all to catch a man who should have been hauled in in Montreal, eighteen months ago. To be frank, the Bureau is trying to save face."

"How the hell am I supposed to trust you?"

"It's a little late for that, isn't it, Roy? You're suspended, you have no law enforcement status whatsoever, you've lifted God-only-knows how many state secrets and furrowed them away somewhere, you're into loan sharks for five thousand. You're sleeping with a twenty-five-year-old Chinese." Brandenburg looked at Kepella contemptuously. "I'd say it's a little late to have doubts about the people running this operation. We're the only ones who can save your ass, Kepella. Don't forget that."

16

Running with the wind, Jay pointed her as high as she would take it. The breeze was perfect, the sea an iridescent green, and Jay had to remind himself he was being paid to do this.

"Fantastic!" he shouted to Marlene, as she clicked the winch another two notches and the jib tightened in the wind. *The Lady Fine* heeled toward the chop and Jay stood up to peer over the bow. She took the wind like a racer, a real go-getter and eager for the strong blow.

Marlene, holding firmly onto a teak runner, edged back toward Jay. "This is the best yet."

He nodded enthusiastically. To port, Mount Rainier dominated the afternoon sky, a monolith filling the horizon, a ring of clouds circling its peak. Spray slapped them both in the face as *The Lady Fine* gathered speed and sliced through the sea. "She's a honey. My God, she's a honey." He looked up to the telltails attached to the stays and said, "Ready?"

Marlene inched forward again. She was wrapped in a yellow robe for warmth against the wind. "Ready," she confirmed, one hand prepared to loosen the line from the cleat, the other holding the winch handle.

"Ready about!" Jay barked, snapping the main sheet loose from the cleat and ducking as the boom swung violently overhead, spinning the wheel with one hand while fishing for a hold on the starboard winch and securing the line on an adjacent cleat. Marlene winched in the jib and tied it off. They were now headed straight for Mount Rainier. It seemed more a fantasy destination than a real mountain only miles away, a place that promised peace and forgiveness and no worldly worries, a Shangri-La, mysterious, floating above the horizon in a sea of indigo sky.

Marlene sat down next to him. The boat cut a foaming white wake through the Sound. "Where did you learn how to sail?"

Jay looked over at her. They both wore sunglasses, so he couldn't see her eyes. "I've sailed all my life. Most every day of every summer as a kid. I started out on Dyer dinghies, moved up to Blue jays, then Lightnings, then my parents' thirty-two-foot ketch. When I was fourteen, my father and I started competing in regattas on weekends. We have a bookcase full of trophies at home. We were very lucky."

"You were comfortable then, as a child?"

"Yes. My father does very well. And you?"

"My father is a Lutheran minister." She twisted her hands together in her lap. "We did not have too much money. We had a great deal of love."

Her mystery, he thought.

She removed her robe and tossed it into the open companionway. It floated down into the galley. She rubbed oil on her arms and abdomen, and quickly over her chest. He felt a twinge in his groin.

"Would you mind?" she asked, turning her back to him and handing him the plastic bottle.

"Not at all."

She reached up and untied the thin straps, lifting her hair out of the way. Jay ran his hands over her smooth back. The boat sailed on. After a while she retied the straps and stretched out on the cockpit seat. She was a long, lean, thing of beauty lying there, eyes closed, legs parted slightly, arms akimbo. Jay stared at her. He could almost feet the sun penetrating her skin, the warmth building up inside her.

He enjoyed the feel of the breeze and the sight of Rainier guarding the Sound. Ten minutes passed before he asked her, "Ready?"

"If we must," she said, sitting up. As she rose, the boat

hit some chop and she lost her footing. Jay jumped up and caught her before she hit her head on the edge of the cockpit. Her skin was warm and slippery. He held her until she had regained her footing, then leaned forward to kiss her. She started to kiss him back, but then pushed him away gently. "No, Jay. We mustn't."

He gazed into her eyes. Her voice said one thing, her vivid green eyes another. Letting go of her, he said, "I told you, Topsiders are a requirement." He pointed to her feet, his insecurity obvious. "Bare feet can kill you."

She ran a finger beneath his lips. His feelings hurt, he shied away from her touch. She went below, donned Topsiders, and put her robe back on. When she was back in the cockpit she brushed the hair out of her eyes and held it in the wind. "If it makes any sense," she began, "I liked that very much. But it would only complicate things."

"I don't think so, Marlene. I think it's inevitable."

She grinned, causing her sunglasses to move on her nose. "Holst is a strange man, Jay."

"So what? Are you his?"

Her smile widened. "No. Of course not."

"Then what?"

"I work for him."

"So what?"

"Do not do this to me, Jay. I can not explain it. I just can not explain it. It would not make any sense." She moved away from him, taking hold of the rail and heading to the bow.

He hollered, "Try me, Marlene. Maybe, just maybe, I'd understand."

She pulled her hair out of her eyes. No, she told him

without a sound, you would not understand.

He loosened the main sheet and roared over the wind, "Ready about. Hard a-lee . . ."

17

On the fourth ring he had finally answered. The conduit. But before Sharon could utter a word, he had given her a different phone number and told her to call in exactly three minutes. Her next phone call proved identical to the first: again he supplied her with a different phone number and told her to call him, this time allowing exactly eight minutes to pass.

He finally answered, "Where are you?"

"I'm staying in a partially burned cabin by a lake on the west side of town, I think, near a church."

"Do you know the name of the church?"

"No, but the church overlooks the lake."

"A small, stone church? Ivy?"

"That's it."

"It's on the east side of town. I know where you are. I'll be right there."

Thirty minutes later a nondescript car pulled up. A man knocked on the cabin door. She opened it cautiously, the Beretta ready.

He stood six feet tall and wore a full, dark beard and wire-rimmed glasses. He appeared to be in his early forties, and she thought him handsome, though tough-looking. He entered the cabin and shut the door. They shook hands.

He sat down in a chair by the soot-covered curtains.

"Let's take it from the top, okay? Tell me exactly what have you done, where you have been, who might have seen you in the last few days? It's important I know."

She told him about the shootings, which he had read about in the papers. "After that I ran. I spent a day ducking in and out of doorways. Eventually, I made it to the other side of town. There are a bunch of cars—a junkyard—over that way, I think," she said, pointing, "and I slept in one for several nights—"

"Food?" he inquired, interrupting her.

"Vegetable gardens. I was careful not to be seen, and not to take enough to be noticed."

"Go on."

"I stole these clothes from a clothesline. I did my best to make it look like wind had blown the clothes from the line. I wasn't sure if it would be convincing, so I moved on."

"That's good."

"They train *women*, too, you know," she snapped sarcastically.

He ignored the comment. "Then what?"

"It took me a day and a night to cross town. I wanted some high ground. I'm down to four rounds. I found this place—good view of the city and surprisingly few people."

"Weekends they come here."

"It's a two-mile walk to the nearest pay phone. I tried to reach you while I was staying at the junkyard, but I couldn't. Once I found this place I waited a day and tried again. Last night I bathed in the lake, it was my first bath in—"

"I'm sorry you had trouble reaching me," he interrupted again. He peered out the glassless window. Fog covered the

129

city. The street below shone with the moisture.

"I was told you would be available if I needed you," she said indignantly.

He shrugged, uncaring. "So far, so good. Let's leave it at that."

"Yes."

"The cops complicate matters. It would be one thing if we were just trying to get you past Fritz Wilhelm's people. Mind you, in this city, that is something like trying to fool the Mafia. But the Regensburg police? They are even worse. It rules out conventional transportation. Both Wilhelm and the police will have everything covered, and not only in Regensburg. No, we'll think of something else. And there's another factor: Wilhelm is thorough. He has bought his way to the top. So there's no telling who to trust." He winked at her. "We'll do this with a few of my people. No one else." His tone of voice bordered on arrogance. The conduit: the one man who could get her out of here.

"So, what do we do?" she asked.

He peered out the crack in the curtains. "Good question."

"A private plane?"

"No, we need something unconventional . . . I did have one idea that might work, but I am not certain . . ."

"What?"

"There are some people in France who can help us. If we are lucky, they can get you aboard a freighter bound for the States. So, we had better get you across the border."

"Won't I be safe once I'm in France?"

"Unlikely, and certainly not worth the risk. Wilhelm's influence reaches far. Too far. And with this police trouble . . ."

"Why can't Washington take care of that? Or Bonn? It was self-defense."

"Because they won't even admit you are here in Germany. They have *proof* you are on holiday in the U.S., in case something like this happened. We *know* that much."

"That wouldn't be true unless I was rated HOT," she said. "You're wrong. That can't be right."

He nodded. "Until we get you home, you don't exist. You've been rated HOT since we lost you the night of Bobby Saks's death."

"That's absurd!"

"Welcome to Operations."

She slumped down into a discolored chair.

He parted the curtains again and looked outside. "Do you have your passport?"

"Yes, but it's a diplo—"

"Get it for me." He let the curtains close and watched as she walked over to her purse. She was a pretty woman. He respected women with guts and smarts. "I should tell you . . . You've done well so far. A lot of women—a lot of agents wouldn't have made it this far. We'll get you out." She handed him the passport and he looked it over. "Okay . . . this is fine. I'll take this with me. I know someone who is good with these. You would be smart to cut your hair very short—like a man's."

"What?"

"Just do it. I'll send a car here at eight o'clock this evening to pick you up. You'll find a wig and some cosmetics in the back seat. Put the wig on immediately. When the driver drops you off, he will point out a building. Walk directly to the building. Don't knock. Let yourself in."

The house, also on the east side of Regensburg, sat alone down a narrow back road and was furnished like a summer cottage. The car, after letting her off, disappeared around the corner. The conduit, dressed in black, locked the door behind her. She worked on her face and wig for twenty minutes. Then she sat for the photo session. The conduit left after taking five photos and didn't return for three hours. When he did, he handed her back her passport. She opened it up. The new photo had been fixed to the front page, a seal embossed atop it. The name read Cheryl Parker. He said, "You're a diplomat's daughter on vacation. It's all in order. You will have no problem at the border."

"You're coming with me, aren't you?"

"Yes and no. You will ride with the same driver who picked you up tonight. I will follow behind as backup in case anything should go wrong."

"Meaning?"

"I told you before: Wilhelm's fingers reach far. There's a network of people after you. We can't rule out anything." He handed her a small paper box that contained one hundred rounds of ammunition for the Beretta. "Anything's possible. Now, reload that Beretta, and carry it on the seat beside you the entire way." She slipped the box into a pocket of her skirt. "I know you're frightened, Sharon. I'm frightened for you. You've done well, *extremely* well so far. I will see you to the border. If I cross, it might arouse suspicion."

"Please. Answer me this: Why did they choose me for this operation?"

132

His eyes became gentle. "Timing, I suppose. You were the only agent close at hand who had Operations training. Because your vacation had already been planned, your absence from the embassy wouldn't arouse suspicion. I would guess that had a lot to do with it. You had all the right qualifications. Being a mule is usually not too difficult—though not without risk. I never knew your contact. He was S.O.—deeply buried. I was told that he was in Regensburg—my territory. I'm too well known in the area to be given this kind of a job. I'm more of a 'clean-up man,' if you will. I handle things like this . . . as well as more undesirable tasks." He walked to the window and looked outside again. "Washington contacted me directly and warned you might call. I was out on assignment. I had to relocate to Regensburg and arrange the proper phone connection. That took a few days. When I arrived I had to make my usual contacts. Then you called. Here we are." He didn't want to frighten her, but the truth was that his orders had come from the director himself. No go-between. Orders never came from the director, which meant this was one hell of an important operation—and Sharon Johnson the key.

"What do I do once I reach France?"

"We've improvised. A magician, just recently in Germany, will help you. His show is in Soultz-sous-Forets Seltz now. He'll try to get aboard a ship. That would be the safest for you."

"A *magician?*"

"Magicians make people appear and disappear . . . isn't that true? Anything is possible given the proper circumstances."

"What are the proper circumstances?"

He withdrew a billfold from an inner pocket of the raincoat he wore. From this he pulled a number of large-denomination bills, German and French. "You'll take this. I have a voucher you have to sign, but I'll do it for you. I want you to listen very carefully and feel free to interrupt at any point. It's very important you know exactly what to do. There is little room for error. Do you understand? Any questions at all, you must ask, no matter how trivial. I'll answer as best I can. Okay?"

He had changed, she thought. He was the devoted professional now, ready to brief her. She knew his insistence on thoroughness resulted not only from his concern for her safety, but for his own service record. She was in his hands now, his responsibility, and he had no intention of failing. She nodded her head and said, "I'm ready."

He winked. "It's no sweat, Sharon. You're almost there."

They were traveling down a two-lane country road, the conduit following in his own car, when her driver stopped the car behind a truck at a stop sign. Sharon had stayed wide awake for the entire drive, only now feeling tired, her head bobbing as she hovered on the edge of sleep. The Beretta lay ready beneath her right hand.

"Lady!" the driver barked, reaching over the seat to rouse her.

She opened her eyes: dusk on the horizon.

"We're stopping for gas in a minute. Last stop before the border—"

The truck had stood still, blocking their way, for almost thirty seconds. Too long. Sharon was looking toward her driver when a soft yellow spurt of light flashed from the side of the truck. Instinctively, she leaned to her left to avoid the shot, her words of warning too late. Both the front and back windows cracked as the bullet tore through them. The driver's body fell slack against the steering wheel, sounding the horn. Sharon struggled to unlock the back door, her fingers searching blindly for the lock as two more shots were fired. It opened. She tumbled out onto the pavement, Beretta in hand.

Another man, short, with a ruddy complexion, was standing by the side of the truck, legs spread, his large hands wrapped around a pistol. Three shots thumped into the open door she was using for cover. Sharon aimed and squeezed the trigger twice. The man was lifted off his feet and collapsed backward. Still.

The conduit smashed his car's interior light and ran in a crouch across the road, drawing the fire of the driver of the truck, as he had hoped. He made it to the edge of the road, leaped into the bushes, righted himself, and got off four quick shots, the last of which winged one of the men.

Following the conduit's lead, Sharon rolled into the bushes on her side of the road, rose to her feet, and hurried forward to a point alongside the truck. A third man she had not seen fired a sawed-off shotgun from the window of the truck. The blast tore a hole in the vegetation in front of her. Two pieces of buck shot embedded in her left arm. The wounds were minor, she realized quickly, and though painful, presented no real problem. She strained to locate the man. There! He was edging his way alongside the truck, gazing into the shrubs.

Sharon gripped the Beretta in both hands, steadied it, and

pulled the trigger. The truck's front windshield exploded—her shot had hit the cab but missed the man with the shotgun. She dropped to a prone position in the dry leaves. Three more shotgun blasts filled the bushes all around her. She was saved from the buckshot by a slight tapering of the road's soft shoulder. She crawled forward GI-style in the direction of the shots.

The conduit heard three more shotgun blasts and made his move. He had no intention of screwing this up. He stood and ran for the back of the truck. The wounded driver, now tucked back into the cab, aimed and fired. The conduit felt the bullet enter his gut. He buckled over, edging behind the shelter of the large truck and struggled to switch clips, reloading his weapon. The man with the shotgun leaped inside the cab and fired two consecutive blasts through the rear window of the cab.

Sharon saw it happen. She saw the conduit run across the road, saw him buckle as he took a slug, saw him reloading. Saw the shotgun blasts. Without knowing exactly why, she charged the truck, jumped up on the runner, and fired point-blank into the surprised face of the man holding the shotgun.

The wounded driver fired once and dove out of the truck. The blindly fired bullet missed Sharon's face by inches. She snapped her head back and fell to the pavement heavily, scrambling to look beneath the truck for his feet. The driver rounded the front of the truck, thinking he had killed her. She rolled under the truck and came to a stop, prone, gun facing front.

The driver's feet paused briefly by the front right wheel. Then he jumped around the truck, ready to shoot a person he thought was prone on the pavement. Sharon tracked his motions with the gun. She would have taken a shot at his ankles if he had given it to her, but he stopped on the far side of the front wheel, denying her the shot. From his hesitation she guessed he was confused as to where she had gone. Was she under the truck, or in the bushes? But his training told him quickly that if she were in the bushes she would have fired. The gun in his hand appeared suddenly and he fired the weapon blindly beneath the truck. His first attempt punctured the oil pan. Black oil poured from the hole and onto the roadway. The next attempt clicked: his gun was empty. As he lunged for the cab to try and get the shotgun, Sharon rolled over once and found herself on the far side of the truck. She moved quickly. Just as the driver pulled the shotgun from his dead partner's hands, she fired, emptying the Beretta into his chest.

She ran now, hard and fast, passing the car she had been riding in and climbing into the vehicle driven by the conduit. She ground the gears, jerking into first, and spun the wheel violently, yanking the car onto the road and pushing the accelerator to the floor. Her training had come back to her. All at once. She was confident now. She had survived. She *would* survive.

The conduit drifted up out of unconsciousness, out of shock. He looked down at himself: he had been peppered with buckshot and was bleeding badly. He couldn't see out of his left eye. He tried to lift himself off the hood. He knew he wouldn't live long if he didn't receive medical attention soon. Then he felt a hand on his arm. He rolled his head to try and see the man speaking German: a tall man with thick lips. "Put him in the van," this man ordered. "We'll want to question him before he bleeds to death."

"What about the others?" a faceless voice asked.

"Check them out. If they're dead, leave them. Burn the truck. I'll call Wilhelm and tell him this one's alive. . . ."

The sun was shining, casting hard shadows. Sharon marveled at the fastidiousness of the French as she watched a merchant sweeping the sidewalk in front of his shop, a clean apron tied about his waist. He smiled perfunctorily at a passerby. She snipped and attached the last piece of adhesive tape to the bandage, thankful that the buckshot had not gone deeper. Thankful it would not scar. The bandage would be off tomorrow.

A few floors below, in the hotel dining room, the luncheon show had begun, a few dozen women in attendance. She pulled down the sleeve of her blouse and buttoned the cuff. When she tugged on the collar to straighten it, a pine needle fell out. She bent over, picked it up, and threw it away.

Many of the tables had been cleared of their services by the time she made it downstairs. Alert, now, she sat down at a table, nodding to the three ladies who looked at her curiously. So far, so good. She thought about the conduit, waiting for the magician to work his way through the routine, realizing she didn't even know his name. To her he was simply the conduit. His plans were dictating her every move.

She sipped her water. The magician, a large bald man with a deep, resonant voice, implored the guests to keep their attention firmly on a large gray box center stage. The conduit had told her to watch the door to the right of the stage. She awaited the signal, her heart beating quickly.

The audience applauded.

The door moved. No, it stopped and closed again. She tuned the rest of the room out, the door all that mattered. A woman appeared in the doorway to the right of the stage, remaining only long enough to glance toward the back of the room and remove the bright red hat she wore.

The signal. Sharon left the large hall and walked down a corridor parallel to it. At the end of the corridor, she knocked on a set of double doors. The right-hand door opened, admitting her. Illusion, she thought, is all I'm after.

A burly man approached her. "Miss, miss," he said in German, "please. There are to be no spectators backstage."

"It is all right, Paul." The magician appeared from behind a curtain. On stage, a woman could be heard explaining the upcoming finale, her voice low and dramatic. The bald magician continued. "Paul, see to the dressing rooms. We are almost finished." Paul hurried off. "The hat?" he inquired.

"Is red," she answered.

He nodded. "I am Hercule. We haven't much time, I'm afraid." He waved an arm toward the back. "This way, please."

She followed behind him, led into the darkness of a prop room, to an enormous box used in one of the disappearing routines. It was difficult to see; her eyes had not fully adjusted. The magician knelt and pushed against a lower section of the box; a hidden door fell open. "It is small. You open it by pulling on one of the straps and then lowering the door to the outside. There is a door on either side. It is the best I can offer. Remain inside for at least one hour once the truck is moving. After that use your judgment—but be forewarned: the truck will be inspected at the docks. It is often no more than a look inside. However, if it is searched, if you are discovered, you are on your own. The driver will admit nothing."

She could hardly see the magician. "And where am I going?"

"If we are successful, you will be aboard ship by this evening. Perhaps sooner. Again, the red hat. You will recognize who to pay by the red beret. He will arrange everything. Now listen: if the driver"—he was hurrying, anxious to be done with her—"knocks twice, it means the rear door will be opened. Three knocks means something has gone wrong. In either case, get inside the box whenever the truck stops. Take no chances. As long as the truck is stopped, remain inside the box until the driver speaks to you directly."

"Yes," she said softly. She handed him a bulky envelope containing the money the conduit had given her. He accepted it.

"Hurry," he said, hearing the applause. "Good luck to you!"

She dropped to the floor and crawled inside. He pushed the door shut behind her. Darkness; muffled applause.

When the magician reached the stage, he looked out into the crowd, a large smile pasted on his face. Then he spotted three tough-looking men at the back of the hall, their eyes searching the room; he bowed.

18

Holst watched as the screen welcomed him to CompuServe. He accessed EMAIL and, when prompted,
retrieved a message.

TO ALBATROSS—RE: J.C. BECKER. BORN COS COB, CT.,
12/28/53. FATHER, ROBERT J. BECKER, STOCKBROKER,
NYSE. BECKER ATTENDED PRIVATE SECONDARY SCHOOL
1967-70. ONE SEMESTER WILLIAMS COLLEGE, FALL OF '73.
HAS LIVED NEW SEABURY, MASS.; BOSTON, MASS.; NYC,
N.Y.; SEATTLE, WASHINGTON. POOR CREDIT RATING. NO
MAJOR CREDIT CARDS; NO BANK LOANS. AVERAGE
YEARLY INCOME $8,540. NO ARRESTS. THREE MAJOR
TRAFFIC ACCIDENTS, '75, '78, '79. ASSETS TOTALING $3,650.
SINGLE. OVERSEAS TRAVEL: PARIS, 3/71; LONDON 4/71—
MARINER.

Holst placed the information in a buffer and then closed
the buffer. He moved through the menus until he could
leave a message. It read:

TO MARINER—MARK HOOKED. $5,000. WILL OWN NOTE
BY WEEK'S END. ADVISE CLIENT: ALL ACCORDING TO
PLAN. EXPECT RENDEZVOUS AS AGREED. WOMAN WILL
MAKE CONTACT SEPT. 3-5. THE LADY FINE—CUTTER-
RIGGED YAWL. CAPTAIN: J.C. BECKER. MAINTAIN AFFIR-
MATIVE ACTION. REPEAT. MAINTAIN AFFIRMATIVE
ACTION.—ALBATROSS

Holst sent the buffer to disc, saving the information on

Jay. He could see his reflection in the computer screen. His lips curled. Not long now.

Sadie, the tall, coarse-featured black woman, arrived an hour later.

"You remember what I have in mind?" Holst asked her.

"I got the message, daddy." She put down her purse and removed her coat. She was dressed in black leather. The jacket was unzipped to her navel. Her large breasts held the coat off her chest; her skin was the color of boot polish.

He handed her an envelope. She counted the bills and put the money in her purse. He saw the gun, a .38, standard police issue. He didn't doubt it was loaded. She walked past him and switched the television on, turning it up. "Sometimes—you know—I make some noise. I try not to. This—you know—helps hide it."

She had the dreary eyes of a junkie and was slightly unstable on her feet. She stood in front of Holst and her pink tongue ran over her large lips. He smacked her hard across the cheek. She lowered her eyes and smiled, seeming to enjoy it.

"Not too much on the face, daddy. That's my calling card."

He struck her again, and he smiled.

Kepella didn't know what to do; he didn't recognize his own face in the mirror. His skin had taken on a ghastly gray and the bags beneath his eyes had doubled and grown puffy. His round face and pronounced jowls made him look like he used to look, back when he had been drinking: Must be the fatigue, he thought. He was frightened. How much longer could he endure?

"What's the matter, Roy?" Rosie was kneeling on the bed, looking like a young girl, her skin brown from the sun, her pubic hair jet black, a bikini shaped wedge of lighter skin surrounding it. Her breasts pointed up and jiggled as she bounced on the bed. An evening mist had collected on the outside of the window. Rain water streaked the panes— a thousand tears falling from a thousand eyes.

"I'm old," Kepella answered. "Rosie, why do you stay with me?" He wanted her out of this. It would grow nasty in the next few days. He had come to like her, despite her obvious involvement in it all. Yes, he wanted her out.

"You not old to me, Roy. Come to Rosie. Come over here."

He wondered how much she knew. She looked like something he might have dreamed about a few months earlier. Cute little Chinese girl—woman, she would insist— naked as the day she was born. Sexy, sassy. His meeting with Brandenburg had been five days ago. How had Brandenburg known about Rosie? Was there a small group of agents assigned to keep him under surveillance? He didn't put it past the Bureau. After all, he had lifted a number of sensitive documents, documents worth tens, perhaps hundreds of thousands of dollars. He was legally separated from any law enforcement. And although this separation had been accomplished to both bait the trap and allow him the flexibility to break certain laws an undercover agent could not break without reams of warrants, it also meant he was a private citizen, barely employed, with an arsenal of state secrets at his disposal. It only made sense that Brandenburg would keep a close eye on him. He moved to the window, trying to peer through the stretched lines of water. The window needed cleaning. To Kepella it seemed like everything needed cleaning; everything needed change. The street below, lit by the glow of an overhead street lamp, shone wet-black in the glare of the bulb. A new van was parked among the others that lined the streets. He wondered if it was a surveillance van.

It actually made him feel more secure, knowing he might be under surveillance. He had felt isolated since his last meeting with Brandenburg—isolated from old friends by his suspension from the Bureau, isolated from new friends by playing the role of an angry man, and used by people like Holst and Brandenburg: all to trap Fritz Wilhelm, a man known by name only, a man without a face, a man who had embarrassed the Bureau by entering and leaving Montreal a free man, when he should have been captured, drugged, and placed on a plane to Boston for interrogation. Now it was Kepella's turn to lead them back to Wilhelm, to try again. Brandenburg waving Kepella under everyone's nose, the stinking piece of fish used as chum.

"Come on, Roy." Rosie stood behind him, naked. He stood by the window, watching the strings of water, wearing a pair of worn boxer shorts. She reached around him and dragged her tiny hands and ruby nails down his chest. He shivered. "Come on, honey. What's wrong. Why you unhappy?" She paused. "Let Rosie please you."

"You scored, didn't you?" he asked her.

"Sure, Roy. Why not?"

He wished he hadn't asked her. She could do what she wanted to do. He was the one trapped. He knew it.

She prepared two large lines of coke on a small hand

mirror. A whiff of instant confidence. She rolled up a five-dollar bill and snorted up the lines. "You sure you don't change your mind, Roy?"

"None for me."

But he did want a drink. What the hell was going on? Damn. Why now? Now, when there was no one to turn to. Rosie was staring at him.

"What is it, Roy? What wrong?"

Act three, scene four. He lifted her off the floor and kissed her. She giggled and roughed up his hair as he carried her to the bed and lay her down. He sat above her, feeling old enough to be her father. He drew imaginary lines on her chest. She moved his hand down lower, her legs open and inviting. He rubbed the soft inside of her thigh. He said, "I'm in trouble, Rosie."

"What kind of trouble?" Her eyes showed concern.

He wondered, Is she that good an actress? Am I in a den of professional actors? "Money problems," he said, then hesitated, according to his script. "I borrowed a lot of money, to get out from under some loans." He stopped caressing her thigh. She closed her legs, trapping his hand. "It is very expensive money."

"What you mean, 'expensive money'?" She sat up, concerned.

"They charge me a wad of interest on the loan."

"Why you do that?"

"I needed to pay off debts."

"Yeah, but why not borrow from a bank?"

"The banks wouldn't loan me the money. It had to be these people."

"It's all right, Roy. You pay them back. I know you will."

"I don't have enough money to pay them back, to buy the food, the apartment . . ."

She bunched her brows. "You try to tell me something, Roy?"

Kepella nodded.

"Don't hand Rosie bullshit, Roy Kepella." She sat up, her neck flushed with anger. "If you don't like Rosie, you say so. Don't hand me bullshit about money. Fuck money. I don't cost you nothing. I don't want to go, Roy. I don't want to go." She bunched her legs up against her chest, glaring at him. "You full of bullshit, Roy Kepella."

"Rosie, if I screw up on these loans, they're gonna come looking for me." He cocked his head. "That makes sense, doesn't it?" She nodded. "And if they come looking here, they might find you." She nodded again. "And these kind of people don't play fair, Rosie. They might take you, hurt you, in order to get to me."

"I know how loan shark work, Roy. You think I growed up on Mercer Island or something? Shit. You don't even know me, do you, Roy?"

Kepella fought to keep the old Roy Kepella out of this. "Rosie, I've been shit for shape lately. I don't have a fuckin' friend on earth, except you. You are kind to me, gentle. You talk to me. We talk. We see a movie now and then—"

"We make good love together, Roy. I mean it. Good love."

He placed a hand on her knee. "Yeah . . . that too, Rosie. That's real nice."

"So what the problem?"

"The problem is that things are going to get rough. I

146

don't want you to get hurt. You give me a couple of weeks. I'll get in touch with you." He shouldn't have said that, he realized; he shouldn't have put it into any kind of time frame. A man in debt was in debt forever. He looked for a way out. "In a couple of weeks I'll know whether I can pay these guys what they want. Once I get back on my feet, we'll get back together."

The hurt covered her face. Her expression was so convincing that Kepella had a difficult time believing she was acting. Maybe both their roles had had their day. Maybe he was being Roy, and she, Rosie. Jesus he hoped not. He hoped this wouldn't become any more complicated than it already was.

"You move in with me, Roy. You know where I live. I take care of you." He looked into her eyes, her agate pupils like tiny black holes pulling him inside her. "Rosie take care of you."

They made love, and later they watched television. Her lovemaking was playful; he moved with all the grace of a three-legged dog.

Then the phone rang.

It was eleven-thirty by the time Kepella dressed. He walked down to Eddy's and had a soda water at the bar. No one behind him. He left Eddy's by the back entrance, which led down a fire alley. Old brick buildings lined the alley, like something off the old Twentieth-Century backlot. Kepella had toured the backlot before they began tearing it down, amazed that one could switch worlds by simply rounding a corner. One minute New York, the next a Wild West or Mississippi shanty town, the next a TV suburb that no one would remember. Not unlike his life, he realized: one minute Holst and Fu and some thug called Peace Brother, the next Brandenburg and his crew cut, then Rosie.

Four blocks later he turned right. He walked another block and turned right again. Then right again. No car followed. No one on foot. He ducked into a porno theater. Two bucks for a couple of hours of skin. The place smelled like piss and puke. He took a seat in the tenth row, his head turning constantly to check the aisle. On the screen two women violated each other. A few rows in front of Kepella, a wino pleased himself. He waited five minutes. No one came in behind him.

Kepella left by the fire exit, a poorly marked doorway up by the screen. He stepped to one side and waited. No one. He wasn't being followed. He slipped out the exit door into the chilly Seattle night air.

The bus pulled up a few minutes later. No one followed him onto the bus. He rode it ten blocks, walked a block north, and opened the door to a Ford four-door with black-walls and mirrored windows. The car pulled away. Thick Plexiglas separated the driver from the back seat. Sound-proof. Nearly bulletproof.

Director Mark Galpin said, "You're late."

"I'm ten minutes late, close enough. What the hell's going on, Mark?"

"Haven't seen you in a while, Roy. Thought we might have a chat."

"Has the board met yet?"

"Next week, though I must say, it doesn't look too good."

"Surprise, surprise."

Galpin's mandible muscles flexed when he wasn't talking, just as they always did. It was as if the man was constantly chewing. He had the same simple face Kepella remembered, the same nervous eyes. The car pulled into a parking garage and parked. The driver left the car. Kepella felt the front door bump shut. He could hardly hear it. Galpin said, "I thought we should be alone. You never know what someone might hear."

"How thoughtful of you, Mark."

"Hold the crap, would you, Roy?" Galpin's neck turned crimson.

"What the hell did you get me out of bed for?"

"To save your butt, friend. Why don't you try to listen for a minute?"

"I'm listening."

"What have you been doing with yourself, Roy?"

"I thought I was listening."

Galpin waited.

Kepella said, "I'm unemployed at the moment."

"I don't mean for work."

"Get to the point, Mark." Kepella was irritable. His thumb involuntarily rubbed against the pad of his index finger.

"Two weeks ago, middle of the afternoon, you were ticketed for speeding."

"What's going on, Mark? Cut the bullshit would you?"

"Why'd you need forty minutes to reach me tonight, Roy? You need time to shake a tail?"

Perspiration ran from Kepella's armpits. His palms were sweating. This was Brandenburg's deal; no one was to be involved. "I was in the middle of a good fuck, if you've got to know, Mark. The old root doesn't stand up all that often anymore. I take advantage of the times it does."

Galpin's jaw muscles flexed. He faced Kepella more squarely. "Okay, let's skip the ticket for a minute. We've been running a narco stakeout over in Ballard. The usual routine. I've got Green, Freeman, and Giapelli on it."

"Narco's not my turf, Mark, you know that. What the hell? It's late."

"A month, two months ago, you would have caught on right away. You would have realized that I knew about the traffic ticket, that would have clicked. You would have figured if I knew what you weren't doing, then I probably knew what you were doing. Your brain's going soft, Roy. You shouldn't be drinking again."

"Earlier tonight I had this feeling you were having me watched."

"Why are you boozing again? You had that licked."

Kepella glowed inside: So even you think I'm drinking again. Great. "You never have it licked, Mark. You have it under control. There's a big difference."

"So what happened?"

"I thought you were having me watched. You get so you can feel it."

"Not watched. I check up on you now and again. I have you followed for a few hours. That's all."

"Oh, is that all? Leave me alone, Mark. I'm doing fine."

"Not the way I see it."

"Damn it, Mark, come to the point."

"Hear me out, Roy." He shifted in the seat, his buttocks numb. "So, we had this spot in Ballard staked. A deal went down. The timing agreed with a tip we had. We thought we were on the major buy."

"What the hell are you doing working narco anyway? That should be DEA."

"We're helping out. Summer vacation time. All the agencies are a little shorthanded. We scratch each other's backs. You know that. Let me finish."

"Go 'head."

"A buyer shows up. Green and Giapelli follow. The buyer is a little Chinese girl. Nice-looking girl they tell me."

Kepella's heart skipped.

"Roy, that nice little Chinese girl returned to your apartment." He let it lie there. "Now, we know she wasn't the major buyer. That deal went down just after Green and Giapelli took off . . . but what's going on, Roy? You care to do a little explaining?"

"No. No explaining, Mark."

"Damn it, Roy. Who is she?"

"A whore I picked up."

"She lives there!"

"I thought you said you only have me watched occasionally."

"Cocaine, Roy? Jesus Christ, you've put me in a hell of a pickle. Your address will wind up in a report—a *narco* report. You know where that puts me? Jesus Christ." His anger flushed into his cheeks. He shifted on the seat, looked out the window at the other parked cars, then back at Kepella. "You have one of the highest security ratings in our department, Roy. Technically I should bring you in now—"

"You can't."

"Just what the hell does that mean?" Galpin shouted.

"Stay out of this, Mark."

"Out of *what*, Roy? That's what I have to know."

Kepella took his turn looking at the parked cars.

"Listen, Roy, policy requires me to arrest you and turn you over to the shrinks. You know how the Agency feels about drug abuse, especially someone with your rating. It won't fly, Roy."

"You're not a policy man, Mark. You never have been. Shove the policy."

Neither man said anything for a few minutes. The heavy silence wore impatiently on Kepella. Galpin seemed accustomed to it. Finally Kepella said, "Leave it be, Mark."

"Leave what be, Roy?"

"Why'd you pull me out of bed at this hour?"

"Leave what be?"

"The girl. Leave her alone."

"Did it ever occur to you that someone might be setting you up? What if this Chinese girl is being run to turn you? It fits perfectly, you know. She gains your confidence, gets you into a little soda, gets you drinking again, your money slides; you start selling little pieces of information, five hundred bucks here, five hund—"

"Knock it off, Mark."

"—red there. Nothing too sensitive at first—"

"Mark, you know me bet—"

"And then the big offer: ten grand, who knows, fifty grand maybe, for some nice juicy tidbit. So you take a look at the history of the department. How often do we actually prosecute? Maybe if the press finds out about it, otherwise you go scot-free and you're tailed the rest of your life—"

"Or someone takes me out . . . I have an accident and happen to die in my bathtub."

"Ridiculous. But look at it from my side. How many go to court? One out of ten, maybe? One out of twenty? A man in your position, good and angry at the department, a suspension that hit the press, you'd make a hell of a target. Admit it! How about it, Roy? Have you been approached?"

"No," Kepella replied honestly, "I haven't."

"Roy, what's going on?"

"Nothing, Mark. I'm screwing a girl half my age. Maybe she plays around with soda. Maybe I look the other way."

"How did you meet her?"

"Always the suspicious one, eh, Mark?"

"They pay me to be suspicious, Roy. You know that. No offense, but you're not the Paul Newman of middle age. A good-looking young chick winds up between your sheets, what should I think . . . that you've bought a new cologne or something? Roy, open your eyes. They may be coming after you."

"Who, Mark? Do you have a name for this ominous 'they'? Or is it just the fellows in the black hats?"

"Christ, Roy! This isn't like you. What the hell is going on?" He paused. "I demand to know." Galpin's fists were clenched.

Kepella thought for a moment. He turned to his former friend and said, "It's coming apart on me, Mark. I'm trying to catch the ball of yarn—trying to pick it up—but all I have hold of is the single strand. I pull and I pull and the ball just keeps running away from me. It unravels and unravels and pretty soon I realize there's nothing in the center, just more yarn. The ball is made up of one long strand." He was shaking his fists in the air. His face vibrated and its loose flesh wiggled. "Christ, Mark. I'm looking for something. But the only thing there is the looking. Do you understand?"

Galpin shook his head. "You're talking in circles, Roy."

Kepella nodded, his face red, his fists still raised. "That's it, Mark! Now you've got it. Good for you. Good for you. We should talk again, Mark." Kepella pulled on the handle, hoping the door would open, hoping the driver had not thrown some master lock and imprisoned him in the back seat. The door swung open. "She's a great lay, Mark. Best lay I've had in years. Makes me feel twenty years younger. I'm living again, Mark. Don't you see? This is what I needed." His face looked tortured. "Exactly what I needed." He slammed the door and walked away.

Galpin remained in the back seat, twisting his hands together in his lap. The driver approached the car and slid in behind the wheel. "Where to, sir?" he asked through the intercom system.

They waited this way, the driver in the front, Galpin in the back, for a full ten minutes. Galpin finally pushed the intercom button. "Just drive, would you? I don't care where. Just start driving." In his mind he saw himself pulling on the end of the yarn. The ball kept rolling away from him.

19

The truck eased to a stop. Sharon Johnson hurried to get inside the box she had been hiding in, pulling the leather strap so the trap door closed behind her. She heard the driver's door bang shut, followed by low voices. Then the sliding door rattled as the driver shook the handle. She heard two loud thumps, which signaled her to remain inside the box, followed by footfalls as a man made a cursory check of the cargo. Her heart raced as she realized how close the inspector was to her. "Move on," she wanted to say. "Go away."

He hollered in French, "Smells like piss 'n the bottle in here. Magicians are scum. Worse than scum." Another unfamiliar voice laughed. The truck rocked as the inspector jumped back down to the pavement. She relaxed. The rear door rattled down and the padlock clicked shut.

The truck rolled on. She crawled out of the box—a maneuver she was growing accustomed to—and sat down atop an adjacent crate. The truck bounced over potholed roads. She could picture the soft French countryside rolling by, the wooden fences, the stone cottages and boundaries. She could feel the sunset stain the horizon a seashell pink. She could imagine children running naked through the vegetable garden while Mama weeded and Papa sat drinking *vin ordinaire* on the mossy patio. Her imagination helped keep her going, distracting her from her ordeal.

If only she had been allowed to telephone the information to Washington. But she understood well enough that this was special courier information—and she was the special courier. No phones. She longed for a hotel room, a hot bath, and some good food. Riding in the back of a truck, in a stage box, alongside your own waste, was about as bad as it gets, she thought.

Hours later the truck stopped again. No one needed to tell her where she was—she could smell the sea. She expected the door to open and the driver to free her. Instead she heard the padlock click open, followed by three loud bangs. Three hits: trouble.

The back door screeched open.

"How long?" she heard the driver's deep voice ask in French. What followed amounted to an impromptu negotiation for a lower price on the unloading of the gear. The driver's main concern was time, and she knew why. If the unloading took too long, the loading would begin, and there would be no time for her escape. She would find herself aboard a cruise ship as a stowaway. The voices bantered back and forth. The driver kept demanding a shorter time period; the other voice protested. More money was offered. It didn't help. The unloading would take at least an hour.

"No, no, no," the driver shouted, banging the truck three times, repeating his signal to her.

Trouble.

The crate moved roughly from side to side. Two men grunted as they struggled with the weight. Sharon slid to a corner of the box, splinters lodging in her buttocks. She had the wind knocked out of her as the box pounded onto the dock. Then she felt a dizzying sensation as it was hoisted and boomed over the waiting ship and lowered into a hold. Intense heat surrounded her quickly. She mopped her forehead and unbuttoned her damp blouse. The crate rocked to the left; she slid to the other side. It bumped into place. She heard something heavy being placed next to the crate. Low voices complained of the heat. Then silence. A long and chilling silence, followed by the loud slam of the hold's doors closing shut.

In absolute darkness, she reached for the strap and pulled to release the hinged panel. The catch freed, but the door stopped immediately. It was blocked. She panicked, turning around to open the opposite panel. But it too was blocked. She pushed against it, then leaned, then kicked it with her feet, but it would not budge. Crates had been placed on either side of the magician's trick box. She screamed, "Help me!" and then covered her mouth quickly, thinking, What am I doing? What am I doing?

At the same moment, while the crew prepared *La Mer Verde* for departure, a man rounded the corner of a warehouse and walked hurriedly toward the ship. As the thick heavy lines were pulled aboard, the man climbed the steep steps to the main deck and showed his papers. He had been sent by the union to replace a crewman who had reported ill at the last minute. He greeted the hard, warm wind with a thin smile. He was a tall man and had thick lips . . .

She had been trapped in the box for hours—to her it seemed more like days—by the time she finally heard footsteps. "Help me," she cried weakly through a crack. Her movements were painful, her joints paralyzed.

"Hello?" He spoke English with a thick French accent.

"Help me, please." Her words were feeble, lifeless.

"Hello?" His voice was closer.

"Over here. I can't get out."

"My God!"

She heard the crate in front of her scrape the deck as it was moved. She smiled wanly. Finally. The trap door fell open and air rushed in on her, smelling as clean as a Maryland spring garden despite its rankness. She stretched an arm through the open door.

He had the firm, calloused hands of a man of the sea. His grip was powerful, and she welcomed this strength, for she had almost none of her own left. He pulled her gently from her prison, her cell.

"My God!" he said again. "A stowaway."

He stared down at her. She was wearing tiny bikini underwear, her unbuttoned blouse hanging off her, her skin flushed with heat rash. He led her to a crate. She pulled her blouse closed and sat down facing him, struggling to button the blouse. Her eyes hurt from the overhead light.

He leaned forward. "Here. Allow me to help."

She pulled away from him.

He didn't seem to care. He drew closer. "I won't hurt you. I promise. Here." He fastened several of her buttons without making any contact. He backed off and fanned the foul air escaping from the crate. She was delirious, her head swimming. He was young and handsome in a Gallic way. He wore no shirt and his dark skin was covered with hair. His teeth were extremely white. "You came on in Le Havre?"

She shrugged, too weak to talk. She took a deep breath and managed to say softly, "You must not turn me in. Please. Please, don't turn me in."

He laughed. "There's not a sailor on this ship who would

turn you in."

She had rehearsed it all so many times, she was able to force the words out. "I have money."

He grinned, though she did not see him do so. Her eyes were pinched closed. He said, "Money. Well, well."

"Yes." She nodded.

"You have belongings?"

She tried to point.

He dropped to his knees and peered inside. The stench overpowered him. He fanned the air in front of him and located her clothes and purse. He pulled them out. The clothes were wet and flattened into an unrecognizable pad of stained fabric. He pulled the pile apart with some difficulty, and helped her into her skirt. He put it on her backward by mistake.

"Can you walk?" he asked her.

She nodded, stood to make the effort, and collapsed. He caught her and picked her up in his arms, cradling her. Her head sagged, and he tried to adjust his hold on her. She reached up and held on around his neck.

He smiled. "You will be fine. Don't worry. My name is François. What is your name, please?"

"Sharon," she told him. "My name is Sharon. What will you do with me?"

He felt her tremble in his arms and saw the desperation written on her face. "You must not worry, Sharon. It is the French sailor's code to help the sick, the injured, not to take advantage of them. Please do not worry. I will help you. Only to help you."

He ascended a long spiral staircase carefully. At the top, an exit led to the crew's quarters, K deck, well below the waterline. He set her down before opening the door and made certain the hallway was clear before carrying her inside. There were always one or two crew members willing to report a stowaway. Stowaways were not that unusual on the Roget Line—several turned up in an average year, each with a different story, a different kind of desperation. The rude or violent were turned over without question. The Sharons were more often protected and nourished.

Claudia lay on her bed reading a book about whales. François knocked and then let himself in, still carrying Sharon. Claudia exclaimed, "What is it, François, *mon dieu,* what have you found?"

"She stowed away in a crate in the Sweat Shop. Been there since Le Havre by the look of her. Can you imagine twelve hours in the Sweat Shop? I thought you and Katrina could . . ."

"Of course. Put her over there." Claudia hopped out of the tiny bunk space. She wore very little clothing but was not the least embarrassed. François took no notice. "She is pretty."

"Yes. I will get her some food. You can help clean her up, find her some clothes. She needs a good bed for a change."

"Katrina and I work in split shifts now. Always a bunk open. You get her the food: some fruit, cheese perhaps, some ice and a glass, bottled water. Oh, and bring her one of those delicious cinnamon rolls. Nothing like a cinny to cheer one up. Hurry off, now. And not a word. I don't trust that new man down the hall at all. We had better keep her to ourselves."

He was nearly out the door when Claudia asked her

name. François told her. Claudia looked over at her guest, who was propped on a chair and hanging onto the corner sink for balance. "Pleased to meet you," she said.

Sharon forced a smile.

20

"Ready?" Jay spun the wheel sharply to port, bringing the bow into the wind, and waited for the sails to luff. He straightened the wheel frantically. "Now," he commanded.

Marlene loosened the jib's halyard and let it go. The jib fell toward the deck, its metal clasps singing against the stay. She bunched it as a woman might remove a bed sheet from a clothesline.

Jay held *The Lady Fine* into the wind, as waves slapped against the hull.

Marlene hurried to the mast and untied the main halyard from the cleat. "All right?" she asked loudly.

"Yes." The mainsail tumbled downward in asymmetric folds. Having released the mizzen's sheet, he stood alongside the cockpit as he and Marlene quickly bunched and rolled the mainsail, furling the tenacious sailcloth. He tossed her several bungie cords and she caught them easily. The two secured the sail. Marlene moved forward to bag the jib. Jay furled the mizzen sail expertly. He switched on the diesel, threw the gear lever forward, and set the throttle low. They were a quarter mile off Shilshole. Their tasks done for now, they met in the cockpit. She was smiling broadly, full of life, gooseflesh running up her arms.

"You're cold," he observed.

"It is chilly all of a sudden."

"Storm's on its way."

"Is that true?"

"Around here, more often than not."

She opened the hatch into the main cabin/galley. "Would you care for a beer?"

"Please. If you're having one."

She returned in her yellow terry-cloth robe carrying two Rainiers. She handed him one. It spit as he popped it open. Sunlight sparkled off the rim of the can. She wanted to touch him. He possessed a confidence she admired; he seemed strong, so unlike herself. She wondered what a person like Jay Becker would do if Iben Holst attempted to blackmail *him*. What would *he* have done, in her place?

"You are very sure of yourself, are you not?"

"Me?" He looked away. "Hardly."

"I embarrass you?"

"Yes, you embarrass me."

"You are a strong person, you see. I admire your strength."

"Me? Strong? You're suffering from heat stroke."

"You make music—you write music—despite the hardships. You decide everything about your life; you leave none of the decisions to others. So many of us, in our jobs, our families, allow others to make the difficult decisions. This is strength."

"Some people might call it pig-headed."

"I am sorry?" She did not understand the expression.

"You know who's strong? Your friend Holst is strong. I know his type. They can be mean sons of bitches. That's why I have to disagree with you. I've been told by several important people in the music business that I'm never going to make it. It's not the music—they insist the music is fine. It's because I'm not hardened enough. If I were stronger then I might stand a chance in the business. I'm not the strong type of personality. I cower when someone becomes forceful."

"Iben, strong?" She laughed. "Iben is a conceited fool. He just wants everyone to think he's strong. He puts on a good show." She looked in toward shore and said, "There is nothing inside Iben Holst. He is a shell of a man."

"Then why do you work for him?"

"We can't all work for ourselves. Sometimes one takes what one is offered. In this case it was a free trip to the United States."

He heard the tension in her voice. "None of my business. Sorry I said anything."

"I am being defensive. I am stupid sometimes. I, too, often wonder why I am working for him."

"Just what does an electronics expert do for the owner of a sporting goods retail chain?"

"Hardly an expert."

"Answer the question."

"Why should I?" She grinned.

"Because I'm jealous."

"Jealous?"

"He's attracted to you, Marlene. I thought at first you were lovers."

She laughed.

"I'm serious. Let me tell you something. You say I'm strong. Not so. Don't shake your head; it's true. Inside every performer is an insecurity. The stage is our place to show everyone that it's not there. I work hard, yes. I have *endurance*—that's true. I've been in this business for years, despite the hardships, as you say. Some people couldn't last in this business days—I'm the first to acknowledge that. But people like Iben Holst scare people like me. I doubt anyone scares him. That's the difference, you see. His strength is very real. He has an intimidating presence that says, 'Don't mess with me.' "

"But he is nobody, inside. He can not carry a conversation for more than five minutes. He is a beast. He uses people to further himself."

"All businessmen do. That's why I avoided business."

"Not like Iben Holst. He is different. You are warm, Jay. Kind. Iben Holst will never be kind."

He saw her choke. "What is it?"

"Nothing."

"Please."

"I miss my home; that is all. I miss my father. He is warm . . . You would like him, I think. He is strong in the way you are strong—no matter what you say." She looked over at him in a way that touched him.

Here is more of her mystery, he thought. He said, "You know, Marlene . . ." She cocked her head. "When I first saw you, I sensed something . . . well, something mysterious about you, like you held a secret you were dying to share. I had the same feeling the first time you mentioned Holst; and again, now, talking about your father."

"You are very perceptive, Jay Becker. That is another of your strengths."

"Will you tell me?"

"There is nothing to tell." She paused. "Honestly."

He studied her, disbelieving.

She said, "Sometime. Perhaps sometime I will tell you."

Jay felt a warmth spread through him. There is a turning point in any relationship, where the masks and acting finally break down. Sometimes the dropping of this mask is seen in physical hints: the burp at the table, passing gas beneath the sheets. There are giggles. Slowly a bond forms and this closeness allows expression. The emotional masks are let down slowly. The affable, jolly friend may be in reality alone and afraid. Jay recognized the moment. They had just passed through this barrier. She was no longer Marlene the goddess. She had just become human.

"Sometime," she repeated. She attempted a smile. She looked terribly pained. He wanted her to open up to him, but didn't dare press, lest she re-tie the mask.

"Ready?" he asked, inspecting the giant mainsail.

"Yes, Jay. You bet. I am ready." Her one quick glance thanked him for not pushing. They had passed beyond friends. The ship rocked; the sails shifted sides; lines tightened; the canvas snapped as it caught the wind.

Jay sipped his beer, which was getting warm. Time to change the subject. It didn't take a genius to realize that. He tugged the boat's wheel back and forth. "You know, the wheel is sticking again. That's not good. We wouldn't want to lose the rudder out there," he said, cocking his head out to sea. "I suppose I should check it out."

Marlene continued to stare toward Shilshole, thinking of her father and what Holst held over her.

"What do you think?" he asked.

"Excuse me?"

"About the steering cable?"

"Yes, a good idea. Is that not what you said?"

"What's wrong?"

She attempted a shrug of indifference, but her face revealed her anxiety.

"Are you mad?"

She placed her beer down, slid quickly over to Jay, and wrapped her arms tightly around him, drooping her head over his shoulder.

"You're frightened. What is it?"

She held him. Trembling. Jay steered with his foot. She lifted her head off his shoulder, their faces close. He could smell the beer sweet on her breath.

He set his beer down and took her cheeks between his strong hands. His right hand was cool from the beer, his left warm from where he had held her. He kissed her gently. She closed her eyes. Her lips were moist and warm, and she kissed him affectionately, pulling him closer and pressing herself against him.

Abruptly, she let go of him and pushed away. "What are we doing?" She glanced around. "We are acting like child—"

"No," he cut in.

"We must not do this. We must not become involved."

"We *are* involved, Marlene. We both know that."

She held her hands to her ears as if she were a child not wanting to hear. "No, Jay. Not here. Not now," she said, suddenly another person.

"Tell me." He knew she wanted to.

She shook her head and pulled him closer again. "No. I wish I could. I wish I could." And then she began to cry.

21

A morning rain was falling, rinsing the buildings, the streets, the air, washing garbage from the gutters. Rosie had gone off to wherever Rosie went off to. Kepella poured himself some Bran Flakes, heaped on the sugar, filled the bowl with 2%, and struggled through it. He would have preferred eggs and bacon, but the plumbing was congested and word had it that Bran Flakes worked wonders.

The knock on the door surprised him. It was early for a visit, though he knew who—at least what—it was before he opened the door. It was *them.* He had failed to pay yesterday. Who else could it be? Knowing this would be the first test, he turned the doorknob. His emotions were not unlike those of the fraternity pledge who willingly bends over, bare-bottomed, to be paddled. Initiation.

"Peace Brother? What the hell—?" The broad-shouldered Chinaman was standing in the door with another huge man. Kepella tried to close the door on the two. He had little problem playing the guilty man—half his life had been spent playing the guilty man.

"Time to pay you visit, Mr. Roy. You put friend of ours in bad place, you know." Peace Brother slurred his words together. "You late, Roy. Whatza matter, you fo-get or somethin'?"

Peace Brother—John Chu—pushed his way inside. Kepella backed away. Behind Chu, the other man, a Samoan with thick round arms and skin the color of an old saddle, followed.

"Come on, fellas. I'm *one day* late with my payment. That's why you're here, isn't it?" Kepella wiped his brow nervously, thinking, The jaws of the lion—wide open and coming to get me.

"Meet Donnie, Mr. Roy. Donnie a friend of mine."

"How ya doing?"

Donnie nodded, threw an arm straight forward, and knocked Kepella five feet back and to the floor. Kepella hit hard.

"What the . . . ?" he hollered.

"You late, Mr. Roy. No good. We come to have a little chat, you know. We come to straighten this out. Make it right," Chu said.

Donnie moved toward Kepella patiently, bent over, and picked him up. Then he hit him in the stomach. Kepella buckled and vomited onto the worn out rug. Bran Flakes and milk. Kepella swung, landing a strong right into Donnie's kidney. The Samoan tilted to his left and gripped his side. He was about to rearrange Kepella's face when Chu stopped him mid-swing and stepped between the two. "Have seat, Mr. Roy."

Kepella didn't budge.

Chu hit him squarely with open palms on both shoulders. Kepella fell back into the couch. "That better. Now, you got the scratch, Mr. Roy?"

Kepella rocked his head back and forth. All he could think about was Donnie. If Donnie had connected with that right . . . He no longer had to act scared. The Samoan was part gorilla—the mean part. "Listen"—Kepella fished for a name—"Peace Brother . . ."

"My name John Chu, Mr. Roy."

"John. I'm only one day late. Gimme a little room, will ya? Come on. I know I have to pay more points. Hey, that's okay. I understand. Who should I see? Mr. Holst? Is that who sent you? Is that who I should see?"

Chu studied him. Donnie was rubbing his sore side, anger gripping his features. "What you got, Mr. Roy? What can you come up with right now? I—we—gotta bring back something."

Kepella searched his pockets and his wallet. He dug up forty-five bucks and change. He stretched out his hand. Chu knocked the money out of Kepella's hands.

"Don't play with me, Mr. Roy. I need one hundred fifty. Please, reconsider your payment."

Kepella searched the room in a panic. He searched the alcove kitchen. Donnie and Chu followed him into his bedroom. It smelled like sour laundry. The bed was a mess, the sheets rumpled and stained. He grew frantic, ransacking his own apartment. He found ten bucks in the pocket of a pair of dirty pants. "I'm tapped out." He looked scared.

"How about this?" Chu waved Kepella's checkbook in the air.

"No such luck. Zero. Overdrawn, actually."

Chu kicked the bedroom door shut, closing all three of them in the small room. He nodded to Donnie. Donnie's hair was black and oily. His gray T-shirt fit tightly and ended inches above his belt, showing a band of dark Samoan skin and a hairy navel. Donnie slapped Kepella hard across the face, splitting Kepella's lip.

"What you do with money?" Chu asked.

Kepella looked around the room and then back at Chu. He knew what had to be done next. He knew the penalty, too. He gathered what little courage remained and charged Donnie. The two moved across the room in slow motion until Donnie slammed into the chest of drawers and Kepella's head sank farther into the man's abdomen. As Donnie rocked forward, Kepella jerked back and slammed his knee upward, catching the Samoan in the forehead. The man swayed and collapsed to his knees. Kepella turned and used what little training he could remember. He lifted his right leg and kicked out at the surprised Chu. But Chu was trained in martial arts. He deflected Kepella's attempted blow effortlessly, spun on his heels, and kicked Kepella in the jaw. Kepella was lifted off his feet and careened into the wall, then crashed to the floor. Donnie staggered over and worked on Kepella's abdomen until Chu pulled him off. Kepella, nearly unconscious, lay sprawled on the floor.

"What did you do with it?" Chu asked.

"Paid back Fu."

Chu nodded. Donnie slugged Kepella hard just above the groin. Kepella screamed.

"That bullshit, Mr. Roy. You pay Fu a thousand bucks. Where the rest of it?"

Kepella didn't need to act anymore. It was all real now; it had begun. "I blew it on the dogs. I thought I had something going, you know. I was up eleven hundred. I got this tip. I placed nearly all of it on this fine-looking greyhound out of Oregon. I thought I had it made."

Chu shook his head in disappointment. "You fucked up, Mr. Roy. I think you gonna have to have little talk with Mr. Holst." He turned to Donnie. "Clean him up."

Donnie dragged Kepella into the bathroom and slammed Kepella's head into the small sink, cutting it. Donnie turned on the water and let it run over Kepella's head before standing him back up. Kepella's head bobbed like a puppet's.

They parked next to a van near the Kingdome. One on either side, they walked Kepella into the vehicle and pulled the door closed. The back of the van was empty and windowless, the floor carpeted. A thick curtain separated the cargo area from the two front seats. Holst lifted the curtain and ducked into the back of the van. He reached up and switched on a small overhead light.

Kepella was still dizzy. He touched his wound and inspected the finger for blood. Nothing.

"You do not look too good, Roy." Holst's heavy accent bounced off the metal walls.

John Chu snuffled. Donnie rubbed his side.

"What the heck, Iben? I'm one day late."

"One day too many, Roy. I tried to warn you. You have to make those first few payments. That is why I asked John to pay you a visit. The people I secured this arrangement through will treat you much worse. If it had been them, Roy, you would be in the hospital, and then it all becomes even more expensive. So you see, I am only trying to help you out."

"You have a funny way of helping people."

"You are angry, Roy. I am sorry to see that. You see," he said to Chu, "it never pays to do business with friends." He glanced back to Kepella. "Never. No matter what the person says." He looked up at the dull green ceiling of the van. "I did try to discuss this with you, Roy. I tried to make you understand. I can leave you for my . . . associates, but I promise they play by an entirely different set of rules. John and his friend here are much more understanding than these other people will ever be. You should have made your first payment. Very important, these first few payments. Now it is time to try and help you through this. I can try to help, or I can go back to my . . . associates, and inform them you have reneged, and that I have—what is it you Americans say?—washed my hands of it? Your choice, Roy. Ah!" He stopped Kepella before he could respond. "But you had better give it some thought. You make the wrong decision now, my friend, and you will find yourself terribly alone. Frightfully alone."

Kepella noted that Iben had delivered all this in a cool, level voice. Yet he sensed an immediacy in the man, an urgency. The two stared at each other in the dimly lit confines of the rear of the van. Traffic moved past outside, tires whirring; a jet flew overhead, grumbling. Kepella touched his injured head and carefully inspected the tips of his fingers—a boy who had fallen down in the playground. "Maybe we can work a deal." Kepella winced as he touched his head again.

"What sort of deal?"

"Maybe you could borrow a little more for me, I could pay my first installment. Everyone is happy."

Astonishment covered Holst's face and he looked around in frustration. "And why would I trust you; Roy? Answer me that if you will."

"What else is there?"

"I told you the options, Roy. All I have to do is leave you off here and drive away. I turn it over to those who made the loan in the first place. You deal with them, or rather, I should say, they deal with you, and I no longer think about it."

"There has to be another way."

Holst studied him. "Perhaps you could liquidate assets? Generate some capital. How about that?"

"No. I don't own anything. I'm in debt to the bank, to this loan. I'm screwed, Iben."

"Your car?"

Kepella shook his head. "Bank owns the car."

"That old heap?"

"Dealer financing. I got it secondhand."

"That much is obvious."

Even Kepella grinned. Another jet flew low overhead. The earth seemed to shake.

Holst said, "There must be something you can sell. Think, Roy, think."

Kepella began nodding his head. Up and down. Up and down. He shut his eyes tightly and bobbed his head repeatedly. Then he seemed to change his mind. He rocked his head side to side. Side to side. "How much do you need?"

"One hundred and eighty dollars, Roy, by six tonight. Two-ten tomorrow."

"Will you give me a few hours? Please? Just a few hours?"

His pleading was wonderfully convincing. He looked back and forth between Holst and the two thugs, who stared at him with blank faces. Back and forth. Sweat covered his brow. His hands were shaking. "Please? A couple of hours, that's all . . . How 'bout it?"

"You would not try to run away on me, would you, Roy? That would be a terrible mistake, as I am certain you know."

"Run away? Me? Come on, Iben. I'd never do anything like that."

Holst nodded patiently. "Okay, Roy. You will have your few hours. You know my room. I will expect you there at exactly six o'clock this evening. Exactly at six. Do you understand?"

"A hundred and eighty bucks. I got it. Six o'clock."

"Fine. See you then." Holst cocked his head and John Chu opened the sliding door to the van.

Kepella scooted over to the door and stepped out into the rain. The air smelled fresh. His body hurt. His head had stopped bleeding. Chu and Donnie got out and walked over to the other car. The van started up and pulled away. The other car followed closely behind. Kepella watched the two cars blend into the procession of traffic. To his left, the Kingdome sat planted on acres of concrete, looking like a huge flying saucer that had landed and taken over the city. Ever so slowly a Cheshire grin stole onto Kepella's face. We're both playing our games, he told himself, and neither is supposed to know the other's intentions. But we both know the bottom line. You know I'm ready to sell. I pretend there is nothing to sell. I can see you drool, you weird German. I can see you think how clever you are, how you will turn the screws and make me give up what I have hidden. And of course you are right.

But everything in its own time. First, you need a little more convincing.

Kepella walked through the rain for several blocks and then turned right, continuing on to the corner of South Jackson and 3rd. King Street Station. He hoped it could work. Drenched by the time he entered the AMTRAK station, he could have easily been mistaken for a bum. His wet jacket drooped from his shoulders, giving him the posture of a tired ape. He ambled toward the ticket counter. John Chu had knocked all his cash out of his hand back at the apartment, so he had no money on him now. But he had a credit card, and if he kept the amount to less than twenty dollars, they wouldn't call in and check his credit—which was long since overdrawn. He knew if he made the trips in short installments he could get quite some distance. Of course, he hoped it wouldn't come to that. But he had to make it look like he was trying to run away. He had to be convincing.

The MasterCard worked fine. Holding the ticket, he looked at the big board: departure in fifteen minutes. He made it about twenty steps, twenty-five at most, before John Chu blocked his path, grabbed his hand, and snatched the ticket, shaking his head in disappointment. "Big mistake, Mr. Roy."

Donnie and Chu escorted him outside. He looked like a wet sheep dog being dragged to the front door by a housewife who had found him curled up on her sofa. Inside, though, he was elated. It was going just as he had hoped. He had gambled and won, knocking what might have been a two-week process down to a little over an hour. The gamble had been a necessity. He knew he couldn't hold up under too much physical abuse. Brandenburg's version would have required several beatings, and Holst was right: some of these guys would beat Kepella to a pulp—or worse—without a second thought. That was unthinkable, an unacceptable solution. No, the solution was to pretend to run, be caught, suffer through one more beating, and then get on with the operation—on with the show. He actually felt good about being escorted out of King Street Station by these two mugs, and he wondered how many other people would feel good knowing someone was about to beat the shit out of them.

They sat Kepella down in the only chair in the room. Holst stood above him, glaring. "You tried to leave the city, Roy. This was very foolish of you. Very foolish. You are lucky again. If I was a different kind of person, I would have these two men break your legs. Then it takes a person longer to get around." Red-faced, he yelled, "I should have had them kill you!" He huffed, lit a cigarette, and paced the room. Donnie and John Chu stood silently by the door. The room smelled like a ripe woman.

"I was going to Kelso to borrow money from a friend."

"Roy, Roy . . . do not lie to me, Roy. You dig your grave more quickly than I can fill it back in."

"I swear, I'll get the money for you. One hundred and eighty by tonight at six. No problem. You let me go and—"

"Shut up!" Holst continued to pace. John Chu smiled viciously, the hound expecting the steak.

"Tell them to leave the room."

"Why should I, Roy?"

"Just do it, Holst. Damn it, do it!" Kepella's face was scarlet. Veins pulsed on either side of his neck. "Do it!"

Holst nodded. Chu opened the door. Holst said, "Wait in the lobby. I'll call. Donnie waits outside the door." Chu nodded. The two left the room.

"Well?" Holst asked.

"Fu lied to you," Kepella said, dropping his head and staring at the floor.

"Go on."

"He told you I wasn't the FBI agent. I am."

"What?" Holst tried to sound surprised. He wasn't very convincing.

"Ex-agent."

"What?"

That time was better, thought Kepella. "The suspended agent."

"I loaned money to an FBI agent?"

"Ex . . ."

"Oh, Roy. You should not have told me this. You have put me in a very—"

"Listen to me, Holst. You're missing the picture here. Give me a chance."

Holst finished the cigarette and lit another. His acting improved with each minute.

Kepella thought, How strange. Both of us acting and only I know it. He said, "I have some things that are worth a great deal of money to the right parties."

Holst studied Kepella carefully, still pacing. "Such as?"

"Information. Information only an FBI man could have access to. Important information."

"To whom?"

"To the right people."

"And who are these people?"

"I thought you might know."

"Me, Roy? Why would I know such things?"

Kepella felt the sweat break out on the palms of his hands.

"You want a drink, Roy?" Holst pulled an unopened bottle of Popov out of the dresser drawer.

"No, thanks anyway."

"What?" Holst inquired. "No drink?" He looked sternly at Kepella, doubting. "Have a drink, Roy." He handed the bottle to Kepella and tossed him a seven-ounce glass.

Kepella caught the glass. He looked at the bottle. All this time pretending. All this time skillfully acting half-drunk, and now this. What could he do? He had to play the role. No problem. To refuse the drink would not be in character.

He unscrewed the cap. The familiar sound of the seal breaking made his heart pound. Excitement pulsed through him, and he wanted to cry out in delight and kill himself, all in the same moment. He poured a couple of fingers' worth, closed his eyes, and gulped it down. Guilt overwhelmed him. His guilt was two-fold: guilt at having put himself in this situation; guilt that it felt so good going down his throat. Yes, it felt good. He wanted another.

"Another," Holst told him.

Kepella poured and swallowed. Warmth filled his gut where only hollowness had been. God, it felt good. The warmth spread through him in seconds—down to his toes and up, up his spine, numbing the base of his brain.

"Have one more," Holst offered.

Kepella poured and drank. When he looked up at Holst, tears filled his eyes. His twisted smile revealed the gleeful agony—the face of a young soldier who has just killed for his first time. So that's why they call them shots, Kepella thought.

"Talk to me, Roy." Holst sat down on the edge of the bed.

Kepella poured himself another small one and drank it. "I protected myself . . . when I left the Bureau."

"How?"

"I took some important documents with me. Information." "Valuable information," he said again.

"So what?"

"So . . . it's worth a shitload of money to the right people. You have contacts, you find someone to buy. I'll sell 'em. I'll pay you your fucking money . . . I'll pay off the whole fucking loan, Holst."

"What kind of valuable information? I have to know who to look for, is that not true, Roy?" he asked, bringing Kepella's attention back from the bottle of Popov.

The top of Kepella's spine felt good and dull. His hands pulsed with a familiar warmth. Very relaxed and controlled. This was the *real* Roy Kepella. "All kinds. I raided the files. I have everything from personality profiles to computer chip designs. We handle the entire Northwest, you know?" he said proudly. "A lot of the high-tech shit comes from Boise. Defense from Boeing, here in Seattle, the shipyards, Navy, you name it."

"Where is this stuff, Roy?"

"Locked away. Yes, sir. Locked away. Nobody gets at it but me. Made sure of that. I'm not fucking dumb, you know?" he said, slurring his words and sounding dumb and pitiful. He stared at the bottle, wanting more.

"Go ahead, Roy," Holst prodded, seeing Kepella's interest.

"No, I better not."

"I don't care if you do, Roy. It doesn't bother me."

"You want one?"

179

Holst thought a moment and decided to break a rule. "Sure." He leaned over to the chest of drawers, picked up the paper-covered glass, and handed it carefully to Kepella. "Pour me a light one, Roy."

Kepella poured them both drinks. They touched glasses. Kepella sucked down the booze and stared at the bottle. Holst sipped and then downed it all in one gulp. He set the glass down next to Kepella's.

"I can't pay you, Iben. I don't have a cent."

"That is what I thought. We will arrange another loan quickly, Roy. How does that sound? Say another five thousand. I will make sure you pay off Fu, and that will leave you some interest money and some spending change. Maybe even enough to play a couple of games."

"I like poker, Iben," Kepella said childishly, trapped somewhere between his cover identity, the sober Roy Kepella, and this, the drunk Roy Kepella.

"What do you say, Roy?"

"Sounds like a winner to me, Iben. Sure, why not?"

"Same terms?"

"Why not?"

"Five thousand?"

"The shit I've got is worth ten times that, twenty maybe. You find me a buyer, Iben. We'll pay these assholes back before the week is up. I'll cut you in for fifteen percent."

"That sounds good, Roy. I will have a look around. How can I reach you?"

Kepella wanted to laugh. "You know where I live."

"You will not run away again, will you, Roy? I would be forced to play rough the next time."

The next time? he wanted to say. Kepella hurt all over,

even half-numb. "No way. I'm here to stay. You find a buyer."

"I will have a look around."

"Too bad these windows don't open."

"Why is that?"

"Because it smells kind of sour in here. Like some broad left her shorts under the bed."

Holst smiled.

But Kepella was thinking, Because, you fucking Nazi, if your window opened I might just jump out and kiss all of you assholes good-bye. I hate this fucking world.

22

You came to me from out of nowhere . . .

Jay heard the lyrics in his head. It wasn't Marlene he was thinking about, it was the approaching storm. They were sailing five miles off the coast and a son-of-a-bitch storm had appeared out of nowhere. To make matters worse, the wheel was sticking. Marlene was dressed in blue jeans and a man-tailored white-cotton buttondown to keep off the chill. He yelled forward, "Drop the jib when I head into the wind."

She looked at him, puzzled, and hollered back, "Why?"

He pointed ahead of them and started to explain, but before his message was over the rain hit. It pelted down hard enough to hurt. With another crew, or even alone, Jay might have continued sailing, but not with Marlene along. This kind of storm would bring strong winds and large swells—too much for the amateur. He pointed *The Lady*

Fine into the wind. The sails luffed, flapping violently. He watched as Marlene dropped the jib. She did a better job of it than last time and quickly had it secured. She was a fast learner. He held the boat into the wind, already soaking wet by the time Marlene pantomimed whether or not the mainsail should come down. Jay nodded. Marlene worked furiously. Halfway down, Jay jumped up and furled it onto the mast to keep it from falling all over the cockpit. He looked up. Marlene, drenched to the bone, had tied off the main halyard and was busy rolling the sail in on itself. Jay crudely tied the sail off in several spots, then moved toward Marlene. The wet shirt clung to her breasts and her stringy hair pressed against her face. Her eyes were haunting in the eerie light beneath the dark gray clouds.

There was no sense to it. Perhaps there is never any sense to such things, Jay thought. The two of them embraced and kissed passionately, rain streaking down their smiling faces. He held her in his arms and hugged her. She giggled. "Go below," he instructed, already leading her toward the cockpit. The rain had become torrential. Jay located two large, cloth sea anchors and, after cleating their lines, threw them overboard. He opened the companionway, stepped inside, and turned to shut it. The boat rocked from the wind; rain blurred the portholes.

Before he turned around she said, "I left a beach towel for you there." He heard her shirt slosh as it hit the floorboards. He turned around. She had moved forward and pulled the door to the head open as a shield, behind which she was changing with her back to him. He saw a bare arm. "Your turn," she said, walking past the door toward him. She was wrapped in a bright red towel, holding it around herself like a giant cape. She walked in tiny steps, like a geisha confined by her kimono. Behind her, Jay saw her clothes in a soggy pile. *All* her clothes.

They were silent, facing each other as the boat tossed in the swells. She stood motionless. Jay inched closer to her. He took her face in his hands . . .

She felt her body trembling as he moved closer, and though she wanted to blame it on the chill from being wet, she knew this wasn't the only reason. It was him. It was the kiss up on deck. It was the rain. Her heart raced as she felt his hands on her face. She had known what would happen before he had come below. She *wanted* it to happen; and that in itself was something of a miracle. But so was Jay Becker. The rain drummed the deck. She opened her lips and, let him kiss her. His kisses were tender and careful, as if he were afraid of breaking her delicate features. She didn't know *how* to kiss. Not really. But her body took over and she quickly felt so lightheaded she thought she might faint. She felt his hands skimming over the surface of the towel, and suddenly the towel was keeping them too far away. She longed for the touch of his skin. Abandoning her attempt to hold the towel shut with crossed arms, she reached to hug him and the towel fell. His hand raced over the bumps of her rib cage, swept across her breast and shoulder, and then slipped below her arms and squeezed her tightly. Their tongues danced together. His wet shirt pressed against her bared chest and yet felt warm. *He* was trembling.

She pulled his shirttail out and slid her hands up his back, pulling him closer. His hands flowed down her back and gripped her buttocks and pulled her against him. God, she thought, she might pass out. Her head was spinning, knees shaking. Then she felt herself choke. She fought the sensation. Not now! Please, God, not now. Does one never stop paying for one's sins? Is this what you are telling a minister's daughter? Must one pay forever? She began to cry, hoping Jay might mistake her tears for water running from her hair. Let him love me, she prayed silently. Leave me alone and let him love me. But the tears continued.

Jay had unbuttoned his shirt and pulled it off. He was about to take her in his arms again when he noticed.

"I am sorry," she sobbed.

Misunderstanding her tears, he said, "No, it's me that should be sorry." He tried a smile. "I guess I got carried away."

She took a step toward him, hooked her fingers in his belt, and pulled him down with her as she lay back on the flooring. Jay pressed against her naked body and they kissed. She pulled his reluctant hand from his side and placed it on her skin, below her breast. He caressed her softly, and then ran his tongue around her nipple. She shivered and sighed. He kissed her lips again and she responded hungrily. She felt so good all over, so wonderfully good, she could hardly stand it. She felt her juices flowing, a warm, swelling pulse between her legs. So good, she thought, wondering what could ever feel better. My God, she thought. My God! And then he touched her there and she jerked. It felt so strange, like they were melting together. She wanted to be part of him. He rubbed her softly and the warmth, the swelling, turned to a hotness that felt as if it might burst. "My God!" she whispered in his ear.

Her sobbing returned immediately, so suddenly in fact, it was more like the storm that had hit them. He pulled his hand away. She rocked her head to one side. "I am sorry, Jay."

"Shhh," he cooed. "Don't worry." He pulled the fallen towel over her naked body and lay by her side, stroking her collarbone with his finger.

Between their two scents, the air smelled electric to her. She wanted to melt into him. "It is not you," she insisted. "This is wonderful. I mean it. I have never, ever . . . Well, that is the point, is it not?" She rocked her head back over and looked him in the eye. His eyes were deep blue. His face seemed boyish this close, and his dark, wet hair shone. She stretched her neck and kissed him once gently. "I must tell you something." He nodded. "It is something I have never told another person, but I *must* tell you. Will you listen?"

"With all my heart," he whispered back.

She wondered what was going through his mind. Could she tell Jay Becker what she had never told another soul? And she knew not only that she *could,* but that she *had* to. She nodded at him, sensing his sincerity, and gathered her strength. "I am twenty-seven years old." She paused, as tears threatened again to stop her. "I have not even kissed a man in eight years. I can not remember what it is like . . . what to do—"

"You kiss wonderfully."

"It is why I am so nervous, I guess." She rubbed his ear with her finger. "When I was eighteen I became ill. I was at university. After a month I became nauseous and my roommate put me to bed. Several weeks of this and my roommate demanded I see a doctor. The doctors ran a dozen tests. It took them two weeks to think of something I had not considered possible." She paused and then whispered, "I was pregnant." She looked away and began crying. Jay waited. She finally looked back at him. "To this day I am not certain when it happened." Then she sobbed again and tried to collect herself. "It was a party. I went with a close friend of mine to this party. I drank the punch. No one told me it was filled with vodka. I never tasted the vodka, I just suddenly felt lightheaded." She paused again, thinking, Like I did just now. "I asked my friend to take me home. He agreed. My roommate asked me the next morning why I had stayed out so late. I felt so horrible, it never occurred to me that I had asked to go home early. Later . . . once I was pregnant, I realized what had become of those missing hours." She cried, but her sobs were partially covered by the pounding of the rain.

"I'd like to kill him."

She tried to smile. "Believe me, I wanted to also." She shook her wet hair from side to side. "No, no, that is not true. I could never kill anyone." She looked back at Jay. "It was too far along for an abortion—besides, my father is a minister and well . . . So, I made an excuse to him about a summer course and I stayed on with my roommate at the apartment and I had the child." A steady stream of tears ran from her eyes. "Before birth, I put it up for adoption," she said, shaking. "I never even *saw* it. I never even saw *my own baby.*" She reached up and threw her arms around Jay's neck, hugging him tightly. "I have never kissed a man since," she whispered into his ear. "I have never allowed myself to even *think* about it. Until you. From the moment

I saw you across the way, on *The Lazy Daze,* somehow I knew you would be the one. I was drawn to you."

She felt Jay squeeze her even harder. She wondered what he could be thinking. Had he sensed her innocence? Had he sensed her secret? Had she spoiled everything by telling him?

"Kiss me," she begged.

He kissed her gently, but without the previous enthusiasm.

"What is it?" she asked, dreading his answer.

"Not like this," he said. "Not here. Not now. It must be done slowly. You need time."

"No, Jay. I need you. I have never even *wanted* the affection. It is so amazing, how I feel right now, I can not tell you. I have *never* felt this way. *Ever!* I will not trap you. Is that not what I am supposed to say? I *promise* I will not trap you . . . but I *need* you. I need your affection. Do you understand?" She kissed his lips and he returned the kiss. She ran her fingers over his chest and again pulled his hand to her breast.

They kissed and touched and explored one another. Then Jay pulled back. Marlene's face tightened. He said, "We shouldn't."

Silence. Her chest heaved up and down with her deep breaths. Her green eyes seemed slightly unfocused. "What is it?"

"We can not make love, Marlene. Not here, not now. Not you and I like this."

"What do you mean? What do you mean, not you and I?"

"We deserve better than this . . ."

"Better than this?"

He laughed. "I don't mean *this* like that."

"You are confusing me."

"I mean, it's better if we wait. It will be even *better* if we give it time." He paused. "I care for you very much, Marlene."

She threw her arms around him.

They sat in the same ice cream parlor, the same chairs, that they had sat in a few days earlier. Five minutes ago it had started to rain again. "I can not remember ever being out in a storm like that," she said enthusiastically, her eyes glassy, cheeks flushed. She looked like the Queen of Health, despite her uncombed hair. The loose foul-weather gear hung off her shoulders and made noise when she shifted in her chair. "I cannot remember ever having two ice cream cones in the same week, either." She smiled, a warmth still pulsing through her. She had never ever felt like this. She wanted to laugh, she felt so good.

Jay's dark hair lay flat against his skull. He looked like a little boy. His eyes nearly matched the vibrant blue of his Gore-Tex jacket, which was slung over a chair behind him. He licked his chocolate cone.

She could still picture them both on the towel, the boat rocking seductively. Exploring. She could *feel* him kissing her. She shuddered, leaned forward, and whispered, "I am glad it rained." Then she blushed. The thin hairs on her neck stood up as a heat consumed her.

He blushed. "Me too. And thank you for sharing that with me. It was one of the most tender moments in my life, Marlene. No one has ever shared something like that with me. I feel privileged."

"I will not pressure you, Jay. You do not need to worry about . . ."

"Marlene . . ."

". . . that. I will be leaving soon, that is, after the regatta." She leaned across the table. She wanted to kiss him. Right here, right now. She wanted him to touch her again. Now. "No matter what, I will always remember today," she whispered, ". . . and you."

"There's more, isn't there, Marlene?"

Astonishment filled her face. "Why do you say this?"

"What is it?"

"I cannot."

"Yes, Marlene. That's the point: You can. You can tell me *anything*. Don't you believe that?"

She ran her fingers through her hair. "I cannot."

"Please."

"I really—"

"Marlene!" barked Holst's voice.

Her face paled. Jay thought she might faint.

She looked toward the door. Holst stood there, neatly dressed, his short hair perfectly arranged. Defined. He cocked his head. She was to come with him. Marlene looked at Jay and shuddered. Her brow knitted and she whispered even more softly, "I must go."

Jay nodded reluctantly. He wanted to pop Holst in the chin. "Thanks," he said quietly.

"Tomorrow," she told him affectionately, standing and holding her cone.

Holst held the door to the small parlor open for her. Once she passed by him he looked down at Jay, who was looking up. The two locked eyes and all was said, right there and then.

The screen door banged shut.

23

Sharon was treated as a guest. François, after leaving her with Claudia and Katrina, had checked in a few times, usually bringing food from the galley. Katrina was a chambermaid; Claudia, a waitress. They went out of their way to shield Sharon and make her comfortable.

In four days of sailing they had had only one close call, when the ship's navigator, who had his eye on Katrina, came looking to ask her for a date. Sharon had stood behind the door while Claudia shooed him away. The Dramamine they gave her quieted her stomach. She was clean, comfortable, and well rested. Since the quarters were crowded and hot, the three of them spent most of the time in tank tops and panties talking, laughing, sharing men stories. It reminded Sharon of the dormitory at Vassar.

Katrina had a low voice, warm and husky. Claudia claimed her roommate was Russian, though to Sharon the accent sounded French, like everyone else's. Katrina said, "It is too bad you cannot go up to the deck, yes? The air is so fresh there. You would like it much," Katrina laughed throatily. "We are to New York soon."

"Are we on schedule?"

"Yes, of course."

"Four more days then?"

"Yes, four days I think. Then it is to New York. You will leave us there?"

Sharon nodded.

There was a quick knock on the door. The handle moved and the door swung open. The navigator saw two females in scanty underclothes: Katrina sitting in front of a mirror applying eye shadow; another girl, unfamiliar to him, sitting on the lowest bunk, very pretty but blushing. If this girl had not shut her legs quickly, he might not have given her a second look, so intent was he on the lovely Katrina. But her movement caught his eye because none of the crew was modest: they shared bathrooms, showers, swimming pools; on deck L, a private crew deck, many of the woman went topless and the men often wore nothing at all—the European way. This woman was not one of them! Not recognizing her, he asked angrily, "Who is she?"

Katrina jumped up, pulled the man inside the tiny cabin, and shut the door. She replied in their native tongue. "Don't you dare say a word, Jean-Paul, or it is the last you've seen of me."

"Who is she?" His anger grew. "A stowaway? Mother Mary, Katrina, do you know what *they* will do to you if they find out?"

"And who's going to tell them?"

"I must tell them."

"Jean-Paul, don't you dare!"

"What choice is left to me?"

"Jean-Paul . . ." Katrina wrapped her arms around his neck and pushed herself against him. "A few more days is all."

He pushed her away, opening the cabin door. "No, Katrina. It is against the rules. I am an officer—"

Sharon interrupted. "It's all right, Katrina." She spoke to

the man. "I will see your captain, but only your captain, do you understand?"

"Impossible."

"It must be your captain, only the captain."

"And why is that, young lady?"

"Because . . ." She hesitated, not wanting to tell anyone. "I am an agent of the United States Central Intelligence Agency—the CIA. It can be checked. I am on an operation. It is imperative that I reach New York without anyone's knowledge. My life is in danger." She made it as dramatic as she could. "I will see your captain, and then you must be sworn to secrecy."

They both stared at her, shock on their faces. Katrina's mouth hung open. Jean-Paul took a step backward through the door. "I won't say a thing," he said in English. "I promise. I never saw you," he added.

Sharon looked over at the stunned Katrina. As she did, a man passed behind the navigator and managed to glance over the navigator's shoulder at the two women inside. He was a tall man with thick lips, though Sharon did not see his face. He raised a hand to shield his face from her and hurried down the narrow corridor. The navigator pulled the cabin door shut.

Alone with Sharon, Katrina recovered and asked, "How did you ever think of that? You sounded so convincing. What a line. You are so clever, Sharon, so very clever." Katrina continued to stare at her new friend, waiting. All she got was a shrug.

An hour later a hurried knock startled both women. The door opened a crack, and a high female voice said in

French, "Katrina, Claudia, a fire in storage room C. We must evacuate immediately. Hurry!"

Katrina turned to face Sharon. "It's quite a ways down. If it threatens this area, I will send François. You are safer if you stay, yes?"

"Yes. Hurry. I will be fine."

Katrina spoke quickly as she donned a robe. "François is in charge of making certain all the cabins are cleared. He'll warn you if it is serious. These things happen frequently. Nothing to worry about." She opened the door and left.

Footfalls padded down the metal corridor past Sharon's door. Voices and confusion continued for another few minutes, followed by silence. Sharon tried to force herself to read.

She saw the door open and thought it would be François, When she saw him, she screamed. It was like a nightmare: the tall man with thick lips; the same man who had chased her the night of Brian's death! How could *he* be on board *La Mer Verde?* Impossible . . . unless the conduit had still been alive and able to talk . . .

The man pushed the cabin door shut and came straight for her, knife in hand. Only then did she see the syringe protruding from his top pocket. He won't cut me, she thought, he'll use drugs and make it look like natural causes, protecting himself. That's to my advantage. Before she could even contemplate a move, he was on top of her, pinning her against the hot metal flooring, the blade held against her throat. He was much to heavy to move. She writhed below him, bucking in an attempt to dump him off her. The man didn't budge. With his left hand, he reached for the syringe.

She had no choice. She rocked forward, the blade cutting her neck, and bit down on his thumb. He moved just slightly, but enough for her to use it. She lifted her right leg and tilted him as he lifted the syringe.

He held the syringe high in the air. Out of the corner of her eye Sharon saw it hovering above her. He would drop his hand now. He would kill her. She bit down even harder, drawing blood.

She saw the syringe stop moving. Then she saw the hairy hand wrapped around her killer's wrist. François took the killer's hair in his right hand and jerked the man's head back, then pinched the man's throat between two strong fingers, choking him. François redirected the syringe until it was an inch from the killer's neck. The killer's eyes opened wide and he tried to shake his head no. He dropped the knife. He wanted to drop the syringe but François controlled his left hand. "No . . ." he gasped in German. "No."

In one quick movement, François shifted his weight and drove the man backward, ramming the killer's head between Sharon's legs and onto the metal floor. The killer went slack, unconscious. François's face was covered in sweat.

Sharon, now sitting upright, still gripped the killer's thumb between her teeth, her neck bleeding. François asked, "Are you all right?"

24

Wind howled savagely across the stays. Rain pelted the decks. Marlene had gone off shopping and was due back in about two hours.

Last night's gig had been a disaster. Books had blamed it on the weather. Jay had blamed it on the band. Something had gone bad, and the music had never jelled. What had started out as a fairly good-sized crowd had ended up ten people and, as a result, the bar manager had let the band off early. Sometimes Jay didn't know why he did it: up on stage, singing personal songs to total strangers, opening himself up, lucky if three people applauded. Oh, there were times when the crowd went wild, fell right into the palm of his hand, was entertained, caught up in the lyrics or the beat. But more often than not, a gig was four hours of indecent exposure, while people treated you like dog dirt and ignored your efforts. Even when the crowd was enthusiastic, Jay often didn't feel right. A part of him didn't belong up on stage. Music was a thankless job. And yet, one day, with the help of a couple of DJ's, it might all change. Critics would ascribe symbolism to the lyrics, others would herald the band's creativity and professionalism; the crowds would come. People would listen and enjoy. Then maybe this decade of lugging heavy gear, ringing ears, impossible group politics, overdue bills, low pay, and bad food, would all be worth it. Maybe.

He devoted his mid-morning to the interior "chrome," as he called it: the stainless steel that covered every latch, knob, and window crank in *The Lady Fine*'s teak interior. Even the so-called stainless would pit from the continual exposure to salt air if it wasn't rubbed down every few days. He finished the job and turned his attention to cleaning the small portholes.

An hour later, the windows clean, Marlene had still not

returned. Running out of things to do, Jay debated washing down the vinyl seat cushions, but then, hearing the hard rain, decided to take her out for a trial run. He had not sailed *The Lady Fine* solo in a storm, and if there was one place a person learned about a boat, it was under adverse conditions. He switched on the diesel and warmed it up, going below to don foul-weather gear. Once topside, he rigged the dodger—a canopy rigging that covered the companionway—unfastened lines, and backed *The Lady Fine* out of her slip. He motored around the massive breakwater and checked his watch, noting that he had at least an hour to kill before Marlene returned. A few hundred yards past the breakwater he pointed her into the wind and kicked her into neutral, moving quickly forward to raise the mains'il. Rain splattered against the thick rubber foul weather gear and he smiled. There was something exciting about sailing in the rain, like skiing in a snowstorm. The mains'il went up easily, and although the rain fell hard, the wind was tolerable, so Jay decided against reefing. He winched it taut and tied it off. He had not sailed *The Lady* alone, and he was loving it.

It was a freak happening. A tremendous gust of wind blew off of windward and kicked the main sheet around the steering column. The same gust pumped into the mains'il, filling it with life and jerking the main sheet hard. The resulting jerk snagged the main sheet and made it fast around the steering column. *The Lady Fine* heeled quickly and cut into the Sound with all the determination of a racer. Jay was thrown off balance—nearly overboard. Jesus Christ, he thought, she should correct herself and steer into the wind. She was rigged to pull herself out of these situations. The wheel should just spin and allow her to head up. He fought to keep his balance, *The Lady* heeling. He threw his weight forward in an effort to reach the rail that ran alongside the companionway. His fingers grasped the wood, and he pulled himself against the main cabin and made his way to the cockpit, the dodger flapping noisily in the wind and rain. Feeling suddenly uneasy, he glanced quickly over his shoulder, over the bow. *The Lady Fine* was headed straight for a finger of rock not a quarter mile away. Another gust rocked the boat as Jay made his move for the cockpit. He lost his footing, swayed, and slipped. He fell to the narrow deck, reaching for anything to stop him. Nothing there. *The Lady* jerked hard, heeling farther over. His feet caught in the rushing water and the drag sucked him overboard. He slipped into the foam beneath the rail, screaming for help. At the last possible second, his fingers hooked around a stanchion and he managed to hold on, still dragging alongside the boat. The foul-weather hat flew off his head, but was held around his neck by its strap. It quickly filled with water, like a bucket held overboard, and the string choked him. He was losing his grip. He pulled hard and took hold with both hands, and then used all his strength to pull himself aboard. He looked up ahead. The boat would hit the rocks in just a few minutes. He fell into the cockpit, reached quickly for the mainsheet, and attempted to free it, noticing for the first time that the mechanism had jammed and tangled, and was hopelessly knotted on itself. He pulled on the steering wheel—and there was the problem. It had jammed. He tugged hard, port, starboard, port—nothing. It was frozen stuck. The rock jetty was only a hundred yards off the bow, *The Lady*

Fine steaming for it. Jay had no choice. He quickly hurried forward, nearly falling overboard again, and uncleated the main halyard. The mains'il tumbled down. The boat righted in the water and slowed. He hurried aft, switched on the diesel, and placed the transmission in reverse, revving the engine. *The Lady Fine* slowed even more, water boiling behind her. Jay hurried below, located a sea anchor, and a few minutes later had it tossed overboard. He punched the transmission to neutral, reducing the engine's rpms. Then he unfastened the foul-weather hat, ducked beneath the dodger, and entered the companionway. The rain fell noisily. He had stopped the boat fifty yards from the rock jetty—too close. Much too close.

Five minutes later, screwdriver in hand, he removed the port shelf in Marlene's aft cabin. On each side of the cabin, removable shelves allowed access to the steering cable. He had inspected the starboard side of the mechanism—the cables branched around either side of the aft cabin via a network of pulleys—and had found everything in order. But as he aimed the flashlight into the port side, he saw it: a rectangular bundle of some sort covered carelessly in a plastic bag that had become hopelessly snagged in the for-ward-most pulley. He tore at the plastic and removed the box. A videotape! Jay was at once furious at whoever had done this. It was by far the most *stupid* place to store video-tapes that Jay could think of. Then he realized they were not being stored; they were being *hidden.* He cleared the plastic bag from the pulley and, a few minutes later, returned the shelf to its proper position, the steering now operational.

He motored back to Shilshole. The sail had been spoiled

and he was soaking wet. When *The Lady Fine* was secure, Jay went below to change into his swim trunks and a T-shirt that he kept in a duffel bag in the forward cabin. He walked past the videotape and couldn't resist. Still in his foul-weather gear he went topside and connected the boat to the pier electricity, went back below, and threw a switch that turned on the VCR. He placed the first of the two tapes inside and ran it while he changed.

A smoke-filled room was illuminated by a single funnel of light over a table. A group of men and an ugly Chinese woman were playing poker. In the lower left-hand corner an arm came into view, carrying a newspaper. The newspaper stopped in front of the camera, close enough to read the date: August 14, two weeks ago. Jay knew he should turn off the tape; this was none of his business. He leaned forward anyway. That's when Iben Holst walked into view on screen, carrying the newspaper. He sat down and spoke with a guy who had a pushed-in face, tacky clothes, and resembled Karl Malden. The Chinaman's voice was hard to understand. He introduced the man to Holst as Roy . . . something. Jay watched a minute and then fast-forwarded the tape, intrigued. The tape cut to a new scene. "Roy," Holst, and the Chinaman were arguing in an office that looked like a compartment in a mobile home. Mr. Roy, as the Chinaman called him, was apparently in debt to the tune of eleven grand and, after a moment, Holst was offering to get him hooked up with a loan shark. Jay wanted to turn the machine off but couldn't. He continued to watch, his heart pounding now. He didn't know who was who in this thing, but either Holst or Marlene had taped it for some reason and had then hidden the tape. It had none of the professional quality that Jay had seen on TV in clips of FBI Abscam cases: there was no clock running in the corner and the sound was poor. Then he realized that the newspaper Holst had been carrying had dated the tape, which explained why it had been held in view for such a long count. Holst was no FBI agent, that much was clear. The German was either protecting himself somehow, or blackmailing "Roy." Jay fast-forward/searched again, holding down a button in order to preview the action at a faster speed. He had managed to shed the wet clothing and, as he let the machine return to play, toweled himself off. The screen blinked and a new scene appeared. Jay let the action return to normal speed.

"Jay?" He spun around, pulling the towel around his waist. Marlene stood on the ladder in the companionway, rain beating down on the overhead dodger, a puzzled expression on her face.

He pushed the stop button. *Click.* "I went for a sail to test her in a gale. The steering stuck. I went overboard—damn near lost *The Lady.*" He picked up the tape box. "This jammed the steering mechanism. That's why it's been sticking lately. It was a stupid place to put tapes, Marlene. I was curious."

"What are they of?"

"Come on! They were in *your* cabin."

"What?"

He hesitated. "What's going on? Tell me."

"In *my* cabin?"

He nodded. "Under the shelf. The plastic bag had jammed the forward-most pulley." Jay became angry.

"What's going on here, Marlene? Tell me."

She stared solemnly at him and inched her way down the steep stairs, then set her bags down.

"Marlene?"

"What are you doing?" she asked incredulously, still unable to believe Holst had hidden the tape on board *The Lady*. Why inside the shelf? Didn't he have *any* sense? And just what was she supposed to tell Jay?

"What is this?" He was holding the empty plastic cassette box in his hand and waving it about aimlessly. "What the hell is this?"

"I don't know."

His face flushed. "Marlene, what's going on? What are you involved in?" He walked over and took hold of her. It seemed impossible that Marlene could be involved in something like blackmail. Not Marlene, his Marlene.

"I have never seen those tapes before. I swear to you."

He shook her gently. "Tell me the truth. Please, Marlene. I need the truth. I can help."

She stared at him, unable to speak.

He stormed past her, turned, and glared. "I'm not coming back, Marlene. Not until you straighten this out. All I ask for is the truth. I have a right to the truth. That wasn't so hard yesterday, was it?" He grabbed his wet clothes and slammed the door to the head behind himself. A moment later he came out and left.

She glanced at the television. It was hissing, gray sparks dancing against a blue background. She walked unsteadily to the VCR and removed the tape from the machine. She saw the torn plastic bag on the cabin floor, picked up the tape box, and did her best at packaging it up. She hurried now, up the stairs, under the dodger, into her cabin. Both shelves were open. Which one had Holst hidden the tape in? She guessed the starboard section, placed the bundled tape inside, and replaced both teak shelves. She looked around the small cabin nervously. Holst had a ferocious temper; if she had guessed wrong there was no telling what he might do . . .

The jukebox played Tower of Power. Behind Kepella a skinny black woman danced topless, a wad of one-dollar bills tucked into her G-string. Kepella, his back to the dancer, sat watching lights flash on an electronic pinball machine a few feet away where a black youth was busy scoring past 458,000. Two balls left. Roy slugged down the remaining vodka, holding the glass firmly in his hand. He swallowed sensually, a connoisseur savoring a fine wine. But this was raw vodka. And this was Roy Kepella's seventh.

Damn peaceful world, he thought. A couple of shots, that nice warm spot in the belly, the nice numb glow at the back of the skull; everyone seemed nice, happy; he felt happy enough, no big worries. Nothing major. He had puked once—nothing major. It left room for another couple of rounds. He wasn't even thinking, really. Oh, a few images would surface and toy around on some level of consciousness, but nothing too pressing. His mind had all the fluidity of setting cement.

Kepella paid for number eight. Ball five on the pinball light show, 678,000. Two free games. New high score. The thin dancer's pelvis was rocking, her tits bouncing. Kepella turned around and tried to focus on her. Nice butt, he thought. Nice strong butt.

He drank number eight painlessly. It was easy now. He was right back in the swing of things. He walked over to the pay phone, put in a quarter, and dialed a number. An answering service answered. Kepella left the pay phone number. A minute later the pay phone rang. He answered it quickly, but with all the coordination of a drunk. "Go," he said, obliged to wait ten seconds. Then he said, "First call," and hung up. He could picture Brandenburg on the other end, smiling perhaps, or nodding into the phone. Kepella had little tolerance for the Brandenburgs of the world. They were too young to have any real experience, yet they tossed their weight around.

He walked over to the black man winning at pinball and slapped him on the back. The man missed a flipper shot; the steel ball rolled into the guts of the machine. Game over, a little light proclaimed. The black man turned and slugged Kepella in the gut, yelling, "Fuck off, man. You fucked up my game." He stood Kepella up and slugged him hard. Two biker types stopped the black man. Kepella rested on his knees, buckled over. The black man struggled. "Hey, you leave me be. This meathead fucked with my game. He fucked my game."

A man who moved with the assurance of a manager helped Kepella to his feet and escorted him to the door. "Sorry, my friend. I think it's time you go home now." He pushed the door open and helped Kepella to the sidewalk. Kepella looked around. First Avenue: the seedy side of Seattle. A bus pulled up and, without even reading the destination, Kepella painfully climbed the steps, pulling himself up along the rail. He reached the driver, searched his pockets, and stumbled back off the bus. He had had a ten-spot folded up in his wallet, tucked behind his driver's license for emergencies. At a buck a drink he should have had two dollars somewhere, but if he did, he couldn't find it.

He started walking in the rain. He was ten blocks toward his apartment before he remembered that Brandenburg had insisted he hide himself once the deal was in full swing. Brandenburg wanted to take all precautions—and after his last meeting with John Chu and the Samoan, Kepella agreed.

He turned around and, dragging his feet, headed for Rosie's.

Rosie opened the door to her apartment. She knew something was wrong. "Where you been, Roy?"

His voice was drunk and angry. "I'm gonna stay with you for a while, if that's all right."

"You drunk," she informed him, her disappointment obvious.

"You right," he replied crisply, mocking her. "Can I borrow a twenty?"

She went into the bedroom, came out, and handed him two tens. He jammed the money into his pocket and, without saying a word, walked past her. Rosie backed up against the wall, frightened of him. She let him leave and shut the door.

Ten minutes later Kepella returned, a paper bag in his hand. A bottle of Papa. He headed straight to the kitchen, withdrew the bottle, unscrewed the cap, loving the familiar sound of a fresh seal being broken, and poured both him and Rosie a few fingers. He thrust the glass at her.

"Your face bruised," she said, accepting the glass

with reluctance.

"Do you mind if I stay with you? I can't go back there."

"They beat you?"

"We had a business meeting. I told you . . ."

"Oh, Roy," she said, setting her drink down and hugging him. As she hugged him, he swallowed half the vodka in the glass. He threw his head back and smiled pathetically at the yellowed ceiling. Without looking at him she said, "Let's leave town, Roy. I have money saved—one hundred ten dollars. We take a bus someplace. Tomorrow morning I take money out of bank." She looked up at him.

Kepella shook his head. "No bus rides, honey."

"I never seen you like this."

"You've never seen the *real* Roy Kepella." He pushed her away, a little roughly. "Rosie, I'd like to introduce you to the *real* Roy Kepella, who, through a unique set of circumstances, has returned from whence he came. Back from the grave, so to speak." He lifted his glass and finished the booze. Back *into* the grave is more like it, he thought. "What? You're not drinking?"

She was staring at him. "You drunk. Why?"

"Why?" he asked, pouring himself another. "But isn't it obvious? I'm drunk because I've been drinking." He laughed ghoulishly. "I thought that would have been obvious."

"I don't think I like you drunk."

"My dear, you join a very long and well-established list of what I must admit are some very prominent people. You are not alone. No, you are not alone."

She crossed her arms defiantly.

"Drink up, Rosie."

"No. I won't drink with a drunk."

"Have your little toot then."

She scowled, reached for the drink, and drank it all at once. She placed it back on the worn counter with a thud. He immediately poured her another. She drank this quickly as well.

"This how you want it, Roy?" She tossed her dark, coarse hair over to one side. Tears welled in her eyes. "This make you happy? What wrong? Pour me another. And another. I drink until I throw up, and then I drink some more. That what you want? That what you do?"

He turned violently and hurled his glass against the wall. It shattered. Then he dropped to his knees and pressed his face against her chest, drooling onto her dress.

She stroked his hair. "Why, Roy? Why?"

He pushed away from her, still on his knees. She lost her balance and tumbled into the door. His moment of self-pity had vanished, replaced by the uncertain anger of a drunk. He poured a deep shot into her glass and drank it down. "Because," he told her. "Because."

She lay on the floor, crying now. "Roy, what they done to you? My dear, sweet Roy. What they done?"

He smiled grotesquely and began to laugh loudly. "The lion's jaws," he said, holding the bottle in front of himself and studying it. "The lion's fucking jaws."

25

The late afternoon sun, hidden behind hazy clouds, glowed like a cat's eye caught in a headlight's glare. Holst, a cup of coffee in hand, watched Marlene move restlessly around the galley. "I will try and arrange a meeting for tomorrow night. Will that work for you?"

"That is fine. The sooner we get this over with the better."

"Is it Becker?"

She snapped her head around. Since Jay had left the boat, Marlene had been a nervous wreck. "What?"

"You are romantic with Becker, are you not?"

"No."

"You have a hard time avoiding men, Marlene."

"Have I had a hard time avoiding you?"

Holst looked away, pretending to have missed her comment. "He is a good worker. I will say that much."

"And a fine sailor."

He looked at his watch. "Where is he? Did you let him off early?"

"No, he did not show up today."

Holst shrugged; for him, all the better. "Are you prepared for the next few weeks?"

"Why do you keep asking me that? I act professional, make him an offer, and verify what he gives us. What is so difficult about that? It is why you wanted me along, is it not? Listen, the sooner the better."

"And you are certain you can verify what he offers us."

"If it is a circuit board, I can tell you what it does. That is why I am here, is it not?"

"Kepella may be hard to handle. He is unpredictable."

"I will be fine. It is a business arrangement. I am very accustomed to making business arrangements. I do it for a living."

"I just wanted to warn you. Be delicate. We do not want him figuring this out. It would dry him up. He may be difficult. It may take several meetings."

Marlene, who had been watching through a porthole as a woman hosed down an adjacent boat, nodded. "You checked into him?"

Holst sipped his coffee. "Becker?"

"Yes."

"We have been over that. I would be remiss if I had not."

"I thought so."

"Why?"

"Because you seem different, like a man playing with a snake he knows is no longer venomous."

"A strange comparison."

"That is how it seems."

Holst shrugged and watched out a different porthole as a Coast Guard launch rounded the jetty and disappeared.

"And what did you find out?"

"He is perfect for us. He has virtually no credit rating. He has lived here, in Seattle, for a few years, playing music. It was good you noticed him. He travels with his band frequently and is basically a nomad. If anything should go wrong, I doubt that—"

"No."

"—anyone would miss him."

"No!" She crossed her arms tightly.

"Be careful, Marlene. What you do and do not tolerate is of no concern to me. Remember that. Besides, all I meant is that if we have to leave him somewhere for a while, no one will miss him. Relax. I am not going to harm anyone. I abhor violence." He looked at her and sighed.

She did not believe a word he said.

They drank their coffees in silence, he at the table, she standing by the small, stainless steel sink. She feared Jay would not be coming back, and she wanted to take it out on Holst, but she didn't dare tell him what had happened. There was no telling how a man like Holst would react.

"I will be going in a minute," he said, standing and leaving the coffee cup on the table.

She followed him out of the galley—something she never did. He turned and asked, "What is it?" Unable to think of what to say, she resorted to an indifferent shrug. He was headed back toward her cabin, not off the boat. Her heart raced. She wanted to stop him, but instead, stopped herself. She stood there listening to him bang around. She put her fingers in her mouth and chewed on the nails. Frantically she turned and hurried into the galley, and went about making more coffee.

Holst entered slowly, angrily, his face red. He barked, "Why was this moved?" He held the tape in his hand.

"Moved?" she tried innocently. "What is it?"

Holst's mind worked like a Swiss watch. "You said he did not come to work today. Was it him?"

She thought quickly and said, "It was not him . . . It was me. I moved it."

Holst hurried down the companionway and grabbed her arm. "He *saw* the tape? Well, did he? Is that why he is not here?"

"No," she said unconvincingly. "It was me."

"Tell me." The pressure of his grip increased.

"No!"

"Tell me." He twisted her arm and forced her to her knees. "You tell me, Marlene. Tell me now, or the tape of your father goes in tomorrow's mail."

"Let go!"

"Did he see the tape?"

"Why did you hide it here? It was so *stupid* to hide it in the steering path. You never *told* me."

His voice became calm. "You *must* tell me, Marlene."

"You did not tell me!" It was as much as a confirmation. "What does he know?"

She shook her head, sobbing, blond hair hiding her face like a curtain.

"What did he see?" He took hold of her arms.

"I do not know. How could I know?" she mumbled. "You should not have hidden it here."

"Where is he?" he asked, shaking her.

"I have no idea. I swear, no idea."

He struck her across the face. She froze, suddenly afraid. He was grinning, his turquoise eyes sparkling.

"Let go of me. Please let go," she begged.

"Where is he?" Holst struck her again. And again.

"Leave him alone!" she tried to say, but the words wouldn't come out right.

He lunged at her. Her head swam, and before she could react he stuffed his handkerchief into her mouth and dragged her toward a drawer where masking tape was stored. In one swift move, he wrapped tape around her mouth and hair, and then around her wrists. She fell to her knees, dizzy. "I've been waiting for this moment," he told her. "Now we will learn who's in charge. It's very important to know who's in charge." He slapped her hard. "When you are ready to tell me, we will make a deal: you will tell me everything you know, and in turn I will not harm Becker. You'll see, everything will work out." He tore her shirt off. "No more on the face. You have such a beautiful face, Marlene." Nodding, he said, "You will learn to obey me." He reached out and moved her chin, forcing her to nod back. "That's a good girl." She shied away, her face badly beaten. She tried to speak, but could not.

Holst made a fist and smiled again.

The morning sun burned a yellow-orange hole in the clouds. Kepella sat in the uncomfortable booth eating a honey-dipped doughnut and sipping coffee, waiting for Holst to speak. Holst spoke confidently. "She needs to know exactly what you are offering. The idea intrigues her, but she needs details."

"Who is this woman?"

"I told you, her name is Marlene. There is no need for you to know any more than that."

"I have to know or I won't meet with her."

Holst frowned. "Then that is the end of our discussion."

Kepella reconsidered. "Okay . . . okay . . . maybe I'll meet with her, and decide from there."

"This is your deal, Roy. I do not want anything to do with it. The sooner I am out of the middle the better."

Kepella was thinking, I bet. "I can get very technical you know." He made this last statement a whisper, scanning the sweet-smelling doughnut shop to make certain no one could hear.

Holst said, "Listen. Before she will even agree to a preliminary meeting, she has to know what *kind* of information you have. That makes sense, does it not?"

"You name it. I've got it." Kepella smiled ruthlessly and rubbed his head, wishing he had had a shot of Popov before coming here.

Holst looked curiously at him, wondering why the man seemed so paranoid. Kepella had switched meeting places at the last possible moment; he eyed each and every person who entered the doughnut shop, even if they just picked up a couple of plains and left. He was whispering and being extremely vague. Holst was dealing with an entirely different man than the one he had befriended at Fu's.

Kepella said, "Listen, Holst, I figure I'm close to twenty, twenty-five thousand in the hole, what with back taxes and delinquent payments. If this broad is for real then chances are she can get this stuff to someone who *really wants* it. You follow me?"

"Meaning?"

"I've had a change of heart. This is worth a fortune to the right people. And right now I need a fortune. You got that?"

"What are you saying, Roy?"

"Listen to me, Holst. You can play as dumb as you like, but the more I sat on this, the more I thought, the more I realized what's going on here."

"Is that so?" Holst said cautiously above the lip of his coffee cup.

Kepella felt he had to play this just right. It wasn't enough to be ignorant; he had to appear blatantly stupid. Blind. "I don't know who you are. And I don't care. And I don't know who this buyer is. But the way I figure it, you're in on both ends. I looked into your sporting goods company . . ." He let the words trail off and went back to his honey-dipped.

"What does that mean?"

"You don't make a lot of dough at that company. So I figure you're taking a percentage both from this broad and from me. Well, that's just fine. You wanna play both ends, that's your business. But don't go trying to screw me. I won't be in this deal long. I won't have her stringing me out. I'll prove I can get good stuff—I'll sell her the big wad—and I'm out. I've seen this shit before, you know. It's always the ones who get hooked in, the ones who get greedy, that get caught. You understand? For me, it's one, maybe two deals—big bucks—then it's back to life as normal. None of this frequent, small-time stuff. Twice—big dough—and out." He tried to sound firm.

Holst had been hanging on every word. For a moment he had thought Kepella had figured it out. He felt like saying, You are an ignorant fool. Instead, he said, "You will not tell her . . . will you, Roy? I mean about the percentage."

Kepella grinned proudly. "No, Iben. I won't say a word. You just explain the stakes, okay? I'm not playing for a couple of K; I'm shooting the moon. I'm going for big bucks and that's that. So this broad better be willing to play along. If she isn't, then we find another buyer. The way I see it, Iben, this kinda makes us partners." Kepella tugged at the honey-dipped and ripped a piece loose. He placed his wadded napkin into the ashtray. "And we don't take any chances. Understand? Every time someone tries one of these deals, they screw up. Not me. We take every precaution there is"—he grinned evilly—"and then some." He continued, "I won't do twenty years for someone else's stupid mistake. This all comes off as smooth as silk, or I find a few Peace Brothers of my own and have them pay back *my* betrayers. You got that, Iben? I go down, everyone goes down. And I won't use the legal system to do it, if you understand me."

Holst thought, You can talk tough with me, Kepella, but if anyone's legs are to be broken, they will be yours. As far as I'm concerned, you are the sludge that floats in the river. My employer has a small army to handle your kind. You mess this up, Kepella, and your ex-wife will be an ex-widow before Christmas. "Whatever you say, Roy. Whatever you say."

"Damn right, Iben. Damn right. Whatever *I* say goes. And you tell this broad that, too. Whatever *I* say. Yes, sir. The ball's in my court now. We play by my rules: one step at a time and steady as she goes." He bit into his doughnut and ripped another piece loose. Kepella's eyes were bloodshot and his hand shook.

Holst knew how to break a woman like Marlene: fear. Fear for her father's reputation, fear for the well-being of her boyfriend, and now fear of survival. Basic instincts. It had taken him nearly forty-five minutes. She had resisted. Cried. But finally she had broken. She was his now. She would do anything he asked.

There was no way he could let Becker go. No, despite what he had promised her, Becker had to be dealt with. Removed. Holst left the doughnut shop and drove to the International district, where he picked up John Chu— Peace Brother. Chu was big enough so that when he sat down in the front seat, the car shifted to the right. Holst asked, "You have the address?"

Chu handed him a piece of the phone book. Holst read the page and eased the car away from the curb. "It is very important to me, John, that we are able to make this look like an accident. A suicide is fine: he is broke, he has lost his woman; that works nicely. But no weapons. In and out—nice and clean."

"I understand. No problem."

"At the very least it should look like attempted robbery, I mean, if something should go wrong."

"I used to do a little B and E. No problem."

Alarmed, Holst said quickly, "You told me you did not have a criminal record."

"I don't." Chu smiled.

"I will wait where I drop you off. When it is over, I want you to nod to me from the corner. Take a bus back. I will contact you later."

"No problem."

A few minutes later John Chu got out of the car and walked west toward Becker's apartment.

Jay heard the freight elevator kick on: a loud pop followed by a grinding. He looked at the bedside clock. For a Saturday, this was a few minutes early for Jocko. Besides, Jocko never used the elevator. Jay sat up on the edge of his bed, waiting for the knock on his door. He heard the elevator stop, the cage slide open. He rubbed his eyes and tightened the drawstring on the surgical pants he wore as pajamas. "I'm coming," he said, expecting the knock.

The door burst open, tearing loose two dead bolts and weakening a hinge. The son of a bitch was huge. He had arms the size of tree trunks and a neck as fat as his head.

He was Chinese, with puffy cheeks and thin slits for eyes. He said, "Gimme yo' money, white trash."

"Hey, what the fuck?"

"Yo' money, man." He came straight at Becker, who did a back somersault, tumbling over the far side of his bed and landing on his feet. Instinctively, he lifted the blanket up like a curtain and tossed it at the intruder. Chu stepped across the bed and took a swipe at Becker, who ducked and ran for the door. But Chu dove from the bed and caught him by one ankle. Becker fell, kicking the man with his free foot. The big man said, "I won't hurt yo' if yo' give me money."

Jay managed one good kick into the Chinaman's nose before Chu took hold of the free foot. Jay tried to scream but couldn't catch his breath. He clawed and scratched Chu's thick neck, trying for the man's eyes. Chu released Becker's feet and slugged him hard in the chest. The blow threw Becker backward and onto the floor. Chu was up and over him. "Yo' money." Jay reared back a leg and kicked him, missing the knee. Chu groaned and collapsed, but again got hold of one of Becker's feet.

Fear overpowered Jay. This man might kill him. Whatever was going on, this monster would certainly win the fight. "Help!" Jay finally yelled, knowing the apartment below him was empty. "Help me!"

Chu leaped forward and drove his knee into Becker's back, knocking the wind out of him.

Jay's chest collapsed beneath the weight. He tried to scream. Nothing. His back hurt. His chest was on fire. The Chinese bastard was dragging him across the floor. A few stray splinters embedded in his back. He couldn't move, he couldn't breathe. He was being dragged across the floor, thinking that if he could only speak he could tell the gorilla where his money was; he could give him his money and get this over with.

Chu dropped his knee into Becker's back again.

Jay gasped for air. He opened his eyes. The room was moving from side to side, like *The Lady Fine* when she was tied up. *The Lady Fine!* The videotape and Holst! Could that be what this was about? Jay suddenly found a reserve of strength, like a second wind after twenty hard miles on *The Streak*. Survival. What if this guy wasn't after cash?

Jay sat up, his breathing ragged, and delivered a good hard right directly into Chu's groin. The blow caught Chu by surprise. He released Becker's feet and grabbed his crotch, stumbling backward. Jay pulled himself painfully to his knees and tried to stand. Chu laced his fingers together, turning his two stubby hands into a single fist. He hammered Becker on the back of the neck, dropping him to the floor, and delivered the blow again.

Jay was suffocating. His dizziness fogged his vision and balance. He lay on the floor, his body numb. Helpless, he watched as Chu calmly opened a window above the alley. His fingers began to tingle—feeling returning. Chu dragged him a few feet, picked him up, and stuffed him out the window, head first.

Jay saw the pavement—the dumpster—three stories down. A gargoyle protruded off the side of the building a few feet below the window. He stretched out his arms, reaching for the gargoyle. He groped for the gargoyle's head . . . only inches . . . precious inches . . .

Chu pushed Becker out the window.

Jocko entered the apartment. "Hey!" he screamed,

crouching into the stance of an experienced street fighter, a switchblade suddenly in his hand. "Come on, junkie," he said, waving the blade.

Chu adopted the same bent stance, his waist sucked in away from the sharp knife. He edged closer to Jocko, unafraid, and dropped to the floor, spinning quickly around and delivering a kick that caught Jocko in the hand. The knife flew from his grip. Chu jumped to his feet and kicked Jocko into a potted tree. He fled quickly, hurrying down the stairs in leaps.

Jocko pulled himself out of the foliage and hurried to the window—drawn morbidly to the window, to one last look at the remains of Jay Becker. Jay was hanging from the gargoyle, hands locked tightly around it. "I'm losing it, man," he told Jocko. "Help."

Jocko leaned out the window but couldn't reach his friend, their hands just inches apart. "Hold on." He looked around for something to help him. Why wasn't his brain working? He couldn't see anything. What could he use? Then he saw the thick orange extension cord. He raced across the room and pulled on it. The terrarium crashed to the floor and Larry the Lizard streaked across the room toward the potted plants. Jocko tied the extension cord off and lowered it to Jay, who looped it around his hand. Jocko pulled him back through the window.

When Jay was safely inside, Jocko announced, "I brought us some doughnuts."

The Department of Public Safety building loomed behind them. Several sea gulls flew by crying.

"I can't believe that." Jocko unlocked the passenger

door for Jay and then walked around the van and got in, closing the door hard. He started the engine. "What a bunch of turkeys. Someone tries to kill you and they don't do a thing."

"Like Flint said, we can't expect them to investigate nothing. There is nothing to investigate. If we'd been able to identify the guy . . ."

"I was sure that was the guy."

"Hey, I thought so, too. But that's when we lost them. We both pick out a man who's been dead for two years. What would you do? That Detective Flint is a nice guy."

"I suppose. I've never liked cops. They think they're hot stuff."

Jay didn't say anything.

"Do you think Flint'll do anything?" Jocko asked.

"He'll file it. That's about all he can do."

"You should have told him about the videotape you found."

"Not until I talk with Marlene."

"That's stupid."

Jay changed the subject. "You may have saved my life just now, you know that?"

Jocko grinned and turned the van left, toward Shilshole. "Yeah, I suppose that's right."

"I owe you."

"You're damn right you owe me."

They both grinned.

"What do I owe you?"

"I'll think about it."

Shilshole seemed oddly quiet. One man was hosing down

a forty-footer over on Pier K. Jay and Jocko sat in the front of the van watching Pier L: *The Lady Fine*. No sign of Marlene.

"Listen," Jay finally said, "I'm going to go see if she's on board."

"No way."

"The guy you're watching for looks like a Nazi. He cuts his hair real short, has one of those 'perfect' faces. You can't miss him. He dresses like Tommy used to dress, you know, black leather jacket, tight jeans, that sort of thing. Honk twice if you see him. I'll swim for the breakwater and meet you over there." He pointed. "I don't know what kind of a car he drives, but keep an eye out. I don't want him to see me."

"This is stupid. What if he's on board?"

"Not this time of day. Besides, we aren't sure he had anything to do with this morning."

"This is stupid. I'll go. No one knows me. I'll check it out."

"Hadn't thought of that. You don't mind?"

"It makes a lot more sense. You sit tight. I'll be right back."

"Okay. Third from the end on the left."

Jocko slammed the door shut. Jay stopped him and handed him the key to Pier L's security gate, then watched as he walked off.

"Knock, knock," Jocko said, tapping on the side of *The Lady Fine*. A moment later she appeared in the cockpit wearing oversized sunglasses and a hat with a wide scarf tied below her chin. The way she had tied the scarf, she was faceless, just two big bug-eyes, a straw hat, and blue silk.

"Are you Marlene?" he asked.

"Yes?"

"Anyone else around." He lifted his eyebrows.

"Who are you?"

"Are you alone?" he demanded.

"What do you want? Where have I seen you before?"

"I'm Jocko."

"The drummer, are you not?"

"That's right."

"Where is he?"

"In the parking lot. In my van. He wants to see you."

She shook her head. "No. Tell him to stay away, Jocko. Tell him I cannot—do not—want to see him."

"I don't think he'll listen to me."

She turned her head slowly—painfully—toward the parking lot, as if she could see him. She reached out for a teak runner and steadied herself. She was suddenly back with Holst: he was beating her, and she was screaming into a rag stuffed in her mouth. She touched the scarf that hid the bruises and began to cry. She had promised Holst she would stay away from Jay as part of their deal. He had promised not to hurt him. She would do whatever Holst said—she would never go through that again . . .

She turned around. Jocko was gone.

When Jay arrived, *The Lady Fine* was locked up tight. He climbed on board and beat on the door to the main cabin. He gave up and beat on the door to her rear cabin. He raised his voice, though not *too* loudly, and told her he knew she was in there. Nothing. He waited for a half hour, knocking on all the windows, the hatches, stomping on the forward deck. Nothing. He left furious, looking back over his shoulder and cursing her, thinking, Goddamnit, now I know I'm in love.

26

They spoke German. Marlene, pressed against the wall of *The Lady Fine*'s galley said, "I didn't think you would keep your word." She was staying as far away from Holst as possible.

Holst was thinking, Your boyfriend went out a window this morning, and you're thanking me? "I don't think I follow you." He walked over to her.

She flinched and drew away from him. "He came by this morning and tried to talk to me."

"Becker?"

"You sound surprised."

"I . . . I . . . I thought you said he told you he wasn't coming back. I *am* surprised."

"I locked the hatch. I wouldn't see him."

"That was our agreement."

"Yes."

Holst wondered what had gone wrong. Chu had reported that he had thrown Becker out the window. Holst had paid him off. Someone was lying. Because Becker's friend had shown up, Holst had ordered Chu to stay out of sight for a few days. He knew the Chinaman didn't have a police record. Still, there was no point in taking chances. Chu was over in the International district, living above a pharmacy. Holst had covered all his bases. He had even planned on meeting Marlene during the local news hour, to keep her from watching the evening broadcast in case the Becker incident was mentioned. He wondered if the police were involved now. He decided to leave Becker alone for a few days. He would watch him, but nothing more than that until the situation cooled off, until he could determine the extent of police involvement. Chu would be the one sought, so there was no need for Holst to switch hotels. At least not yet. To be safe, Holst had traded his rental car for another color, another model. He wasn't worried.

"What time did he come by?"

"Just before noon."

"Probably wanted his job back."

Marlene was tempted to say, He wanted me. Instead, she asked, "What time do I meet Kepella?"

"Seven-thirty, a little over an hour from now."

"I had better get ready."

He cornered her and walked over to her slowly. She looked away. He stopped in front of her. "You haven't forgotten our agreement, have you?" She shook her head. He reached over and tapped her bruised cheek, watching her face intently, smirking. She closed her eyes, her face in pain. He said, "No, I don't think you've forgotten."

Rain blurred the windshield. It was coming down harder than the usual drizzle—"Seattle dew" as the natives called it. Holst had rented her a sporty little AMC Eagle. At the stoplight she studied her face in the rearview mirror. The cosmetics covered the bruises well. She turned left and immediately right onto Greenlake.

The Greenlake Grill had an oak bar separated from the dining area by a partition. The decor was art deco and spare: black-and-white checkerboard floor tile, white linen tablecloths, wicker-and-stainless-steel chairs, a few healthy well-placed plants relieving the starkness with splashes of lush green.

She parked across from the restaurant in the parking lot of a Baskin-Robbins. Once under the awninged portico of the Greenlake Grill, she collapsed her umbrella. The maitre d', an acne-scarred man with gentle eyes, escorted Marlene into the bar. She removed her raincoat and drooped it over an arm, carrying her black umbrella. She wore a cream-colored raw silk jacket, a pleated lavender blouse with curved collar, a thin alligator belt, and a skirt that reached just below her knees and matched the jacket. Her hair curled under, the left side clipped back. Her lips were a soft, wet, glossy red; her eyes, brilliant green. The gardenia pinned above her breast emitted a faint perfume.

She felt like two different people: the Marlene who was Holst's captive and the Marlene here to do a job. She had tried so hard to block the memory of the beating from her mind that she had little trouble assuming the identity of a smooth professional. She was an actress, acting out her role, now the object of Holst's rage, now the business professional. To save her father's reputation she had a job to do—this was why she had come. Her ability to be convincing, to do the job well, was the key to protecting her father's reputation, and quite possibly the reputation of an entire political party. If she failed, then he failed. And if there was one person on this earth Marlene would do *anything* to protect, it was her father. He could do no wrong. That Holst had proof her father had broken German law meant only that Holst had to be stopped from making it public. In her mind, her father *must* have had his reasons. Now all that mattered was doing her job and protecting her father.

What, only two months earlier, had been a life of routine was suddenly a life filled with danger and purpose. And although following the beating she had resigned herself to obey Holst, she had not ruled out getting even. Every time she saw the man she plotted a new way to inflict on him what he had inflicted on her. The bruises would heal—this she knew—but the memory of that night would linger on. He had violated her with his brutality and he would be made to pay, either by God or a person doing God's work. Yes. He would pay.

She knew the most direct harm she could do would be to sabotage the deal he had struggled so hard to put together. She could walk into the Greenlake Grill and mess it all up. But then her father would pay, not Iben Holst. No. There had to be another solution. For now, she decided, she would play the role and get this over.

She recognized Kepella immediately as the sad man with the permanently punched-in nose and flat lips. He was drinking a clear cocktail, vodka or gin, which was obviously not his first. His eyes were bloodshot, and he was chewing his lips as he stared at the table. She stopped at his table and clicked the tip of her umbrella impatiently on the tile, her raincoat still folded over her arm. She was thinking, It will be over soon. Home to father, soon.

A few drops of water dripped to the floor. Kepella looked up, slack-jawed at her stunning looks. "Marlene?"

"Marlene Johanningmeir. You are Roy?"

He stumbled to his feet and pulled a seat out for her.

They shook hands. His was warm and greasy. She sat down as he took her coat and umbrella, depositing them on the chair next to him. "You're ah . . . well, you're younger than I thought you would be."

A freckled waitress approached the table and a minute later went after Marlene's rum sunrise. When she was well away, Marlene said, "I understand you may have something I might be interested in." All business.

"Later, if you don't mind?" Kepella asked—demanded —looking into her eyes. "Not here." He hesitated. "You're in Seattle on business?" he asked.

Her brow creased. She wanted to get this over with, not talk small talk. "Yes, I am." All business.

He nodded. His eyes darted about nervously. "Good."

His eyes were steel balls bouncing back and forth between bumpers in a pinball machine. She could almost hear the bells going off. "Are we going to talk business, Mr. Kepella? I am on a busy schedule."

"What?" He flashed his red eyes at her. "No! Not here, Ms. Johanningmer."

She didn't bother to correct his mispronunciation. "Then where?"

"Don't you want your drink?"

"No thank you. I would prefer to do business."

Her drink was delivered. The glass, was sweating—like Roy Kepella.

His words were slightly slurred. "There's a phone booth across the street, in the parking lot." He turned and pointed to where Marlene had parked. "Over there. I'll meet you there in one minute." He up-ended the vodka and finished it. It had been a long afternoon.

Marlene nodded, irritated at the arrangement. She stood, and he handed her her coat and umbrella.

Outside, Marlene put up her umbrella and stepped out from under the awning. She crossed the street, dodging the water running at the curb, and waited by the glaring white light of the pay phone. It wasn't a booth, but a phone with a small stall around it.

Kepella wore a felt hat and a Gore-Tex jacket. His legs were wet to the knees by the time he reached her. He raised his voice over the roar of the rain striking her umbrella. "I won't take any chances, Marlene. It's stupid to take chances. So we'll talk in a neutral zone." He leaned in front of her and hurried through the Yellow Pages. Then he stepped back. "Shut your eyes and stab the book, Marlene. That's where we'll meet."

"What?" She could hardly hear him over the sound of the rain.

"Just stab the book with your eyes shut."

She did as he said.

"Hold your finger there."

She opened her eyes.

Kepella leaned forward and read the name. "Puget Motor Motel. We'll talk there. I know where it is. You want to ride with me?"

Marlene was dumbstruck. "Whatever you like, Mr. Kepella."

"Sure. Come on. Ride with me."

He led her across the street and opened the door for her. The Puget Motor Motel was ten minutes away.

He left her in the car while he went inside the office. Room

12. He opened the door for her, explaining, "This way you couldn't wire the place, and neither could I."

She leaned her umbrella against the cheap set of drawers and folded her raincoat, laying it on the bed. "Very well, Mr. Kepella—"

"Roy."

"Roy. What is it you have to offer? As I explained, I am in a hurry."

He sat down in the chair and ran his hand through his rain-soaked hair. "Take off your clothes."

"I beg your pardon?"

"Disrobe, Miss Johanningmer." Again mispronouncing her name. "I'm sorry, but I must insist on it. I will not talk until I am certain you are not wired for sound."

"You are out of your mind." Not another maniac, she thought. Not another like Iben Holst.

He sniffed. He was getting a cold. "You're right. But I must insist. I have been in law enforcement for over twenty years, Ms. Johanningmer. I know most of the tricks and how to avoid them. I am forced to take precautions. You'll take off your clothes, right now, or we won't even start talking a deal."

She shook her head back and forth. She had to talk a deal, but this request appalled her. "Very well." She headed toward the bathroom.

"No, Miss Johanningmer. Not in there. Sorry, but I have to be able to see you." He rubbed his eyes.

"I thought you are to search my clothes?" she said indignantly.

Kepella was loosening his tie and unbuttoning his shirt. "They wire people on their skin, too, Marlene. Sorry, it's all the way down, or no deal." He looked over at her. "It goes for me, too, if that helps any." He removed his shirt. "The sooner we're through with this, the sooner we can talk."

Marlene was stuck with it. "Very well." She was furious. She removed the silk jacket and began unbuttoning her blouse, feeling uneasy and strange, and thinking, If he tries something, I'll kick him in the groin. She wondered what he would make of her bruises. She turned around and continued undressing. A moment later she was down to her bra and pantyhose. She was facing away from Kepella, but knew the mirror allowed him a view of her anyway. She heard his pants come off, and then his underwear. God, his underwear.

"All of it, Marlene, and turn around please."

"This is absurd."

"Perhaps, but I'm not doing it for kicks. I'm not going to jail for fifty years because of your modesty. Now turn around, and remove the rest of it."

She had to sit on the bed to remove the pantyhose.

"What happened to you," he asked.

"I . . . ah . . . I fell down some stairs."

Kepella grunted.

Marlene felt a rush of anger. She had lied for Iben Holst. She had compromised herself even further. Where does it end? she wondered. How can I do such a thing? What am I doing here? Her father's face appeared before her, as clear as Kepella's flat nose.

Kepella fumbled with the articles she had removed, squeezing and searching the seams, standing three feet from her, naked.

She was close to tears. She kept thinking of Holst, wondering if he had somehow put Kepella up to this. As he handed back her clothing, piece by piece, she dressed quickly. "You have humiliated me, Mr. Kepella."

"Hey, listen, lady! I'm telling you: Roy Kepella takes no chances. Understand? I apologized. That's the best I can do. It can't be helped. Part of the job."

A few minutes later they were dressed and facing each other, Marlene sitting on the bed, Kepella in a plastic-upholstered chair. He tugged at the sleeve of his sport jacket. "What is it you are after?"

"My clients are interested in a variety of merchandise. What is available?" Her voice was clipped.

"Name it."

"It can hardly be that simple," she said condescendingly.

"Listen. You want information on employees out at the sub base, I have it; you want to know about communication satellites based over the Pacific, I have it."

"And what about computers?"

Kepella smiled. So Brandenburg had been right. "What about them?"

"We need some parts to Crays. Spare parts. We need some Zycorps terminals."

"I know where the inventory is kept. I know the names of several Customs officials and have TRW credit runs on them. If that's what you mean."

"And what could I purchase this information for?"

"Fifteen thousand dollars."

She smiled professionally. "I was thinking more in the area of five."

"Fifteen."

Holst had given her specific instructions: a small amount

of money first for a small piece of information. Check out the information and determine its accuracy. Up the stakes at each trade. "What if you were to supply only a sample from a warehouse, for say three thousand."

"Nothing doing. You want to hit a warehouse that's your business. I can supply inventory information, maybe some security advice, and a line on a passage through Customs. Pulling it all off is your people's job." He waited and then said, "Marlene, this is not going to be a long relationship."

"Mr. Kepella, you know these things take time. First we must evaluate the quality of your information before we can authorize large payments."

"I'm telling you, three, four trades at most, and I'm out. I know from experience. So you had better check my *quality* quickly. I won't be around too much longer."

She thought it over. "Five thousand for the location of one warehouse, its contents, security, and schedule."

"Ten."

"Six."

"Eight."

"Agreed." She stood. "When can you have the information?"

"Tomorrow noon at the earliest, evening perhaps. How do I reach you?"

She gave him the phone number of Holst's briefcase cellular phone, which was aboard *The Lady Fine*. "If you can't reach me," she said, "contact Holst."

"The least number of people involved, the better."

"Yes, but he is involved."

"In what way?"

She shrugged, confused. "He introduced us."

"That hardly constitutes involvement."

The sun had set by the time he left her back at her car. He drove up the road and hid the Dodge amid cars parked at a softball game.

She drove past a few minutes later, and he followed. She didn't seem like the type to spot a tail, but even so, he stayed a good distance back, just another set of headlights in the throng of moving traffic. She turned onto I-5, drove south to 45th, west until Leary, and on out to Shilshole Marina. He dropped well behind her as they approached the marina—they were the only two cars on the road. He drove past as she turned and parked. The road climbed a steep hill toward Golden Garden Park. He stopped and watched her tiny silhouette pass beneath one lamp after another. He counted docks: five over from the little hut. She boarded, three ships from the end, on the left. Then he noticed the car below, on the side of the road. It was the same car he had first noticed on 45th. So, they had followed him as well. Just as he had thought. He wanted them to see him. When he was sure they had, he drove off. He hadn't had a drink in hours and his head hurt.

"I would not say that I am involved."

"That is exactly what he said."

The Lady Fine rocked in the light chop. Again they spoke their comfortable German. "He's right. You must keep me out of this, or he may become suspicious."

"Where is the TV?"

"Being modified. If Kepella's information checks out, we'll hide the chips inside the television." It was only partly the truth. He had also removed it because Marlene, who was not a newspaper reader, usually watched at least part of the evening news. Soon enough, Becker would have to be dealt with. If Becker made the news and Marlene saw it, it could ruin everything. He and Marlene had made a deal. His job was to keep up appearances, to see this operation through, and that was just what he was doing. "Tell me more."

"I have told you it all. He seemed drunk, extremely drunk. How can we take his word on anything?"

"He is falling apart, Marlene. By selling stolen information, he is doing the one thing he probably always told himself he would *never* do. And now look at him. I would be drinking, too."

"I do not trust him."

"But you *will* be able to confirm the authenticity of the merchandise?"

"Of course. But he will not give us the merchandise, only the warehouse information, as I have told you."

"I already have the warehouse information."

"Then why ask for it?"

"I need the terminals and the chips. Kepella's information will help me there. They will have to be stolen. That has already been arranged. His information on the Customs personnel is critical. He offered it as a package; we buy the package. It serves as a good first test. We get some information we already have, which gives us a chance to measure the quality. We also gain some information we did not have. From here on out, Marlene, it becomes a very delicate game. Kepella could change his mind overnight. He could even turn against us—though we have protected ourselves well there. You are his contact now. You must treat him gently, but from a position of strength. I am sorry that he put you through the ordeal of undressing, but you see, that really proves he's a professional. He is protecting himself. When he stops protecting himself, we become wary. You have to watch for the slightest change in personality, remember everything he says and does."

"What about more video?"

"Yes, that will help us keep him working for us, but that motel trick of his was clever. I will have to think of a way to beat him there."

"You enjoy this, don't you?" She could see it in his eyes.

"Yes. I enjoy it very much." He studied her carefully. He thought, Marlene, you *don't* understand, do you? You still haven't figured out why we chose *you*: an only child, your mother dead, your father unaware of where you are. "We take very few chances, Marlene. That is how we stay in business."

"Meaning?"

"It will be over soon enough."

She changed the subject. "I would like the television back."

"It will take a few days . . . Be patient."

The briefcase phone rang. Holst said, "If it is Becker, find out where he is."

She looked strangely at Holst and answered the phone. "For you," she told him.

After he had hung up he said, "You were followed."

"By Kepella?"

"Yes."

"I'm sorry. I looked for—"

"No. It is good. I would have worried if he had not fol-

234

lowed you. He wants to know who all the players are. If he has any Agency friends left, and I'm sure he does, he'll check you out."

"Me? What could he possibly find out about me?"

"By noon tomorrow he will know everything about you. Everything we want him to know."

"And just what is that?" she said, annoyed.

"That you have worked for several important electronic companies. Your education, family history, the usual."

"And what else?"

"That you took a trip to Iran in 1977, Libya in 1979, toured Central America last year."

"But that's not true."

"To him it will be. That is all that is important."

27

Night clouds floated over Manhattan, illuminated by billions of watts of light that poured from street lamps, marquees, apartment windows, headlights . . . Passengers fanned themselves with the small sightseeing pamphlets that had been distributed to each cabin when the ship had docked an hour ago.

Sharon sat patiently in the small waiting room where the Customs official had asked her to wait. After a time the door swung open and the paunchy man who had detained her announced, "You may leave. Please sign here."

She signed the form and stopped to exchange her remaining deutsche marks for U.S. currency. Three phone calls and a taxi ride later, she was on her way to

Washington, D.C.

She arrived at Dulles at 11:45 on a hot and humid August night. She was picked up and driven to Langley and moved quickly through the security area. A few minutes later her first debriefing began. The debriefings lasted three full days, and finally, on the afternoon of the third day, a limousine drove her to the Senate Office Building.

Now Sharon paced outside a room where *the* meeting was to take place. She was nervous. Due to logistics and politics, neither director would agree to meet in the offices of the other, and so the meeting had been moved here, onto neutral ground. The others had been inside for a little over thirty minutes when an aide summoned Sharon.

She told them what Brian had asked her tell no one else: that a double agent existed inside the FBI and was running agents for Fritz Wilhelm. "He had heard that Seattle was next. It was explained to him that Seattle's office held files not accessible to agents here. Brian was certain they would go after someone in Archives."

The men mulled this over and sent their aides off. But the most important information Sharon had—the image of the mole in the FBI—was trapped inside her head. The two directors agreed that the first order of business was to try and glean the image of the mole from Sharon's mind via the talents of a police sketch artist. The meeting broke up shortly thereafter.

The first session had been scheduled for early evening.

Sharon tried to relax. She had been working with the bald and quiet sketch artist for over an hour and they weren't even close. The forehead was wrong, the chin was off, the eyes didn't fit at all. Her problem was that she kept confusing the face in the photograph with the face of the thick-lipped man. The sketch came out more like the latter, and struggle as she might—concentrating on the image of the photograph in her head—the two faces superimposed each other. "No. I'm sorry. I think the forehead was thinner."

The sketch artist was accustomed to this. He could tell in the first five minutes if his subject had it or not. This one didn't have it. She wasn't sure. He was a professional, however, and wasn't about to rattle her. His art was patience: he waited while people tried to remember. He knew, though, that she wasn't going to remember. But they paid him to sit here and do his best and that's what he was doing. He used the gum eraser to rub out the top of the man's head. The picture now looked like one of those porcelain mugs with a man's face on the outside and an open hole where the top of the head should be. He lowered the forehead and added the hair, spinning the pad around for Sharon to examine. "Any closer?"

They went at it for another two hours. It was on a coffee break that Sharon was approached by the director. "I understand you're having some difficulty," Maxwell said.

"I can't separate the two faces. I'm trying, but they both blend together." She fought back tears of frustration. The last thing she wanted to do was cry in front of *him*. "It's a bit like sampling perfumes, I'm afraid," she said, attempting a smile. "After a while you can't smell a thing."

"The last thing we want to do is rush you, Sharon. You've been through an awful lot these past few weeks. You're a very capable agent. I have the utmost confidence in you. When you're ready, you'll be able to see that face as clear as day. Take a couple of days off. Don't think about it. Clear your mind. That's the best route. After that we'll try again. The worst thing for you is frustration. I can feel you're upset about this. No need to be. This happens to us all. Don't ever think that you're letting the Agency down. We're proud of you, and I mean that sincerely. When you feel well rested, we'll give it another try. If that doesn't work, we have a few other tricks up our sleeves. You'll see. It will all work out." He patted her on the shoulder, but the gesture seemed patronizing. He was simply not the kind of man to see men and women as equals. He was of another age. He would never fully understand his women agents.

She nodded and thanked him and headed home. She did feel tired, he was right about that. And she knew he was right about her anxiety, too. If she could only relax, the face would become as clear as day. They had not put her into the file photos yet. That gooed up your mind even worse. She figured if she failed another time with the sketch artist, then it would be on to the photos. Days and days of turning pages of Agency employees, face after face, hour after hour, in hopes she might spot the mole. But she feared this would only confuse her all the more. If she was ever to help it would be with the sketch artist.

If, if, if—the only word she said to herself anymore—a word she was beginning to hate.

28

Kepella slipped quietly out of bed. Rosie slept soundly beside him. He walked into the kitchen, unscrewed the cap, and downed two gulps of Papa straight from the bottle. His head throbbed and the booze would settle it down. As long as there was someone to blame for his drinking—in this case, Holst—he had no trouble with it. It was when he blamed himself that it hurt. Somewhere in the back of his mind he *knew* it would get to that—a week, a month, a year from now—but this morning he skirted that thought easily. The vodka hit bottom as he slipped into his unpressed trousers and pawed through the closet for a shirt. Unable to find a clean one, he donned another he had worn two days ago, thinking it would be cleaner than yesterday's. Warmth crept up his spine. His fingers tingled; the headache abated. He smiled and burped foully. He was glad to be free of the deception. Pretending one is drinking when one is not is too much effort. Swishing vodka in your mouth like mouthwash was, for an alcoholic, like getting hot for a broad who turned out to be a transvestite. No, now he could catch a glow without having to fake it.

"You're a crazy fool."

"Hold that steady, would you?"

Jocko repositioned the police bar and held it steady while Jay marked a hole to drill. "You should stay at my place."

"This is my home," Jay said seriously. "I live here. They won't scare me away. I've got my plants, I've got Larry the Lizard; I'm not going anywhere."

"So you buy a police bar and think that's that?"

"When I'm here, and this thing is in place, nobody is going to get in. Read the box. This mother is tested."

"And when you aren't here?"

"I admit, my security system is lacking. A couple more

days and this place'll be sealed tight. No sweat."

"I'd still buy a gun if I were you."

"You already own a gun."

"That's my point. You remember the time—"

"Yeah, yeah, I remember. One shot into the ceiling and the guy took off." He looked at Jocko as he set down the steel bar and reached for the electric drill. "Truth is, I don't have the same head as you. I'd blow somebody away. I know I would. I'd panic and I'd blow the guy's head off."

"How about a knife? What if I hadn't had *my* knife the other day."

"I thought he kicked it out of your hand."

"He did. But it grabbed his attention. You can't deny it grabbed his attention."

Jay grinned. "Listen, man, you're a different person than I am. You're the urban survivor type. I'm plants and animals. You beat drums for a living, I write love songs. Weapons and I just don't work."

"Well, I'm sticking close to you, then. You're gonna need me."

"You may be right about that."

"I'm serious."

Jay started the drill and ran the bit deep into the wood. The drill wound down. He stepped back and examined the work. Jocko raised the steel bar and Jay inspected the angle. He lifted the metal fixture the bar fit into and began fixing it to the door with screws. "This thing'll stop *anyone*."

Jocko looked at the windows and the skylights. "*If* whoever it is tries to come through the door."

"Hey, enough. You'll make me paranoid. You'll have me

240

boarding up the place."

"Or staying with me."

They finished the work twenty minutes later. Jocko stepped outside and jumped against the door. It didn't budge. Just like the box said.

Jay had been riding hard for fifteen minutes. He crossed the Ballard Bridge, turned onto Ballard Way, and headed out to Shilshole. *The Streak* had fifteen gears. Jay could hold her at thirty without much problem and was expert at weaving through traffic. He kept his back arched and head low, to help his aerodynamics. He wore a helmet and peered over the low handlebars to spot any problems ahead. He could bring her to a stop in twenty-some feet. He could even dump her—if he had to. He jammed on the back brake and came to a stop for a red light. Ballard people looked different to him from Seattle people. He couldn't figure why. The handful of pedestrians who crossed the intersection looked kind of melancholy. The light changed and a car honked at him. He hunkered down and rode on.

Kepella arrived at Shilshole just before eleven o'clock, drove past it, and parked in Golden Garden Park. He had a pair of high-powered binoculars with him. He walked through the lovely park, past banks of bushes, and found a spot with a good view of the marina. He focused in: Marlene was polishing the rail at the rear of the ship. Sailboat? Bow? Stern? Kepella didn't know beans about boating terms and didn't care. He took out the pint, unscrewed the cap, and sucked down a finger or two. Damn it felt good . . . nice and warm on a hot, muggy summer day . . .

Kepella saw a handsome man in his early thirties let himself onto the dock using a key. He hadn't figured on a pass key. It would complicate things. He watched the dark-haired man through the binoculars as he walked hurriedly to the ship Marlene was on and she looked up. The guy looked like a young Clark Gable.

"Hello, there," Jay said in his most pleasant voice.

She snapped her head around and raised her hand to her mouth. Her eyes shifted to the open hatch midships.

"Don't run away from me," he said. "I knew you were in there yesterday. Why didn't you answer me?"

"You must leave, Jay. You must leave quickly." She looked down the dock, tugging on her hat and scarf.

He wanted to tell her about the goon trying to throw him out a window, but feared she would run for the hatch and lock herself inside. "Can't we talk?"

"No, we must not see each other."

The words tumbled out of his mouth before he knew what he was saying. "I'm in love with you, Marlene. You're all I can think about." He wanted to kiss her. He wanted to be back *there*.

She fought back tears. "No, Jay. I do not love you. I do not. I am seeing Iben, Jay." It was one of the hardest things she had ever had to say.

"What do you mean, 'seeing'?" His face had turned red.

"Having relations," she lied, turning her face away.

"Relations?" he blurted out. His throat tightened. "What do you mean, relations?" He swallowed, backing away. She said nothing. He turned and walked briskly down the dock.

She burst into tears. Oh, how she wanted to stop him! How she wanted to tell him the truth! How she wanted out of Holst's operation and into Jay's life. "Jay!" she called out.

But he did not hear.

Kepella ran to his car, feeling dizzy by the time he reached it. He fired up the engine and headed back for Shilshole, wanting to know all the players, and needing a key to the security gate. Perhaps this young man was his answer. But the man was riding a bicycle, a fast bicycle, and Kepella had no experience with such things. He caught up to the bicycle quickly and passed it. A few minutes later he turned into a gas station about halfway through Ballard. The rider pedaled by almost immediately. Kepella gave him a good lead and then pulled back into traffic, going at bicycle speed, just a bit slower than the rest of the traffic. Cars passed them. Together they moved across Ballard Bridge.

Twenty minutes later, Becker glided to a stop at what appeared to be an old factory building that had been converted to apartments. He carried the bike inside. Kepella drove past and parked. He waited a minute and entered the building. There were three mailboxes, two with names—the middle box without. He heard the elevator stop. It was an old freight job with the sliding wooden gates that looked like prison bars. It had stopped on the third floor.

Kepella checked the mailboxes. J. Becker was the only name listed for the third floor. The place had chipped plaster walls, crooked stairs, dim lighting, and no security.

In any other lexicon it would have been called a tenement.

The phone pole outside the building told him more. It bore a poster with a picture of the guy on the bike dead center in a group of freaks. The name below the photo, in bold lettering, was The RockIts. The poster had been tacked on top of a bunch of others, for the sake of history, no doubt, with the most recent listing the engagements for August. Kepella read down the list quickly—the band played often, and at popular spots. Tonight's show was at Charlie's, 9:00 to 1:00. Kepella decided to return about ten o'clock and have a look around. He didn't want to stumble in the dark, so he walked the perimeter of the building. On the far side he found a fire escape, old and rusted, which appeared to reach the third floor. No problem. The adjacent building was a retail outfit of some sort, so no one would be the wiser if Kepella used the fire escape later that night. Access was by a metal ladder mounted into the brick wall.

He told himself he was stopping for lunch. He stopped in a sleezy strip joint on First Avenue, ordered a burger with cheddar, fries, and a vodka gimlet, up. The dancer at the moment was a white girl with nice legs. Her breasts were ridiculously large; she seemed to be beating and strangling herself with them at the same time, using them as props for her individual style of dance. He drank five gimlets by two-thirty, drove to Rosie's, and slept two hours in the car, in the driveway. Just he and his Dodge. Nice and cozy.

Freddie the Firebug liked speed. It bothered John Chu the way this guy never stopped moving. His every joint was in constant motion, even sitting down. The guy was as white as Wonder Bread. Chu thought all white people were dumb. No history. No culture. Nothing but war. The Chinese were the most developed race on earth. "A C-note. That's a lot of speed, Freddie."

"Speed, man?" The thin man's eyes darted around. Freddie liked to pop it, shoot it, snort it, whatever was handy. He lived for his next hit. He was so thin he disappeared when he turned sideways, and he had teeth as rotten as a caveman's. His hair, dark and constantly greasy, hung over his eyes. He couldn't look at Chu for more than a heartbeat.

"It has to be at three-clock in the morning. Has to be, Freddie."

"I'm cookin' some pork, eh, yellow man?"

"Could be, Freddie."

"What flo' the pork on?"

"Third floor, Freddie. Second-floor apartment is empty."

"You want the second floor, not the basement? Shit, man, you askin' for trouble. They spot that as a torch in about two seconds, man."

"How about both?"

"Now you thinkin', yellow man. Now you thinkin'."

"Can you do it?"

"Sheeit. You name it man. I drop a box in five minutes or five hours. However you like. Cost you more with pork inside."

"Two bills is all I got."

"Show me."

"Half now, half in the morning."

The wisp of a man smiled. Chu ran his own tongue across his teeth, wondering what a mouth like that felt like—jagged little brown plugs, looking like a city skyline.

Freddie said, "What's the address?"

"What do we do this for?"

"You're bummed out, Jaybone, don't take it out on the band."

"We bust our hump up there. Do these people give a shit? Look at them. The place is packed, everybody getting drunk and trying to get laid."

"What else is there? I haven't had some leg in over a week."

"I'm serious!"

"So am I."

"No. I mean it. I'm serious."

"Listen, Jay. On any other night you would think this is great, okay? That's the truth. We've got a full house, lots of nice T and A, those two over there have been staring at us for the last ten minutes and giggling. You're just pissed off."

But Jay had his dreams. He knew he had passed the big three-oh, was still unmarried, still making fifty bucks a night. Here he was, doing the same old thing, still waiting for the big break. He'd lost Leith, God only knows why; he'd thrown Linda to the dogs; now Marlene was sleeping with Captain Nazi.

Jocko was right. It was Marlene. Any other night, it would have seemed like a great crowd. The forty-five had yet to reach all the stations, and he had received word that some of the smaller stations were playing it often, so who knew, maybe there was still a chance. He was usually optimistic. He believed in his own abilities and the power of perseverance. You could make anything happen if you were willing to work for it hard enough, long enough. But doubt crept in at times. And tonight was one of those times. As a performer, he tried to avoid acknowledging *those* nights, fearing he might eventually throw in the towel. He knew it was a delicate balance: you had to live in the real world, but with your own sense of what was "real"—your own goals and targets—and you couldn't let anything beat you down.

Jay spotted the man by accident. *The* man he had seen on Holst's video was sitting at the bar drinking a clear drink, one eye on Jay. He couldn't believe it! Their eyes met, and Jay immediately started moving toward the bar. The man looked heavier in person, and he had a pushed-in face and a big nose and was sweating. Damn, it *was* crowded. Jay, not particularly tall, stood on his toes. The guy was gone, his drink empty. Then he caught a glimpse of him: the back of his head moving quickly toward the front door. "Hey!" Jay shouted. A few heads turned. A pretty girl smiled at him and stepped in his way. "Excuse me," he said, and brushed past her. "Hi," she said warmly. His quarry made it to the door and disappeared. Jay pushed past the remaining people and popped open the door. It was an unusually warm night. The man was jogging into the parking lot. "Hey," Jay called again. He began to run, even as he thought, What am I doing? What am I supposed to say? The man reached a beat-up car, yanked the door open, and jumped in. He backed out quickly and drove away. Jay couldn't read the license plate because the guy had kept the lights off. The car turned left at the end of the lot, passed some parked cars, left again, and headed back toward the club, toward the exit, with its lights still off. "Hey," Jay hollered. The clunker bounced over the curb and pulled out into traffic. The lights came on too far away for Jay to read the plate. Gone. Jay stopped at the edge of the parking lot out of breath.

When he walked back into the bar the band was on stage waiting for him. He pushed his way through the crush of bodies and jumped up on stage. A couple of people clapped because they knew the show was about to start.

The vocal monitor amp blew on the fifth song. Jay could hear his voice in the mains, but the monitors were gone. He glanced at Jocko, who shrugged in the middle of a complicated drum fill. Jocko was like that: he had the coordination of three people. Jay sang a mean version of Stevie Vaughn's "Cold Shot." The last line was, "We let our love go bad," and Jay sang the line with feeling. The crowd danced slowly to the number. It was a good night suddenly. Seeing the guy had changed everything. On any other night, just losing the monitors would have wrecked Jay. But not now. Something was cooking, and Jay was involved. He felt as if he'd walked into a Hitchcock movie: fighting through the crowd to reach the guy; the guy disappearing, roaring out of the parking lot; Jay empty-handed. No doubt about it, something was up. The rest of the set went well. Jay could feel the band's enthusiasm grow as his own increased. Playing music was great that way: all the band members felt the presence of the other players—especially the leader—and when you leaned into it, everyone would follow, and all of sudden it sounded like twenty guys, a wall of sound, churning out an infectious beat, good strong melody, and dazzling harmonies. The dance floor filled. They *felt* it. The music was hot.

"The set ended. Jay wiped the sweat onto the sleeve of his shirt and set his guitar down.

"What do we do?"

"I get my stereo amp. Can I use the van?"

"Sure. You mind if I hang? I think I've got a date with that redhead."

"Go for it," Jay said as Jocko walked away. "Hey, Romeo?" Jocko turned around. "Keys?" Jay asked.

The night sky, bleached by the city lights, showed only a handful of stars, but across the way Jay could see a jet pass behind the Space Needle. It looked beautiful. Jay punched in the cassette and listened to an old Stevie Wonder cut.

Mark Galpin's assistant had great respect for his boss. Who else would still be at work at eleven o'clock? The Skipper was about as dedicated as they come, and as loyal to his agents as one could ask.

The telex had come through less than an hour ago, "eyes only" for the director. It had been decoded by Galpin's desktop computer. Because of his habit of grinding his teeth, Galpin appeared nervous to many of the agents that didn't know him well. He maintained the image of the whip-cracking superior, which was just as well. His assistant knew better. The real Mark Galpin was the man who displayed the color photo of his family proudly in the center of his desk, the Skipper, who loved a fifteen-knot wind on the weekends and water to maneuver in. He had a heart of gold, and right now his concern was for Roy Kepella.

"I'm going to share this with you, Bristol," Galpin told

the man. "It doesn't leave this room."

"Yes, sir."

"I have reason to suspect that Roy Kepella has been set up to drain the Agency of classified information. It is a reverse sting, in effect, and if it's true, then we have a priority problem on our hands. Clear?"

"Yes, sir."

"Just between the two of us, Roy Kepella is a good friend of mine. I'd hate for him to take the fall on this one. But that's how it will go down if we don't locate him immediately. I want to give extra time to this one. I want you to check his computer logs and see what, if any, information he might have requested in the days just prior to his suspension. I want you to get a few of the more closed-mouth agents combing the streets for him. I ran Parker and Carter out to his apartment, and he's not around. They have it staked out, but I don't have a lot of hope on that. Check the gambling bars. I know, I know," Galpin said in response to his assistant's curious expression. "We may not know of all the places, but find out. Roy likes cards. Check around at security agencies and private detectives. He might have applied for a temporary job at one of them. He did that the last time we suspended him. I don't want our hand tipped if we locate him. Contact me immediately. And remember, when you're sending agents onto the street, use the newest we have. Roy knows the Agency well. He can spot any of us three blocks away. Maintain a low profile and put everyone on this we can afford. The last thing we need is a mess like this. The sooner this is over the sooner we can get back to business as normal. Make that clear to the men. Overtime shifts are available until we locate Kepella. Have Walters bring me an updated schedule the minute he has it. I want to increase our manpower by twenty-five percent minimum, and I want the schedule tonight."

Special Agent Bristol kept up with Galpin, his pencil running across the page as he furiously took notes.

"Have you got all that?"

"Yes, sir."

"We've handled worse than this before. We've worked and eaten with this man for over eight years. We ought to know him well enough to find him quickly. I'm putting you in charge of coordination."

"Yes, sir."

"So if anyone gets a bright idea, go with it. All ideas run through you; you report directly to me."

"Do we know who he is working with, sir?"

"No. Washington is working on it. That's all we know. No, Bristol, I think we should assume we're on our own here. We don't want the boys in Washington thinking we have our thumbs up our butts, now do we?"

Bristol shook his head. "No, sir, but it seems to me we have very little to go on." He read from his list, trying to show his boss the assignment was a tough one. "Gambling halls and the like. We bust any of those we find. He's not in his apartment, so he could have left town. We'll put some agents on that, but you know how long it takes to check the various shifts at the trains, buses, and airports. That's a full-time job in and of itself—"

"I don't want to hear how tough this is, Bristol. I want some results. Now if you have any *questions* I'd be happy to answer them, otherwise . . ."

"Right." Bristol hurried from the office.

Roy Kepella looked up at the clock behind the bar, suddenly frantic. He had killed forty minutes drinking. He paid for his three drinks and hurried outside. He had only intended to settle his nerves with a quickie. Instead he had obliterated his nerves with three long ones. He reached Becker's apartment just as a jet flew overhead. He climbed the fire escape carefully and slowly, and still reached the top floor out of breath. The window latch opened easily with his penknife—he slipped the blade between the two pieces of wood, pushed gently, and rocked the old-fashioned catch out of the way. The window stuck about eighteen inches open, and rather than get noisy, he stuffed himself through and into the apartment.

He stepped on a plant and squished it. The place was like a forest. He clicked on his small penlight and wormed his way past a dozen more plants. Kitchen was a mess. Three envelopes on the table, all addressed to Jay Becker. He rifled a few drawers. Salvation Army utensils: no two forks matched. Same with the pans. Becker liked spaghetti, tuna, cereal. The icebox had veggies and something called tofu in it. Half-gallon of milk. Haagen-Dazs vanilla Swiss almond, half gone.

A cheap desk had papers in it. Bills mostly. Pink notices. Credit due, balance due. A bunch of papers on The Rocklts, including a pile of the posters he had seen on the lamppost, but with no dates filled in. He found an old pipe that smelled like old pot—hadn't been smoked in a long time. Then he saw the key he was looking for, in a pile of change on a dresser by the door. He pocketed the key. It looked like

Becker had installed a police barricade bar earlier in the day: there was still sawdust on the floor. Kepella continued toward the couch, passing some dirty laundry on a chair. Below, a car honked loudly. An empty bag of chips lay discarded on the coffee table. Empty beer can. The couch had stains on it. Behind the bookshelf—behind the couch—the bed was unmade, the sheets clean. A nice-looking stereo sat alongside an impressive record collection. The stuff looked fancy enough. A photo over the bed showed a guy in a body suit crossing a finish line on a bicycle. It was Becker, younger by a good ten years. A dozen sports trophies stood tarnished and dust-covered on top of the bookshelf—sailing and bicycling.

The elevator made a loud pop as it stopped. Kepella heard the cage open. He wondered how he had missed hearing it start up. Probably during the car honking, he thought. A key in the door. He started for the window, stopped, and pushed himself back into the corner by the bed. Despite his years on the Bureau, he had never done anything like this. His heart was pounding. Christ, he thought, the old ticker's gonna blow.

The door opened. A blade of light from the hallway's bare bulb cut across the forest of plants. Kepella didn't hear the door close. Becker had left it open. That was a good sign: he obviously didn't plan on staying long. Kepella held his breath, then let it out slowly, trying to calm down. Becker rounded the corner, having not turned on a light. He came straight for Kepella. He reached for the lamp by the bed, and paused . . .

Kepella made his move. He leaped to his feet and mowed Becker down. Becker screamed at the top of his lungs, reached out, and tripped the intruder. The guy fell hard. Becker rose and dove onto the Kepella's back. "You son of a bitch," he said, pounding on the man's back.

Kepella rolled in the dark. He kicked wildly and felt Becker fall off. His mind was working well now. He stood and hurried toward the door, taking a split second to knock all the change off the dresser, knowing it would give him a chance to slip the key beneath the door later, which, if he was lucky, would not tip Becker to the fact that he had taken it in the first place. He ran to the dimly lit stairwell and took it in leaps and bounds.

Jay wasn't about to follow. He sat up and watched the man rush out the door. His neck hurt where the kick had landed. He rubbed it. That certainly hadn't been the Chinese dude. Too soft. In fact, even in the darkness the intruder had looked for just a second like the man with the pushed-in face. The man at Charlie's. Was his mind grabbing onto that image? he wondered. Or had it *really* been the face from the video? He turned on all the lights in the place and looked around quickly. Nothing missing. Fear suddenly struck him and he hurried. This was no longer fun. He was frightened and alone. Quickly, he dismantled the stereo and tucked the amp under an arm. Heading out the door, he took a last look around and saw the open window. His heart jumped. He set down the amp, hurried to the window, and closed and latched it. He noticed the crushed fern and felt a quick stab of pain in his heart, greater than the pain he had felt in his neck. He was mad. He locked the door behind himself and checked it. Twice.

He picked up the amp and entered the elevator.

The band was waiting on stage.

29

Kepella, excited from his encounter with Becker, headed straight for a bar. He sucked down two quick shots of Popov, then headed for Burt and Bane's gun shop down by the waterfront. Burt and Bane's stayed open until midnight, and besides selling about every weapon ever made, the store also had a key cutting machine in the back. Seventy-five cents—a little high—and you could copy your key.

He passed the bow-and-arrow rack, the camouflage coveralls, the Army-surplus boots, the line of counters displaying dozens of handguns. Beyond the displays, hundreds of rifles, single-shot bolt-action to semi-automatic clip, were lined up, looking like a row of marching soldiers.

The Shilshole key took about two minutes to copy.

Phase two of his plan involved some *real* detective work. Kepella enjoyed this more and more now. This was what an FBI agent was supposed to do. She had left him a phone number, which either meant she didn't live on the boat or she somehow had a phone on board. He drove to the Shilshole parking lot, took out his binoculars, and stepped into the pay phone booth. He left the door open so the light wouldn't go on, because the light would interfere with his view of the ship through the binoculars. She answered on the third ring.

"Marlene?"

"Speaking."

He liked the sound of her accent. "This is . . . your friend. I wonder if we might be able to arrange a meeting this evening. Very short. I'm sorry to call so late."

"I was not asleep. Yes. Where you would like to meet?"

"Where we met the first time . . . at the bar, that is. Say in about thirty minutes?" He knew it would take her about twenty minutes to drive to the Greenlake and park. He also assumed she would need at least ten minutes to get organized.

"I may be a few minutes late, but yes, that sounds fine. See you there."

"Oh, Marlene?"

"Yes?"

"I hope you'll have that little something for me."

"I will try, R—" She caught herself, stopping before she called him by name. "I cannot promise at this hour. Goodbye."

Kepella climbed back in the old bomb and drove up the hill to a set of worn stone steps that ascended into Golden Garden Park. He crept up the steps until he reached a hedge, and then sat down on the cold stone, training the binoculars on the *The Lady Fine*. The night air felt wonderfully warm to him, or perhaps it was the two shots of Papa. The ships looked so beautiful under the glow of the lamps lining the docks, their masts reaching into the night sky, tiny white lights flickering from the topmost points. Most of the ships were dark and quiet, but on one ship a party raged, people waving drinks and enjoying themselves. Seeing the party gave Kepella a pang. He had not been to a *real* party in how long? Before he had quit drinking. It had been his own idea—avoid temptation: deliver us from evil—and now, suddenly, he was painfully aware of his renewed drinking. He had started again. Goddamnit, he had started again. Even worse, he liked it. And he knew, for him, it was disaster. Guilt overwhelmed him. He felt his throat tighten, his stomach knot, and then the tears came. He sobbed pitifully. Guilt. Pain. Tears. He knew the booze would kill him. He was killing himself: a long, slow suicide. How could he be two people at the same time? How could he *know* and still keep drinking?

But he couldn't let the guilt destroy him. He wiped the tears from his face and raised the binoculars to his eyes. She hurried topside, straightened her clothing, and left the pier.

He hurried down the stone steps, climbed into his car, and drove toward Shilshole, pulling off the road at the Vine Boat Ramp. Marlene drove away moments later in an AMC Eagle. Kepella waited a minute and drove into the parking lot.

The duplicate key opened the security gate to Pier L without trouble. He strolled casually to the end of the dock, climbed aboard *The Lady Fine,* and stepped carefully down into the cockpit. It didn't occur to him that the boat might be locked up. But it was. Using his penlight he looked for a key. He couldn't find one. After several minutes of searching, he realized there was another cabin at the rear of the ship. It was unlocked. He let himself in. The sight of a tiny light blue two-piece hanging to dry made him smile. Marlene's cabin.

He guessed Marlene would just be arriving at the Greenlake Grill now. He stopped and watched a couple leave the party over on Pier M. They both walked unsteadily—a bit high.

He went through Marlene's clothes, feeling a bit

ashamed. He toyed through them carefully, so as not to disturb anything. In the bottom drawer, he found her large leather passport billfold. He opened it up. It was her photo, all right. Her last name was Jenner.

Kepella had asked her for the money. Holst had it at his hotel. The drive downtown took fifteen minutes longer than she expected. By the time she reached the Washington Plaza's lobby she caught herself tapping her Italian-leather shoe impatiently on the veneered marble floor. She wore the same hat and scarf, covering her face. She had used extra eye shadow to hide her growing black eye. The added cosmetics cheapened her appearance.

Holst finally emerged from the elevator carrying a briefcase. He looked at her and felt triumphant. He had done this to her. He had broken her. She was his. He led her around a corner and out of sight of the registration desk to two overstuffed chairs bracketing a mock fireplace.

They hardly talked. All he said was, "When you leave, you will pick up the valise. Now say something."

So she told him that she wanted the television back and she wanted to know how long this would all take. She was tiring of it.

She thought about Jay incessantly. The wonderful sexual glow she had been feeling—saving—for Jay, had been extinguished by this vile man. What chance would she ever get to be with Jay again?

She picked up the briefcase and left.

Freddie the Firebug had all his professional gear in his knapsack. His wiry frame danced down the street charged by the speed he had mainlined only ten minutes ago. He loved to work on speed. He worked fast, real fast, he could hear a pin drop; and he could run fast, real fast. The meth made him quick as a jackrabbit, quick as Bugs Bunny. Freddie loved Bugs Bunny.

He checked the address twice. Freddie had only loused up the address once, had torched the wrong box, but the dude had refused to pay him, so from then on Freddie always checked the address twice. This was the place. A screwdriver got him through the basement door, nice and quiet. Whew! That had been a hummer of a hit of speed. He was cranked; cooking with gas. Yessir, he felt *fine*.

Freddie preferred paint thinner or lacquer thinner for basement jobs. It made the investigator's job real tough. Basements were favorite spots for storing paint, rags, thinner. And if you used the right fuse, the right timer, then it was damn near impossible to tell the place had been torched. Of course, in a job like this it was more tricky, because the yellow man had wanted both the basement and the second-story apartment to go. Yeah, that was more tricky, but not impossible.

Freddie liked the organic method. None of this electronic crap for him. Electronics stuck out like a sore thumb. Sift through the rubble, you could spot a timer every time. He carried a couple of household wall-timers, but rarely used them. Otherwise, Freddie preferred to use fuses that burned up in the blaze. Burn your evidence: that's what his pal Elmore had told him at the JD center all those years ago; burn your evidence and there's no way to trace it to you. Freddie used punks. A punk is like an odorless incense stick—that's how Freddie thought of them. He only used one brand: Takanini from Japan. Best punks available. For a job like this he would time four or five sticks. He would sit around home for an hour or more watching the punks burn down, measuring the length they covered in various time periods. He had it down. He loved to watch things burn. He used two makes of candles as well, and he had invented the "Freddie Chimney": a modified coffee can that allowed a candle to burn without the flame being seen. For a job like this—a three-hour burn—he would use both candles and punks. He had the rigs with him.

To his delight, he found what every torch loves to find: an entire corner of the basement devoted to old paint products. Christ, he thought, I lug two gallons of paint thinner all the way over here, only to find a shitload of materials available. I should have cased the place, but yellow man insisted on no casing. In and out, he had said. So, in and out is what he would get. Freddie worked fast. He filled a couple of paper paint pails with paint thinner, soaked the rags he had brought, and made a nice long fuse over to a pile of stacked furniture. On one of the chairs, he placed a paper pail full of thinner. His wet rag-fuse led to the pail. He opened all the cans of paint and placed them around three open pails of thinner, over in the corner. The paint cans looked to Freddie like a circle of covered wagons. He used another quart of thinner to make a fuse to some bedding stacked close by under some wooden floor joists. Freddie loved the sight of wood.

He had cut one of his candles to a two-hour-and-forty-five-minute-burn length, leaving enough wick to light the punk. He had marked circles on the punk to indicate five-minute burn periods. He set up the Freddie Chimney and laid the fourth ring over the edge of the first pail of thinner. Then he left the basement and headed for the second-story apartment.

Freddie was all set to use the screwdriver on the door when he turned the handle and it opened. He grinned. He liked easy jobs. No fuss, no muss. Mr. Clean will burn your whole house and everyone that's in it . . .

This wasn't as easy to fudge as the basement. The apartment had been stripped clean. Bare as a baby's bottom. He set down his knapsack and was about to unload all his gear when he had a thought. He walked over and opened the gas valve to the room heater. The utilities were on the landlord—the gas worked. He grinned. Freddie rarely used flashlights of any kind—too risky; he preferred to let his eyes adjust to the dark. He patrolled the room, checking the windows for leaks. One was stuck open a crack, so he used his screwdriver to jam it with a rag. Freddie was something of an expert with gas. He knew exactly how long a line would have to leak to fill a given size of space with enough gas to blow the box. It was just something he knew. He didn't use a calculator; he simply looked around and started poking pinholes in the gray-plastic tube that ran from the regulator to whatever unit it happened to be—in this case the kitchen range. He poked about fifteen pinholes. The thin plastic skin on the connectors not only saved money for the gas company, they also made Freddie's job a hell of a lot easier. Yeah, fifteen holes. In a couple of hours the place would be full of gas, and ready to blow. All it needed was a little flame.

Freddie left the apartment, shut the door, and took two minutes to stuff the bottom crack with one of his rags. It looked fine. Just right. He calmly returned to the basement, checked his Casio watch—it had a light built into it when you pushed the upper right-hand button—and moved the punk one more ring up the edge of the pail full of paint thinner. Then he lit the candle. If he figured right, the second-floor apartment would blow quite a while after the basement lit, which to any bystander (how many bystanders would there be at three in the morning? he wondered) would fit with the way a fire might run. Yup. It was a real clean job. Just right. Freddie put the Freddie Chimney over the candle, sat down, and rolled up his sleeve. He always liked to keep an eye on things for the first few minutes, but he was dying for a nice hot vein full of speed . . .

Kepella wrote down all the vital information: passport number, date and place of birth, full name, countries traveled to and dates. He returned the pen to his pocket, took the penlight out of his mouth, and climbed back off the boat carefully.

He was so damned pleased with himself he decided to stop for a drink before trying to catch up with Marlene. One drink. He stopped at the first nice-looking place he saw. Oscar's Corner Pub. The place was dark and quiet—just the way Roy Kepella liked it. It was a men's bar. The tube was on in the corner, exhibition game between the Seahawks and Houston Oilers. Seahawks were all over them.

The bartender, a happy sort of fellow, asked Kepella if he wanted another. Kepella was absorbed in the game. "Sure, why not?" he replied. It was late in the fourth quarter before he looked at his watch.

The band sounded great; the crowd moved to the beat. Jay leaned back and watched a delicate blonde bounce to the pounding of Jocko's bass drum as Jimmy cut loose on a dazzling solo, full of bends and screaming high Bs. Jay let out a hoot and walked across the stage, egging on Jimmy, the lead guitarist, as a coach might cheer from the sidelines.

The power failed. The room went dark.

It was the third power failure in a week. Several high voices moaned their complaints. The band's gear went dead in the middle of a chorus: only the drums and horns dribbled on for a measure before realizing what had happened. The emergency lights came on. Jay ad-libbed, hollering, "Looks like we melted the circuits. We'll be with you in a minute." A good part of the crowd laughed, mostly out of nervousness, Jay thought. People don't like the dark unless they're paired off. Someone came in from outside and yelled to the crowd, "The whole area's out. Looks like most of the city." Applause and laughs.

The manager, who had been standing by the back room, saw a number of people head to the door and, knowing this could trigger a mass exodus, called out, "One round of drinks on the house! For everybody!" The bartender flashed the manager a confused look—the boss was not the generous type. The crowd heaved toward the two bars. Waitresses, on orders from the manager, delivered additional candles to each table, and the crowd settled into one of those "we're-all-in-this-together" moods. Jay, never one to be outdone, told Jocko to get out the brushes and had Books get out the accordion they used on the Cajun songs.

He went backstage and uncased his acoustic guitar, and when he came back to front and center, Jimmy was already waiting with a chair. He handed Jimmy the guitar, turned to the horns, Books, and Jocko, and said, " 'Further on Down the Road.' " Rob, the bass player, set down his bass and stood alongside Jay, knowing that without the P.A. they would both have to sing the melody. Jocko counted off the song and the band started playing.

Now they owned the place. The crowd exploded into applause, impressed by a band willing to keep playing, and within seconds the dance floor was packed with couples slow-dancing. Jay looked back at Jocko, who nodded, a cigarette dangling from his lips. The nod said, *Jay, you're something else.* Jimmy looked over, smiled, and started singing along. "Further on down the road, you will accompany me," went the song. Jimmy had arranged it, and it was one of those tunes that gave you goosebumps, because the message was right.

These were the moments Jay lived for, he realized. It had nothing to do with dreams of money or the big time. If the truth be known, he was afraid of the big time. What he liked was feeling an entire crowd come together, making people forget their day-to-day problems, and watching them be carried away by the music. Jay liked to transport people into a four-hour fantasy, where there was little sense of time, little sense of the outside world, just a room full of music, a pretty girl, and time to kill. He leaned back and laughed in the middle of the song. This was what he lived for. This moment. This was it.

30

By the time Kepella phoned her, the blackout had ended. Marlene, having given up waiting, returned to the boat. The briefcase phone rang. "Hello?"

"I thought I was being followed. I didn't want to take a chance. Can we try again?" Kepella said.

"Where?"

"You pick. Where are you located?"

She thought, You followed me here the other night. You know exactly where I am. But she played along. "I will meet you at the Jazz Alley, over in the University section."

"Fifteen minutes?"

"It is open only another forty minutes."

"I'll hurry," he told her.

"I will meet you there. Oh yes . . . I have what you requested."

Kepella had not trusted his own memory to keep track of the various files he had lifted and where each had been stored, so he had made an inventory of them and had stashed it in an envelope, in a briefcase, in a coat room, at the Pacific Regency Hotel. He had three keys on his key-chain: one to his car, one to his apartment, and one to a rented storage area. In the rented storage area he had hidden a small bag containing an assortment of keys, each of which opened a different hiding place. He had been careful to make this as difficult a procedure as possible, so he could not be followed to one particular place. Any plan could be compromised, of course, but he and Brandenburg had agreed on a system that was complex but not ridiculously complicated. The most sensitive information had been placed in safe deposit boxes around town. The less sensitive material, some on cassette, some on paper, was stored in rental storage bins or checked at the bus depot.

Kepella stopped at the Regency and studied his list to locate where he had put the printed information on spare computer parts. He had left it in another briefcase in a coat room only a few doors away. Brandenburg had emphasized that this was something they would come after, so Kepella had an envelope all prepared. The odd thing was, this was public information anyway. A few hours in a library, cross-referencing a variety of technical magazines, a run downtown and a look at the various properties owned by the various companies, and one could put it all together. Therefore, Kepella reasoned that this was a test. They—Wilhelm, via Holst, via Marlene Jenner—wanted to see what Kepella could bring them. He suspected they already had much of this information. They were baiting him, and eventually would seek bigger fish.

Jazz Alley had a high ceiling, painted black to hide the water pipes and emphasize the stage lighting. Small tables were covered with blue-checked tablecloths and had wooden chairs pulled up to them. A platform stage was built against the far wall. A bar ran straight down one side of the club. Kepella paid his two bucks, cued the bartender, and up-ended a shot of Popov. He gestured for a refill. He finished the second shot of booze and, feeling warm, leaned back against the bar, looking for Marlene. She wasn't at any of the tables, but he noted a deep alcove to the left of the stage. He threaded his way through the listeners—serious, attentive types—during the middle of a bass solo. The musician was pretty good. He received a

266

warm round of applause before the drummer took over. Kepella had never liked drum solos.

He spotted her sitting all the way in the back of the alcove, empty tables between herself and the closest couple. He edged his way toward her, thinking how lovely she looked in the dim light of the room. She noticed him approaching and offered the flick of a smile. Tolerant. He knew she probably loathed him after he had forced her to strip; but Roy Kepella had to play this as Roy Kepella would. He sat down, placing his briefcase next to hers. A waitress approached and Kepella ordered a vodka gimlet, up. Marlene ordered a white wine.

When the waitress had left, Marlene asked, "You were followed earlier?"

"It's possible. I must be careful. One can't be too careful."

She looked down at her briefcase. "Half now. Half on confirmation. How do I reach you?"

"I'll reach you. Tomorrow?"

"Yes. Tomorrow is fine. I am interested in some other merchandise."

He raised a hand to stop her, turned a napkin to face her, and handed her a pen. "Please," he said.

She wrote it out slowly, in a precise, European hand. When she spun the napkin around it read: *Deployment of green laser communication.*

He knew that so-called green lasers, the latest laser technology, would soon enable the Pentagon to communicate with the United States nuclear sub fleet at any ocean depth. The research had been underway a long time. If the U.S. nuclear deterrent was to be completely effective, the green laser system had to be deployed. The Navy had feared they had lost the technology to the Soviets in the Walker spy case, but were later relieved to find out the Walkers had not gained access to it. The most available public information put deployment in the late 1980s. Those in the know, like Roy Kepella, knew better. The question that had been raised in technical journals—and no doubt in the minds of foreign powers as well—was whether the Navy would go with land-based or satellite deployment. Kepella knew the answer as he sat staring at her. How far should he go? Dared he risk giving away this kind of information?

"Who are you working for?" he asked.

"What?" she stammered.

"Who are you acting for?"

"You must be joking."

"Listen, Marlene. This is how I'm going to play this. For everything I turn over from now on, I not only want payment, I want information. The wrong information and I dry up." This had nothing to do with his Brandenburg deal. This was strictly Roy Kepella. A drunk or not, Roy Kepella was patriotic. He had served his country twenty-one years plus—and if he was going to turn over this kind of information to Wilhelm, orders or not, he wanted to make damn certain he knew who was ultimately receiving it. In the event Brandenburg's people failed to bring in Wilhelm, as the FBI had failed in Montreal, Kepella would have some hard information and quite possibly a trail worth following.

The drinks arrived. Kepella and Marlene stared at each other, and the waitress, had she been attentive, would have realized this wasn't love.

"This is not possible."

"Marlene, listen to me." He drank half the gimlet in one gulp. "I worked for the Bureau for many years. I have what we call a sixth sense. No matter what you say, I know you are being forced into this." Brandenburg had suggested that most of the runners were outsiders, experts in a given field but having nothing to do with Wilhelm's network. More often than not, these runners simply disappeared. "Don't shake your head. I *know*, Marlene."

"I don't know enough to help you."

"Let me be the judge of that." He sensed it: she was on the verge of telling him something. His palms sweated. Damn, he thought, I'm an operative . . . this is amazing. Her eyes were glassy and she had put both hands into her lap because she couldn't hold them still. "What do they have on you?"

"No. I cannot. Please."

"Okay. You think about it. I'm doing what I'm doing because I have to, Marlene. Just like you. I have to. I worked my butt off for my department and they gave me a bum deal. They owe me. I still have friends over there, Marlene. You don't work twenty-one years without making some friends. When this is over—soon—I will probably have to leave the country. I will hide. But what about you, Marlene? My friends could help you. They could protect you. But they will need something from you. This for that, you understand? I will have to have some-thing to trade with. You think about it carefully."

Without saying a word, she picked up the briefcase he had brought and left the table.

"Don't screw it up, Marlene," he called after her.

She stopped and looked over her shoulder. She opened

her mouth, but no words came out. She felt so alone. She had felt her best around Jay, but Jay was gone now. She was alone again. And here was another person reaching out to her—the very person she was supposed to be compromising. She was strongly tempted to tell him everything she knew, which wasn't much. Marlene needed a friend.

Kepella bought a pint of Papa from a bartender on 47th. It had been nearly a year since he'd bought a bottle here, but the man behind the bar pretended it had been last week. He put the bottle in the glove compartment and drove slowly over to Jay Becker's loft apartment, hoping to drop off the key he had taken earlier. The sooner the better. The lights in the loft were on and a fairly new van was parked illegally in front of the entrance. He drove around the block so he could park on a corner with a good view of the apartment.

"I'm shitty with women."

"No you're not."

"I've always been shitty with women."

"That's bullshit. You're a stud. They fall all over you."

"Let me tell you something, Jocko. I always feel that women think I'm an ugly egotistical son of a bitch."

"I feel the same way. I just don't think about it much. I see some single, beautiful girl and I figure she wants company as badly as I do."

Jay said, "But we're different, you and I. You go after women physically. I'm scared of the physical. I go after the romantic, or the challenge. The truth is, women know how to handle the physical approach. They can say yes, or no. They can read books on body language and start batting their eyes or crossing their legs. The romantic approach throws them off. They think, Jesus, this guy is strange. They don't understand it when I don't go for their clothes. I should have been born a hundred years ago."

"You're right. We're different." Jocko paused. "The problem is that women have been told to look out for the *serious* relationships. That used to mean the guy wanted in their shorts, but over the years it's been lost in translation. Now everybody wants in everybody's shorts. They just don't want anything *serious*. You're a freak, that's all. You write songs about your women, you put the name of their cats in songs; you take them to museums, to fancy dinners—and when it comes time for a good night kiss, you fall apart. You've told me so. You fall so head-over-heels for them that you start coming unglued—and you mess up all the signals. *Believe* in yourself. I've seen you go through three heavy relationships. In all three the girl was hooked on *you*, not the other way around."

"You're twisting what I meant to say. You have a way of doing that."

"Thank you." Jocko lit a cigarette, and Jay didn't complain. "They fall all over you, Jay. You just don't see it."

"Not true."

"You see? You don't believe it. It's the truth. I'm envious, man. Sure, I get a girl in the sack from time to time—but you get women who have something upstairs. You're sensitive. There aren't many sensitive males left in this world. It's mostly Marlboro Men drinking Miller beer and driving four-wheel-drive trucks."

Jay smiled. "But I met Marlene on the job, not at a gig. She doesn't look at me that way."

"Bullshit." Jocko grinned. "You carry it on your face like

a sign: It says, 'I'm intelligent, handsome, and sensitive—inquire within, girls beware.' Your problem is, you're a much more powerful person than most people expect you to be. Your modesty won't accept that. The sooner you get used to that, the better."

"I walked away from her."

"You tend to dive into things before you test the water."

"Meaning?"

"Meaning when you like something you go after it, often without knowing much about it. Also meaning, if I were you I'd hire a private detective."

"You're worried. I'm touched."

"I'm serious."

"Jocko, you are anything but serious. You're a good-looking Jew who has too much money and too much time. Never too serious."

"I didn't ask."

"True. I, on the other hand, am broke, without credit, and I owe the city a wad, and it's driving me batty."

"You can borrow from me. I really don't mind a bit."

"No."

"How much have you saved?"

"A few hundred."

Jocko yawned. "I gotta go."

"You just got here."

"I got here an hour ago. It's late. I'm beat. Come over with me. Spend the night. Play it safe."

"Nah. Thanks anyway."

"Come on."

"What happened to your redhead, anyway?"

"I got her phone number." He hesitated. "I've got a bottle

of Scotch at my place."

"No thanks."

"Don't go see her. Don't be stupid."

"Sure." Jay shrugged.

"If you change your mind . . ." He stood. "I'll be up drinking Scotch and dreaming of redheads."

"Don't stain the couch."

"Funny." Jocko pulled the door shut behind him.

Jay heard him clomping down the stairway—Jocko never used the elevator. He took out a pad of paper, thinking of the rich party-goers on *The Lazy Daze*. The strong, overhead light bothered him. He switched it off and sat back down. The light from the street was enough to see by. If he had one steady companion in this world, it was his music. He began scribbling:

I see you with your long dress on,
drinking from your fine, fine crystal.
Sipping your white wine
thinking everything is fine.

But there's one thing you're missing . . .
It's a real good kissing.
Go on, go on: call me a liar
But you don't know me.
I am the Lord of Desire

For tonight,
I am the Lord of Desire.

Ray Bans and suntans

and co-co-nut lotion.
Stories you've never lived but
wished you had.
You can say and he can hear,
but no one listens.
And don't forget, no don't forget
I know what you're missing . . .

For tonight, I am the Lord of Desire.

He had a good strong tempo and nice melody going in his head. He sang it through a couple of times and then worked out a last verse, thinking of Marlene.

Bat your eyes
turn your head,
But you let me see.
You may be fooling someone
honey
But it ain't me

For tonight
I am the Lord of Desire . . .

That did it: he had to see Marlene, Now.

Kepella saw the young guy drive the van away, and then a minute later, the light in Becker's apartment window went off. Kepella thought Becker had gone to sleep. Good time to replace the "borrowed" key. A bearded man wearing a T-shirt and sweat pants ran by in a full sweat. Strange to see a man jogging at damn near three in the morning. Takes all kinds.

Kepella had put away close to half the pint of Papa by a few minutes before three. He had given Jay plenty of time to fall asleep. Kepella didn't want any more trouble. He slipped out of the borrowed car and decided to walk around the block once, just to check things out. The lap took five minutes; he walked right past Freddie hiding in a doorway.

Kepella climbed the stairs to Jay's apartment. He planned to slip the key quietly under the crack, leaving it on the floor. The loose change on the floor shouldn't arouse too much suspicion. As he knelt by the door to the loft apartment, Kepella heard the shower running. First a guy jogging at two-forty-five in the morning, now a kid in the shower at three. He slipped the key under the gap in the door and shoved it in further using a folded dollar bill. He walked quietly back down the stairs.

As Kepella walked across the street, he noticed the skinny bum in the doorway. He didn't want to be mugged at three in the morning.

The fire took quickly. Before Kepella was half a block away, he turned and saw the blaze jumping from the rear of the building. Becker! he thought, pressing his back against a wall and watching the fire grow. What to do? If he allowed Becker to fry, then what was the purpose of any of this? He had to move. Fast.

He had enough sense not to use the stairway, even though, as he ran past the front door, the fire seemed not to have reached the front of the building. He hurried around to the alley and the fire escape. He was huffing by the time he began to climb the ladder. He reached the first landing.

From here it was obvious the fire would consume the building within minutes. He pulled himself up the rusted fire escape. Sweat broke out across his forehead. He felt the booze in his veins. Dizzy. He stopped. He looked down, feeling even more dizzy, and then started to turn back, torn between up and down: the story of his life.

Jay had showered off the cigarette smoke he collected every night playing the bars. He had changed into fresh jeans, a clean pair of socks, and his running shoes. He noticed the Shilshole pass key lying there. Had that been there before? He was just buttoning his Hawaiian shirt when he smelled smoke. Then he spotted a faint curl coming under the door. Smoke! He picked up the key and ran to the phone. Nothing. Dead. Just like he would be in another minute if he didn't do something. He ran over to Larry the Lizard's repaired terrarium and fished Larry out. A window broke behind him. Glass flew into the room. Jay dropped Larry and ducked behind a group of ferns.

"Kid," a gravel voice called out. "The building's on fire. Becker?"

Jay stood up and shouted, "Who *are* you?" He could see half a face, its skin orange from the flames. A pushed-in face and a bulbous nose. It was him. No doubt. The same guy. The guy who had broken into the apartment. The guy on the videotape the Chinaman had called "Roy." "What do you *want*?"

Kepella peered through a hole in the jagged glass. "The fire!"

Smoke was filling the room quickly. Jay switched on a light. He could barely see. "Larry!" he called hopelessly. "Larry!"

The fire built quickly across the side of the building. Kepella shouted, "Kid, use your head. Get outa there. Now!"

Jay panicked. He removed the police bar and opened the door a crack.

"No, kid. Don't be stupid . . ."

Thick smoke. No flames. An orange light danced in the shaft of the freight elevator. Jay took hold of *The Streak,* hoisted its light frame above his shoulder, and ran through the smoke toward the stairs.

Kepella hurried down the fire escape. Stupid kid. The building was going up like tinder.

Jay reached the bottom of the stairs. As he opened the entrance door, he turned, remembering the Kramers. He ran into the corridor and pounded on their apartment door. No answer. Vacation, he remembered. He ran to the front of the building. Smoke poured from the freight elevator. Jay took one last look. As he came out onto the street carrying *The Streak* he saw the guy running up the hill. He shouted, but the guy kept running. He climbed on *The Streak* and pedaled hard. The guy got in a car and slammed the door.

Jay had the bike really moving by the time the second-story apartment blew. The force of the explosion knocked him off. He looked back at the flames. His home was destroyed. He had scuffed his right arm, but managed to get back on the bike. At the corner he tripped a fire alarm.

The car raced off. Jay tucked his head low, shifted gears up, and started gaining on him. He was only twenty yards behind him, pedaling hard along the flat, head tucked low, hidden by the darkness and his aerodynamic position. The car turned right. Jay turned right. The car turned, left. Jay turned left. The car sped up. Jay sped up. They traveled this way, car and bike in tandem, for a few minutes. Then they hit a red light. Jay braked, dismounted, and jumped the bike up onto the sidewalk to avoid being seen in the rearview mirror. He watched through the car window as the guy chugged from a pint of something. Who the hell was this guy?

Five blocks later, the car pulled into a short driveway on Cedar, up near Broad. Jay pedaled past and pulled over, noting the address. Jocko's place was three blocks away. He waited ten minutes. A light went out in a lower window. Jay thought of his loft—the jungle—all of it gone. Burned. He saw before his eyes all that he would never see again, and sighed: no tears, no tight throat, just one deep sigh.

Burned. All of it gone. Forever.

31

Jocko delivered a cup of tea, poured himself a Scotch, and sat on the springy couch opposite his friend, who had a blanket draped over his shoulders.

"I left Larry up there."

"You left a lot of things up there," Jocko responded. "You can do what about it? This I would like to know."

Becker tried to smile. "You sound like your father."

Jocko just smiled.

"You know, when I found that videotape, I thought, Shit, this is *exciting!* I really *enjoyed* it for a while." He tried to laugh. "I don't know if the guy on the fire escape was trying to save me or kill me, but this stuff has got to stop."

"You'll have to talk to the cops. We should go down there now."

"Now maybe they'll listen. What if there's nothing they can do about it?"

"There has to be something."

"What if there isn't?"

"Then I pay off your debt and I fly you the hell out of here, until whatever this is is over. Should have done that in the first place."

"If I got the cops the tapes, then they'd listen."

"Don't even think about it—"

"But it might involve Marlene. I have to get Marlene out of this."

"You have to get yourself out of this first."

"I'm sick of that attitude! When do we think about the other person? I *care* for her, damnit!"

"This is no time to get righteous."

"What if I got the videotape, got Marlene off *The Lady Fine,* and told Holst to leave us alone? What the hell could he do?"

"Kill you."

"I'm serious. I leave the tapes with a lawyer . . . in the event of death, and all that."

"Too many flicks."

"What?"

"You've been watching too many flicks."

"Look who's talking. You're the tube freak, not me."

"We settle your debt. You get the hell out of town. No more 'I Spy.' "

"But it might work," Becker thought aloud.

"The first thing we do is rig you up with a piece, laws or no laws."

"I'd end up shooting myself. We've been over that."

"Then a blade." Jocko reached down and pulled a switchblade out of a small leather strap fixed around his calf. "You can use Mildy."

"What about you? You can't sleep without that thing."

"Let's not get testy. I have Mildy's predecessor around here somewhere. I retired it in favor of Mildy's ebony handle and safety catch. You're better off with Mildy. She's a safer model." He opened and closed it twice to demonstrate how it worked, and handed the strap and knife to Becker.

Jay tried it and did fine. "I don't know. This seems ridiculous."

"Better safe, and all that. Remember, if you have to use it, make sure you pull it back out. You don't leave a blade in an opponent. They can use it on *you*."

"That's disgusting. You're the martial arts freak. I don't know anything about this stuff."

"Stab the other guy, pull it out, and run like hell. That's how you use a blade."

Jay sipped the tea.

"How are you feeling?"

On the couch, in front of a lamp, Becker's face was in shadow and his hair glowed. The frustration in his voice could be seen in the twisting of his hands, the nervous tapping of his right leg, his knee jumping, as if he was listening to the beat of a fast song. Jay leaned forward and the harsh light flooded the right side of his face, throwing the shadow of his nose across his left cheek. "We've been in the business ten years, and what have we got to show for it?"

Jocko blew cigarette smoke away from Becker, and didn't answer.

"How much money have we brought in?" Jay asked.

"You mean over the last ten years?"

"Yeah."

"Somewhere around four hundred grand, I'd say. Maybe a little bit more."

"I've never had more than two hundred dollars in my account. You know that? Never topped two hundred bucks and we've made damn near half a million."

"There's been a lot of us, Jay."

"I make what, six to eight grand a year? It costs me that much to squeak by. I've washed dishes, I've tended bar, I've played duo gigs with Jimmy, I've taught sailing lessons . . ."

"I know what you're saying."

"Not really. Not really, Jocko. I don't mean to sing the blues, but you and I have different situations. You don't *need* the money. I do."

"I know that. What am I supposed to say to *that*?"

"I don't know. How should I know? I don't expect you to say *anything*. I'm just complaining, that's all." He moved and his face returned to shadow.

"Am I supposed to talk you into playing?"

"I don't know. So many people, you know, they look at me a certain way. Oh, they never say anything—one reason or another—but they're *thinking*, Poor slob, should get outta this business. What the fuck? Most people don't even consider it a business. They think we're screwing off up there. They think we're a bunch of hacks."

"They're jealous."

"Maybe."

"They are. They see all the attention we get, and they think they'd like it. They misunderstand."

"How many clubs do you think we've played?" Becker asked, breaking a short silence.

"Three hundred maybe."

"How many gigs?"

"Gigs? I don't know . . . a thousand?"

"Tonight was twelve hundred forty-seven."

"Is that right?"

"How much longer am I supposed to keep doing this? How much longer do I live with fifty bucks in my checking account, saving money to buy strings and gas and all the shit you have to buy? I'm going out of my mind."

"It's good for you. Last time I saw you like this, you wrote a couple of great tunes. Remember, man, you write the tunes. If this ever does take off, *you* make the publishing dough. The rest of us earn wages. There's a big difference. You want somebody to tell you how fucking great you are, how we can't do The RockIts without you, how you hold the whole damn thing together by just being who you are—not me, not tonight." He smiled, because Jay had smiled. Jay needed to be reminded of his value now and then. Jocko always did it in a strange way.

"The life-style sucks."

"Basically, you're right."

"We're living in a dream world."

"Another reason why they're all jealous," he said, twisting what Jay had meant.

"What if it never breaks? What if it never goes?"

"That scares you, doesn't it?"

Angry now—jealous—Jay said, "You're damn right that scares me, man. I haven't got your kind of dough."

Jocko twisted the cigarette into the ashtray. Smoke curled away from him. The red ember glowed a moment and then turned gray and lifeless. "If you did, you wouldn't write the songs you do. If you did, you wouldn't sing better and better. You would become complacent. Believe me, Jay. I know about these things. Why the fuck do you think I drink so much damn Scotch?"

Jay studied his friend, noticing for the first time his own shadow stenciled against the arm of the opposing couch. The shadow distracted him. "I'm tired."

"I know."

"It's been a long, long time."

"It certainly has."

"Sometimes I wonder if it's worth it."

"Me too."

"I meet a woman like Marlene and I wish I could take her out to fancy dinners, cruise town in a Porsche. Sometimes that stuff's important."

"To whom?"

Jay watched the shadow against the couch. "You're saying it shouldn't be."

"I don't know what I'm saying."

"That's probably right. 'We are who we are,' and all that."

"No more. No less."

Becker smiled. It felt right to smile. "You're a good shit, Rocks."

"A fuckin' genius."

The cynicism bothered Jay. "You afraid of the future?"

Jocko looked over at his friend. He wanted to tell him how much he envied Jay's talent, his looks, his ability to take it all so damn lightly most of the time. He wanted to remind him of how lucky the last ten years had been: people—total strangers at the time—giving the band money to pay bills, to make tapes, loaning them vehicles, offering them places to stay; and all because they knew the band had it . . . they knew *Jay* had it. You could *feel* it. Something different. The future? What future? Jay's future? Jocko had no fears about Jay's future. The fucking world was blind—and deaf. At some point it would happen. It would simply happen. And then all the bar owners, all the managers, all the record people, would kick themselves, saying, "He was in here once. I passed up that kid."

"No, I'm not afraid of the future. I'm afraid of *myself*. Always have been . . ."

"What's that supposed to mean?"

Jocko lit another cigarette and stared down at the Scotch. "We'll talk in the morning. I have some ideas on how to better protect you—"

"Don't be ridiculous."

"You realize we'll finally be having breakfast over here."

"That means I buy the doughnuts."

"You're damn right." Jocko pulled the door to his room shut.

Jay looked over at the empty couch. The knife seemed huge. He reached over and touched it. It was still warm from pressing against Jocko's leg. Jay withdrew his hand quickly and stared at it, thinking, What if?

32

Kepella ordered a cab to pick him up at the Space Needle at 8:15. He drove to the monorail, and taking the same precautions as before, waited to board last. Arriving at the Seattle Center, he walked quickly to the waiting cab, climbed in, and barked to the driver, "Get moving."

Brandenburg wore a peach bathrobe. His Oriental maid was frying up some eggs and hashbrowns. At Brandenburg's recommendation, Kepella asked for and received a glass of fresh-squeezed orange juice. Kepella had worn his hair as short as Brandenburg's during his stint in Korea. He had hated it. Kepella sipped at the OJ. Minute Maid was a treat for Kepella; this was luxury.

"You look tired."

"You look like a goddamned king, if you don't mind my saying so."

"But I do, Roy." Brandenburg bit into some crisp toast and flicked crumbs from his lap. "I'm on vacation. I work hard. I play hard. That's my prerogative."

"Vacation?"

Brandenburg looked away. "Officially, I'm on vacation. It seemed an appropriate cover to myself and the director. You needn't be bothered with the details. Fill me in, now. Where do we stand?" He lifted an eyebrow and sipped at the orange juice, obviously savoring the pulp, chewing it slowly.

Kepella took out a slip of paper. On it were two names written in an unsteady hand. A few weeks ago Kepella had prided himself on his penmanship. No longer. It looked like the hand of an old man, and that's how he felt—like an old man.

Brandenburg picked up the piece of paper. "J. Becker, Marlene Jenner, passport number . . . What's this?"

"I want you to run those names for me. I want to know everything there is to know about both of them."

"Who's this Becker?"

That's odd, Kepella thought. Why had Brandenburg only singled out the kid? "He may be involved."

"How?"

"I'm hoping you can help answer that."

Brandenburg waved the paper in the air. "This may take a while."

"I want it sooner than later."

"My point is—"

"I don't give a damn what your point is, Brandenburg. These people are involved in this and I want to know how deeply. Now get me the information or count me out of this."

"Roy . . ."

"Don't 'Roy' me, Brandenburg. Don't mix it sweet for me, buddy. I'm putting it all on the line out there. I'm an old fart, right? Right? And I don't care for this one damn bit, you got that? Not one damn bit." His hands were shaking. He needed a shot of Papa. There was a bottle in the car . . . "Don't screw with me, mister." He shoved his hands into his lap.

Brandenburg was staring. "I'll look into it, Roy."

"You're damn right you'll look into it," Kepella whispered, ashamed now.

"It shouldn't be long now, Roy."

"It better not be." Still a whisper.

"You've passed the first group—"

"They want the green laser deployment next. Can you figure that?"

"They don't go for the small stuff, I'll say that."

"It's like they know."

"What's that, Roy?"

"It's like they know exactly what you and I talked about."

"What we discussed in the briefing was information I had, Roy. That's why it strikes you as odd."

Kepella wanted to say, *You* strike me as odd, Brandenburg. Instead he said, "I want the information on the kid and the woman. I need that. You got that?"

"A certain degree of informality I will tolerate, Roy. Let us not forget position, shall we?"

Kepella wondered if Brandenburg might have a nip stashed around here somewhere. He desperately wanted to ask.

"I'm running *you*, Roy. Not the other way around." He paused between each word, "I . . . say . . . jump . . . you . . . say . . . how . . . far. Clear . . . ?" He raised his voice. "Clear?!"

Kepella cowered. He was sweating badly, sitting on his hands to keep them still. He felt weak, his mouth sour. He thought he might throw up. Just a nip. Just one shot and all would be well. "Seeing as you're on vacation and all"— Kepella's attitude had done an about-face, his tone, his entire disposition was suddenly submissive—"you wouldn't happen to have a belt around?"

"A belt?"

"Never mind."

"Oh." Brandenburg smiled, turning his wrist and glancing at his watch. "You mean a toddy?"

How many people wear watches while still in their bathrobe? Kepella asked himself This guy was one strange bird.

"Over there." Brandenburg pointed without looking, directing Kepella as he might direct a servant. "I'll join you. Vodka isn't it?"

Kepella already had the cabinet open. "You don't seem too surprised."

"Why should I?"

"I was dry."

"You're a drunk, Kepella." His tone was contemptuous. "A drunk is never dry for long."

Kepella placed the bottle back in the cabinet and shut the door, his hand trembling. He remained kneeling. He wanted to show Brandenburg—or was it himself?—how strong he was; he didn't need a drink . . . But then he reopened the cabinet and brought the bottle of Smirnoff over to the dining room table.

The window was open: another clear day. The air smelled clean and moist. It would be another scorcher. Brandenburg slowly unscrewed the bottle cap, watching Kepella watch him. He poured a tiny amount into his orange juice and slid the bottle over to Kepella. Kepella poured a decent-sized shot. It mixed with the pulp that had stuck to the sides of the glass. He drank it without looking at Brandenburg.

"To your health," Brandenburg said, sipping his spiked OJ.

The vodka hit bottom and Kepella relaxed. He told himself if he could just cut down, he would be able to regain control. Mornings were the worst: the queasy stomach, the dry heaves, the shakes. But he had to start somewhere.

"You're doing a fine job, Roy. Really quite good. I think you'll be happy in Washington . . . D.C. that is. Washington could use some fresh blood."

"I brought the money with me."

"I wondered what that was."

"The first advance."

"Yes. Well, let's a take a look." He signaled Kepella to hand him the briefcase. Roy obeyed, now hoping the man might recommend another "toddy." Brandenburg opened the briefcase. "New bills." He looked at Kepella. "You should have specified old bills."

"I forgot." Spoken like a child to a parent. It was the truth; Kepella never remembered discussing it.

"The point is, Roy, the bills I have are *old* bills, as I thought you understood. We can't very well make a switch now, can we? If this fellow Holst is supplying her with the cash, well then, he would be suspicious if you turned around and paid off your debt with different bills, now wouldn't he?"

"I could pay him a small amount, like I had deposited it and later withdrawn this amount."

Brandenburg just stared at Kepella, waiting for him to see the flaw in the idea.

Kepella finally said, "No, that's no good. Why the hell would I deposit a few grand in cash?" He shook his head. A child.

"Why don't I give you a thousand of the marked bills. You can say you woke up this morning, went out to play

289

the dogs, and finally won."

"Good idea."

"But for Christ's sake, Roy, make certain you find out which dogs did win, in case he asks you." Brandenburg left the room. When he returned he handed Kepella the marked money.

Then Kepella remembered. "How did you know about Rosie?"

"What?"

"Rosie. The last time we met, you mentioned Rosie. How did you know about her?" Brandenburg suddenly seemed nervous. Imagine that. Old flattop nervous.

Brandenburg said, "You told me about her. You mentioned her. How else would I know about her?"

Kepella knew he had never said anything. He nodded as if this explained it. He figured Brandenburg didn't want to admit to having him followed, or didn't want to admit having met with Mark Galpin, which Kepella was sure he must have. "The dog thing is a good idea."

"Another?" Brandenburg tapped the edge of the bottle. It chimed a dull note.

Kepella had to work to control himself. He looked at Brandenburg and shrugged. "Why not?" He poured one for himself. Brandenburg had barely touched his laced OJ. Kepella's hands tingled; the base of his brain was warm. "When can you have the information on the two?"

"I told you it may take a while."

"I want it today."

"Impossible."

"This evening then." Kepella rose. "No later than this evening."

"These things take time, Roy. You know that."

"Listen, Brandenburg. I don't much like you. You're an arrogant son of a bitch. I figure you're keeping from me about as much as you're letting me in on. I figure it was you who put Galpin up to having me followed, because I know Mark Galpin, and he wouldn't do something like that without a direct order. So I figure you know when I eat, shit, and sleep. That's your business. But I need to know who the hell those two people are. That's important to me. I wanta know whether or not I should be on guard with them, that sorta thing. And I happen to know that profile runs take about forty-five minutes maximum. So, for once you better listen to me. I want those profiles. I'll give you 'til this evening. I want this damn job over with. Another few days at most. You had better hope Wilhelm is already on his way, because I won't play along much longer, Washington or no Washington. I've lost my friends—what few I had—and my self-respect; I'm boozing again; and I'm beginning to think that if I play too much longer, either someone's gonna waste me or I'll lose any faint chance I may have at straightening out my life. If you screw up, if you *miss* Wilhelm again . . ." He paused. "*I'm* the one who lifted all the documents. I'm the one who'll have all the explaining to do. Christ, even if I wanted to, I couldn't *prove* you were running me."

"I'd back you up, Roy."

"Get me those profiles." He huffed away, smelling like vodka. Brandenburg didn't even turn his head. He pushed his orange juice aside and rang the silver bell on the table.

33

Evening. The sun hung low in the horizon, ready to set out over the Pacific. Shilshole was picturesque. A postcard. White masts glimmered in the soft light; halyards clapped against wood and aluminum, a constant dull applause mixing with the low whistle of wind across stays. Marlene finished painting clear nail polish onto her little fingernail. Holst worked at the small, folding table that was covered in newspaper, soldering the second of two wires to a DC convertor.

"Are you sure that will work?" Marlene asked, blowing her nail dry.

"Yes. The only problem is whether or not you can stall him."

"That is not a problem."

"You *will* go through with it, will you not?"

"We have been over this. What choice do I have? Leave me alone."

He wondered if she was up to this. Perhaps he had pushed her too far by beating her. It was something he couldn't control. There was nothing to be done about it now. He had hoped that with Marlene, a beating would have forced her final defeat, her surrender. Perhaps she is stronger than most, he mused. In a while—in a few days— I will lower you over the side for the last time. That will be the end of your defiance.

He knew that Kepella controlled the game at the moment, and like it or not, they were now playing by his rules. Holst was soldering a way around that, and if Kepella did not deliver exactly as he promised, then Roy Walter

Kepella also had little time left on this earth.

Holst finished soldering, unplugged the iron, and approached Marlene with a tiny bottle in his right hand. He spoke German. "I put it into a bottle of nail polish. It's a clear liquid, like what you just put on, so even if he checks, he won't know the difference. Tip your finger now, and if you have the chance, again later." He handed her the bottle. She unscrewed the cap carefully and inverted the small bottle, wetting the end of her index finger. It dried instantly.

She asked, "And you are certain this will work?"

"Yes. I tried it myself. It works."

Kepella and Marlene met again at the Greenlake Grill. This time Kepella waited in his Dodge until Marlene arrived, and then pulled alongside of her Eagle and rolled down his window. He appeared slightly drunk, a smile pasted on his leathery lips, his eyes glassy. "Hop in."

A block behind, Holst watched.

"Should we not select a motel again?" Marlene asked Kepella while nervously scratching the back of her hand.

"Not here. In a minute. Please, no questions." Kepella had to maintain his role of paranoid informer. It wasn't too difficult anymore.

She opened the car door and slipped into the front seat. She smelled like wildflowers.

The sky held a sliver of orange in the west, seemingly placed there by the brush of a careful artist. Then suddenly the brush stroke was gone; the sky glowed gray-blue.

Kepella crossed the opposite lane and pulled into a Shell station, parking in front of a pay phone stall. "I pick, tonight," he announced.

"What?" Marlene exclaimed, realizing the blacklight fluid on her fingertip would be useless—Holst's plan defeated.

Kepella missed the surprise in her voice.

"I thought I would be allowed to pick," Marlene said.

He shrugged. "My turn."

They both stepped out of the car. Kepella pulled his raincoat closed and tied the belt. He opened the Yellow Pages to the motel section, closed his eyes, and stabbed the page. Marlene saw her chance. "Which is that?" she asked. She reached down and carefully placed her chemically coated fingertip on the name of the motel—The Westside Motel—and rotated it once, as Holst had schooled her.

Back in the car, she said, "Roy, do you suppose we might stop somewhere and have a drink or two?"

He glanced over at her, a line of sweat caught in a crease of his forehead. "Why?"

She thought, Why indeed? "I could use a drink."

"Me too." Kepella pulled into Tommy's Steaks and parked. He was thirsty.

It felt as if it might rain.

Jay sat around Jocko's apartment all day, his boredom mounting with each passing hour, thinking about the fire. Jocko had gone off for a bucket of chicken. Jay couldn't help thinking of what he had lost: some love letters; lyrics to several dozen songs, now kept only in his head; family memorabilia; photos; correspondence; thrift store clothes with memories of a decade of performances woven into the seams. None of this was earth-shattering. Nonetheless, he was devastated. Larry the Lizard had died in the fire; "the forest" was ashes—his green friends he had cared for were gone.

Jocko had doted on him like a good Jewish mother. Drink this. Eat this. Think this. Finally, he had sulked out, grumping about doing some shopping.

The heart, Jay realized, is the only true test of anything. Your heart knows what matters. His heart told him that Marlene was innocent and in trouble. In over her head. She needed him. He no longer believed she was sleeping with Holst. That had been a clever line to get rid of him. And it had worked. He strapped the switchblade to his left calf as Jocko had shown him, and left the apartment, climbing aboard *The Streak* and heading off toward Shilshole. He would change things, once for and all.

He rode for fifteen minutes. Once there he hid behind a Winnebago that was parked on the far side of the parking area, directly across from Pier L, and waited, trying to build up his nerve. The sun sat above the horizon ready to be extinguished by Puget Sound. As he was trying to decide what to do, he saw Marlene leave *The Lady Fine* and start in his direction. Holst followed slowly behind her.

The two climbed into separate cars and caravanned out of the parking lot, Marlene's Eagle in the lead. Jay jumped onto *The Streak* and set off at top speed, helmeted head down, pedals flying. Both cars traveled down Market Street. Due to the unusually heavy traffic Jay was able to stay with them, electing to remain a block behind. By Oswego he had sweated through his shirt and the seat of his pants and thought he might blow a ventricle.

When Holst finally pulled over, Jay hopped off *The Streak* and jogged in place to keep his legs from cramping.

He watched as Marlene transferred to an old junker of a car. It was Roy's car—the same car he had followed the night before. A few blocks later she and Roy got out at a Shell station and a minute later they were back on the road. There was no way to follow them without passing Holst, so he swallowed his urge and decided to stay with the German instead. Now he knew they were all connected. But how? Marlene was obviously involved in something, just as Jocko had said. Tonight she was dressed to kill, and suddenly Jay didn't necessarily want to know the rest.

Holst drove across the street to the phone booth at the Shell station. Ah-ha, Jay thought, a message. Iben Holst removed a vacuum cleaner—or something—from his car and took it with him to the phone booth. A minute later he got in the car and drove away.

The chase began again.

Fifteen minutes later Holst pulled into The Westside Motel, parked, and entered the office. Three or four minutes later, he emerged and pulled his car around to one of the rooms and parked again. Lugging some gear, he disappeared into a room. Jay leaned *The Streak* against a tree and hid in the bushes. A motel?

Holst had spent the better part of the day working on his false identification. His only real problem had been finding a convincing badge, a problem he solved by renting a police hat from a costume shop. The hat's badge looked authentic enough for a quick flash. He had pinned the badge into a thin identification wallet and had practiced flipping it open. His performance was convincing. Once he flashed the badge, the woman night clerk, a nervous Oriental, agreed to his every request.

He took his gear first to room 114. He placed the voice-activated tape recorder inside a towel under the bed, hoping the sound on the video would be enough but wanting this as a backup in case. The video camera presented a bigger problem. He measured the wall carefully and worked speedily, knowing he had only thirty or forty minutes. He drilled a two-inch hole in the sheetrock, removed the insulation from the stud wall, and then drilled into the wall directly behind where the mirror had hung. He brushed away the sawdust and mounted a two-way mirror he had bought. Mylar on Plexiglas. It looked fine: as cheap as the rest of the place. From room 115, he trained the video camera through the newly drilled hole and focused. When the TV had warmed up, he was looking at a dark picture of an empty room 114. He adjusted the camera's aperture.

Marlene wore a white dress with blue fleur-de-lis in neat and patterned rows. Her hair was in a bun and held in place with a jeweled skewer. Her smile, contrived as it was, sparkled in the soft light of the cocktail lounge. A piano player earned his keep in the corner. Kepella lifted his glass and drank. "Did you think about what I said?"

She stared at the table, a thick coat of polyurethane covering the imitation boat hatch. "A great deal."

"And?"

"I do not know how to help."

"Holst is running the deal, isn't that right?"

She shook her head. "I do not understand why you would care to know any of this."

"To protect myself. To protect both of us. If something

goes wrong—if I'm busted—I need a way out of all of this. I told you before, we both may need a way out."

"Nothing will go wrong."

"I wish I had your confidence. Don't forget I used to work for the Bureau."

She placed her hands in her lap. She wanted Holst stopped. She knew that much. But if she missed *her* chance at him, then who would punish him? "Holst runs it."

Kepella kept the smile off his face. She had broken. Just as he had guessed, she was no professional; she was being used; she was all alone. He knew the feeling. "They're using you, aren't they? What do they have on you, Marlene?"

"Why do you keep asking that?"

"I assume you are what we call the 'resident expert.' You're the one who can verify what I give you. Isn't that right?"

"It might be." She sipped the drink nervously and finished it, her second. She wasn't accustomed to two mixed drinks.

Kepella raised a hand, ordered them both another. The base of his skull was warm and numb. "So they're using you . . ."

She wanted to say, You don't know the half of it. Instead, she said, "No."

"What do they have, Marlene? Personal? Family? Business?"

"Family," she admitted.

Now we're getting somewhere, he thought. "You want to tell me about it?"

"No. What do they have on you?"

"A gambling debt. It's very large. That's why I suspected Holst. I think he rigged the games."

"He did. That is all I am going to tell you, Mr. Kepella. No more. Now you will trade?"

"Of course." He raised his glass to hers and they toasted. "I'm far too much in debt, and to the wrong people, not to play along. Like you, I have no choice." He waited. "And the kid? How does he fit into it?"

She spilled some of her drink. She told herself not to drink anymore, but took a sip anyway. "I don't know who you are talking about."

"Jesse Becker."

She glared across the table. "Jay had nothing to do with this."

"But . . ."

"No more, Mr. Kepella. Ask me no more questions, please." She checked her watch. A red flag went up in Kepella's dulled brain. He thought it odd she should check her watch. "Can we please leave now?" she asked.

"This was your idea," he reminded her.

"Please."

Kepella paid for the drinks and helped her with her jacket. He felt like kicking his heels together. Progress at last. It was beginning to fit together.

Kepella opened the door to 114 with the key the Oriental desk clerk had given them.

Marlene flicked on the light. The bed occupied most of the room, save for a chest of drawers and a color television. The bathroom was at the far end of the room, behind a white door. Kepella closed the door. She opened her briefcase, and the two of them sat side by side, examining the papers Kepella had given her. She seemed concerned only with two or three specific computer boards that drove the laser, and Kepella realized how knowledgeable she was. He answered a few questions and she paid him the balance of the money.

"What about the method?"

Kepella resisted. He *felt* like a traitor now—no more role-playing. He was giving away state secrets—that fact was inescapable. He felt his palms sweat, his pulse increase. "Satellite," he said.

She removed a small notepad and pen from the briefcase. "Deployment?"

He looked around the room, trying to avoid giving the answer. Funny, he thought, there's a strip of paint beneath the mirror that hasn't faded. Somebody probably broke the mirror and the motel had replaced it. Shitty-looking mirror, though, dull and gray. "Space shuttle deployment of the first working model is scheduled for September."

She looked up. "Are you certain?"

"They will let it leak that it's another spy satellite. All the attention will be on Florida. A second shuttle will be launched from the California site at the same moment. They hope to catch the Soviets with their pants down."

"I beg your pardon?"

"Just an expression. Off guard . . . they hope to surprise them."

"Yes. I see." She took notes, a shorthand Kepella didn't recognize. "September?"

"Barring any other shuttle delays. Yes, last week in September, I believe."

"Do you have working plans?"

"No, not complete plans. They have them spread around the country to prevent any one supplier from seeing the full picture. We have Zelco Industries here. They provide the gasses. I can give you that. That's all I have." He took off a shoe and handed her the folded paper.

She studied it for several minutes. "This is excellent. I will see they pay you a bonus for this."

"They?" he tried.

She looked quickly over her shoulder, toward the mirror. Kepella made the connection then. Glancing down, he saw traces of saw dust on the rug, below the chest of drawers. He might have missed it if the mirror had fit.

He jumped up, hurried out the door, and, before Marlene could react, kicked in the door to room 115. He rushed over to the VCR. Just as he reached for it he heard, "Do not touch the equipment, Roy. It would be a fatal mistake."

Holst stood in the doorway, a small semi-automatic pistol in hand.

"Bastard," Kepella spit.

"I could not take your word, now could I, Roy? Insurance, is what it is. Marlene told me you were thinking of cutting our business deal short. I cannot allow that, Roy. You are far too valuable. Now, with this tape, you will help me until I say stop. Is that clear?"

"Bastard."

Holst waved Kepella away from the equipment with the gun, and then shut the door. "Go back inside, Roy. Marlene will tell you what we want next."

"And what if I refuse?"

"I will kill you so that it looks like suicide. I will expose

301

an edited version of the tape."

Kepella, a little drunk, walked back into 114 and shut the door. Marlene's eyes said, *Now you know how it feels . . . how it really feels.*

Holst checked to see that the machine was still running. No use losing good footage. He could see the resignation written on Kepella's face. He stepped out for a cigarette. It was then he heard the sneeze. Someone was in the bushes . . .

Jay felt the sneeze coming. Christ! He tried everything, pinched his nose, sucked air through it, even rammed a finger up his nostril, trying to quell the itch. He had seen the whole thing: Roy furious; Holst with a gun.

And then he sneezed. He saw Holst look up toward him.

"Stop!" Holst shouted.

Jay scrambled up the hill toward *The Streak,* jumped on, and pedaled away.

"Stop!"

He heard the car fire up and the tires squeal. Holst was coming after him.

He headed west on 57th Street, making ninth gear by 33rd Avenue. In the twilight, in the tiny rearview mirror mounted on his helmet, he suddenly saw Holst's car. A horn blasted in his left ear. He looked up just as he ran a red light. A car was approaching from his left, another from his right. Nowhere to go. He squeezed the rear brake gingerly and laid *The Streak* down into an intentional fall. The car on his left swerved and missed him. He kept his balance perfectly, sitting on the high side of the bike as it skidded on a pedal and handlebars, holding on with all his strength to keep it from bucking into a somersault. The car to his right swerved as well, and was suddenly aimed right for him. He ducked. His shoulder grabbed the pavement as he slid under the car's front bumper, his helmet hitting the front license plate. He slid to a stop, his scuffed-up shoulder bleeding. The leg of his jeans was shredded and pain screamed from his right knee. Then the pain disappeared—he felt only adrenaline pumping. He looked around. Holst was out of his car, looking into the jam of traffic. Their eyes met. Jay popped the wounded *Streak* back up, threw his hurt leg over the bar, and took off. The pedal was bent slightly, as was the brake handle, but the bike had come through it surprisingly well. He looked back. Holst's car pulled out and jumped up onto the sidewalk, bypassing the congested traffic. It knocked over a newspaper vending machine.

Jay shifted gears.

Holst passed the third car back.

Jay looked behind again, pumping now as hard as he could. He began passing cars on the right, eyes alert for anyone pulling out in front of him. He put several cars between himself and Holst. Then Holst made his move. He swung into the oncoming lane of traffic and took three cars to his right, jamming his way back into traffic amid a flurry of horns.

Jay shifted again and leaned forward across the handlebars, keeping his head low to cut the wind. He took two cars. Holst picked up another car, and was only three cars back.

Then Jay saw trouble ahead. A car had pulled out from a parking lot and was waiting for a break in traffic. Jay took a second too long to judge the distance. No way to beat the car; no way to squeeze by. He grasped the rear brake handle and made it bite, locking, releasing, locking, releasing—tight little controlled skids. When he had slowed sufficiently, he threw *The Streak* into a right turn, his leg ready to break his fall if she slipped out from under him. He cleared the rear bumper by inches and made a swift arc in the parking lot, realizing this was exactly the right tactic. Now he was headed in the *opposite* direction from Holst. He poured it on, downshifting and cutting through the lot to 37th. He backtracked on 60th and turned right onto 35th.

No sign of Holst. Jay did one of his controlled bike lifts, jumping the curb at a slow speed, and hurried down an alley beside The Tam, a club he had played a few years ago. He braked to a stop, locked *The Streak* to a fire escape, and pounded loudly on the rear fire door, which was also the stage door. Otis Read, a string bean of a man who played left-handed guitar, opened the door. Otis cracked a joke about Jay Becker of The RockIts trying to steal the show. Jay had interrupted Otis's set. The crowd laughed. Noticing Jay's bloodied shoulder and knee, Otis told him to go get a drink and clean himself up. The crowd laughed again.

34

"I'm gonna do it." Jay pulled on a pair of Jocko's jeans. His shoulder hurt. His knee hurt. His knuckles hurt. He balled his hands together and blew into them to warm the knuckles. That helped.

"What is it with you?"

"Somebody's got to get her out."

"So who chose you?"

"I did."

"I don't get it."

"Listen, Rocks. You and I have been debating my life for the past few nights. We both agreed that the choice is a simple one: I can choose to do things for *me* and put on the coat and tie and go earn a decent salary in some office with wall-to-wall and an IBM PC; or I can hang in there—play music—and continue to do it for *them*, the proverbial *them*. So maybe I'm close to a decision."

"You've fallen for Marlene, haven't you? You've lost it."

"That's rhetorical. I have to talk to her. The question is: Are you going to help or not?"

"Of course. I'll follow you in the van."

"Now I don't follow you."

"If we ride together, we're screwed. If I back you up, maybe I can call in the cavalry."

"You're a good shit, Jocko."

"I know."

Jay had been tossed out a window and his apartment had been burned, yet something in him refused to walk away from this. He didn't want to call it love—to him it was more like seeing something through. A single moment, now several weeks back, had changed everything: he had cracked up a friend's car, gone into debt, and taken a day job. He looked up at his friend. "What the hell do we live for if we can't help someone like Marlene?"

"Ourselves," Jocko returned.

"I'm serious."

"You're morose when you're serious."

"What if she needs us?"

"Hey, I'm not arguing with you. But don't forget: she may not want help. I'll go as far as supporting you to find out. But you've got to keep your eyes open. If she's into something and she's using you, then you've got to see that and get the fuck out of this. These guys are playing serious. I've been around shit like this; you haven't. Helping Marlene to get out is one thing. Becoming involved would be a big mistake."

"What's the difference?"

"I suppose we'll find out, won't we?"

"That's a hell of an answer."

"That's the truth."

Holst's car was nowhere to be seen. Jay locked *The Streak* on the far side of Shilshole's lot, well away from where it might be noticed. He kept in the shadows and stepped onto the large sidewalk that fronted all the docks, at Pier R. At Pier L he looked up at the parking lot and located Jocko's van. The parking lights blinked once. If Holst arrived, Jocko would sound the horn twice and Jay would slip over *The Lady*'s side.

He pulled open the door to her cabin.

"Who is there?"

"Me." He hurried down the steps. She was in bed. He couldn't see her well.

"Not here! You must leave."

An ivory light bled through the tiny porthole windows, throwing shadows across her face. "We have to talk," he said.

"Not here. Please leave." She feared he might see her bruises. She had removed the cosmetics before going to bed.

He tried to maintain a tone between anger and forcefulness. "I saw you tonight."

"Tonight?" Puzzlement.

"With Roy, the man I saw on the videotape."

"At the motel?" Astonishment now.

"I followed you—you and Holst."

"To the motel?"

"Yes."

"You were right," she said, "before. We *are* blackmailing that man. You must get out of this."

He waited.

"There is no reason to tell you what we are after, but I wanted you to know that I am not doing this of my own accord. No. There. That's all I have to say to you. I did not want you thinking . . ."

"They tried to kill me."

She shifted and the sheets rustled.

"Twice. Maybe three times. You told him about the videotape?"

"No! I put it back in the wrong section. You should not have left so quickly." Her tears started slowly. Holst had lied. He had beaten her, agreed to a deal . . . he had lied.

Jay waited, then stopped her by saying, "Holst tried again tonight. The police can't help—not until I have more information. I need that tape. I think I can get you out of this if I have that tape."

"When I told you that he and I . . . When you left that day . . . It was not the complete truth . . ."

"I know."

He had to see her eyes—eyes never lie. He had to know if what she was saying was the truth. He switched on the lights.

She had been beaten. Badly. "Marlene!"

She flinched and looked away.

"Jesus." He knelt by her bed, reached out, and touched her arm gently. "Holst?" he asked.

Still refusing to look at him, she said, "You must leave, Jay. It is not safe for you here."

"You're coming with me, Marlene." He turned her head gently toward him, seeing her faint bruises more clearly, wincing. "My dear Marlene."

She trembled. Grief filled her face, a sad, distant grief full of pain and loathing.

Jay turned and pulled up the port shelf. No tape. Gone. He reached across her and pulled up the starboard shelf. Again, no tape.

"It is my father," she whispered.

"What?" Jay could barely hear her.

"He has another tape. My father is a minister, active in what some call radical politics. He is an honest man. But not completely honest, I guess. Holst has a video of him giving money to a politician. The party he supports stands a good chance in our next election. Such a tape would ruin everything he has worked for. He would be discredited. You have to leave, Jay. I *must* do this for Holst. Then it will be over. All I want is for it to be over. Please"—her green eyes begged—"do this for me."

"We have to find that tape I had before. We'll trade the tape he wants for the tape of your father."

"No. There is no trusting him."

"Get dressed. We have to find that tape." He searched the shelf across from her again: no tape.

"It is not in there," she said, pointing.

"Did he come on board with you tonight . . . after the motel?"

"Yes, for a few minutes."

"And did he have the tape when he arrived?"

She squinted. "He must have."

"And when he left?"

"Let me think."

"It's here somewhere."

"Why do you think so?"

"He doesn't seem like the type to take chances. You're working for him, right?"

"Yes." She moved restlessly.

"What do you do?"

She stared at him.

"Tell me."

"I am a contact, a middleman."

"He protects himself. See? He uses you as his front. He maintains a safe distance. I followed him as he followed you and Roy . . . I *know* that much. So, where would he put the tape? Certainly not in his car, not wherever he's staying—it would only implicate him in all of this. No, if anything goes wrong, it has to be you, so, he has to hide them where *you* are. You see?"

She nodded reluctantly.

"Where was he tonight, when he was on board *The Lady*? Where's he been?"

"I remember looking out my window as he left. I didn't

see the tape. Before that, he was forward, in the galley."

"Get dressed. Help me find it." He hoped a task might pull her out of her depression. He left her in the cabin, peered over the rear cabin's companionway, inspected the dock and parking lot, and hurried through the cockpit and down into the main cabin. He began tearing the place apart. As he searched, he planned.

He would find the tape, take it and Marlene to the van, and turn them over to Jocko, who would drive to an out-of-town motel. He would then ride downtown and locate Detective Flint, even if he had to wake him up. He would have Jocko call in the name of the motel to the answering service that took band calls. He and Flint would go out to the motel and they would run through the whole thing, top to bottom. They would have Flint copy the tape—cops must have equipment to do that sort of thing. Then Jay would take the original and make a deal with Holst to trade tapes: the one of Marlene's father for the one of Roy. When the trade went down, Flint would bust it and that would be that. Everyone would live happily ever after.

Nothing. He couldn't find the tape anywhere. He checked the floorboards, the storage beneath all the seats, including the forward holds, the closet, the drawers, the cabinets. Nothing. He was headed up the stairs when Marlene appeared above him, her face stained by tears. "Nothing," he said.

"How?" she asked.

"What's that?"

"How did he try to kill you? Are you sure it was him?"

"The tape, Marlene. We have to find the tape." He stopped at the top of the companionway just inches from her. "Come on!"

She grabbed him with more strength than he knew she had. She shook him. "I must know. I must know for certain."

Jay nodded, frightened by her outburst. "All right. Easy does it. A Chinese goon tried to toss me out my window. I thought he was a junkie. Last night someone set my apartment building on fire. The fire inspector blamed it on a messy basement and a gas leak. It was no gas leak, Marlene. Someone torched the place. It was all over the TV news . . . didn't you see it?"

"The television!" she exclaimed.

Jay looked over. "He took the TV?"

"Yes, the day after—"

"The VCR?"

"Excuse me?"

"The video machine?"

"No, just the television."

Jay looked back into the galley/cabin. He had trashed it. "That's it!" He jumped down the stairs, nearly falling, and stopped at the console that held the stereo and video machines. Next to the video machine a number of black plastic videotape boxes sat stacked in a long line. Jay turned to Marlene, who had followed him down. "Without a television, he knew you couldn't watch these," he said, pointing to the tapes. "Do you know the saying, 'The best place to hide something is the most obvious place'?"

She looked at him curiously.

"He overlooked something," he said, reaching behind the stereo. "To a rock musician, knowing audio electronics is more important than knowing scales." He unplugged a wire from the back of the stereo and plugged it into the side of the VCR. "Sometimes it pays to be a musician." He switched on both the VCR and the stereo. "We may not be able to see them, but we can listen to the soundtracks."

He pushed in the first videotape and fast-forwarded. Marlene joined in the action. She unboxed the tapes while Jay fast-forwarded and then pushed play. He looked at her for a response. She shook her head. " 'The Today Show.' I made that one."

He tried the next, handing her the reject.

"No," she said. "Jane Fonda."

On the fifth tape, Jay cried, "Pay dirt!" Cocktail party sounds with someone dealing cards. They both listened. They heard a woman's gravelly voice say, "Hit me." Jay advanced the tape. They heard Kepella and Marlene talking in the motel.

Marlene said, "That's it!"

He ejected the tape. Marlene slipped it into the box.

"Are you willing to try this?" he asked.

She took one step toward him and hugged him impulsively, hugged him hard. She held him until, finally, he gently pushed her away. She had tears on her face again, this time tears of joy. She kissed him. "I missed you."

He smiled and whispered quietly into her ear, "Ready about." He turned her around squarely by the shoulders, until she was facing the stairs.

"Hard a-lee," she returned. And she laughed—for the first time in ages.

35

Holst was ten minutes away before he realized he had left his driving gloves on the boat. He had turned around and driven back. But as he approached Pier L, he saw the two of them walking down the dock arm-in-arm. Becker! Holst crouched, like a hunter waiting for the approach of his prey, waiting for the kill. Becker had seen the tape; Becker had seen an actual meeting; Becker had to be dealt with.

Behind him, a car horn honked twice just as Marlene stepped through the gate. He reached out and grabbed her. She screamed as Holst pinned her arms behind her.

Jay heard the horn a second too late. He ducked his head and charged Holst, who fell, releasing Marlene. "Run, Marlene!" Jay shouted.

Together they ran into the parking lot, Jay limping slightly from his injured knee. Marlene screamed again as she crashed to the pavement. Jay turned. Holst had tackled her by the ankles. A sparkling sea mist swirled across the parking lot, dancing beneath the overhead lights. The sound of a television emanating from a Winnebago parked in the far corner echoed across the lot. Jay froze. What to do?

Holst pulled out a gun.

The van appeared suddenly. Jocko threw the passenger door open. "Get in," he yelled. Jay obeyed without thinking. He found himself racing out of the lot, looking back at her as Holst manhandled her toward the boat.

Some hero! he thought. "We've got to go back for her!"

"Forget it."

"Turn around!"

"Forget it! We have to think this out." Jocko turned right, snaking the van up the curving road that ran along the perimeter of Golden Garden Park.

"I got the tape," Jay announced, waving it in the air. "Wait till he discovers that."

"Oh, shit," Jocko moaned, seeing the tape.

"What's your problem?"

"We're in this thing now, man. I'm not so sure that was so sm—" A jet headed out over the Sound, its roar carrying across the water like rolling timpani. Jay missed Jocko's last word, but he knew what his friend had said. He stared at the tape in his hand and suddenly wished he hadn't taken it. There was no way out now. They would come looking for him; he had made certain of that. "What am I doing?" he asked Jocko.

"I've been asking you that for the last week. Not a whole hell of a lot we can do about it now, is there?"

Jocko paced the living room, staring at the phone. "And you're sure she has this number?"

"She has both numbers: this and the answering service."

The phone rang. Both men jumped for it. Jocko acquiesced, letting Jay answer. "Hello?"

"Becker please," said the strident German voice.

Jay felt light-headed. He sat down. Just the way Holst spoke gave him the creeps. "Speaking."

"You have something I seem to be missing."

"Likewise."

"Excuse me?" Said politely and patiently.

"Marlene. I want to speak with Marlene."

Her voice came on the line. "Hello?" She sounded scared. "Don't do thi—" Jay heard her gasp as Holst struck her.

"You see?" Holst's voice said calmly. "Everything is fine. We will trade, you and I: Marlene for my tape. No police, no trouble of any sort. Agreed?"

Jay tried to think, but couldn't. The only thing he could think about was Holst slapping Marlene. He would kill the bastard.

"I asked if you agree. I will only remain on the phone another ten seconds."

"Agreed!" Jay snapped. Jocko shook his head, disagreeing. Jay shrugged.

"Golden Garden Par—"

"Not a chance." Jocko had warned him about this. He had said, "If they suggest a desolate location, they only have one thing in mind. Make it a public place. Force their hand." Jay said, "Murphy's bar, twenty minutes."

"I don't know where Murph—"

"Look it up in the phone book." Then he hung up. Jocko had been adamant about this as well—"The person who hangs up first is the one who controls the situation. Don't let him hang up on *you*. *You* hang up on him."

"I did it," Jay said.

"What?" Jocko asked wildly.

"Hung up on him."

"Good."

"Murphy's bar in twenty minutes. No cops, no nothing."

"This is outrageous."

Jocko had picked up on Jay's excitement. But Jay felt only fear now. He said, "The guy is dusty in the attic, man.

There's no telling what he will do."

"You gonna call Flint?"

"No way."

"I thought that was the whole purpose of this?"

"Not as long as they have Marlene. If we were trading for tapes, fine. But I don't trust Holst. He's fried in the brains."

"But that's the point."

"Absolutely not. We do it your way. You back me up."

"Me? I don't know what I'm doing. This is stupid."

"This is all we've got. Bring your gun. You'll hang out in the van and keep an eye peeled."

"You've got Mildy?"

Jay grinned, bent down, and touched the knife strapped to his calf. "Mildy's fine." He felt the surge of excitement begin again. The same surge he had felt a few hours after the Chinese goon had tossed him out the window: a mixture of adrenaline and fear.

Like a man who knew what he was doing, Jocko said, "We keep him waiting. That's the way it's best. Let him sweat it out for a change. Let him feel what it's like."

"I'm scared shitless."

"Me too."

Consumed with guilt at having abandoned Marlene at Shilshole, Jay thought, Can't do that again. Jocko pulled the van onto I-5. Next time, I stay and fight it out, win or lose. No more running. "I shouldn't have left her," he said.

"No other choice."

The Streak bounced in the back of the van. The plan was to let Jay off a few blocks from Murphy's so that Jocko wouldn't be spotted when he parked. The evening mist had become a light fog that now enveloped the city. It swirled in front of the headlights, slowing traffic. Two wrecked cars sat in the breakdown lane, taillights flashing. Jay considered the fact that somehow, one stupid traffic accident had changed the last month of his life, and quite possibly his entire future. He would never be the same again; he would suspect people first, trust them later. Some people— ghetto kids, perhaps—learned this at an early age. Hell, he had waited until thirty. In fact, he realized, he had waited until thirty to learn a lot of things—most of them about himself.

Marlene had once called him strong, and yet he had left her in a parking lot in the hands of a man that had beaten her. Strong? He felt like several people rolled into one: the performer; the insecure boy; a man full of intentions. He liked to think of himself as a man who cared about other people. But how much of that was bullshit? How much of that was him fooling himself? Sure, he liked to entertain people, but he also liked the adulation from the crowd. And he *loved* the struggle. He had picked one of the most difficult professions one could find. That was no coincidence. Jay Becker liked struggles.

Jocko turned right off the highway and immediately left again. A man and woman passed in front of the van on bicycles. Nice machines. The woman, a redhead, wore a skimpy halter top and looked comfortable on wheels. Her partner was too tall for his rig and Jay could tell that the bike had been packed incorrectly. It leaned to the left, unbalanced by the weight in the rear panniers. The couple cut right, lights fading into the fog. Jay had not been on a good bike tour in quite a while. Perhaps it was time to sort this all out on a tour—head down to northern California, do the coast.

"You've got Mildy?" Jocko asked again. Jay heard him and nodded. "You sure you won't take this?" Jocko pulled the handgun out from beneath his shirt. It was a stubby black revolver.

"No thanks."

"Suit yourself." The van stopped.

Jay climbed over the engine mount and into the back of the van. He picked up *The Streak* and slid the van's door open. Warm fog caressed his face.

"Give me a minute to find a spot."

"How long is that?"

"Give me five . . ."

"Yeah, okay."

"You alright, man?"

"No."

"We don't have to do this, you know."

"I do, Rocks. I *have* to."

"If it looks wrong, I'm coming after you. So if something goes down, use your head. We won't get a second chance."

"Listen, Rocks, in case something happens . . ."

"Hey, fuck the sentimental stuff and shut the door." Jocko drove away down the clouded street without looking back.

Jay walked his bike for half a block, giving Jocko a head start. His shoes sponged on the slick sidewalks, squeaking and smacking. The bike clicked along beside him. Cars purred past, wheels whining through the light water, tossing spray onto the row of parked cars between the street and sidewalk. The fog, lit by the signs and street lamps, felt like a low ceiling in a smoke-filled room. Jay liked this weather: *this* was Seattle.

Slightly damp, he reached Murphy's and chained the bike to a lightpost. He tried to collect himself, remembering Jocko's instructions: appear confident and be prepared for anything. He spotted Jocko's van parked down the street and the sight instilled him with confidence. He took a deep breath and pulled open the door.

The wind was knocked out of him instantly. His first thought was that some drunk had hammered into him while trying to get out the door. Then he felt the arms wrap around him—thick arms. He saw the strange tattoo of a mushroom cloud. The man lifted him off the ground and carried him away from the door. Jay attempted to break the goon's grip. The guy's viselike arms were choking the wind from him, pinning his arms helplessly to his sides. His first scream nearly made a noise, but ended up more a gush of air. Then he couldn't breathe, much less scream.

A big man, escorting a pretty woman, complained, "Hey!"

John Chu said, "Dusted, ya know. Angel dust, he's freaked out bad . . ."

The couple backed off and moved around them as Chu fought to stuff Jay inside a panel van double-parked in front of the bar. He finally got him in and squeezed in behind. Donnie sat behind the driver's wheel. As Chu took hold of Jay again, Holst barked, "Drive."

"Where?"

"Shipyards. This side of the canal."

Christ, Jay could see it coming. They were going to

carve him up into pieces and dump him. End of the line. Holst was confident and relaxed—strong—kneeling in the back of the windowless van, rocking from side to side. He asked, "Where is the tape, Jay?"

Jay looked around. No Marlene. He'd been conned. Roached. Jay didn't have the slightest idea what to do. Jocko's few suggestions became tangled into a kind of mindless running dialogue between Jay and himself. Eyes alert. What else? *You* choose topics to discuss. What else?

"Where is the tape, Jay?" Holst repeated calmly.

"Where's Marlene?"

Holst nodded. They had planned for this. Chu took hold of his feet and dumped Jay onto his stomach so that he lay facing Holst. The rug in the van smelled like cat urine. Chu sat down heavily on Jay's back and yanked his arms out in front of him. Holst repeated, "Where's the tape, Jay?"

"You said you would trade," Jay gasped.

Chu pinned Jay's arms to the floor of the van. Jay sucked for air, inhaling the rank smell.

Holst touched the back of Jay's hands. "The deal we had is altered, is it not? You would be well advised to inform me as to the whereabouts of the videotape."

Jay said nothing. The van lurched on its springs as Donnie took a corner quickly. The floor was warming from the transmission, bringing with it noisome odors. Where's Jocko? Jay wondered. Where the hell is Jocko?

"Musicians need their hands, do they not?" Holst continued to stroke the backs of Jay's hands affectionately. Without warning, he snapped Jay's smallest finger to the side, breaking it easily. Jay screamed and jerked, trying to move Chu. His head spun. Holst snapped the ring finger of the same hand. Jay wailed.

The van slowed. "Yes, musicians need their fingers. They need their hands, don't they? Men who like to touch pretty women need their hands too, no? Especially this finger," and Holst broke Jay's middle finger at the knuckle. It didn't break well, so he tugged on it, and snapped it again. Nice and clean. Jay moaned, unable to think, to hear. He opened his eyes and could hardly see. "No more. No more. The tape is in the back of my amp at Charlie's. Up on stage. No one is playing tonight. My amp is the Fender Twin Reverb, next to the drums. Jesus! no more!"

Holst smiled thinly, a sliver of white teeth showing. "Are we there?"

"Shipyard all around us. Canal to our right," replied Donnie.

"All clear?"

"All clear."

"Pull over and stop."

"Yes, sir."

"Well, Mr. Becker. I can't say that I've enjoyed knowing you. Quite frankly, you have been a headache for me from the beginning." He thought to himself, You're the Albatross—you brought the bad luck. "We both appreciate her, you see, you and I. Both in our own ways—and there is seldom room for two men with one woman."

"What if I lied about the tape?" Then Jay said, "I lied about the tape." Insisting.

"You are out of your element, Mr. Becker. You did not lie. Believe me, I have learned the difference. No, I am quite certain that tape is exactly where you told me it is. Quite certain."

"You bastard," Jay managed, his thoughts clearing. His left hand—*his left hand* the most *important* guitar hand— looked like a wheel that had sprung some spokes. Mildy, he thought. Right there, strapped to his leg—the switchblade. Chu, still sitting on Jay, struggled with a length of heavy chain.

The collision knocked Chu off of Jay and into Holst. Something had hit the van hard. And then Jay knew: Jocko! Donnie rocked back and then forward. His head broke the windshield, knocking him senseless. The momentum lifted Jay up off the carpet. He reached down, withdrew the switchblade, pushed the release, and plunged the knife deeply into the first piece of human he saw: Holst's arm. Holst yelled. Jay stabbed him again. It felt good. It felt right to do this. He wanted to plant the thing in Holst's back. He raised the knife . . .

The front door flew open. Jocko pulled Donnie from the driver's seat onto the pavement and kicked him in the groin. He waved his gun around before poking his head inside the van. Chu stirred.

"Book it!" Jocko declared, reaching around the steering shaft and removing the keys. Jay moved the switchblade between the thumb and index finger of his mangled hand. He opened the van's side door and scrambled out. Chu started to move but stopped when he heard gunshots.

"No, Jocko," Jay hollered, picturing the driver with a slug in his head. "Come on," he ordered, climbing into Jocko's van. Then he saw Jocko shoot the rear tire as well. The van rocked to the left as the air blew out of the tire.

Jocko climbed in, the van still running. "Yee-ha!" he shouted maniacally, throwing the van into reverse, the tires screeching. "Fucking A!"

Jay leaned back, gripping his hand. The van roared away.

Jocko switched on the overhead light and, looking over, saw Jay stroking his broken fingers. "Oh God," he said. "Oh my God."

"They got me," Jay agonized. "They really got me."

36

The doctor counted slowly to ten, and at six the woman with the sandy brown hair fell under his control. "Tell me your name."

"Sharon Johnson," she said quite clearly.

"Occupation?"

"Special Agent for the Central Intelligence Agency, presently assigned to the American Embassy in Bonn, West Germany, telex code name, WINDFIRE."

"Are you comfortable, Sharon?"

"Yes." She smiled.

He brought her back to the night agent Robert Saks had died in Regensberg. Her brow creased as she recalled his desperate last moment. "He pulled the photograph from his inside pocket, and then his fist tightened on the photograph. I tried to pull it loose and he gripped it even harder. I turned his wrist and I saw the man in the photograph. It had been taken in an office, with several other men. He had drawn a circle around one of the faces. I assumed that was the man he had told me about—the double agent."

"I want to stay right there for a moment, Sharon. I want you to go back to that first instant you saw the face in the photograph. I want you to push all other thoughts from your mind . . ." He adjusted the flow of fluid into her arm by turning a small valve on the plastic tubing. "That very instant you first saw the face. Only the face. You see only the face." He paused. "Now, do you see him? Do you see the man in the picture?"

"Yes," she answered, her voice more distant.

The doctor looked over at the Agency artist, raised his eyebrows, and asked, "Are you ready?" The artist nodded back.

The doctor said to Sharon, "I want you to open your eyes when I tell you to. I want you to compare the face in your mind with what you will see and I want you to carefully tell me the difference." Again, he paused. "Can you do that for me?"

"Yes."

"Very well then." The doctor slid out of the way, allowing the artist to face Sharon. "Open your eyes."

Fifteen minutes later she had corrected the drawing. Five times the doctor asked her to make absolutely certain the face in her head matched the artist's sketch. She responded to the last of these requests by saying, "The photograph was taken at a distance. It is not perfectly clear. This man I see here is very similar. Very similar." Her sentences were becoming too long, he was losing her. He brought her out carefully and let her rest.

Director Maxwell had a short meeting with the doctor and seemed pleased with the results of the session. He invited Sharon into his spacious office, which overlooked a leafy canopy. A sea of green. She sat down, intimidated by the flags, the photographs, and the man.

He said, "I think you've done it, Sharon. How do you feel?"

"Fine, sir. I hope I did it right."

"We will send this out to Seattle and get the wheels rolling. I wanted to personally thank you for all you've been through. I know these last few weeks are some you would probably rather forget. I would doubt you would ever see that kind of operation again. We don't get too many of those, I assure you. Thank God. But I want you to know that you have provided the Agency and your country a great service by your sacrifice and dedication to duty, and as a token of gratitude I am permitted to promote you two grades higher, and that is exactly what I shall do this afternoon. It is a promotion well deserved. Again, thank you."

He stood, and she understood. They shook hands, and she left the office thankful it was all over. As she reached the door she turned and asked, "Excuse me, sir?"

"Yes, Sharon?"

"Well, I wonder if I could be informed if we catch the man. I feel close to this assignment, and I think I would rest easier if I knew the outcome—good or bad."

"I think that can be arranged."

She nodded, wondering what went on inside Maxwell's mind. What did he have to live with every night? As she pulled the door shut, she hoped she might never find out.

37

Kepella reached the Rainier bank's Stoneway branch at three-thirty. He signed the safe deposit register and handed the woman his key. A moment later he was in a private booth opening the small box. He pulled out a pocket of folded papers. In his hands were the entire northern Pacific schematics for the Navy's SOSUS listening system: a string of submerged microphones that could "hear" and tri-angulate the exact location of enemy submarines. It was among DOD's most sensitive information—just the kind of bait Kevin Brandenburg knew would attract Wilhelm.

The sun stung his face as he left the bank. Seattle at its best: hot, humid, beautiful. The air smelled wonderful, like a million flowers. The streets bulged with athletic types: joggers, bike riders, kids on skateboards. Kepella reached into the glove compartment and exercised his elbow, drinking down three big gulps of vodka. Today marked an improvement. He had waited until after ten o'clock to have his first nip. It had been nine yesterday, and right out of bed the day before that. He felt he improved with each day.

Less than ten minutes later he pulled into Rosie's short driveway, the warm spot beginning to form at the base of his skull. Rosie looked worried as she stood in the kitchen fixing herself a bowl of granola, dressed only in cotton bikini underwear and matching camisole. Her thin body moved fluidly to Kepella. They embraced.

He located his briefcase and said, "I have to make a call."
She looked worried.

"Business." He studied her. She looked like a child. For the first time he found himself doubting that Rosie *was* involved in Holst's operation. Could it be she had nothing to do with this? He tried not to think about that, realizing what it meant if she was here of her own accord. He placed a call, which rang Holst's portable briefcase phone. After a short conversation he hung up, turned to Rosie, and said, "I have to go."

"You had drink this morning."

"Yes," he admitted, somewhat ashamed of himself. "Nerves."

"No more today, okay, Roy?"

"We'll see. I can't promise."

"Please?"

"I'll try, Rosie. I don't know. I'll try. Can't promise."

"Something wrong, Roy." Tears welled in her eyes.

"What is it, Rosie," he asked, pulling her close, feeling his groin stir. Jeez, he'd grown fond of her. Too fond.

"Something wrong, Roy. I can tell. Don't go. Please, don't go."

"I have to, baby." He pushed away from her gently. "I'll be all right. Last job for a while." He knew he shouldn't have said that—bad luck to call anything the last—but he couldn't help himself. "After this we'll take a trip. I'll show you the Olympic Peninsula, like I promised."

She nodded and wiped away her tears, trying to smile. She didn't believe a word. Something was wrong. Roy Kepella wasn't coming back.

As Kepella left Rosie's, he didn't notice the car following him. Jocko had rented two cars, one for Jay and one for himself: his van's radiator was bashed in from last night's collision. Now he was at Shilshole keeping watch. Jay had driven to the apartment he had followed Roy to the night of the fire. Now, he was right behind the guy.

At first, Kepella had been surprised that Holst would return to The Westside Motel. Then he realized it was the last place he would have thought of looking for him. He checked his pocket for the SOSUS papers and left his car.

The drapes had been pulled and Kepella had to adjust his eyes to the darkness as he entered the room. The air was musty and smelled of perspiration. Marlene sat on the bed, her hair messed, her face badly bruised, her shirt torn at the shoulder, which was also bruised. She kept her swollen eyes fixed on the carpet and did not move as Kepella entered.

Holst's shirt was torn, his left arm bandaged. He was perched on the edge of a chest of drawers, shirt unbuttoned, a slight grin on his lips as he gazed at Marlene. "Shut the door."

Marlene was nearly catatonic. Kepella noticed scratches on Holst's neck. Fingernail scratches. Her legs were bruised and discolored, her lips, though covered with too much lipstick, swollen and split.

"Sit," Holst demanded.

Kepella sat in the only chair. He couldn't stop looking at Marlene, who still had not looked up.

"Tell him, Marlene."

She obeyed immediately, though her voice was toneless and defeated. "There was nothing in the plans you delivered to indicate an adequate power supply for the laser, if satellite-based. Explain this please."

Kepella shrugged. "I don't understand all the bullshit." He looked to Holst. "That's all we have. If there's something missing, that only makes sense. No one location has the whole picture. You must know that."

Holst said, "And you are certain it is to be satellite-deployed?"

"In this job, one is never certain. You know how well the different services use blinds. This whole thing could be bullshit. As far as *I* know, this stuff is legit. It is to be deployed by satellite in late September, early October. I told her all that. That's all I know."

Marlene still had not looked up. "You brought the SOSUS papers?" Holst asked. Kepella nodded, still watching Marlene. "Show it to her," Holst demanded.

Kepella handed the folded papers to Marlene. She unfolded them slowly and studied the first page, then turned to the next page.

"Is that it?" Holst asked.

"Patience," she said. She glanced at Kepella, a full conversation in the single glance. She was telling him, Help me. Please help me, without saying a word.

Kepella's eyes shifted back and forth between the two. Holst grew anxious. He slipped off the chest of drawers and approached Marlene. He struck her hard across the head. "Answer me!"

She appeared not to feel the blow. She turned the page and looked into Holst's eyes. Her voice was flat. "I am trying to read."

Perplexed, Holst faced Kepella, the gun apparent in his hand for the first time.

Kepella could feel it coming. Holst had lost a screw. He was going to kill Kepella, maybe even the girl. Whatever had happened prior to his arrival had damaged them both, but only Marlene showed it. Kepella reached an instant decision. Brandenburg's deal, was, for the moment, down the tubes. Kepella's efforts had come down to this: three of them in a motel room, no backup, and a crazy German with a weapon in his hand.

Kepella leaped from his chair and knocked the gun from Holst's hand. He drove the German into the chest of drawers and raised his hand to deliver a right to the man's throat. Holst drilled his knee into Kepella's crotch, pushing the overweight agent back onto the bed. Marlene lunged to the carpet, grabbing for the gun. Holst slammed his foot down onto her wrist. Bones crunched loudly. Marlene screamed . . .

The heavy sliding glass door and the hanging drapes muffled the voices inside. Jay found it impossible to discern any of the words. He closed his eyes and concentrated. Then it sounded like a struggle. He pulled on the door. Locked. His eyes lit on a stack of metal-wire milk crates two doors down. As he reached the stack, he heard Marlene scream . . .

Holst picked up the gun and fired. Kepella's body jumped with the silenced shot, and he collapsed, his eyes staring unfocused at the dirty wall. Marlene screamed again.

The glass shattered into a thousand pieces, spraying the back of the drapes. Jay's first and only experience with courage had been in the back of that van. For his entire life he had considered himself a coward—he had never even been in a fist fight. Even so, he charged through the drapes, not realizing that with three homemade finger splints on one hand he had little with which to attack.

The exploding window surprised Holst. As he prepared to fire another bullet into Kepella—to make sure—something, someone, flew through the drapes to his right. His gun moved as he pulled the trigger and the bullet hit the wall.

Jay charged, stumbled, and smashed the milk crate into Holst. The impact knocked the gun loose and threw Holst into the chest of drawers, knocking the wind out of him. Jay saw Kepella's open eyes and panicked. He grasped Marlene's hand—she screamed—and dragged her until she began to run. Then he couldn't stop her. Together, they fled through the hole where the sliding door had been.

A window across the courtyard exploded as a bullet hit it. They ran harder, turning right at the first corner. Jay said quickly, "We'll separate. Meet at Gasworks Park, ten o'clock tonight."

"No," she wailed, slowing. "My hand."

"Hurry!" he demanded. "Yes. Now get in." He stuffed her into the driver's seat of his rental, reached around her, jabbed the key into the ignition, and started the car. "Drive!" he commanded, noticing for the first time that she held a thick set of papers in her good hand. Separated, at least one of them could escape Holst. She looked at him curiously, the life gone from her face. She gripped the wheel, dropping the papers onto the seat. "Go!" he thundered. And off she went.

Jay tucked his hurt fingers against his body and sprinted like he had never sprinted before. He turned right, ran down the street, crossed it, turned left down an alley, right at the end of the alley, crossed another street, right again, left again. He dove into a thick hedge, winded. A car had followed him, followed his every turn. Thinking it had to be Holst, he listened as it drove by.

38

Mark Galpin had never liked hospitals. He had too many memories associated with the familiar smell, the rows of rooms like rows of prison cells. When he came to a hospital it was usually to visit the morgue. He hated it. A few years back—fifteen years into his service—he had still wondered why he had chosen this particular route through the labyrinth of life. What had compelled him to try and fight a war against crime that could never be won? What had compelled him to try and lead men through such a war? But he hadn't had a single thought along those lines in the past few years. A switch inside him had been thrown. He had accepted his position in life. There was to be no more questioning, only service. Soon the twenty years would be up. Soon it would be retirement, sailing, a family life, and relaxation. God willing, he would have a good twenty to thirty years of life remaining to do the things he had always wanted to do. For now it was service.

The door to the room appeared no different than any of the others. He pushed it open, noticing that his watch read 8:45 P.M.

Roy Kepella lay in the bed closest to him; the window bed was empty. The surprised expression on Kepella's face said it all. He had a bandage on his chest. Neither man said anything as Galpin dragged a chair over close to the bed and sat down.

Galpin said softly, "In going through your wallet they found your business card. They called the Bureau."

Kepella nodded with his eyelids. "Figures."

"How's it feel?"

"Piece of cake. Missed the lung. No big deal."

"You want to tell me about it, Roy?"

"I can't, Mark. I'd like to, but I can't. I'm on orders. It's kind of hard to explain."

"Perhaps I could clear things up for you."

"I don't follow you."

"I received a priority call a few days ago from Washington. A CIA agent who had been sent to Germany as a mule returned to the States with some vital information. The word was that Fritz Wilhelm, a middleman arms and technology dealer for the Soviets based in West Germany, had set his sights on Seattle. He was going after some spare computer parts for the Iranians, the green-laser communication technology for the Soviets, and the SOSUS map of the Pacific, copies of which are all kept in our archives. Any of this sound familiar, Roy?"

"Can't say that it does, Mark."

Galpin's jaw muscles flexed and he nervously tugged the cuff of each shirt sleeve to protrude exactly half an inch past the end of his navy blue sports jacket. "Wilhelm has a mole in the Bureau, Roy. We believe this man intended to pose as a top-level official running an inside sting using one of our Seattle agents." He saw Kepella's already pale face drain of all color. He was talking to a ghost. "It would operate as a standard sting, is how we see it. He would convince the agent that this was the only way to get Wilhelm. The agent would then fall out of favor with the department in order to appear an attractive catch by Wilhelm's people. Only Wilhelm's people would know what was going on the whole time. The sting was really being played on the agent they decided to use. Ideally, they would obviously look for someone with access to the Bureau's files." He stopped. He'd said enough.

Kepella stared at his friend. He looked at the man trying to think of something to say. "The agent calls himself Brandenburg. I took a sick day and flew to Washington to meet him."

"Go on."

"He met me at a hotel outside of D.C. He told me it was just between him and the director and myself." He shook his head and closed his eyes. "I should have seen it. Christ, they gave me enough hints." He paused. "He reimbursed my air ticket with *cash* and explained it away to secrecy. He knew *exactly* what items they would be coming for . . . I should have seen it."

Galpin sighed. "We don't hold you responsible, Roy. You know our position. We want to make the best of a bad thing." He reached into his breast pocket and withdrew a folded sheet of paper. Unfolding it, he passed it to Kepella. "This is an artist's sketch of the man we think is the mole. Any resemblance to your Brandenburg?"

Kepella looked at the photocopy of the sketch, nodding. "It's close enough. His face isn't that wide, and the chin is much different, but the eyes and nose are right on. That's him." He handed the paper back to Galpin, who accepted it and returned it to his pocket.

"That's the best news I've had in days. Excuse me a second." Galpin used the phone, passing the information onto his office, which in turn would pass it on to Washington. When he had hung up, he sat back down in the chair and asked Kepella to tell him the whole story. Kepella took it from the first Brandenburg interview and caught Galpin up to date. It took him nearly an hour.

Galpin digested the progression of events, referring to a notepad he had filled while Kepella talked. He asked, "So this musician left the motel with Marlene, and you're fairly sure she had the SOSUS papers?"

"Like I said, I kept my eyes open in order to fool them. Holst took another shot anyway, to make sure. As I remember, Becker knocked Holst down, grabbed Marlene, and fled. It seems to me she was carrying the papers in her hand. I can't be sure." He swallowed some water. "Holst went right after them. I made it over to my car. I was losing a lot of blood. I passed out in the emergency room. I woke up here."

"That checks out." Galpin looked helpless. "So either this Marlene or Becker or both have the SOSUS papers?"

"That would be my guess."

Galpin used the phone again. The downtown office was advised to put an all-points bulletin out on four people, including Holst and Chu. Fu Won's was to be kept under surveillance, as was *The Lady Fine*. He addressed Kepella. "And what about the computer parts?"

"I don't follow you."

"A couple days back, Tuesday, I think it was, someone got away with four of ZyCorp's computer terminals and several boxes of spare parts that would work in Crays. Since we heard from Washington, and began looking for you, we were certain it was all connected."

Kepella frowned. "I gave them that information, Mark. On Monday, I think. They got me drinking again, Mark, and well, my memory is kinda shot. I had no idea they had hit the warehouses. I thought it was a test of some sort—

you know, see how accurate my information was. I didn't realize they hit the warehouses. I wouldn't know where the parts are, but I would guess they're on that boat. Just a gut feeling, you understand, but I kept trying to figure out why Holst would involve a person like Becker in all of this. Why bring in someone new? The only thing I could come up with was that he needed someone other than himself to sail that boat somewhere. Why else would he risk involving a stranger? But if he did hire a skipper, then all sorts of things come to light. We know Wilhelm has never entered the States, but he's been spotted in Canada several times—"

Galpin interrupted. "Yes, so Holst has Becker sail the boat across the border on one of the busiest sailing week-ends of the year. If all goes well, the stuff ends up in Canada. If something goes wrong, if the Coast Guard searches the boat, Becker's the one with the explaining to do. Holst is long gone. That's possible."

"That's how I'd do it." Kepella supplied Galpin with every conceivable place to look for Becker, explaining the band's poster on the phone pole and how someone from the band might know how to find him. Then he asked, "What about Brandenburg?"

"We'll sit on that address. We don't want to alarm him. If he's still there, he may lead us to Wilhelm or Holst."

"What if we sting him back? At the moment you don't have anything on him, except the word of a drunk who's been suspended from the Bureau and has given away state secrets. Let me help, Mark. Give me a chance to prove myself."

"How's that?"

"Wire me for sound. If he's in communication with Holst at all, then he thinks I'm dead, right? So what happens if naive Roy Kepella comes wandering back into the nest, explaining the whole thing went sour and that Holst has gotten away? We'd at least be able to confirm that Brandenburg was running me, and I have the feeling I'm going to need all the help I can get. What do you say?"

"It's a thought." Galpin hashed it over in his mind. "We could set up a strike force outside, in case it goes sour." He rose. "Do you feel up to it?"

"Shit, this thing is barely a scratch—cut a hole in some muscle is all. Believe me, Mark. I'd do anything to get Brandenburg after all this. I can certainly have a ten-minute conversation."

"I'll check with your doctor and call Washington. I like it. It might even give us a lead. You rest up, Roy. I'll contact you later. You get some sleep." He walked toward the door and turned. "Oh, and by the way . . . I'm glad he missed. It's good to have you back." He shut the door. Hospitals still bothered him.

39

At ten o'clock, Gasworks Park, the tiny knoll of grass with its cluster of eerie refinery pipes that overlooks the north end of Lake Union, was empty. He followed a paved path up to the knoll to the giant sundial, a location that offered him a better view of both the entrance to the parking lot and Lake Union. As he waited, facing the lot, the tangled-metal labyrinth of the former gasworks sat off to his right. Far behind it, out on the street, a few lights managed to slip past the elbows, valves, and nozzles. The wind stung his cut face.

He checked his watch. Ten past ten. No Marlene. What had gone wrong? She was supposed to meet him here. He waited. Twenty past ten. He was worried. He watched the reflection of boat lights stretched into long rippling rails that ran across the water. Ten-thirty. He could picture Holst beating her. Ten-forty. He hurried out to Northlake, walked into a sailor's bar, and called a cab.

What would Holst do next? Did he have Marlene? With Roy dead, Holst's blackmail was over. Jay tried to put himself in Holst's position: Seattle would hardly be a place to hang around. Holst would get out of here, either taking Marlene with him . . . or leaving her behind . . .

Where would the German take her? Christ, it's a big city, Jay thought, glancing around and seeing the thousands—millions—of lights: the houses, the office buildings, the shops, bars, restaurants, theaters, the Space Needle, the boats on Lake Union, the headlights and taillights milling about the hundreds—thousands—of streets, lanes, avenues, and drives. Good luck finding anyone out there. A jet flew silently over the Sound, its lights blinking. Was Holst on that jet? Had he already done away with Marlene and was now fleeing the city? The country?

Time to find Jocko. Maybe even search *The Lady Fine*.

The cab dropped him by Pier A, so he could approach the parking lot from the boats. Less conspicuous, he figured. The faint, continual drone of a busy city could be heard all around him, drifting out to sea. The strong overhead lights illuminated the colorful cars. Set against the glowing sky and still night air, it looked to Jay like a glossy photograph.

He walked along the sidewalk that fronted the docks, keeping his head low. He ambled up a row of cars and made his way along the third row. He glanced to his left, eyes searching for the Chinese goon or Holst. Nothing.

He strained to see beyond Jocko's rental. He jerked his head to the left, thinking he saw a movement. His eyes scanned the parked cars. It had seemed like a person ducking back down behind a dash or behind a car. He waited, hoping to spot the movement again. Nothing. He stepped quickly between two cars and yanked on the handle to Jocko's rental. It was locked.

He tapped quickly on the window, feeling like someone was watching him. He thought, Come on, Jocko, open the goddamned door. He tapped again, louder this time. He bent over quickly, unable to see clearly inside the dark car, but well enough to see that Jocko had fallen asleep, head against the steering wheel. Jocko, known for the sleep of the dead, would not wake from a simple tap on a window. Jay hurried around the rental to the driver's door. It opened. He bent and punched Jocko in the arm. Nothing. He shook him, stepping back quickly, throat tightening, knowing without wanting to know. Jocko slipped over in the seat, his head rotating as he fell. His chest was covered with blood; his throat had been slit. His eyes were glued open. In his right hand he held the butt of his unfired gun.

Jay fell to his knees. Tears rolled down his face. Then he stood and screamed in his loudest voice, "You fucking assholes! You motherfuckers! Come and get *me,* you fucking assholes." He dropped back down to the pavement, crying, his chest heaving.

Had they done this to Marlene, too? Did they plan on doing this to him? He pushed Jocko over in the seat. The lifeless body slipped and fell to the floor. Jay pushed his dead friend's legs out of the way of the pedals and then sat down in the driver's seat. He picked up the revolver and laid it on the front seat next to him. Then he saw the face, a face painted in blood on the plastic of the dashboard. It was four simple lines: a straight line for a mouth, a vertical line for the nose, and two slanted lines for the eyes. A Chinaman. *The* Chinaman.

He started the car and pushed the pedal to the floor. Thirty seconds after he raced from Shilshole's parking lot, the first two FBI agents arrived in their plain, gray sedan.

40

He drove to Jocko's in case Holst or Marlene had left a message on the answering machine. If he could brave it, he could remove the keys from Jocko's pocket and get into the apartment. Then he could decide to go talk to the cops or take some other course of action.

He pulled the car to a stop in front of the apartment building and put the car in park, engine running. He slid over in the seat, noticing for the first time that he had sat in some of Jocko's blood. The sight of the awkwardly placed body turned his stomach. He reached over and closed his friend's eyes, feeling his own throat tighten. The keys were in the right-hand pocket.

He climbed the stairs, pulling with him not only the weight of his body but memories of hundreds of other times he had climbed these stairs. Jocko had been sick a few years back and Jay had doted on *him* for a change. He had spent the better part of two weeks here, for Jocko was basically helpless when he got sick. Having been raised under the tender guidance of an over-protective Jewish mother, he was accustomed to being waited on, and only became more ill if left on his own. There was no healing Jocko now. His body was cold, lying in an inhuman position on the floor of the front seat of the rental, on the street below.

One moment, either way . . .

Jay wondered how such a thing could have happened. Jocko was street-wise. And yet somehow the Chinaman had surprised him, had overpowered him and had . . .

He fiddled with the set of keys, searching for a match. Before opening the door he decided that the police would not be involved in this. It had gone well beyond that. There was no point in relying on criminal justice to punish the Chinaman. He had no faith in criminal justice. No faith in the law. And he knew that several days ago, even several hours ago, given a different set of circumstances, there would have been no way that Jay Becker could have convinced himself that he had the inner strength to kill another human being. Even being thrown out a window had not instilled it in him. But now he had no doubts whatsoever. He knew what had to be done, win or lose, and his only worry was that he might never find the Chinaman again. He might never get the chance. But if given the chance he would kill the man—and he would use any means possible.

There was no *fair* in this. No gentlemanly code of conduct.

He turned the key. The apartment, warm and stuffy, was silent. No loud stereo like there usually was whenever Jay entered through this door. He locked himself in and headed straight to the answering machine, concentrating on what lay before him, trying to keep the memories locked away. "One cannot dwell on the past," Jocko had once told him. "One must live for today alone."

Marlene's voice was on the tape. She gave a phone number and an extension and asked for Jay to call her immediately. He dialed the number. After three rings a voice answered, mumbling a name of some sort. Jay gave the extension, too hurried to pay attention to what was said. She answered, "Jay?"

"Yes."

"I have been waiting for your call."

They killed Jocko, Marlene, he wanted to say, but stopped himself. "Where are you?" he asked instead.

"At a motel. I miss you. I couldn't make it to Gasworks Park because the doctors kept me longer than I thought."

"Doctors?"

"My wrist is broken. I had a cast put on. It is not important. I want you to listen to me carefully, Jay. And I want you to understand that no matter how strongly you feel about what I am about to tell you, there is nothing you can do to change my mind. You can either help me, or I will do this alone. But I am going to do this as I see fit, and you must understand that from the beginning. You should never have been involved in any of this. This is between Iben Holst and myself, and it must be settled between us. If you will do me this one favor, then I feel I cannot lose, but I will not listen to arguments. There is no time for that. If you try and argue I will hang up and do this myself."

He thought, You once called me strong. Now look who's talking. "Let's be reasonable, Marlene."

"No, Jay. Not reasonable, either."

"They killed Jocko." There. He had said it. He hoped it might change her mind.

She paused for so long that he almost thought she had hung up. Finally, she said, "I am sorry for you. I am more sorry than you will ever know. I love you, Jay Becker, but I will not let anything change my mind. I am going to trade with Holst. The tape of my father for *The Lady Fine*. Everything he wants is aboard the boat. What I ask is that you sail the boat to someplace nearby but away from the marina. Without *The Lady* he cannot harm me. And if I do not know where the boat is, then he can not make me tell him, can he?" She was explaining it quickly, and Jay could sense she was about to hang up. In his head he kept hearing her telling him that she loved him, and he had to focus on her words to retain what she was planning. He was both proud of her and angry with her: proud because she had found a strength she had been searching for, angry because this was the wrong place to find it. He knew that if he tried to interrupt, the line would go dead. Her final words were, "I will call you on the radio. You will tell me where you have sailed to and then you will leave *The Lady* and get safely away before they arrive. When it is all over, I will leave a message on your band's answering service or on Jocko's machine. I have both numbers. I know you will do this for me. I do love you, Jay. You know I do." And then she hung up.

Jay reviewed her plan, trying to poke holes in it. There was no telling how Iben Holst would react to Marlene trying to put conditions on him. Jay didn't trust that she could do this alone. He called back the motel and got the address from the desk clerk.

She was at the Castle Rock Motel in Ballard. He couldn't face another ride with Jocko's corpse, so he called a cab. Then he saw another major flaw in her plan: someone could be guarding Shilshole. Someone could try on him what they had tried on Jocko. He wondered if she had thought of that. He wondered if she had figured a way around that. He told the cabbie to hurry, promising to pay any ticket, but the cabbie just grunted and drove at his own speed. The miles dragged by, the whole time Jay picturing her leaving the Castle Rock and heading off to a rendezvous with Holst. Stay where you are, Marlene. Stay where you are.

"Can't you drive this thing any faster?" he asked, tapping his foot nervously on the rubber mat.

"Hey, back off, mister. This is how I earn a living. This ain't no joy ride. You'll get there when I get there. You got that?" He turned a corner. "You're here. See, wha'd I tell ya? Four-forty."

"Here's ten bucks," Jay said, handing the man the money. "Park it for a few minutes. I'll be right out."

The bald driver took the ten. "I'll give ya a few minutes for five bucks. That's all. One honk and then I'm down the road."

Jay ran into the office. The clock read midnight. The manager was a nice enough fellow. The only reason Jay swore

344

at him was because Marlene had left ten minutes earlier.

A party on *The Lazy Daze* was just breaking up as Jay approached Pier M. Again, he had been let off up by Pier A, several hundred yards away, on the other side of the boathouse, so as not to be noticed in case someone was keeping eye on Pier L. He only had to wait a few minutes before an intoxicated couple came strolling down the pier and opened the gate. He made it look as though he was about to use a key on the gate. He entered as they left, and pulled Jocko's blue tam down as he walked up to the thinning party. He leaned against the boat, smiling, his attention on *The Lady Fine* just across the narrow lane of water that separated the two piers. There were no lights turned on aboard *The Lady*, no motion to her whatsoever. Only now did he realize he had left Jocko's gun with the body. He had the switchblade, but that didn't give him a great deal of confidence. He walked to the end of Pier M and, fully clothed, swam the short distance to Pier L. "Shark!" somebody joked from *The Lazy Daze*, pointing at Jay, and the few who remained at the party laughed, quickly returning to their small talk. He pulled himself up onto Pier L and approached *The Lady* carefully. He rocked her, ready to flee, but it was obvious no one was aboard.

He went below and switched on the radio. The portable cellular phone was gone. The television had been returned. He didn't like motoring at night, especially without the running lights on. But he was taking every precaution not to be spotted. She should have waited until morning. She should have remained at the motel. She should have.

He rounded the breakwater with no problems and then

switched on the running lights, headed out around the point, north, past a stretch of fine waterfront homes on a course that would take him around Meadow Point to Carkeek Park. At Carkeek, he would still be within the city limits, and that appealed to him.

He wondered what she was doing at this moment. He wondered if he would ever see her again. He wished her luck, rose up on his toes, and steered for the flashing marker off Meadow Point.

Marlene dialed the number of Holst's portable phone, and he answered. She wasn't going to be stupid. She demanded the meeting be at a public place, somewhere where Holst could not abduct her. She told him to meet her at the Garden Lounge of the Olympic Four Seasons. She drove the rental Jay had pushed her into at the Westside. She couldn't find anywhere to park. She drove around the block twice and finally resorted to the parking garage across the street from the elegant Four Seasons. It was only as she turned off the engine and looked around at the stark confines of the third level of the parking facility that she became frightened. She hurried to the elevators and grew impatient waiting for it. When the doors opened and it was empty she heaved a sigh of relief. In a few minutes she would be inside the elegant Garden Lounge. There was no way anyone could do anything to her there. She was angry at herself for not having driven here first and then making the call. It would have made much more sense.

The elevator hummed gently, moving slowly. She grew restless. When the doors opened, John Chu was grinning at her. She wanted to call for help, to scream, but nothing came out. He took one long stride into the elevator and pushed a foul-smelling rag into her face. She felt herself falling to her knees, and then she heard the elevator doors bump shut. John Chu was laughing.

Jay was having trouble staying awake. He was working on his third cup of coffee when the voice on the radio listed The Lady Fine's name and call letters. Sixty seconds later the call was put through. Suddenly he was wide awake. "Hello? Over."

"I have what you want, Becker. That should make it clear enough. Over."

Holst's voice. Jay felt dizzy. He reached out and took hold of the narrow countertop. His worst fear had come true, and he knew that Marlene would not have volunteered any information without serious persuasion—and Holst had known to call on the radio. He didn't like the feeling that was swelling inside him: now he wanted two people dead. "Go ahead," he said. "Over."

"You have The Lady Fine. I have the lady. You will motor the boat north to Freeland. Over."

"I know where that is. Over."

"I will contact you there. Keep the radio on at all times. I trust you are not foolish enough to involve others in this. I will expect you by noon tomorrow. Out." He disconnected.

Jay put down the receiver, his hand trembling from lack of sleep, lack of food and nerves. Why would Holst have him sail The Lady Fine? Why not demand to know the location and come take the papers off the boat? What was there to gain?

Then he remembered Jocko. He had no intention of leaving his buddy on the floor of a parked car. He decided to turn Jocko's body over to Detective Flint.

If he used the ship-to-shore, Flint would know he was on a boat, and Jay had no desire to screw this up. It took him fifteen minutes to inflate the rubber raft stored on board *The Lady*. He paddled into Carkeek and found a pay phone by the parking lot that faced the Sound. The phone rang twice and was answered. The desk sergeant asked who was calling. Jay gave his name. After a lengthy pause the man told him, "Detective Flint's on another line. You'll have to hold."

"Yeah, okay." He held. It felt like two minutes before Flint finally answered.

"Becker?"

"Right."

"What's up?" Flint sounded tired.

"Two people have been killed tonight. I want you to handle the bodies for me. I'm indisposed."

"Slow down! It isn't that easy. I think we better talk. You know how that goes."

"No talk. No time. One is a guy named Roy. He's out at the Westside. A German named Holst killed him. I saw it. The other is my best friend. He's in a parked car in front of 609 Crocker Street West. You'll have to contact his mom and dad. I wouldn't know what to say."

"Now wait a minute, Becker. You know as well as I that I can't let you skate on this without asking some questions. If you don't turn yourself in, then a warrant will be issued. That won't look good to a judge. Think about that. You don't want to send a judge crossed signals."

Jay paused to think. What choice did he have? He thought he heard a car behind him, but when he turned around he couldn't see anything in the dark due to the reflection from the inside light of the booth.

"Becker?" Flint asked.

"Still here. Listen, all I can tell you is that I'm involved in something, kind of indirectly, if you follow me. A friend of mine's been kidnapped. I can't involve you guys. You do what you have to do, and I'll take whatever you dish out. But I gotta do this without you guys or my friend will be killed. If I understood any of this, I might explain it better. But that's all for now. Take care of Jocko for me. He was my best friend." He set the receiver down into the cradle.

When he turned around, two police officers were standing outside the phone booth.

"You tricked me." Jay sat on the far side of Flint's cluttered desk in an office the size of a broom closet. The clock read two-fifteen. Flint handed him a cup of coffee and lit a cigarette.

"You mind?" Flint asked, waving the cigarette.

"As a matter of fact, I do."

Flint shrugged and killed the butt. "Have it your way. They're no good for me anyway."

"While you had me on hold you traced the call?"

"Afraid so. We've been looking for you for hours, kid."

"I didn't see it coming."

"I was counting on that." A buzzer rang. He picked up the phone, said, "Okay," and hung up. "Someone here to see you. This is where I get off the bus." He rubbed his eyes.

"What's going on?" Jay felt his heart pounding—a different kind of fear this time.

"He'll explain it all. They don't tell us much."

"They?"

Flint rose from his chair, attempting to neaten some papers. The desk remained cluttered. He picked up his cigarette pack and the plastic lighter beside it. "Hang in there, kid, you're not in any trouble. Just cooperate, okay? You'll make it easier on all of us."

Jay followed Flint with his head. A nervous-looking man stood in the doorway.

"He's all yours," Flint said.

"What about Jocko?" Jay interrupted.

"Got that taken care of," Flint assured him. "Remember what I said."

The other man entered the room and closed the door. He was a good-looking man with nice clothes. He flexed his jaw muscles continually. He reached out his hand. Jay shook it unenthusiastically. "My name is Mark Galpin. I'm the director of Seattle's FBI regional office."

"Is this about Roy Kepella?"

"Why do you say that?"

"Flint told me the guy was with the FBI. I told him he was killed; he wouldn't believe me."

"He's *alive,* Jay. He survived the bullet wound."

"Not possible. I saw him. He was dead."

"He was well trained, is what he was. He's in the hospital, but he's gonna be fine. He kept his eyes open to try and fool Holst. He credits you with saving his life. He says if you hadn't barged in when you did, he'd have been killed for sure. He can thank you later. Right now, you and I have some business to attend to."

"I'll tell you what I told Flint. A friend of mine has been kidnapped. I can't involve you guys. If I do, she'll be killed."

"Are we talking about Marlene?"

"Could be."

"What do they want to trade for her, Jay?"

"I told you; can't do it."

The man's face grew scarlet, the color spreading onto his neck. "You're not holding as many cards as you might think. We have half a dozen charges we can hold you on. If we hold you, you can't help her. Now why don't we both cooperate and see what we can come up with? There's more involved here than you might think."

"Tell me about it. You know, you and Flint aren't so different. You both have badges for blinders and a tone of voice that makes me sick. This isn't one of your games. This isn't one of your stings. This is my woman's life we're talking about."

Galpin pushed back in the chair. "Let's look at it this way, Jay. How well have you done so far? Answer me that honestly." He studied Jay's blue eyes. "What would you do if you were me?"

"Let me go. Protect Marlene's life."

"Would you really? Think about it." He stood. "I've got time, if Marlene does. You stay right here and consider your position. If you cooperate, all we're going to do is keep an eye on you. That's all. If you don't, we'll hold you right here. You think." Galpin left the room.

Jay watched over his shoulder as Galpin walked to a water dispenser and filled a cone-shaped paper cup. Galpin turned around and looked back at Jay. Jay looked back at the cluttered desk.

Five long minutes later Galpin sat back down and said, "So what do you say?"

"If they see you following me, they'll kill her. I believe that. What we have is a stalemate."

"What we have is technology, Jay. We can be several blocks behind you, no one the wiser. All we want to do is protect you and Marlene. There's no use in you being killed, too."

Jay slipped into laughter. His fatigue stretched it out unnaturally. "A few blocks behind, eh? I won't be in a car, Mr. Galpin. I'll be in a boat. How you gonna pull that off?"

"Believe me, Jay. We can pull anything off. I believe that. I'm asking you to as well. We've handled hundreds of these, Jay. How many have you handled?" He paused. "Am I getting through to you?"

"Loud and clear."

"Then you'll cooperate?"

Jay nodded. "Not a hell of a lot of choice, is there?"

41

Becker motored due north for two and a half hours, until he spotted Cultus Bay and Possession Point off the starboard bow. He had had little sleep. An unmarked car had dropped him off at Carkeek Park with the small black box just after 3:00 A.M. He was instructed to install the box aboard *The Lady Fine* and to unravel a long copper wire, which would act as an antenna. It had taken half an hour, so his restless sleep had been reduced to a little over two hours.

His head ached and his eyes felt dry and hot, even behind sunglasses and under the brim of a hat. Rigging the boat took longer than usual because of his hurt fingers. He was miserable.

He set a new compass course to bring him alongside Freeland. At ten till noon he identified a point of lush green land that jutted into the Sound. Just around that point lay Freeland. A small plane passed overhead. Damn, they're clever, he thought, thinking this was the FBI and feeling much safer. He knew that one of the many sailboats he could see was manned by special agents, though he couldn't tell which one. He also knew his transmitter was only good for a mile or two; so there would be flyovers as well as the other sailboat to track his location. The Labor Day mobs jammed the waterways. Without the transmitter he would be easily lost. He hated to admit it, but he felt better knowing the FBI was tuned into the transmitter as well as the ship-to-shore frequencies.

As he approached Freeland he heard a nasal female voice from below decks—the radio. He went below and answered it.

Holst said, "You will continue northwest to San Juan Island, and anchor overnight off of American Camp. Do you have that?"

"Yes."

Holst hung up. Anxiety flooded through Becker. The San Juan chain was close to Canada. The FBI had no power in Canada. And Jay had no faith in quick solutions to complicated jurisdiction problems where bureaucracies were concerned. How long would it take Galpin to notify the Canadian authorities? The anxiety passed as another small plane took off from Whidbey Island, flying nearly directly over *The Lady Fine.* That must be a signal, Jay thought. Everything's under control.

It was a commuter plane.

Kepella edged quietly around the far side of the house, keeping close to the tall vegetation. He had spotted the car in the garage: Brandenburg was home. His shoulder hurt badly and was bleeding again.

Behind him, on the other side of the hedge and across the street, two agents listened to his heavy breathing, ready to signal the five others who were trimming trees in Pacific Bell workmen's uniforms.

Kepella moved quickly. Galpin had told him that as far as they had determined, Rosie had nothing to do with Holst's operation. Both John Chu and Donnie Mota had growing bank accounts. Rosie had a little over a hundred bucks to her name. All this while Kepella had assumed Rosie was being paid to keep an eye on him. Now he was forced to see it in a different light. She had hidden him. She had tried to stop him from drinking. She had cried *real* tears for him. Rosie was a gift from God, and if Roy Kepella got himself free of this, Rosie would be around more often. Maybe for good. But Brandenburg—he was another story.

Kepella slid the glass door open. He heard the television as he stepped inside. He passed through the dining room, stopping in the doorway to the small den. Brandenburg didn't see him, his eyes glued to the tube. "They tried to kill me," Kepella said dramatically.

Brandenburg jumped. He reached down and, using the remote control switch, shut off the television. He had a weapon upstairs, another in the liquor cabinet, and another hidden in the kitchen's refrigerator.

"Jesus, Roy, you should have knocked. You scared the hell out of me."

"You mind?" Kepella asked, pointing to the chair facing the couch.

"How about the dining room? More air out there," Brandenburg said as he rose, and indicated for Kepella to lead the way. He saw the bulge. Kepella was carrying a gun. The closest gun for Brandenburg was in the liquor cabinet in the dining room. Fair was fair. If Kepella turned nasty, Brandenburg wanted to be prepared. As they sat at the table he asked, "So come again, Roy?"

"I delivered the SOSUS papers, as you and I agreed . . ." He paused, trying to lead Brandenburg into it.

"Right," Brandenburg acknowledged.

Kepella thought, Step one accomplished. "But something was wrong. He had beaten the woman badly. She was damn near catatonic, and Holst started waving the gun around like a madman. I had to make one of those decisions . . . so I jumped him. I knew it was bad for our operation but what choice did I have? He could have killed us both."

"He beat up Marlene?" Brandenburg asked incredulously.

"I hope I haven't wrecked the operation," Kepella tried again.

"No, no, Roy. Christ, I'd say it works perfectly. You acted like yourself. If you had just sat there, then he might

355

have become curious. Maybe he was testing you."

"It was no test. He's lost a few screws. If you ask me, that woman has something to do with it. I thought you should know. I came here as quick as I could. They fixed me up at the hospital last night. I figured you'd know what to do."

"You should probably go back to Fu's in a few days, something like that."

"I went by the marina . . . I thought that might be a good idea, but the boat is gone." It had actually been Galpin who had explained the series of events to Kepella.

"Is that right?"

Kepella didn't see the least bit of surprise in Brandenburg's face. "So, what does that mean? Have we missed Wilhelm again, or what?"

"I'm gonna come clean with you, Roy. We have the whole thing under control. We've had the boat under surveillance for days. Right now it's being sailed to the rendezvous. We've got Wilhelm in the bag. The director is going to be very impressed with your part in all of this. Very impressed indeed."

"I'm glad you called me to Washington and set this all up. I'm proud to have been involved in this operation."

"You've been a tremendous asset, Roy. Couldn't have done it without you. How about a drink? Let's celebrate."

Now Kepella turned angry. "No booze. Not for me." He watched Brandenburg kneel by the cabinet. Kepella grew more angry by the second. The lies. The booze. Being treated like dogshit. Brandenburg should pay for all of this, he decided. What would the law do? Slap a wrist? If he could only make him pull a gun, he could kill him in self-defense. Kepella slipped his weapon out, hidden below the table. Would Brandenburg allow himself to be provoked into using a weapon, or was he too calm an individual?

"You really had me going for a while," Kepella started. He wondered what the boys in the van would do once he got into this. Would they wait it out, or would they kick the door? He decided to make it quick, before they had time to rally.

"What's that, Roy?" Brandenburg asked, slipping the gun into his pants pocket hidden by the open door of the cabinet.

"I should have caught on with the cash. When you paid me cash for the plane ticket. That should have alerted me."

Brandenburg came over with two drinks in hand. He held them on a tray, the tray hiding the bulge in his pocket. He slipped into his chair expertly, Kepella never seeing the bulge. He passed a drink across to Kepella, who pushed it off the table onto the carpet.

"No thanks."

"What's going on here, Roy?"

"I said I should have caught on when you paid me cash for my airline tickets. That was a mistake."

A noticeable shake filled Brandenburg's hand as he sipped his drink. The ice rattled.

Kepella continued, enjoying it more. "Really the whole plan was quite brilliant. Who pays you, Holst or Wilhelm?"

"Now listen here . . ."

"No, mister. I'm done listening to you. It's your turn to listen to me." He knew this was not at all what Mark Galpin had in mind. Galpin would have strung Brandenburg along and tried to follow leads and tried to fit it all together. But this was personal. No matter how wrong to

357

Mark Galpin, this is what Kepella had had in mind all along. He was thinking, Pull a gun on me, asshole. Give me the excuse.

"Wait just one minute," Brandenburg objected.

"I know the whole damn thing, mister. How many other agents have you set up over the years? Five, ten? How many other lives have you wrecked? I figured it out the other day," he lied, in order to keep Brandenburg thinking only he knew the secret, to draw him into a contest. "No help at all. You knew too much. You knew about Rosie before I barely did. You knew about Holst. I checked the files, shithead," he said, improvising, "and *no one* knows about Holst's connection to Wilhelm. Only you. What do you think about that?"

Brandenburg was stunned. He tried to keep his cool as he reached for the gun in his pocket. "So what's next, Roy?"

"This is." Kepella raised his gun above the table.

Brandenburg fired from beneath the table, squeezing off two rounds and sending Kepella over in his chair. Kepella shot the ceiling, dropping the gun on his way over, throwing it out of reach. His knee was on fire. The second bullet had missed him completely. Brandenburg stood and fired again, but Kepella rolled toward his gun and the shot missed.

The picture window slid open and an agent dove through the door while another shouted, "FBI, put down the weapons!"

Brandenburg spun around. He looked at the agent aiming at him and then at Kepella scooting across the carpet, still going for the gun. Wilhelm had promised the wife would be taken care of if anything like this ever happened. Brandenburg had no intention of spending his life in an eight-by-eight cell.

"Put down your weapon!" the agent shouted.

Brandenburg stuck the barrel in his mouth and pulled the trigger.

Jay made American Camp at 7:45, exhausted. Night would arrive soon. The tide was shifting. He remained well off-shore to allow for the outgoing tide.

He dropped anchor in a light fog and fought his fatigue until the frosty-pink rim of fading sun stung the horizon. He ate half a can of cold tuna and fell asleep in the forward cabin, which he considered safest, as it had two exits—an overhead hatch in the forward compartment or through the galley and out the companionway. Beneath his pillow he had *The Lady*'s flare gun and a sizable kitchen knife. He had taped another knife to his calf. He closed his eyes.

When he opened them it was morning. He had slept like a log. The same red ray of sunlight now peeked out from the opposite horizon, turning the ominous clouds salmon-pink. *Red sky at morning, sailor take warning.* He winced at the pain in his fingers. A paramedic at the police station had splinted them for him. He had been told they would be fine in time. He wasn't so sure.

But when he looked outside again, he realized that his order of business had changed. *The Lady Fine* was nowhere near American Camp. He hurried topside. The island was a tiny dot to starboard. He worked his way up to the bow and hauled in the morning line. It had been cleanly cut with a knife while he had slept. The strong outgoing tide had drawn him miles west of San Juan Island and probably into Canada.

Holst was taking no chances. But why had they let him live? he wondered. If they had been this close to him, why not kill him and take the boat themselves. The answer hit him: Holst wanted someone else to sail whatever was aboard *The Lady* into Canada.

By law Jay was required to register *The Lady* with Canadian customs at either Friday Harbor or Bedwell Harbor. Since Friday Harbor was well behind him now, it would have to be Bedwell. There was a twenty-five-percent chance the boat would be searched by Canadian authorities at the Customs dock. If, however, Jay decided to bypass Customs, counting on the heavy holiday boat traffic, and was spotted by a patrol, the boat would definitely be searched. He'd seen that often enough. The Canadians were thorough. They waited until just before sunset and then patrolled most of the favorable coves and bays along the border. On a weekend like this the job would be formidable; but it would also be a weekend with extra law enforcement manpower. Jay decided to find out what was on the boat, and where it had been stored. There was no use in being surprised.

He searched forward first, tearing apart the floorboards and ransacking the storage areas that held the sails and skin diving gear. Nothing. He searched methodically through the galley. When he reached the television, he got an idea. He attached the twelve-volt adaptor and plugged in the television. It didn't work. He checked his connections twice. It didn't work. So, he figured Holst had hidden something inside the television. He continued through the galley area frantically, unable to find anything new.

Once inside Marlene's cabin, he searched every drawer, including the area where he had found the videotape of Roy. Then he noticed that the storage area below Marlene's bunk was locked with a new padlock and clasp. He ran into the cockpit and got the tool box. After bending two screwdrivers, he finally broke the clasp off by tearing loose the screws. Inside were four unopened cardboard boxes, each with the name Zycorps printed on the side. Computers.

He heard the voice faintly—a marine operator. He raced out of Marlene's cabin, through the cockpit, and jumped down into the galley. He answered out of breath.

A moment later Holst said, "You recall the night you sat with Marlene and me at the Blue Sands? Over."

"Yes. Over."

"Check your charts. Go to the buoy whose number corresponds with the date of that meeting. Your final instructions are there. Out."

Jay racked his brain. Had it been a Wednesday or Thursday? He checked a calendar he carried in his wallet. A Wednesday. Wednesday the 17th. Buoy #17.

He checked the charts, his fingers racing from marker to marker, icon to icon. Number 17 was just south of Saltspring Island, British Columbia.

He was right. He was being used to ferry the computers into Canada. Holst had been careful, in case someone was listening in—which they were.

He ate a quick breakfast, spent a few minutes on the head, and set a course for buoy #17. Running a fine craft like *The Lady* under power instead of sail was a sin. Jay hated it, but his schedule demanded it.

An hour later, a lightning storm began.

Mark Galpin couldn't believe his ears. His assistant moved nervously in the chair across from him. "Two hours ago, you came in here and told me that *The Lady Fine* disappeared during the night. And now you're telling me that not only have we lost his signal, but even our Air Force can't pick it up. You expect me to believe that?"

"We can't control the weather, sir. That transmitter doesn't behave well in electrical storms. If the storm abates, I'm confident we can locate him again. We have someone now trying to raise a member of his band who might know what night that was. If we can find that out, we'll know which buoy he's heading to. That's the best we can do until the weather cooperates."

"That kid is counting on us. Do you understand that? He knows damn well they intend to kill him, and he's counting on us to stop it. Now, I don't care who you have to involve. I want that transmitter signal located. Get a Coast Guard cutter out there, something, anything. Just find that boat!"

The assistant leaned forward. "I'm not trying to beat a dead horse, sir, but the technology does not work in that kind of storm. Even if a Coast Guard cutter could locate the signal—which is unlikely—they would have no means of triangulating the position without the storm clearing. They would still be chasing what's known as a ghost signal. That can take days—like searching for an airline's black box on the bottom of the ocean floor. It's a needle in a haystack."

"What are you telling me?"

"That we have to wait out the storm."

"And what's the forecast?"

The assistant frowned. "Not good. There are embedded cells all over the area. They're strung out in a line sixty-miles long in a storm moving at ten miles an hour."

"Six hours?"

"At the very least, sir. With the summer heat off the Olympic Peninsula, it could go on all night."

"Damn." Galpin rubbed his temples. "And how about Roy Kepella?"

"He won't walk for a few months. The bullet shattered his kneecap. He'll be in the hospital a few days."

"Did you mention the Washington transfer to him?"

"Yes, sir, just as you asked."

"And what did he say to that?"

"He said he wouldn't transfer there for all the money in the world. He said something about retiring. He was joking with a Chinese woman about starting a restaurant in Palo Alto. I couldn't tell if he was serious or not."

Galpin grinned.

"He said he was going to call it Rosie and Roy's."

Galpin laughed. The assistant had never heard him laugh. Galpin sobered quickly. "Put as many men as needed on locating these band members. And arrange a helicopter for me out to San Juan Island. And on your way out, tell Emily to connect me with the RCMP, British Columbia. We're going to need a little cooperation here."

The assistant hurried out the door. As it shut, Galpin laughed again. Rosie and Roy's. He could just picture it.

Jay took his chances and didn't check in with the Canadian Coast Guard. The message on buoy #17 instructed Jay to sail farther north, to a cove on the southern point of Salt-

363

spring Island and wait for dusk. He was to await a flare that would signal him to row into shore. Marlene would be there.

Marlene.

The trip took him longer than expected due to the furious storm. The seas weren't terribly rough, but the lightning was constant and intense. Every few seconds the thunder would sound like a cannon.

As he motored narrowly between two rock outcroppings, he switched off the running lights. Sunset was still an hour off, but the storm had darkened the sky considerably. He knew they would be looking for *The Lady*. Any element of surprise would work to his advantage. And if he could stall, it would only give the FBI more time. He wondered if they were landing a few men on the island right now, setting the trap they had promised him. He had seen a sea plane flying low an hour before, weaving dangerously low through the lightning. Perhaps it was them.

It was so difficult to see in the available light that Jay fixed his attention on the point of land opposite the cove. He knew they couldn't see *The Lady* from shore, and if he could motor it across to the opposite shore before dark, he might be able to make shore and sneak up on them.

With his attention on the point of land, the noise of the engine droning in his ears, and the rattle of booming thunder and pelting rain, he never saw the small Zodiac raft appear from behind the outcropping of rock. Its silent, electric outboard engine gained steadily on the cumbersome *Lady*.

Jay planned his sneak attack, picturing the FBI or the Mounties on the far side of the island and closing in. He squinted to see the far away shoulder of land.

The Zodiac continued to gain on him.

Something pulled his attention from shore. He glanced over his shoulder, his eyesight partially blocked by the hood of the foul-weather gear. He looked right at the approaching Zodiac and didn't see it.

And then, all at once, the sky cleared. The sun beat through from the west. Rain continued for another minute, as an arching rainbow created a bridge of color between Saltspring and the east. And except for the fading fireflies of the flashing lightning to starboard, one would never have known it had stormed at all.

He pulled off the foul-weather gear. And when he looked up, he was face-to-face with John Chu.

The Chinaman was standing on the stern.

Jay yelled. Chu attacked, springing toward Jay.

Instinctively, Jay leaned to his left and swung from the boom, his fingers in pain, dropping onto the far side of the cockpit. He turned. Chu seemed confused. Jay saw his advantage: he was comfortable on a boat; Chu was not. Jay kicked the gear lever forward, keeping his balance. Chu slipped on the slick deck but quickly regained his stance. *The Lady Fine* motored ahead, its wheel unmanned. Jay hurried forward—he needed a weapon. The flaregun! Chu pulled a long hunting knife and brandished it in the air, following Jay up toward the bow on the opposite side. Jay moved easily, beating the cautious Chu by several paces. He lifted the forward hatch and dropped into the forward cabin, quickly grabbing the flaregun where he had left it. He squatted and turned to fire. Chu's face appeared over the hatch. Jay squeezed the trigger.

A bright, burning ball of orange flame rocketed through the hatch, barely grazing Chu's left cheek and igniting his black hair. Chu dropped the knife onto the deck, slapped his head frantically, and hollered. The orange flare arced lazily into the sky, falling back toward the water.

Jay fumbled for the remaining three cartridges—blue, red, yellow—and stuffed them into his pocket. With his free hand he picked up the butcher knife, remembering he still had the smaller knife taped to his calf

The Chinaman. Jay could still see the crude stick drawing Jocko had smeared on the dash in his own blood. The Chinaman.

Jay jabbed the blue cartridge into the flaregun as he hurried aft and up through the companionway. He reached the big wheel and spun it violently to starboard. The change in direction dropped Chu, who was headed back toward Jay. He leaned out over the rail, his hand only finding the tiny stay at the last second to prevent his going overboard. Jay rushed ahead, planted his elbows on top of the companionway hatch, and squeezed the trigger. The ball of fire roared into Chu's left shoulder, bounced off, fell to the deck, and hissed as it tumbled into the water.

Chu tore at his smoldering T-shirt as he rushed Jay. Jay tried to reload the flaregun but dropped the red cartridge. He bent to retrieve it, setting down the butcher knife, but the shell rolled away from his groping hands, spinning and winding its way around the floor of the cockpit.

Chu jumped into the cockpit.

Jay dove out, face first, onto the starboard decking and clambered to his feet. He felt Chu's grip on his ankle. Kicking hard, he tore loose, simultaneously knocking the knife from Chu's hand. The knife bounced once on the deck and fell into the water. Chu followed it with his eyes. Instinctively, Jay reached down, withdrew the blade from his calf and rammed it with all his strength into Chu's chest, letting go and stepping back. Chu stared down at the knife. Then Jay heard Jocko's voice: "Never leave the knife in the opponent, or you give him a chance to use it against you."

Chu yanked out the weapon without a whimper. Blood ran from the wound. His black eyes glistened, and a peculiar smile spread across his face. He lunged at Jay, nicking his arm and drawing blood. Jay scooted backward in terror, unable to take his eyes off Chu. Thoughts flooded his brain, along with a building guilt. He had tried to *kill* another man. He backpedaled, worming his way around the edge of the rear cabin as Chu moved slowly toward him, bleeding badly but readying himself for the kill. Chu knew knives. That much was obvious.

He did not know boats, however. Jay crouched, hurried to a point beyond the rear mizzen boom, and stood up quickly—a move Chu mimicked. Then Jay leaned with all his strength into the boom and smashed it into Chu like a giant, slow-moving baseball bat. Chu raised a hand to fend off the boom. Jay dropped back to his knees, hooked a forearm around Chu's right ankle, and pulled violently. Chu was lifted off his feet and smashed onto the deck, his shoulder striking a large cleat. He let out a guttural cry.

Jay ran around the port side of the rear cabin and leaped into the cockpit, grasping the butcher knife and picking up the flaregun. Withdrawing the one remaining flare from his pocket, he rammed it into the gun just as Chu landed on both feet in front of him. He spun and side-kicked Jay in the chest, hurling him back with such force that Jay hit the lip of the hatch and tumbled awkwardly into the galley, crashing to the floorboards on his broken fingers.

The searing pain blotted out everything, so that conscience no longer existed in Jay Becker, only instinct. He ran forward below-decks and waited for Chu's move, waited to see if Chu would come down or stay on deck.

Chu leaped into the galley, avoiding the teak steps altogether. The radio barked static. Chu tore the radio off the wall.

Jay did not look behind. When he heard Chu, he reached up through the forward hatch and pulled himself up painfully, rolling onto the deck. He slammed the hatch closed and moved quickly back to the cockpit.

Cat and mouse, he thought. Cat and mouse.

He expected Chu to come back toward the cockpit. Jay picked up the flaregun from the floor of the cockpit and aimed, waiting for Chu. Then he saw that Chu had opened the hatch and climbed through. He was standing at the bow. Jay fell toward the throttle and pulled it forward, doubling the engine speed. Still on his belly, his arm bleeding, Jay scooted forward and spun the wheel with all his strength.

The boat lurched forward as Jay yanked the throttle and Chu lost his balance. The boat jerked to starboard, and Chu, trying too quickly to regain his balance, was totally unprepared for the sudden change in direction. Jay rammed his fingers into the spokes of the moving steering wheel to stop it, screaming at the top of his lungs; he spun the wheel in the opposite direction and, hooking his foot over the gear lever, pulled violently, grinding the gears into reverse.

Chu stumbled backward, toward the bowsprit, confusion written on his face. His foot caught on the anchor mount and he went over the bow of *The Lady Fine*. Jay rose to his knees and straightened the wheel, immediately kicking the gear lever forward. Instinct. He turned the wheel slightly to port. He felt the man's body bump underneath the port hull. He pulled hard to starboard and heard the diesel groan as the boat lurched heavily, throwing Jay into the steering wheel and banging his head against it. He had run the Chinaman over with the throttle wide open. He scurried to the stern, hanging onto the rail, gasping for breath. The mangled corpse surfaced twenty feet back. Jay turned his head to look away. He had never seen anything that grotesque . . . the Chinaman was dead.

42

He dropped anchor, though not where Holst's note had told him to. Were Holst and the Samoan goon waiting for him on shore? Was this the end of the line? When Chu did not return, what would Holst do? Too many questions.

His wound was not deep, not even too painful. He wrapped it and the bleeding stopped.

He took *The Lady*'s flaregun and its one remaining shell with him. He wore a pair of Marlene's blue jeans—unbuttoned at the waist—and a black turtleneck as he climbed into the Zodiac raft and motored silently through the darkness toward shore, keeping an eye on the area where moments earlier he had seen the flare in the woods.

The water was still. The raft glided along effortlessly. A

quarter-moon crept above the horizon, its dim blue-gray light kissing the tops of the tall Saltspring Island cedars. Jay kept his head low in case Holst had spotted the Zodiac. The short trip seemed to take forever. Somewhere on this island Marlene was being held hostage. He looked down at his butchered fingers, and, at the same time, thought of Jocko.

The shore was littered with fist-sized stones. Jay rocked the motor forward and dragged the heavy raft ashore. In a half-crouch, he scurried into the woods and waited for sights or sounds. Nothing. Perhaps they had not seen him. He looked out at the anchored *Lady Fine*, admiring her lines in the moonlight. What was Holst thinking now? Could he see the boat from where he was, or was he waiting at a point up the shore, around one of the jagged points of land? Jay walked northeast, following the edge of the trees for perhaps ten minutes, when he spotted a dark cabin off to his left, nestled in a small clearing. He approached the cabin cautiously, detouring well around to the left, in order to arrive from the island side, expecting that if anyone was guarding the place, it would be from the water side. The cabin had a single chimney and two small windows in front. Jay stepped from tree to tree, easily hiding himself, until he was within a few yards of the cabin. He crouched again and ran to the south side, heart pounding, and pressed his body flat against the windowless log wall. He was light-headed from fear and anticipation. He edged around the west side of the small building, keeping low until he was below a window. He mustered his courage, rose quickly, and peered inside. The cabin, dark and still, showed no signs of life. He moved to the next window. Nothing.

Wrong cabin.

He stayed higher in the woods for the next few minutes, moving steadily, parallel with the shoreline, from tree to tree, pausing, listening, pausing. He guessed he was about half a mile from the first cabin when he detected the muffled sounds of shouting. The sound of voices made him feel safer; anxiety had built up while he crept through the dark, overgrown forest, and voices—*any* voices—were a comfort.

He moved toward the sounds until he spotted a second cabin. It looked much like the first, old and decrepit, except it was larger and of frame construction, with shingled siding instead of logs. Two chimneys jutted upward, one on either end. There were two windows to the left of the front door and a single window to the right. Yellow lantern light shone from every window. He hid behind a tree and watched two silhouettes move with seeming randomness inside the room to the left of the front door. He proceeded tree by tree around to the right of the building, away from the windows, and again, ran to the side wall, flattening himself. He moved toward the water and rounded a corner. The clearing stretched down to a short dock with a rowboat upside down upon it. Jay realized a point of land did indeed block sight of *The Lady Fine* from here, and wondered if Holst knew it was anchored just beyond. He peeked through a crack in a curtain. There was Marlene, asleep in a chair, her face battered, all alone in a room. He pushed silently against the window, but it didn't budge. He wondered where Galpin's backup was. *Hurry up*, he thought.

His heart raced. He held the flaregun in his right hand and eased his way carefully onto the back landing, twisting the doorknob slowly. The door opened silently and he stepped into the dark kitchen, hearing Holst's voice more clearly now. A door from the kitchen led to a small entranceway that had two other doors leading to small rooms off of it: one to the right, with Holst and whomever arguing, the other, to the left, with Marlene inside. Becker stood in the kitchen. The two men continued to argue. He stepped through the hallway and into the room where Marlene was sleeping.

She awakened; her head swung toward him. He raised the flaregun to his lips, indicating silence. Her face and legs were badly bruised. A deep sadness swept through him. It wasn't pity, or fear, but simply a deep, lingering sadness. He loved her—not infatuation, not friendship—but love. Their eyes met. She tried to hide her face from him.

The arguing stopped. The Samoan stomped into the kitchen and the back door slammed. Jay turned.

A board creaked in the hallway. Jay stepped back and knelt behind a chest of drawers. Then he realized he had laid the flaregun down on the small table. Holst entered the room. He stood alongside the table, sensing something, his hand nearly brushing the flaregun. Then he spotted it.

"Now!" Marlene shouted, and Jay jumped up quickly, dumping over the chest of drawers. He charged Holst, who yelled, "Donnie!" and Jay thought, I'm screwed; I'll be outnumbered.

Holst grabbed the flaregun and fired. But Jay was already diving to body-block Holst at the shins. Holst collapsed to the floor. The flare started a small fire on the bed beyond Marlene. Jay lunged at Holst. Then he heard the Samoan throw open the kitchen door. Jay scrambled to his

372

feet and fled through the living room, out the front door, running hard. He heard Holst yelling for the Samoan to get moving. The Samoan had not followed.

He sprinted, dodging trees, ripping through sections of dense underbrush, and in what seemed like two minutes, reached the other cabin. Still running, he angled toward the water, slowing as the footing became more rocky. He tripped over a fallen log, banging his aching hands into a bed of small rocks. He rolled, bruising his left shoulder, and lay panting on the shoreline. He couldn't hear anyone behind him, but he was terror-stricken just the same, his heart pumping hard from the sprint, his teeth chattering with fear. Get hold of yourself! he demanded, unable to move, lying frozen on a bed of rocks. Slowly, he managed to get to his feet and then, summoning what little courage he had, he searched the shoreline for the Zodiac and found it. Don't think about the Samoan; don't think about the German; don't think about that flare missing you by inches; don't think about leaving Marlene with them again. But it wasn't that simple.

43

He needed a weapon. He motored the Zodiac back to *The Lady Fine*. He came up with a plan and went about implementing it. He spent five minutes sabotaging the Zodiac, unhooking the battery from its electric motor and tossing it overboard. If, through the moonlight, Holst had seen him return to *The Lady*, then the presence of the Zodiac would convince him that Jay was still aboard. But with the Zodiac out of commission, whoever rowed out to the sailboat would also have to row back in, thus giving Jay more time. He turned on a light, making it look as though he was aboard. He changed back into shorts, keeping his Topsiders on. Then it struck him that this was it. He was going to go wait it out on shore. If someone came out toward *The Lady* then maybe he would try something; if they didn't, then he would wait for Galpin. Either way, he decided it wasn't worth the risk of leaving the computers on board. If something went wrong now, if he failed, then at least Holst would fail, too. He punched two holes in all four cardboard boxes and watched the machines gurgle into the depths. The television followed in case it had something important, too. He hoped it was the right thing to do. But it was done. The spearguns were stored forward with the skin-diving gear. He took the biggest speargun from the hold and slipped overboard, praying it wouldn't be the last time he saw *The Lady Fine*.

Where the hell was Galpin?

The water was very cold. He swam to shore in ten minutes, and had been sitting against a log for another ten when he spotted the vague shape of a dory round the point, oars moving like slow wings. He decided to make his move. If they had gone for the gear and found it missing, Holst might kill Marlene. Jay had forced his own hand. His ruse had obviously worked: they thought he was aboard. He knew he now had the element of surprise. But not for long. How long to row out and back? Ten minutes? Twenty?

He crouched and stitched his way through the fallen timber, taking the same route back toward the cabin. Adrenaline filled him and his heart pounded hard. He had a speargun. He had used a speargun before. The only question in his mind now was whether or not he could use it on a human. He wouldn't dare try a leg shot: too little target, he thought, as he moved quickly toward the cabin, wondering who would be guarding Marlene. He reached the front yard and moved silently toward the cabin. He stretched the speargun's rubber cord back to the farthest notch and edged over to the window. The Samoan, ten feet from Marlene, was pacing the room nervously. That meant Holst was in the dory—climbing on board *The Lady* about now. He noticed the room's single lantern. If he could only get inside and break the lantern, he might buy enough time to get her out . . .

Becker turned the handle to the front door. Its rusty hinge squeaked. He flung the door open, stepped inside, and spread his feet apart, aiming the speargun, waiting.

The Samoan hurried into the front room, stopping abruptly at the sight before him. He fumbled for something in his pocket.

Jay saw the bulge in the Samoan's pocket. He aimed and pulled the trigger, releasing the spear. The contraption made a snapping sound, the spear whirred through the air, and the Samoan roared as it embedded deeply into his abdomen, buckling him over. As he spun around, Jay saw the spear protruding out his back. The Samoan staggered, then fell to the floor, breaking an arm off a chair on his way down.

Jay hurried over to Marlene, stepping over the Samoan, who was unconscious but breathing. As he began to cut through the rope that bound Marlene, he heard a helicopter approaching. *Finally,* he thought, *finally they've come to help.*

44

Hearing the helicopter, seeing the lights overhead, was the first true relief Jay had felt in weeks. He wrapped an arm around Marlene, a smile pasted on his face. "It's the FBI," he said. "They followed me the whole way."

But Marlene knew Holst's plans. "I don't think so, Jay," she said.

"Yes, it is. A man named Galpin. They caught me at Carkeek Park, where I had taken *The Lady*. I didn't want to do it. They gave me no choice . . ." His voice faded into the roar of the chopper. It was still twilight, and though the chopper had been silhouetted against the sky, as it passed below the tops of the tall evergreens, descending to the small opening that fronted the cabin, Jay couldn't see any government markings. The smile disappeared from his face. He turned as Marlene broke loose from him and ran to the Samoan's still body.

"It's Wilhelm, Jay. He's the boss. Help me. Please, help me." She was trying to drag Mota's body into the only closet in the tiny foyer.

Jay stood numbly at the window. He saw the helicopter—with pontoons instead of wheels—hovering as a man jumped to the ground. The chopper climbed back into the sky. The man approached the cabin with a briefcase in hand.

"Jay!" she hissed at him. "Hurry."

He ran to her side and helped her drag the Samoan's body into the closet. Jay bent over, frantically searching the Samoan's pockets. "The gun!" he whispered.

"Holst has it." She pulled on his shirt, tugging the confused Jay out of the closet, then threw the speargun on top of the body and closed the closet door. "Hide over there." She pointed to the door. "I will stall him. He expects me to meet him here." Marlene pulled a dusty throw rug over the bloodstains and sat down quickly in the only chair in the room, facing the doorway.

Jay took his last hurried step as the door opened. He watched the man's back through the crack. He had broad shoulders and was wearing a Gore-Tex jacket and what looked like an old hunting hat. A walkie-talkie was strapped to his waist. He stopped as he saw her and set down the briefcase. "You must be Marlene."

"Yes, and you, the Mariner," she said, using the code name that she had been directed to use.

He nodded and looked up, as if he could see through the roof of the house. "The helicopter must refuel in Nanaimo. It will return shortly," he explained. "It will land out by the boat, and we will board it there. Where is Albatross?"

"He is on the boat, checking the merchandise."

"How long has he been gone?"

"A few minutes is all. He will be a while."

"It all went smoothly then?"

"Hardly smoothly, but it is over."

"Then I owe you this." He pulled out a videotape and set it on the pitted tabletop next to him.

The sight of the videotape distracted Marlene. "How do I know that is the only copy?"

"You don't. You'll just have to trust me."

She coughed a laugh.

"You don't trust me?" he asked.

Jay saw the man's right hand slowly creep up under the

back of his coat and then the handle of a small revolver appeared. Jay pushed against the door, shoving his weight into it and catching Wilhelm by surprise. Wilhelm toppled over, dropping the revolver. It skidded along the floor into the sitting room. Jay ran for it, but as he passed Wilhelm, the big man reached out and tripped him up. Jay fell face first to the floor, landing on his bad hand and screaming. Marlene took one step toward Wilhelm. But the big man was fast and already on his feet. He backhanded her effortlessly and sent her reeling into and over the chair. She collapsed into the corner.

Jay was on his knees and crawling for the gun. He flattened straight out and took hold of it as Wilhelm dove on top of him, knocking the wind out of him and grabbing hold of his arm. The two wrestled for control of the weapon, but it flew from Jay's hand and into the far corner. Wilhelm's gaze followed the gun, providing Jay with an opening. He rolled and delivered the back of a fist into Wilhelm's ear. The big man tumbled off him. This time Wilhelm scurried for the pistol.

For Jay, unable to breathe, Wilhelm's actions seemed to slow to a crawl. Suddenly every second was thirty seconds. Wilhelm inched toward the pistol, tossing furniture out of his way, unable to see the gun. Jay's attention fixed on the kerosene lantern on the mantle, just above him. He struggled to his feet. Wilhelm knocked a chair out of his way, still unable to find the weapon. Jay was standing. He reached up and grabbed hold of the glass lantern. He tapped it against the stone hearth, trying to crack the glass. Wilhelm was bent over, frantic now. Unable to find the gun, he took hold of the inverted chair and threw it at Jay, quickly looking down again for the weapon.

The flying chair struck Jay squarely in the back. The pain was intense. The lantern bumped the stone hearth and cracked. Jay had known, without thinking about it, that if he simply threw the lit lantern at Wilhelm it wouldn't spread flame until it broke and the burning wick touched the spreading fuel. But if he could crack the glass then the flames might start the moment the lantern connected with its target. He cocked his arm back, elbow locked, and launched the dripping lantern at Wilhelm, who had just found the gun.

A surprised Wilhelm rose to fire the weapon. His instincts were good. At the last possible second, he spun around, his finger already squeezing off a shot, as the flames engulfed his back.

Jay watched, unable to move or look away.

Wilhelm reacted quickly, dropping the gun and peeling off the burning jacket. He dove to the floor and rolled toward Jay, beating his burning pant legs furiously. Flames spread into the corner and across the furniture, and the walls caught fire. Wilhelm miraculously extinguished the flames on his pants and jumped to his feet.

Jay ran from the room. He turned to look at Marlene, who was just coming to her senses in the corner. He pushed through the door into the kitchen, Wilhelm right behind him. As he cleared the doorway, he stopped, spun around, and kicked as hard as he could, catching Wilhelm between the legs. Wilhelm howled and fell forward. Instinctively, Jay bunched his broken fingers into a fist and slugged the man in the face, screaming with the contact. He struck him again, and as Wilhelm began to fall further, Jay kicked with all his might and broke the man's jaw. Wilhelm hit the floor unconscious, his pants still smoldering, the back of his shirt burned off.

The flames had spread quickly, pushing smoke out of the room and into the foyer. Jay reached Marlene, who was on her knees in the corner.

The fire set off all the bullets in Wilhelm's gun at once, confusing them both. Jay threw himself over her. She hugged him with all her strength. Then Jay heard the helicopter approaching. He ran into the kitchen and peered through the dirty window. He couldn't see the chopper, but he did see the approaching dory.

"It's Holst," he said to Marlene, frightened. "He's back."

She stood in the kitchen doorway, holding the videotape and briefcase. "I will get the speargun," she said.

He said, "No, get away from here. Hide! I'll do my best." He stared at her. "Okay?"

She nodded.

Jay ran out the back door, crouching low, hearing the chopper in the distance, but still unable to see it. As he reached the beginning of the old, crippled dock, Holst bumped the dory against the far end and tied the skiff to a wooden post. Jay tucked himself behind a huge fallen tree, his left hand searching for and finding a good-sized stick. He took it in both hands like a baseball bat and concentrated on Holst, who was running cautiously up the dilapidated dock, eyes on the broken slats of wood, jumping over the holes. Holst paused at the end of the dock, taking two steps into the wet field grass. He held a revolver in his right hand.

When his back was to Jay, Becker rose. "Holst!" he

hollered. And as the surprised man turned to fire the gun, Jay delivered a home run blow to the side of the German's face.

Holst collapsed, but was able to roll and squeeze the trigger, and Jay felt a burning in his left shoulder. He'd been hit. He dove over a fallen tree. Holst pumped off two more rounds, splintering the log above Jay's head. The German staggered to his feet, his jaw pushed ungainly to one side, a large, open welt across his neck and cheek, his left eye a mess. He inched forward, ever closer to Becker.

Jay took hold of a stone and blindly threw it over the log, missing Holst but distracting him and causing him to fire another shot. Two left, Jay thought, and he rolled along the smooth stones to his left, moving behind the log, his shoulder beginning to burn more fiercely. He poked his head up quickly and ducked as Holst turned and fired. As he crouched waiting, he tried to decipher the image imprinted on his mind. Had he seen the briefcase and the tape laying in the grass? Had Marlene actually been coming up behind Holst with the loaded speargun? Was that possible? Distract Holst, he thought. Don't let him sense her! One bullet left! Jay threw another rock over the log, and another. No shots. He rolled back to his right—Holst's blind side—and peered over again. Fire the bullet! he wanted to shout. He screamed at the German, who had not seen him.

Marlene pulled the trigger. The spear shot forward and into Holst's lower back. The German straightened up and spun to see who had ambushed him. He raised the gun, then looked back at Jay, swinging the gun around, uncertain which of them to shoot. He swayed on his feet, waving

381

the gun like a drunk man.

Shots rang out and bullets riddled Holst's body. He slumped forward, collapsing onto the fallen log, only feet from Jay. The agents swarmed from out of the woods, thick black vests with the letters RCMP across their chests. There must have been a dozen of them.

Epilogue

Jay's arm was in a sling. He sat on the pad in the cockpit. Marlene's green eyes peered over the bow from her position behind the wheel. She was intent on what she was doing.

"You've got an awfully serious expression on your face."

"I want to do this right."

"Considering your wrist, you're doing fine. The lady's fine," he added.

She smiled at him, eyes bright. "How does it feel?"

"The shoulder?"

She nodded, her blond hair failing across her shoulders.

"Like someone shot me, I suppose. I hurt all over. I slept fourteen hours last night. It was nice of Galpin to let us see each other."

"Yes, he is a good man."

"So?"

She looked at Jay curiously.

"So what's he say? Where do you stand? I've been kept in the dark for nearly a week."

"They have been debriefing me—I think it is called. I

have told them everything, from the first day Holst approached me in Germany, to the night on the island."

"And?"

"You mean punishment?"

"You know exactly what I mean."

"They call me state's evidence. If I will tell the courts what I have been telling them, then they will try and get a suspended sentence. No promises. I take whatever they give me."

"And Wilhelm?"

"He has not told them a thing. Did they tell you about the money?"

"No." Jay sat up.

"The briefcase was filled with cash. They may give you a reward. I had a meeting with Kepella and a woman named Sharon Johnson. She was very nice. They were here for debriefing as well. She is with the CIA in Washington. She told me it is customary to give a ten-percent reward when cash is found in a case like this. Kepella said he would testify on your behalf."

"How much was in the suitcase?"

She smiled and moved the wheel so *The Lady Fine* pointed into the wind.

"What's going on?" Jay asked.

She hurried forward and expertly lowered both the mainsail and the jib. Jay watched her, impressed. She had learned well. She let the anchor overboard and pulled on it to make sure it was secure. They were on the far side of a small island. Not a boat for as far as the eye could see. She walked back, confidently, and unfastened her yellow terry-cloth coverup, slipping it off over her cast. She went below and, after a few minutes, returned with a large beach towel. She spread it on the floor of the cockpit, took Jay by the hand, and sat him down on the towel. She leaned toward him and kissed him gently on the mouth.

He kissed her back, though shyly.

She unbuttoned his Hawaiian shirt and slipped his arm out of the sling.

He watched her, a smile on his lips. "What's going on?" he asked.

She lowered her eyes demurely and unfastened the top of her sky blue lycra suit. "I am working on being a stronger person."

He helped her to lay back and kissed her hungrily, touching her soft skin.

"I love you," she whispered in his ear.

The wind caught the unfurled sail and snapped the boom hard to port. The sailcloth tumbled down into the cockpit, covering them both. They laughed.

Jay said, "Ready about, hard a-lee."

Center Point Publishing
600 Brooks Road ● PO Box 1
Thorndike ME 04986-0001 USA

(207) 568-3717

US & Canada:
1 800 929-9108